THEY MAKE PLANET CALLS

The only connecting link between countless colonized planets are the Med Ships—lone starships, each carrying only one man and one beast. These trained super-medical engineers risk their lives at every planetfall.

The human enemies they face are just as dangerous as any interplanetary plague!

This is THE MED SERIES, the classic adventure epic from the dean of science fiction writers, Murray Leinster.

THE MED SERIES

MURRAY LEINSTER

ACE SCIENCE FICTION BOOKS
NEW YORK

THE MED SERIES

PRINTING HISTORY
Ace edition / May 1983

ISBN: 0-441-52360-9

Ace Science Fiction Books are published
by Charter Communications, Inc.
200 Madison Avenue, New York, New York 10016.
PRINTED IN THE UNITED STATES OF AMERICA

THE MUTANT
WEAPON

I

"The probability of unfavorable consequences cannot be zero in any action of common life, but the probability increases by a very high power as a series of actions is lengthened. The effect of moral considerations, in conduct, may be stated to be a mathematically verifiable reduction in the number of unfavorable possible chance happenings. Of course, whether this process is called the intelligent use of probability, or piety, makes no difference in the facts. It is the method by which unfavorable chance happenings are made least probable. Arbitrary actions such as we call criminal cannot ever be justified by mathematics. For example . . ."

Probability and Human Conduct—Fitzgerald

CALHOUN LAY ON his bunk and read Fitzgerald on *Probability and Human Conduct* as the little Med Ship floated in overdrive. In overdrive travel there is nothing to do but pass the time away. Murgatroyd, the *tormal*, slept curled up in a ball in one corner of the small ship's cabin. His tail was meticulously curled about his nose. The ship's lights burned steadily. There were those small random noises which have to be provided to keep a man sane in the dead stillness of a ship traveling at very many times the speed of light. Calhoun turned a page and yawned.

Something stirred somewhere. There was a click, and a taped voice said:

"When the tone sounds, breakout will be five seconds off."

A metronomic clicking, grave and deliberate, resounded in the stillness. Calhoun heaved himself up from the bunk and marked his place in the book. He moved to and seated himself in the control chair and fastened the safety belt. He said, "Murgatroyd. Hark, hark the lark in Heaven's something-or-other doth sing. Wake up and comb your whiskers. We're getting there."

Murgatroyd opened one eye and saw Calhoun in the pilot's chair. He uncurled himself and padded to a place where there was something to grab hold of. He regarded Calhoun with bright eyes.

"Bong!" said the tape. It counted down. *"Five . . . four . . . three . . . two . . . one . . ."*

It stopped. The ship popped out of overdrive. The sensation was unmistakable. Calhoun's stomach seemed to turn over twice, and he had a sickish feeling of spiraling dizzily in what was somehow a cone. He swallowed. Murgatroyd made gulping noises. Outside, everything changed.

The sun Maris blazed silently in emptiness off to port. The Cetis star-cluster was astern, and the light by which it could be seen had traveled for many years to reach here, though Calhoun had left Med Headquarters only three weeks before. The third planet of Maris swung splendidly in its orbit. Calhoun checked, and nodded in satisfaction. He spoke over his shoulder to Murgatroyd.

"We're here, all right."

"Chee!" shrilled Murgatroyd.

He uncoiled his tail from about a cabinet handle and hopped up to look at the vision screen. What he saw, of course, meant nothing to him. But all *tormals* imitate the actions of human beings, as parrots imitate their speech. He blinked wisely at the screen and turned his eyes to Calhoun.

"It's Maris III," Calhoun told him, "and pretty close. It's a colony of Dettra Two. One city was reported started two Earth-years ago. It should just about be colonized now."

"Chee-chee!" shrilled Murgatroyd.

"So get out of the way," commanded Calhoun. "We'll make our approach and I'll tell 'em we're here."

He made a standard approach on interplanetary drive. Naturally, it was a long process. But after some hours he flipped over the call switch and made the usual identification and landing request.

"Med Ship *Aesclipus Twenty* to ground," he said into the transmitter. "Requesting coordinates for landing. Our mass is fifty tons. Repeat, five-oh tons. Purpose of landing: planetary health inspection."

He relaxed. This job ought to be pure routine. There was a landing grid in the spaceport city on Maris III. From its control room instructions should be sent, indicating a position some five planetary diameters from the surface of that world. Calhoun's little ship should repair to that spot. The giant landing grid should then reach out its specialized force field, lock onto the ship, and bring it gently but irresistibly down to ground. Then Calhoun, representing Med Service, should confer gravely with planetary authorities about public health conditions on Maris III.

It was not expected that anything important would turn up. Calhoun would deliver full details of recent advances in the science of medicine. These might already have reached Maris III in the ordinary course of commerce, but he would make sure. He might—but it was unlikely—learn of some novelty worked out here. In any case, within three days he should return to the small Med Ship, the landing grid should heave it firmly heavenward to not less than five planetary diameters distance, and there release it. And Calhoun and Murgatroyd and the Med Ship should flick into overdrive and speed back toward headquarters, from whence they had come.

Right now, Calhoun waited for an answer to his landing call. But he regarded the vast disk of the nearby planet.

"By the map," he observed to Murgatroyd, "the city ought to be on shore of that bay somewhere near the terminus. Close to the sunset line."

His call was answered. A voice said incredulously on the spacephone speaker, *"What? What's that? What's that you say?"*

"Med Ship *Aesclipus Twenty*," Calhoun repeated patiently. "Requesting coordinates for landing. Our mass is fifty tons. Repeat, five-oh tons. Purpose of landing: planetary health inspection."

The voice said more incredulously still, *"A Med Ship? Holy—"* By the change of sound, the man down on the planet had turned away from the microphone. *"Hey! Listen to this!"*

There was abrupt silence. Calhoun raised his eyebrows. He drummed on the control desk before him. There was a long pause. A very long pause. Then a new voice came on the spacephone, up from the ground, *"You up there! Identify yourself!"*

Calhoun said very politely, "This is Med Ship *Aesclipus Twenty*. I would like to come to ground. Purpose of landing: health inspection."

"Wait," said the voice from the planet. It sounded strained.

A murmuring sounded, transmitted from fifty thousand miles away. Then there was a click. The transmitter down below had cut off. Calhoun raised his eyebrows again. This was not according to routine. Not at all! The Med Service was badly overworked and understaffed. The resources of interplanetary services were always apt to be stretched to their utmost, because there could be no galactic government as such. Many thousands of occupied planets, the closest of them light-years apart, couldn't hold elections or have political parties for the simple reason that travel, even in overdrive, was too slow. They could only have service organizations whose authority depended on the consent of the people served, and whose support had to be gathered when and as it was possible.

But the Med Service was admittedly important. The local Sector Headquarters was in the Cetis cluster. It was a sort of interstellar clinic, with additions. It gathered and disseminated the results of experience in health and medicine among some thousands of colony-worlds, and from time to time it made contact with other headquarters carrying on the same work elsewhere. It admittedly took fifty years for a new technique in gene selection to cross the occupied part of the galaxy, but it was a three-year voyage in overdrive to cover the same distance direct. And the Med Service was worthwhile. There was no problem of human ecological adjustment it had so far been unable to solve, and there were some dozens of planets whose human colonies owed their existence to it. There was nowhere, nowhere at all, that a Med Ship was not welcomed on its errand from headquarters.

"Aground there!" said Calhoun sharply. "What's the matter? Are you landing me or not?"

There was no answer. Then, suddenly, every sound-producing device in the ship abruptly emitted a hoarse and monstrous noise. The lights flashed up and circuit breakers cut them off. The nearest-object horn squawked. The hull-temperature warning squealed. The ship's internal gravity field tugged horribly for an instant and went off. Every device within the ship designed to notify emergency clanged or shrieked or roared or screamed. There was momentary bedlam.

It lasted for part of a second only. Then everything stopped. There was no weight within the ship, and there were no lights. There was dead silence, and Murgatroyd made whimpering sounds in the darkness.

Calhoun thought absurdly to himself, *According to the book, this is an unfavorable chance consequence of something or other*. But it was more than an unfavorable chance occurrence. It was an intentional and drastic and possibly a deadly one.

"Somebody's acting up," said Calhoun measuredly, in the blackness. "What the hell's the matter with them?"

He flipped the screen switch to bring back vision of what was outside. The vision screens of a ship are very carefully fused against overload burnouts, because there is nothing in all the cosmos quite as helpless and foredoomed as a ship which is blind in the emptiness of space. But the screens did not light again. They couldn't. The cutouts hadn't worked in time.

Calhoun's scalp crawled. But as his eyes adjusted, he saw the pale fluorescent handles of switches and doors. They hadn't been made fluorescent in expectation of an emergency like this, of course, but they would help a great deal. He knew what had happened. It could only be one thing—a landing-grid field clamped on the fifty-ton Med Ship with the power needed to grasp and land a twenty-thousand-ton liner. At that strength it would paralyze every instrument and blow every cutoff. It could not be accidental. The reception of the news of his identity, the repeated request that he identify himself, and then the demand that he wait . . . This murderous performance was deliberate.

"Maybe," said Calhoun in the inky-black cabin, "as a Med Ship our arrival is an unfavorable chance consequence of something—and somebody means to keep us from happening. It looks like it."

Murgatroyd whimpered.

"And I think," added Calhoun coldly, "that somebody may need a swift kick in the negative feedback!"

He released himself from the safety belt and dived across the cabin in which there was now no weight at all. In the blackness he opened a cabinet door. What he did inside was customarily done by a man wearing thick insulated gloves, in the landing grid back at headquarters. He threw certain switches which would allow the discharge of the power-storage cells which worked the Med Ship's overdrive. Monstrous quantities of energy were required to put even a fifty-ton ship into overdrive, and monstrous amounts were returned when it came out. The power amounted to ounces of pure, raw energy, and as a safety precaution such amounts were normally put into the Duhanne cells only just before a Med Ship's launching, and drained out again on its return. But now, Calhoun threw switches which made a rather incredible amount of power available for dumping into the landing-grid field about him—if necessary.

He floated back to the control chair.

The ship lurched. Violently. It was being moved by the grid field without any gentleness at all. Calhoun's hands barely grasped the back of his pilot's chair before the jerk came, and it almost tore them free. He just missed being flung against the back of the cabin by the applied acceleration. But he was a long way out from the planet. He was at the end of a lever fifty thousand miles long, and for that lever to be used to shake him too brutally would require special adjustments. But somebody was making them. The jerk reversed directions. He was flung savagely against the chair to which he'd been clinging. He struggled. Another yank, in another direction. Another one still. It flung him violently into the chair.

Behind him, Murgatroyd squealed angrily as he went hurtling across the cabin. He grabbed for holding places with all four paws and his tail.

Another shake. Calhoun had barely fastened the safety belt before a furious jolt nearly flung him out of it again to crash against the cabin ceiling. Still another vicious surge of acceleration, and he scrabbled for the controls. The yanking and plunging of the ship increased intolerably. He was nauseated. Once he was thrust so furiously into the control chair that he was on the verge of blacking out; and then the direction of thrust was changed to the exact opposite so that the blood rushing to his head seemed about to explode it. His arms flailed out of control. He became dazed. But when his hands were flung against the control-board, he tried, despite their bruising, to cling to the control-knobs, and each time he threw them over. Practically all his circuits were blown, but there was one—

His numbing fingers threw it. There was a roar so fierce that it seemed to be an explosion. He'd reached the switch which made effective the discharge circuit of his Duhanne cells. He'd thrown it. It was designed to let the little ship's overdrive power reserve flow into storage at headquarters on return from duty. Now, though, it poured into the landing field outside. It amounted to hundreds of millions of kilowatt hours, delivered in a fraction of a second. There was the smell of ozone. The sound was like a thunderclap.

But abruptly there was a strange and incredible peace. The lights came on waveringly as his shaking fingers restored the circuit breakers. Murgatroyd shrilled indignantly, clinging desperately to an instrument rack. But the vision screens did not light again. Calhoun swore. Swiftly, he threw more circuit restorers. The nearest-object indicator told of the presence of Maris III at forty-odd thousand miles. The hull-temperature indicator was up some fifty-six degrees. The internal-gravity field came on faintly, and then built up to normal. But the screens would not light. They were permanently dead. Calhoun raged for seconds. Then he got hold of himself.

"Chee-chee-chee!" chattered Murgatroyd desperately. *"Chee-chee!"*

"Shut up!" growled Calhoun. "Some bright lad aground thought up a new way to commit murder. Damned near got away with it, too! He figured he'd shake us to death like a dog does a rat, only he was using a landing-grid field to do it with. Right now, I hope I fried him!"

But it was not likely. Such quantities of power as are used to handle twenty-thousand-ton spaceliners are not controlled direct, but by relays. The power Calhoun had flung into the grid field should have blown out the grid's transformers with a spectacular display of fireworks, but it was hardly probable it had gotten back to the individual at the controls.

"But I suspect," observed Calhoun vengefully, "that he'll consider this business an unfavorable occurrence. Somebody'll twist his tail too, either for trying what he did or for not getting away with it! Only, as a matter of pure precaution—"

His expression changed suddenly. He'd been trying not to think of the consequences of having no sight of the cosmos outside the ship. Now he remembered the electron telescope. It had not been in circuit, so it could not have been burned out like his vision screens. He switched it on. A star-field appeared over his head.

"Chee-chee!" cried Murgatroyd hysterically.

Calhoun glanced at him. The jerking of the ship had shifted the instruments in the rack to which Murgatroyd clung. Clipped into place though they were, they'd caught Murgatroyd's tail and pinched it tightly.

"You'll have to wait," snapped Calhoun. "Right now I've got to make us look like a successful accident. Otherwise, whoever tried to spread us all over the cabin walls will try something else!"

The Med Ship flung through space in whatever direction and at whatever velocity it had possessed when the grid field blew. Calhoun shifted the electron telescope's field and simultaneously threw on the emergency rocket controls. There was a growling of the pencil-thin, high-velocity blasts. There was a surging of the ship.

"No straight-line stuff," Calhoun reminded himself.

He swung the ship into a dizzy spiral, as if innumerable things had been torn or battered loose in the ship and its rockets had come on of themselves. Painstakingly, he jettisoned in one explosive burst all the stored waste of his journey which could not be disposed of while in overdrive. To any space-scanning instrument on the ground, it would look like something detonating violently inside the ship.

"Now—"

The planet Maris III swung across the electron telescope's field. It looked hideously near, but that was the telescope's magnification. Yet Calhoun sweated. He looked at the nearest-object dial for reassurance. The planet was nearer by a thousand miles.

"Hah!" said Calhoun.

He changed the ship's spiral course. He changed it again. He abruptly reversed the direction of its turn. Adequate training in space combat could have helped plot an evasion course, but it might have been recognizable. Nobody could anticipate his maneuvers now, though. He adjusted the telescope next time the planet swept across its field, and flipped on the photorecorder. Then he pulled out of the spiral, whirled the ship until the city was covered by the telescope, and ran the recorder as long as he dared keep a straight course. Then he swooped toward the planet in a crazy, twisting fall with erratic intermissions, and made a final lunatic dash almost parallel to the planet's surface.

At five hundred miles he unshielded the ports, which of necessity had to be kept covered in clear space. There was a sky which was vividly bright with stars. There was a vast blackness off to starboard which was the night side of the planet.

He went down. At four hundred miles the outside-pressure indicator wavered away from its pin. He used it like a pilot-tube recording, doing sums in his head to figure the static pressure that should exist at this height, to compare with the dynamic pressure produced by his velocity through the near hard vacuum. The pressure should have been substantially zero. He swung the ship end-for-end and killed velocity to bring the pressure indication down. The ship descended. Two hundred miles. He saw the thin bright line of sunshine at the limb of the planet. Down to one hundred. He cut the rockets and let the ship fall silently, swinging its nose up.

At ten miles he listened for man-made radiation. There was nothing in the electromagnetic spectrum but the crackling of static in an electric storm which might be a thousand miles away. At five miles height the nearest-object indicator, near the bottom of its scale, wavered in a fashion to prove that he was still moving laterally across mountainous country. He swung the ship and killed that velocity too.

At two miles he used the rockets for deceleration. The pencil-thin flame reached down for an incredible distance. By naked-eye observation out a port, he tilted the fiercely roaring, swiftly falling ship until hillsides and forests underneath him ceased to move. By that time he was very low indeed.

He reached ground on a mountainside which was lighted by the blue-white flame of the rocket blast. He

chose an area in which the treetops were almost flat,
indicating something like a plateau underneath. Murgatroyd was practically frantic by this time because of his
capture and the pinching of his tail, but Calhoun could
not spare time to release him. He let the ship down
gently, gently, trying to descend in an absolutely vertical
line.

If he didn't do it perfectly, he came very close. The
ship settled into what was practically a burned-away
tunnel among monstrous trees. The slender, high-velocity flame did not splash when it reached ground. It
penetrated. It burned a hole for itself through humus
and clay and bedrock. When the ship touched and settled, there was boiling molten stone some sixty feet
underground; but there was only a small scratching
sound as it came to rest. A flame-amputated tree limb
rubbed tentatively against the hull.

Calhoun turned off the rockets. The ship swayed
slightly and there were crunching noises. Then it was
still on its landing fins.

"Now," said Calhoun, "I can take care of you,
Murgatroyd."

He flicked on the switches of the exterior microphones, which were much more sensitive than human
ears. The radiation detectors were still in action. They
reported only the cracklings of the distant storm.

But the microphones brought in the moaning of wind
over nearby mountaintops, and the almost deafening
susurrus of rustling leaves. Underneath these noises
there was a bedlam of other natural sounds. There were
chirpings and hootings and squeaks, and the gruntings
made by native animal life. These sounds had a singularly peaceful quality. When Calhoun toned them down
to be no more than background noise, they suggested
the sort of concert of night creatures which to men has
always seemed an indication of purest tranquility.

Presently Calhoun looked at the pictures the photorecorder had taken while the telescope's field swept over
the city. It was the colony-city reported to have been
begun two years before to receive colonists from Dettra

Two. It was the city of the landing grid which had tried to destroy the Med Ship as a dog kills a rat, by shaking it to fragments, some forty thousand miles in space. It was the city which had made Calhoun land with his vision plates blinded; which had drained his power reserves of some hundreds of millions of kilowatt-hours of energy. It was the city which had made his return to Med Headquarters impossible.

He inspected the telescopic pictures. They were very clear. They showed the city with astonishing detail. There was a lacy pattern of highways, with their medallions of multiple-dwelling units. There were the lavish park areas between the buildings of this planetary capital. There was the landing grid itself, a half-mile high structure of steel girders, a full mile in diameter.

But there were no vehicles on the highways. There were no specks on the overpasses to indicate people on foot. There were no 'copters on the building roofs, nor were there objects in mid-air to tell of air traffic.

The city was either deserted or it had never been occupied. But it was absolutely intact. The structures were perfect. There was no indication of past panic or disaster, and even the highways had not been overgrown by vegetation. But it was empty—or else it was dead.

But somebody in it had tried very ferociously and with singular effectiveness to try to destroy the Med Ship.

Calhoun raised his eyebrows and looked at Murgatroyd.

"Why is all this?" he asked. "Have you any ideas?"

"Chee!" shrilled Murgatroyd.

II

"The purpose of a contemplated human action is always the attainment of a desired subjective experience. But a subjective experience is desired both in terms of intensity and of duration. For an individual the temptingness of different degrees of intensity-of experience is readily computed. However, the temptingness of different durations is equally necessary for an estimate of the probability of a given person performing a given action. This modification of desirability by expected duration depends on the individual's time sense; its acuity and its accuracy. Measurements of time sense . . ."

Probability and Human Conduct—Fitzgerald

EVENTUALLY CALHOUN LEFT the ship and found a cultivated field and a dead man and other things. But while in the Med Ship he found only bewilderment. The first morning he carefully monitored the entire communications spectrum. There were no man-made signals in the air of Maris III. That was proof the world was uninhabited. But the ship's external microphones picked up a rocket roar in mid-morning. Calhoun looked, and saw the faint white trail of the rocket against the blue of the sky. The fact that he saw it was proof that it was in atmosphere. And that was evidence that the rocket was taking photographs for signs of the crater the Med Ship should have made in a crash landing.

The fact of search was proof that the planet was inhabited, but the silence of the radio spectrum said that it wasn't. The absence of traffic in the city said that it was dead or empty, but there were people there because they'd answered Calhoun's hail, and tried to kill him when he identified himself. But nobody would want to destroy a Med Ship except to prevent a health inspection, and nobody would want to prevent an inspection unless there was a situation aground that the Med Service ought to know about. But there should not be such a situation.

There was no logical explanation for such a series of contradictions. Civilized men acted either this way or that. There could only be civilized men here, yet they acted neither this way nor that. Therefore—and the confusion began all over again.

Calhoun dictated an account of events to date into the emergency responder in the ship. If a search call came from space, the responder would broadcast this data and Calhoun's intended action. He carefully shut off all other operating circuits so the ship couldn't be found by their radiation. He equipped himself for travel, and he and Murgatroyd left the ship. Obviously, he headed toward the city where whatever was wrong was centered.

Travel on foot was unaccustomed, but not difficult. The vegetation was semi-familiar. Maris III was an Earth-type planet and circled a Sol-type sun, and given similar conditions of gravity, air, sunlight, and temperature range, similar organisms should develop. There would be room, for example, for low-growing ground-cover plants, and there would also be advantages to height. There would be some equivalent of grass, and there would be the equivalent of trees, with intermediate forms having in-between habits of growth. Similar reasoning would apply to animal life. There would be parallel ecological niches for animals to fill, and animals would adapt to fill them.

Maris III was not, then, an "unearthly" environment. It was much more like an unfamiliar part of a known planet than a new world altogether. But there were some oddities. An herbivorous creature without legs which squirmed like a snake. A pigeon-sized creature whose wings were modified, gossamer-thin scales with iridescent colorings. There were creatures which seemed to live in lunatic association, and Calhoun was irritably curious to know if they were really symbiotes or only unrecognizable forms of the same organism, like the terrestrial male and female firefly-glowworm.

But he was heading for the city. He couldn't spare time to biologize. On his first day's journey he looked for food to save the rations he carried. Murgatroyd was handy here. The little *tormal* had his place in human society. He was friendly, and he was passionately imitative of human beings, and he had a definite psychology of his own. But he was useful, too. When Calhoun strode through the forests, which had such curiously unleaflike foliage, Murgatroyd strode grandly with him, imitating his walk. From time to time he dropped to all four paws to investigate something. He invariably caught up with Calhoun within seconds.

Once Calhoun saw him interestedly bite a tiny bit out of a most unpromising-looking shrub stalk. He savored its flavor, and then swallowed it. Calhoun took note of the plant and cut off a section. He bound it to the skin of his arm up near the elbow. Hours later there was no allergic reaction, so he tasted it. It was almost familiar. It had the flavor of a bracken shoot, mingled with a fruity taste. It would be a green bulk food like spinach or asparagus, filling but without much substance.

Later, Murgatroyd carefully examined a luscious-seeming fruit which grew low enough for him to pluck. He sniffed it closely and drew back. Calhoun noted that plant, too. Murgatroyd's tribe was bred at headquarters for some highly valuable qualities. One was a very sensitive stomach—but it was only one. Murgatroyd's metabolism was very close to man's. If he ate something and it didn't disagree with him, it was very likely safe for a man to eat it too. If he rejected something, it probably wasn't. But his real value was much more important than the tasting of questionable foods.

When Calhoun camped the first night, he made a fire of a plant shaped like a cactus barrel and permeated with oil. By heaping dirt around it, he confined its burning to a round space very much like the direct-heat element of an electronic stove. It was an odd illustration of the fact that human progress does not involve anything really new in kind, but only increased convenience and availability of highly primitive comforts. By the light of that circular bonfire, Calhoun actually read a little. But the light was inadequate. Presently he yawned. One did not get very far in the Med Service without knowing probability in human conduct. It enabled one to check on the accuracy of statements made, whether by patients or officials, to a Med Ship man. Today, though, he'd traveled a long way on foot. He glanced at Murgatroyd, who was gravely pretending to read from a singularly straight-edged leaf.

"Murgatroyd," said Calhoun, "it is likely that you will interpret any strange sound as a possible undesirable subjective experience. Which is to say, as dangerous. So if you hear anything sizable coming close during the night, I hope you'll squeal. Thank you."

Murgatroyd said, *"Chee,"* and Calhoun rolled over and went to sleep.

It was mid-morning of the next day when he came upon a cultivated field. It had been cleared and planted, of course, in preparation for the colonists who'd been expected to occupy the city. Familiar Earth plants grew in it, ten feet high and more. And Calhoun examined it carefully, in the hope of finding how long since it had received attention. In this examination, he found the dead man.

As a corpse, the man was brand new, and Calhoun very carefully put himself into a strictly medical frame of mind before he bent over for a technical estimate of what had happened, and when. The dead man seemed to have died of hunger. He was terribly emaciated, and he didn't belong in a cultivated field far from the city. By his garments he was a city dweller and a prosperous one. He wore the jewels which nowadays indicated a man's profession and status much more than the value of his possessions. There was money in his pockets, and writing materials, a wallet with pictures and identification, and the normal oddments a man would carry. He'd been a civil servant of the city. And he shouldn't have died of starvation.

He especially shouldn't have gone hungry here! The sweet maize plants were tall and green. Their ears were ripe. He hadn't gone hungry! There were the inedible remains of at least two dozen sweet maize ears. They had been eaten some time—some days—ago, and one had been left unfinished. If the dead man had eaten them but was unable to digest them, his belly should have been swollen with undigested food. It wasn't. He'd eaten and digested and still had died, at least largely of inanition.

Calhoun scowled.

"How about this corn, Murgatroyd?" he demanded.

He reached up and broke off a half-yard-long ear. He stripped away the protecting, stringy leaves. The soft grains underneath looked appetizing. They smelled like good fresh food. Calhoun offered the ear to Murgatroyd.

The little *tormal* took it in his paws and on the instant was eating it with gusto.

"If you keep it down, he didn't die of eating it," said Calhoun, frowning. "And if he ate it—which he did— he didn't die of starvation. Which he did."

He waited. Murgatroyd consumed every grain upon the oversized cob. His furry belly distended a little. Calhoun offered him a second ear. He set to work on that, too, with self-evident enjoyment.

"In all history," said Calhoun, "nobody's ever been able to poison one of you *tormals* because your digestive system has a qualitative analysis unit in it that yells bloody murder if anything's likely to disagree with you. As a probability of *tormal* reaction, you'd have been nauseated before now if that stuff wasn't good to eat."

But Murgatroyd ate until he was distinctly potbellied. He left a few grains on the second ear with obvious regret. He put it down carefully on the ground. He shifted his left-hand whiskers with his paw and elaborately licked them clean. He did the same to the whiskers on the right-hand side of his mouth. He said comfortably, *"Chee!"*

"Then that's that," Calhoun told him. "This man didn't die of starvation. I'm getting queasy!"

He had his lab kit in his shoulder pack, of course. It was an absurdly small outfit, with almost microscopic instruments. But in Med Ship field work the techniques of microanalysis were standard. Distastefully, Calhoun took the tiny tissue sample from which he could gather necessary information. Standing, he ran through the analytic process that seemed called for. When he finished, he buried the dead man as well as he could and started off in the direction of the city again. He scowled as he walked.

He journeyed for nearly half an hour before he spoke. Murgatroyd accompanied him on all fours now because of his heavy meal. After a mile and a half, Calhoun stopped and said grimly, "Let's check you over, Murgatroyd."

He verified the *tormal*'s pulse and respiration and temperature. He put a tiny breath sample through the part of the lab kit which read off a basic metabolism rate. The small animal was quite accustomed to the process. He submitted blandly. The result of the checkover was that Murgatroyd the *tormal* was perfectly normal.

"But," said Calhoun angrily, "that man died of starvation! There was practically no fat in the tissue sample at all! He arrived where we found him while he was strong enough to eat, and he stayed where there was good food, and he ate it, and he digested it, and he died of starvation: Why?"

Murgatroyd wriggled unhappily, because Calhoun's tone was accusing. He said, *"Chee!"* in a subdued tone of voice. He looked pleadingly up at Calhoun.

"I'm not angry with you," Calhoun told him, "but dammit—"

He packed the lab kit back into his pack, which contained food for the two of them for about a week.

"Come along!" he said bitterly. He started off. Ten minutes later he stopped. "What I said was impossible. But it happened, so it mustn't have been what I said. I must have stated it wrongly. He could eat, because he did. He did eat, because of the cobs left. He did digest it. So why did he die of starvation? Did he stop eating?"

"Chee!" said Murgatroyd with conviction.

Calhoun grunted and marched on once more. The man had not died of a disease, not directly. The tissue analysis gave a picture of death which denied that it came of any organ ceasing to function. Was it the failure of the organism—the man—to take the action required for living? Had he stopped eating?

Calhoun's mind skirted the notion warily. It was not plausible. The man had been able to feed himself and had done so. Anything which came upon him and made him unable to feed himself . . .

"He was a city man," growled Calhoun, "and this is a damned long way from the city. What was he doing out here, anyhow?"

He hesitated and tramped on again. A city man found starved in a remote place might have become lost, somehow or other. But if this man was lost, he was assuredly not without food.

"He belonged in the city," said Calhoun vexedly, "and he left it. The city's almost but not quite empty. Our would-be murderers are in it. This is a new colony. There was a city to be built and fields to be plowed and planted, and then a population was to come here from Dettra Two. The city's built and the fields are plowed and planted. Where's the population?"

He scowled thoughtfully at the ground before him. Murgatroyd tried to scowl too, but he wasn't very successful.

"What's the answer, Murgatroyd? Did the man come away from the city because he had a disease? Was he driven out?"

"Chee," said Murgatroyd without conviction.

"I don't know either," admitted Calhoun. "He

walked out into the middle of that field and then stopped walking. He was hungry and he ate. He digested. He stayed there for days. Why? Was he waiting to die of something? Presently he stopped eating. He died. What made him leave the city? What made him stop eating? Why did he die?"

Murgatroyd investigated a small plant and decided that it was not interesting. He came back to Calhoun.

"He wasn't killed," said Calhoun, "but somebody tried to kill us—somebody who's in the city now. That man could have come out here to keep from being killed by the same people. Yet he died anyhow. Why'd they want to kill him? Why'd they want to kill us? Because we were a Med Ship? Because they didn't want Med Service to know there was a disease here? Ridiculous!"

"Chee," said Murgatroyd.

"I don't like the looks of things," said Calhoun. "For instance, in any ecological system there are always carrion eaters. At least some of them fly. There would be plain signs if the city was full of corpses. There aren't any. On the other hand, if the city was inhabited, and there was sickness, they would welcome a Med Ship with open arms. But that dead man didn't come away from the city in any ordinary course of events, and he didn't die in any conventional fashion. There's an empty city and an improbable dead man and a still more improbable attempt at murder! What gives, Murgatroyd?"

Murgatroyd took hold of Calhoun's hand and tugged at it. He was bored. Calhoun moved on slowly.

"Paradoxes don't turn up in nature," said Calhoun darkly. "Things that happen naturally never contradict each other. You only get such things when men try to do things that don't fit together—like having a plague and trying to destroy a Med Ship, if that's the case, and living in a city and not showing on its streets, if that is occurring, and dying of starvation while one's digestion is good and there's food within hand's reach. And that did happen! There was dirty work at the spaceport, Murgatroyd. I suspect dirty work at every crossroad. Keep your eyes open."

"Chee," said Murgatroyd. Calhoun was fully in motion, now, and Murgatroyd let go of his hand and went on ahead to look things over.

Calhoun crossed the top of a rounded hillcrest some three miles from the shallow grave he'd made. He began to accept the idea that the dead man had stopped eating for some reason, as the only possible explanation of his death. But that didn't make it plausible. He saw another ridge of hills ahead.

In another hour he came to the crest of that farther range. It was the worn-down remnant of a very ancient mountain chain, now eroded to a mere fifteen hundred or two thousand feet. He stopped at the very top. Here was a time and place to look and take note of what he saw. The ground stretched away in gently rolling fashion for very many miles, and there was the blue blink of sea at the horizon. A little to the left he saw shining white. He grunted.

That was the city of Maris III, which had been built to receive colonists from Dettra and relieve the population pressure there. It had been planned as the nucleus of a splendid, spacious, civilized world-nation to be added to the number of human-occupied worlds. From its beginning it should have held a population in the hundreds of thousands. It was surrounded by cultivated fields, and the air above it should have been a-shimmer with flying things belonging to its inhabitants.

Calhoun stared at it through his binoculars. They could not make an image, even so near, to compare with that which the electron telescope had made from space, but he could see much. The city was perfect. It was intact. It was new. But there was no sign of occupancy anywhere. It did not look dead, so much as frozen. There were no fliers above it. There was no motion on the highways. He saw one straight road which ran directly away along his line of sight. Had there been vehicles on it, he would have seen at least shifting patches of color as clots of traffic moved together. There were none.

He pressed his lips together and began to inspect the nearer terrain. He saw foreshortened areas where square miles of ground had been cleared and planted with Earth vegetation. This was a complicated process. First the ground had to be bulldozed clean, and then great sterilizers had to lumber back and forth, killing every native seed and root and even the native soil bacteria. Then the land had to be sprayed with cultures of the nitrogen-fixing and phosphorous-releasing microscopic organisms which normally live in symbiosis with Earth plants. These had to be tested beforehand for their ability to compete with indigenous bacterial life. And then Earth plants could be sown.

They had been. Calhoun saw that inimitable green which a man somehow always recognizes. It is the green of plants whose ancestors thrived on Earth and which have followed that old planet's children halfway across the galaxy.

"There's a look to a well-tended field," said Calhoun, after a long look through binoculars, "that shows what kind of people cultivated it. There are fields up ahead that are well laid out, but nobody's touched them for weeks. The furrows are straight and the crops healthy. But they're beginning to show neglect. If the city was finished and waiting for its population, there would be caretakers tending the fields until the people came. There's been no caretaking done here!"

Murgatroyd stared wisely about as he considered Calhoun to be doing.

"In short," said Calhoun, "something's happened that I don't like. The population must be nearly zero or the fields would have been kept right. One man can keep a hell of a lot of ground in good shape, with modern machinery. People don't plant fields with the intention to neglect them. There's been a considerable change of plans around here. Enmity to a Med Ship is something more than a random impulse." Calhoun was not pleased. With the vision screens of his ship burned out, a return to headquarters was out of the question. "Whoever was handling the landing grid doesn't want help. He doesn't even want visitors. But Med Service was notified to come and look over the new colony.

Either somebody changed his views drastically, or the people in charge of the landing grid aren't the ones who asked for a public health checkup."

Murgatroyd said profoundly, *"Chee!"*

"The poor devil I buried even seems to hint at something of the sort. He could have used help! Maybe there are two kinds of people here. One kind doesn't want aid and tried to kill us because we'd offer it. The other kind needs it. If so, there might be a certain antagonism . . ."

He stared with knitted brows over the vast expanse toward the horizon. Murgatroyd, at this moment, was a little way behind Calhoun. He stood up on his hind legs and stared intently off to one side. He shaded his eyes with a forepaw in a singularly humanlike fashion and looked inquisitively at something he saw. Calhoun did not notice.

"Make a guess, Murgatroyd," he commanded. "Make a wild one. A dead man who'd no reason for dying. Live people who should have no reason for wanting to spatter us against the walls of our Med Ship. Something was fatal to that dead man. Somebody tried to be fatal to us. Is there a connection?"

Murgatroyd stared absorbedly at a patch of brushwood some fifty yards to his left. Calhoun started down the hillside. Murgatroyd remained fixed in a pose of intensely curious attention to the patch of brush. Calhoun went on. His back was toward the brush thicket.

There was a deep-toned, musical twanging sound from the thicket. Calhoun's body jerked violently from an impact. He stumbled and went down, with the shaft of a wooden projectile sticking out of his back. He lay still.

Murgatroyd whimpered. He rushed to where Calhoun lay upon the ground. He danced in agitation, chattering shrilly. He wrung his paws in humanlike distress. He tugged at Calhoun, but Calhoun made no response.

A girl emerged from the thicket. She was gaunt and thin, yet her garments had once been of admirable quality. She carried a strange and utterly primitive weapon. She moved toward Calhoun, bent over him and laid a hand to the wooden projectile she had fired into his back.

He moved suddenly. He grappled. The girl toppled, and he swarmed upon her savagely as she struggled. But she was taken by surprise. There was the sound of panting, and Murgatroyd danced in a fever of anxiety.

Then Calhoun stood up quickly. He stared down at the emaciated girl who had tried to murder him from ambush. She was panting horribly now.

"Really," said Calhoun in a professional tone, "as a doctor I'd say that you should be in bed instead of wandering around trying to murder total strangers. When did this trouble begin? I'm going to take your temperature and your pulse. Murgatroyd and I have been hoping to find someone like you. The only other human being I've met on this planet wasn't able to talk."

He swung his shoulder pack around and impatiently jerked a sharp-pointed stick out of it. It was the missile, which had been stopped by the pack. He brought out his lab kit. With absolute absorption in the task, he prepared to make a swift check of his would-be murderer's state of health.

It was not good. There was already marked emaciation. The desperately panting girl's eyes were deep-sunk, hollow. She gasped and gasped. Still gasping, she lapsed into unconsciousness.

"Here," said Calhoun curtly, "you enter the picture, Murgatroyd. This is the sort of thing you're designed to handle."

He set to work briskly. Presently he observed, "Besides a delicate digestion and a hair-trigger antibody system, Murgatroyd, you ought to have the instincts of a watchdog. I don't like coming that close to being shot by a lady patient. See if there's anybody else around, will you?"

"*Chee,*" said Murgatroyd shrilly. But he didn't understand. He watched as Calhoun deftly drew a small sample of blood from the unconscious girl's arm and painstakingly put half the tiny quantity into an almost microscopic ampule in the lab kit. Then he moved toward Murgatroyd. The *tormal* wriggled as Calhoun made the injection. But it did not hurt. There was an insensitive spot on his flank where the nerves had been blocked off before he was a week old.

"As one medical man to another," said Calhoun, "you've noticed that the symptoms are of anoxia—oxygen starvation. Which doesn't make sense in the open air where we're breathing comfortably. Another paradox, Murgatroyd! But there's an emergency, too. How can you relieve anoxia when you haven't any oxygen?"

He looked down at the unconscious girl. She displayed the same sort of emaciation he'd noted in the dead man in the field some miles back. Patients with a given disease often acquire a certain odd resemblance to each other. This girl seemed to be in an earlier stage of whatever had killed the civil servant in the corn field. He'd died of starvation with partly eaten food by his hand. She'd tried to murder Calhoun, just as persons unknown, in the city, had tried to kill both Calhoun and Murgatroyd in the Med Ship some forty thousand miles out in space. But her equipment for murder was not on a par with that of the operators of the landing grid. She didn't belong in their class. She might be a fugitive from them.

Calhoun put these things together. Then he swore in sudden bitter anger. He stopped abruptly, in concern lest she'd heard.

She hadn't. She was still insensible.

III

"That pattern of human conduct which is loosely called 'self-respecting' has the curious property of restricting to the individual, through his withdrawal of acts to communicate misfortune, the unfavorable chance occurrences which probability insists must take place. On the other hand, the same pattern of human conduct tends to disseminate and to share chance favorable occurrences among the group. The members of a group of persons practicing 'self-respect,' then, increase the mathematical probability of cultures in which principles leading to this type of behavior become obsolete. A decadent society brings bad luck upon itself by the operation of the laws of probability . . ."

Probability and Human Conduct—Fitzgerald

SHE CAME VERY slowly back to consciousness. It was almost as if she waked from utterly exhausted sleep. When she first opened her eyes, they wandered vaguely until they fell upon Calhoun. Then a bitter and contemptuous hatred filled them. Her hand fumbled weakly to the knife at her waist. It was not a good weapon. It had been table cutlery, and the handle was much too slender to permit a grip by which somebody could be killed. Calhoun bent over and took the knife away from her. It had been ground unskillfully to a point.

"In my capacity as your doctor," he told her, "I

must forbid you to stab me. It wouldn't be good for you." Then he said, "Look, my name's Calhoun. I came from Sector Med Headquarters to make a planetary health inspection here, and some lads in the city apparently didn't want a Med Ship aground. So they tried to kill me by buttering me all over the walls of my ship with the landing-grid field. I made what was practically a crash landing, and now I need to know what's up."

The burning hatred remained in her eyes, but there was a trace of doubt.

"Here," said Calhoun, "is my identification."

He showed her the highly official documents which gave him vast authority—where a planetary government was willing to concede it.

"Of course," he added, "papers can be stolen. But I have a witness that I'm what and who I say I am. You've heard of *tormals?* Murgatroyd will vouch for me."

He called his small and furry companion. Murgatroyd advanced and politely offered a small, prehensile paw. He said *"Chee"* in his shrill voice, and then solemnly took hold of the girl's wrist in imitation of Calhoun's previous action of feeling her pulse.

Calhoun watched. The girl stared at Murgatroyd. But all the galaxy had heard of *tormals*. They'd been found on a planet in the Deneb region, and they were engaging pets and displayed an extraordinary immunity to the diseases men were apt to scatter in their interstellar journeying. A forgotten Med Service researcher made an investigation of the ability of *tormals* to live in contact with men. He came up with a discovery which made them very much too valuable to have their lives wasted in mere sociability. There were still not enough of Murgatroyd's kind to meet the need that men had of them, and laymen had to forego their distinctly charming society. So Murgatroyd was an identification.

The girl said faintly, "If you'd only come earlier . . . but it's too late now. I—I thought you came from the city."

"I was headed there," said Calhoun.

"They'll kill you."

"Yes," agreed Calhoun, "they probably will. But right now you're ill and I'm Med Service. I suspect there's been an epidemic of some disease here, and that for some reason the people in the city don't want the Med Service to know about it. You seem to have it, whatever it is. Also, that was a very curious weapon you shot me with."

The girl said drearily, "One of our group had made a hobby of such things. Ancient weapons. He had bows and arrows and—what I shot you with was a crossbow. It doesn't need power. Not even chemical explosives. So when we ran away from the city, he ventured back in and armed us as well as he could."

Calhoun nodded. A little irrelevant talk is always useful at the beginning of a patient interview. But what she said was not irrelevant. A group of people had fled the city. They'd needed arms, and one of their number had gone back into the city for them. He'd known where to find reconstructions of ancient lethal devices— a hobby collection. It sounded like people of the civil service type. Of course there were no longer social classes separated by income. Not on most worlds, anyhow. But there were social groupings based on similar tastes, which had led to similar occupations and went on to natural congeniality. Calhoun placed her now. He remembered a long-outmoded term, "upper middle class," which no longer meant anything in economics but did in medicine.

"I'd like a case history," he said conversationally. "Name?"

"Helen Jons," she said wearily.

He held the mike of his pocket recorder to pick up her answers. Occupation: statistician. She'd been a member of the office force which was needed during the building of the city. When the construction work was finished, most of the workmen returned to the mother world Dettra, but the office staff stayed on to organize things when the colonists arrived.

"Hold it," said Calhoun. "You were a member of the office staff who stayed in the city to wait for the colonists. But a moment ago you said you fled from the city. There are still some people there, at least around the landing grid. I've reason to be sure of it. Were they part of the office staff too? If not, where did they come from?"

She shook her head weakly.

"Who are they?" he repeated.

"I don't know," she said drearily. "They came after the plague."

"Oh," said Calhoun. "Go on. When did the plague turn up? And how?"

She continued in a feeble voice. The plague appeared among the last shipload of workmen waiting to be returned to the mother world. There were then about a thousand people in the city, of all classes and occupations. The disease appeared first among those who tended the vast fields of planted crops.

It was well established before its existence was suspected. There were no obvious early symptoms, but those affected felt a loss of energy and they became listless and lackadaisical. The listlessness showed first in a cessation of griping and quarreling among the workmen. Normal, healthy human beings are aggressive. They squabble with each other as a matter of course. But squabbling ceased. Men hadn't the energy for it.

Shortness of breath appeared later. It wasn't obvious, at first. Men who lacked energy to squabble wouldn't exert themselves and so get out of breath. It was one of the medical staff who drove himself impatiently in spite of what he thought was a transient weariness, and discovered himself gasping without cause. He took a metabolism test, suspicious because the symptoms were so extreme. His metabolic rate was astonishingly low.

"Hold it again," commanded Calhoun. "You're a statistician, but you're talking medical talk. How's that?"

"Kim," the girl said tiredly. "He was on the medical staff. I was—I was going to marry him."

Calhoun nodded. "Go on."

She seemed to need to gather strength even to talk. She did not go on. Shortness of breath among the plague victims was progressive. Presently they gasped horribly from the exertion of getting to their feet, even. Walking, however slowly, could be done only at the cost of panting for breath. After a certain time they simply lay still. They could not summon the energy to stir. Then they sank into unconsciousness and died.

"What did the doctors think about all this?" demanded Calhoun.

"Kim could tell you," said the girl exhaustedly. "The doctors worked frantically. They tried everything— everything! They could get the symptoms in experimental animals, but they couldn't isolate the germ or whatever it was that caused the disease. Kim said they couldn't get a pure culture. It was incredible. No technique would isolate the cause of the symptoms, and yet the plague was contagious. Terribly so!"

Calhoun scowled. A new pathogenic mechanism was always possible, but it was at least unlikely. Still, something that standard bacteriological methods couldn't track down was definitely a job for the Med Service. But there were people in the city who didn't want the Med Service to interfere. The girl had referred to them once, when she spoke of a flight from the city, and again when she said someone ventured back for weapons. And she'd used a weapon on him, thinking him from the city. The description of the plague, too, was remarkable.

It was able to hide from men, which was something no other microorganism could accomplish. It was an ability that would offer no advantage to a disease germ in a state of purely natural happenings. Disease germs do not encounter bacteriological laboratories, as a rule, often enough to need to adapt to escape them. It would not help an average germ or microbe to be invisible to an electron microscope. There would be no reason for such invisibility to be developed.

But more than that, why should anybody want to keep a Med Service man like Calhoun from investigating a plague? When infected people fled from the city to die in the wilds, why should people remaining in the city try to destroy a Med Ship which might help to end the deaths? Ordinarily, well people in the middle of an epidemic are terrified lest they catch it. They'd be as anxious for Med Service help as those already infected. What was going on here?

"You said about a thousand people were in the city," observed Calhoun. "They tended the crops and waited for the city's permanent inhabitants. What happened after the plague was recognized to be one?"

"The first shipload of emigrants came from Dettra Two," said the girl hopelessly. "We didn't bring them to ground with the landing grid. Instead, we described the plague. We warned them away. We quarantined ourselves while our doctors tried to fight the disease. The shipload of new people went back to Dettra without landing."

Calhoun nodded. This would be normal.

"Then another ship came. There were maybe two hundred of us left alive. More than half of us already showed signs of the plague. This other ship came. It landed on emergency rockets because we had nobody left who knew how to work the grid."

Then her voice wavered a little as she told of the landing of the strange ship in the landing grid of the city that was dying without ever having really lived. There was no crowd to meet the ship. Those people who were not yet stricken had abandoned the city and scattered themselves widely, hoping to escape contagion by isolating themselves in new and uncontaminated dwelling units. But there was no lack of communication facilities. Nearly all the survivors watched the ship come down through vision screens in the control building of the then-useless grid.

The ship touched ground. Men came out. They did not look like doctors. They did not act like them. The vision screens in the control building were snapped off immediately. Contact could not be restored. So the isolated groups spoke agitatedly to each other by vision screen. They exchanged messages of desperate hope.

Then, newly landed men appeared at an apartment whose occupant was in the act of such a conversation with a group in a distant building. He left the visiphone on as he went to admit and greet the men he hoped were researchers, at least, come to find the cause of the plague and end it.

The viewers at the other visiphone plate gazed eagerly into his apartment. They saw the group of newcomers enter. They saw them deliberately murder their friend and the survivors of his family.

Plague-stricken or merely terrified people—in pairs or trios widely separated through the city—communicated in swift desperation. It was possible that there had been a mistake, a blunder, and an unauthorized crime had been committed. But it was not a mistake. Unthinkable as such an idea was, there developed proof that the plague on Maris III was to be ended as if it were an epizootic among animals. Those who had it and those who had been exposed to it were to be killed to prevent its spread among the newcomers.

A conviction of such horror could not be accepted without absolute proof. But when night fell, the public power supply of the city was cut off and communications ended. The singular sunset hush of Maris III left utter stillness everywhere—except for the screams which echoed among the city's innumerable empty-eyed, unoccupied buildings.

The scant remainder of the plague survivors fled in the night. They fled singly and in groups, carrying the plague with them. Some carried members of their families who were too weak to walk. Others helped already-doomed wives or friends or husbands to the open country. Flight would not save their lives. It would only prevent their murder. But somehow that seemed a thing to be attempted.

"This," said Calhoun, "is not a history of your own case. When did you develop the disease, whatever it may be?"

"Don't you know what it is?" asked Helen hopelessly.

"Not yet," admitted Calhoun. "I've very little information. I'm trying to get more."

He did not mention the information gathered from a dead man in a corn field some miles away.

The girl told of her own case. The first symptom was listlessness. She could pull out of it by making an effort, but it progressed. Day by day more urgent, more violent effort was needed to pay attention to anything, and she noted greater weakness when she tried to act. She felt no discomfort, not even hunger or thirst. She'd had to summon increasing resolution even to become aware of the need to do anything at all.

The symptoms were singularly like those of a man too long at too high an altitude without oxygen. They were even more like those of a man in a non-pressurized flier, whose oxygen supply was cut off. Such a man would pass out without realizing that he was slipping into unconsciousness, only it would happen in minutes. Here the process was infinitely gradual. It was a matter of weeks. But it was the same thing.

"I'd been infected before we ran away," said Helen drearily. "I didn't know it then. Now I know I've a few more days of being able to think and act, if I try hard enough. But it'll be less and less each day. Then I'll stop being able to try."

Calhoun watched the tiny recorder roll its multiple-channel tape from one spool to the other as she talked.

"You had energy enough to try to kill me," he observed.

He looked at the weapon. There was an arched steel spring placed crosswise at the end of a barrel like a sporting blast-gun. Now he saw a handle and a ratchet by which the spring was brought to tension, storing up power to throw the missile. He asked, "Who wound up this crossbow?"

Helen hesitated. "Kim—Kim Walpole," she said finally.

"You're not a solitary refugee now? There are others of your group still alive?"

She hesitated again, and then said, "Some of us came

to realize that staying apart didn't matter. We couldn't hope to live anyhow. We already had the plague. Kim is one of us. He's the strongest. He wound up the crossbow for me. He had the weapons to begin with.''

Calhoun asked seemingly casual questions. She told him of a group of fugitives remaining together because all were already doomed. There had been eleven of them. Two were dead now. Three others were in the last lethargy. It was impossible to feed them. They were dying. The strongest was Kim Walpole, who'd ventured back into the city to bring out weapons for the rest. He'd led them, and now was still the strongest and—so the girl considered—the wisest of them all.

They were waiting to die. But the newcomers to the planet—the invaders, they believed—were not content to let them wait. Groups of hunters came out of the city and searched for them.

"Probably," said the girl dispassionately, "to burn our bodies against contagion. They kill us so they won't have to wait. And it just seemed so horrible that we felt we ought to defend our right to die naturally. That's why I shot at you. I shouldn't have, but . . .''

She stopped helplessly. Calhoun nodded.

The fugitives now aided each other simply to avoid murder. They gathered together exhaustedly at night-fall, and those who were strongest did what they could for the others. By day, those who could walk scattered to separate hiding places, so that if one was discovered, the others might still escape the indignity of being butchered. They had no stronger motive than that. They were merely trying to die with dignity, instead of being killed as sick beasts. Which bespoke a tradition and an attitude that Calhoun approved. People like these would know something of the science of probability in human conduct. Only they would call it ethics. But the strangers—the invaders—were of another type. They probably came from another world.

"I don't like this," said Calhoun coldly. "Just a moment."

He went over to Murgatroyd. Murgatroyd seemed to

droop a little. Calhoun checked his breathing and listened to his heart. Murgatroyd submitted, saying only *"Chee"* when Calhoun put him down.

"I'm going to help you to your rendezvous," said Calhoun abruptly. "Murgatroyd's got the plague now. I exposed him to it, and he's reacting fast. And I want to see the others of your group before nightfall."

The girl just managed to get to her feet. Even speaking had tired her, but she gamely though wearily moved off at a slant to the hillside's slope. Calhoun picked up the odd weapon and examined it thoughtfully. He wound it up as it was obviously meant to be. He picked up the missile it had fired, and put it in place. He went after the girl, carrying it. Murgatroyd brought up the rear.

Within a quarter of a mile the girl stopped and clung swaying to the trunk of a slender tree. It was plain that she had to rest, and dreaded getting off her feet because of the desperate effort needed to arise.

"I'm going to carry you," said Calhoun firmly. "You tell me the way."

He picked her up bodily and marched on. She was light. She was not a large girl, but she should have weighed more. Calhoun still carried the quaint antique weapon without difficulty.

Murgatroyd followed as Calhoun went up a small incline on the greater hillside and down a very narrow ravine. Through brushwood he pushed until he came to a small open space where shelters had been made for a dozen or so human beings. They were utterly primitive —merely roofs of leafy branches over framework of sticks. But of course they were not intended for permanent use. They were meant only to protect plague-stricken folk while they waited to die.

But there was disaster here. Calhoun saw it before the girl could. There were beds of leaves underneath the shelters. There were three bodies lying upon them. They would be those refugees in the terminal coma which, since the girl had described it, accounted for the dead man Calhoun had found, dead of starvation with food plants all around him. But now Calhoun saw something more. He swung the girl swiftly in his arms so that she would not see. He put her gently down and said, "Stay still. Don't move. Don't turn."

He went to make sure. A moment later he raged. It was Calhoun's profession to combat death and illness in all its forms, and he took his profession seriously. There are defeats, of course, which a medical man has to accept, though unwillingly. But nobody in the profession, and least of all a Med Ship man, could fail to be roused to fury by the sight of people who should have been his patients, lying utterly still with their throats cut.

He covered them with branches. He went back to Helen.

"This place has been found by somebody from the city," he told her harshly. "The men in coma have been murdered. I advise you not to look. At a guess, whoever did it is now trying to track down the rest of you."

He went grimly over the small open glade, searching the ground for footprints. There was ground-cover at most places, but at the edge of the clearing he found one set of heavy footprints leading away. He put his own foot beside a print and rested his weight on it. His foot made a lesser depression. The other print had been made by a man weighing more than Calhoun. Therefore it was not one of the party of plague victims.

He found another set of such footprints, entering the glade from another spot.

"One man only," he said icily. "He won't think he has to be on guard, because a city's administrative personnel—such as was left behind for the plague to hit— doesn't usually have weapons among their possessions. And he's confident that all of you are weak enough not to be dangerous to him."

Helen did not turn pale. She was pale before. She stared numbly at Calhoun. He looked grimly at the sky.

"It'll be sunset within the hour," he said savagely. "If it's the intention of the newcomers—the invaders—to burn the bodies of all plague victims, he'll come back here to dispose of these three. He didn't do it before lest the smoke warn the rest of you. But he knows the shelters held more than three people. He'll be back!''

Murgatroyd said *"Chee!"* in a bewildered fashion. He was on all fours, and he regarded his paws as if they did not belong to him. He panted.

Calhoun checked him over. Respiration way up. Heart action like that of the girl Helen. His temperature was not up, but down. Calhoun said remorsefully, ''You and I, Murgatroyd, have a bad time of it in our profession. But mine is the worse. You don't have to play dirty tricks on me, and I've had to, on you!''

Murgatroyd said *"Chee!"* and whimpered. Calhoun laid him gently on a bed of leaves which was not occupied by a murdered man.

''Lie still!'' he commanded. ''Exercise is bad for you.''

He walked away. Murgatroyd whined faintly, but lay still as if exhausted.

''I'm going to move you,'' Calhoun told the girl, ''so you won't be seen if that man from the city comes back. And I've got to keep out of sight for a while or your friends will mistake me for him. I count on you to vouch for me later. Basically, I'm making an ambush.'' Then he explained irritably, ''I daren't try to trail him because he might not backtrack to return here.''

He lifted the girl and placed her where she could see the glade in its entirety, but would not be visible. He settled down himself a little distance away. He was acutely dissatisfied with the measures he was forced to take. He could not follow the murderer and leave Helen and Murgatroyd unprotected, even though the murderer might find another victim because he was not being trailed. In any case Murgatroyd's life, just now, was more important than the life of any human being on Maris III. On him depended everything.

But Calhoun was not pleased with himself at all.

There was silence except for the normal noises of living wild things. There were fluting sounds, which later Calhoun would be told came from crawling creatures not too much unlike the land turtles of Earth. There were deep-bass hummings, which came from the throats of miniature creatures which might roughly be described as birds. There were chirpings which were the cries of what might be approximately described as wild pigs, except that they weren't. But the sun Maris sank low toward the nearer hillcrests, and behind them, and there came a strange, expectant hush over all the landscape. At sundown on Maris III there is a singular period when the creatures of the day are silent and those of the night are not yet active. Nothing moved. Nothing stirred. Even the improbable foliage was still.

It was into this stillness and this half-light that small and intermittent rustling sounds entered. Presently there was a faint murmur of speech. A tall, gaunt young man came out of the brushwood, supporting a pathetically feeble old man, barely able to walk. Calhoun made a gesture of warning as the girl Helen opened her lips to speak. The slowly moving pair came into the glade, the young man moving exhaustedly, the older man staggering with weakness despite his help. The younger helped the older to sit down. He stood panting.

A woman and a man came together, assisting each other. There was barely light enough from the sun's afterglow to show their faces, emaciated and white.

A fifth feeble figure came tottering out of another opening in the brush. He was dark-bearded and broad, and he had been a powerful man. But now the plague lay heavily upon him.

They greeted each other listlessly. They had not yet discovered those of their number who had been murdered.

The gaunt young man summoned his strength and moved toward the shelter where Calhoun had covered an unseemly sight with branches.

Murgatroyd whimpered.

There came another rustling sound, but this had nothing of feebleness in it. Branches were pushed forthrightly out of the way and a man came striding confidently into the small open space. He was well-fleshed, and his color was excellent. Calhoun automatically judged him to be in superlative good health, slightly overweight, and of that physical type which suffers very few psychosomatic troubles because it lives strictly and enjoyably in the present.

Calhoun stood up. He stepped out into the fading light just as the sturdy stranger grinned at the group of plague-stricken semi-skeletons.

"Back, eh?" he said amiably. "Saved me a lot of trouble. I'll make one job of it."

With leisurely confidence he reached to the blaster at his hip.

"Drop it!" snapped Calhoun from behind him. "Drop it!"

The sturdy man whirled. He saw Calhoun with a crossbow raised to cover him. There was light enough to show that it was not a blast-rifle—in fact, that it was no weapon of any kind modern men would ordinarily use. But much more significant to the sturdy man was the fact that Calhoun wore a uniform and was in good health.

He snatched out his blast-pistol with professional alertness.

And Calhoun shot him with the crossbow. It happened that he shot him dead.

IV

"Statistically, it must be recognized that no human action is without consequences to the man who acts. Again statistically, it must be recognized that the consequences of an action tend with strong probability to follow the general pattern of the action. A violent action, for example, has a strong probability of violent consequences, and since at least some of the consequences of an act must affect the person acting, a man who acts violently exposes himself to the probability that chance consequences which affect him, if unfavorable, will be violently so."

Probability and Human Conduct—Fitzgerald

MURGATROYD HAD BEEN inoculated with a blood sample from the girl Helen some three hours or less before sunset. But it was one of the more valuable genetic qualities of the *tormal* race that they reacted to bacterial infection as a human being reacts to medication. Medicine on the skin of a human being rarely has any systemic effect. Medication on mucous membrane penetrates better. Ingested medication —medicine that is swallowed—has greater effectiveness still. But substances injected into tissues or the blood-stream have the most effect of all. A centigram of almost any drug administered by injection will have an effect close to that of a gram taken orally. It acts at once and there is no modification by gastric juices.

Murgatroyd had had half a cubic centimeter of the girl's blood injected into the spot on his flank where he could feel no pain. It contained the unknown cause of the plague on Maris III. Its effect as injected was incomparably greater than the same infective material smeared on his skin or swallowed. In either such case, of course, it would have had no effect at all, because *tormals* were to all intents and purposes immune to ordinary contagions. Just as they had a built-in unit in their digestive tract to cause the instant rejection of unwholesome food, their body cells had a built-in ability to produce antibodies immediately if the toxin of a pathogenic organism came into contact with them. So *tormals* were effectively safe against any disease transmitted by ordinary methods of infection. Yet if a culture of pathogenic bacteria, say, were injected into their bloodstream, their whole body set to work to turn out antibodies because their whole body was attacked, and all at once. There was practically no incubation period.

Murgatroyd, who had been given the plague in midafternoon, was reacting violently to its toxins by sunset. But two hours after darkness fell he arose and said shrilly, *"Chee-chee-chee!"* He'd been sunk in heavy slumber. When he woke, there was a small fire in the glade, about which the exhausted, emaciated fugitives consulted with Calhoun.

Calhoun was saying bitterly, "The whole thing is wrong! It's self-contradictory, and that means a man, or men, trying to meddle with the way the universe was made to run. Those characters in the city aren't fighting the plague—they're cooperating with it! When I came in a Med Ship, they should have welcomed my help. Instead they tried to kill me so I couldn't perform the function I was made for and trained for! They're going against the way the universe works. From what Helen tells me, they landed with the purpose of helping the plague wipe out everybody else on the planet. They began their butchery immediately. That's why you people ran away."

The weary, weakened people listened almost numbly.

"The invaders—and that's what they are," said Calhoun angrily, "have to be immune and know it, or else they wouldn't risk contagion by tracking you down to murder you. The city's infected and they're not alarmed. You're dying and they only try to hasten your death. I arrive, and I might be of use, so they try to kill me. They must know what the plague is and what it does, because their only criticism of it seems to be that it doesn't kill fast enough. And that is out of the ordinary course of nature. It's not intelligent human conduct."

Murgatroyd peered about. He'd just waked, and the look of his surroundings had changed entirely while he slept.

"A plague's not pleasant, but it's natural. This plague is neither pleasant *nor* natural. There's human interference with the normal course of events—certainly the way things are going is abnormal. I'm not too sure somebody didn't direct this from the beginning. That's why I shot that man with the crossbow instead of taking a blaster to him. I meant to wound him so I could make him answer questions, but the crossbow's not an accurate weapon and it happened that I killed him instead. There wasn't much information in the stuff in his pockets. The only significant item was a ground-car key, and that only means there's a car waiting for him to come back from hunting you."

The gaunt young man said drearily, "He didn't come from Dettra, which is our planet. Fashions are different on different worlds, and he wears a uniform we don't have. His clothing uses fasteners we don't use, too. He's from another solar system entirely."

Murgatroyd saw Calhoun and rushed to him. He embraced Calhoun's legs with enthusiasm. He chattered shrilly of his relief at finding the man he knew. The skeletonlike plague victims stared at him.

"This," said Calhoun with infinite relief, "is Murgatroyd. He's had the plague and is over it. So now we'll get you people cured. I wish I had better light!"

He counted Murgatroyd's breathing and listened to his heart. Murgatroyd was in that state of boisterous good health which is standard in any well-cared-for lower animal, but amounts to genius in a *tormal*. Calhoun regarded him with deep satisfaction.

"All right!" he said. "Come along!"

He plucked a brand of burning resinous stuff from the campfire. He handed it to the gaunt young man and led the way. Murgatroyd ambled complacently after him. Calhoun stopped under one of the unoccupied shelters and got out his lab kit. He bent over Murgatroyd. What he did, did not hurt. When he stood up, he squinted at the red fluid in the instrument he'd used.

"About twenty cc's," he observed. "This is strictly emergency stuff I'm doing now. But I'd say that there's an emergency."

The gaunt young man said, "I'd say you've doomed yourself. The incubation period seems to be about six days. It took that long to develop among the doctors we had on the office staff."

Calhoun opened a compartment of the kit, whose minuscule test tubes and pipettes gleamed in the torchlight. He absorbedly transferred the reddish fluid to a miniature filter-barrel, piercing a self-healing plastic cover to do so. He said, "You're a pre-med of course. The way you talk—"

"I was an intern," said Kim. "Now I'm pre-corpse."

"I doubt that last," said Calhoun. "But I wish I had some distilled water . . . this is anticoagulant." He added the trace of a drop to the sealed, ruddy fluid. He shook the whole filter to agitate it. The instrument was hardly bigger than his thumb. "Now a clumper . . ." He added a minute quantity of a second substance from an almost microscopic ampule. He shook the filter again. "You can guess what I'm doing. With a decent lab I'd get the structure and formula of the antibody Murgatroyd has so obligingly turned out for us. We'd set to work synthesizing it, and in twenty hours we would have it coming out of the reaction flasks in quantity. But there is no lab."

"There's one in the city," said the gaunt young man hopelessly. "It was for the colonists who were to come.

And we were staffed to give them proper medical care. When the plague came, our doctors did everything imaginable. They not only tried the usual culture tricks, but they cultured samples of every separate tissue in fatal cases. They never found a single organism, even with electron microscopes, that would produce the plague.'' He said with a sort of weary pride, ''Those who'd been exposed worked until they had the plague, and then others took over. Every man worked as long as he could make his brain serve him.''

Calhoun squinted through the glass tube of the filter at the light of the sputtering torch.

''Almost clumped,'' he said. Then he added, ''I suspect there's been some very fine laboratory work done somewhere to give the invaders their confidence of immunity to this plague. They landed and instantly set to work to mop up the city—to complete the job the plague hadn't quite finished. I suspect there could have been some fine lab work done to make plague mechanism undetectable. I don't like the things I'm forced to suspect!''

He inspected the glass filter tube again.

''Somebody,'' he said coldly, ''considered that my arrival would be an unfavorable circumstance to him and what he wanted to happen. I think it is. He tried to kill me. He didn't. I'm afraid I consider his existence an unfavorable circumstance.'' He paused, and said very measuredly, ''Cooperating with a plague is a highly technical business; it needs as much information as fighting a plague. Cooperation could no more be done from a distance than fighting it. If the invaders had come to fight the plague, they'd have sent their best medical men to help. If they came to assist it, they'd have sent butchers, but they'd also send the very best man they had to make sure that nothing went wrong with the plague itself. The logical man to be field director of the extermination project would be the man who'd worked out the plague himself.'' He paused again, and said icily, ''I'm no judge to pass on anybody's guilt or innocence or fate, but as a Med Service man I've authority to take measures against health hazards!"

He began to press the plunger of the filter, judging by the wavering light of the torch. The piston was itself the filter, and on one side a clear, mobile liquid began very slowly to appear.

"Just to be sure, though—you said there was a lab in the city and the doctors found nothing."

"Nothing," agreed Kim hopelessly. "There'd been a complete bacteriological survey of the planet. Nothing new appeared. Everybody's oral and intestinal flora were normal. Naturally, no alien bug would be able to compete with the strains we humans have been living with for thousands of years. So there wasn't anything unknown in any culture from any patient."

"There could have been a mutation," said Calhoun. He watched the clear serum increase. "But if your doctors couldn't pass the disease—"

"They could!" said Kim bitterly. "A massive shot of assorted bugs would pass it, breathed or swallowed or smeared on the skin. Experimental animals could be given the plague. But no one organism could be traced as giving it. No pure culture would!"

Calhoun continued to watch the clear fluid develop on the delivery side of the filter piston. Presently there was better than twelve cubic centimeters of clear serum on one side, and an almost solid block of clumped blood cells on the other. He drew off the transparent fluid with a fine precision.

"We're working under far from asceptic conditions," he said wryly, "but we have to take the chances. Anyhow, I'm getting a hunch. A pathogenic mechanism that isn't a single, identifiable bug—it's not natural. It smells of the laboratory, just as uniformed murderers who are immune to a plague do. It's not too wild a guess to suspect that somebody worked out the plague as well as the immunization of the invaders. That it was especially designed to baffle the doctors who might try to fight it."

"It did," agreed Kim bitterly.

"So," said Calhoun, "maybe a pure culture wouldn't carry the plague. Maybe the disaster-producing apparatus simply isn't there when you make pure cultures. There's even a reason to suspect something specific. Murgatroyd was a very sick animal. I've only known of one previous case in which a *tormal* reacted as violently as Murgatroyd did to an injection. That case had us sweating."

"If I were going to live," said Kim grimly, "I might ask what it was."

"Since you're going to," Calhoun told him, "I'll tell you. It was a pair of organisms. Separately, they were so near harmless as makes no difference. Together, their toxins combined to be pure poison. It was synergy. They were a synergic pair which, together, were like high explosive. That one was the devil to track down!"

He went back across the glade. Murgatroyd came skipping after him, scratching at the anesthetic patch on his side.

"You go first," said Calhoun briefly to Helen Jons. "This is an antibody serum. You may itch afterward, but I doubt it. Your arm, please."

She bared her pitifully thin arm. He gave her practically a cc of fluid which—plus corpuscles and some forty-odd other essential substances—had been circulating in Murgatroyd's bloodstream not long since. The blood corpuscles had been clumped and removed by one compound plus the filter, and the anticoagulant had neatly modified most of the others. In a matter of minutes, the lab kit had prepared as usable a serum as any animal-using technique would produce. Logically, the antibodies it contained should be isolated and their chemical structure determined. They should be synthesized, and the synthetic antibody-complex administered to plague victims. But Calhoun faced a group of people doomed to die. He could only use his field kit to produce a small-scale miracle for them. He could not do a mass-production job.

"Next!" said Calhoun. "Tell them what it's all about, Kim."

The gaunt young man bared his own arm. "If what he says is so, this will cure us. If it isn't so, nothing can do us any more harm."

And Calhoun briskly gave them, one after another, the shots of what ought to be a curative serum for an unidentified disease which he suspected was not caused by any single germ, but by a partnership. Synergy is an acting together. Charcoal will burn quietly. Liquid air will not burn at all. But the two together constitute a violent explosive. The ancient simple drug sulfa is not intoxicating. A glass of wine is not intoxicating. But the two together have the kick of dynamite. Synergy in medicine is a process by which, when one substance with one effect is given in combination with another substance with another effect, the two together have the consequences of a third substance intensified to fourth or fifth or tenth power.

"I think," said Calhoun when he'd finished, "that by morning you'll feel better—perhaps cured of the plague entirely and only weak from failure to force yourselves to take nourishment. If it turns out that way, then I advise you all to get as far away from the city as possible for a considerable while. I think this planet is going to be repopulated. I suspect that shiploads of colonists are on the way here now, but not from Dettra, which built the city. And I definitely guess that, sick or well, you're going to be in trouble if or when you contact the new colonists."

They looked tiredly at him. They were a singular lot of people. Each one seemed half-starved, yet their eyes had not the brightness of suffering. They looked weary beyond belief, and yet there was no self-neglect. They were of that singular human type which maintains human civilization against the inertia of the race, because it drives itself to get needed things done. It is not glamorous, this dogged part of mankind which keeps things going. It is sometimes absurd. For dying folk to wash themselves when even such exertion calls for enormous resolution is not exactly rational. To help each other to try to die with dignity was much more a matter of self-respect than of intellectual decision. But as a Med Ship man, Calhoun viewed them with some warmth. They were the type that has to be called on when an emergency occurs and the wealth-gathering type tends to flee and the low time-sense part of a population inclines to riot or loot or worse.

Now they waited listlessly for their own deaths.

"There's no exact precedent for what's happened here," explained Calhoun. "A thousand years or so ago there was a king of France—a country back on old Earth—who tried to wipe out a disease called leprosy by executing all the people who had it. But lepers were a nuisance. They couldn't work. They had to be fed by charity. They died in inconvenient places and only other lepers dared handle their bodies. They tended to throw normal human life out of kilter. That wasn't the case here. The man I killed wanted you dead for another reason. He and his friends wanted you dead right away."

The gaunt Kim Walpole said tiredly, "He wanted to dispose of our bodies in a sanitary fashion."

"Nonsense!" snapped Calhoun. "The city's infected. You lived, ate, breathed, walked in it. Nobody can dare use that city unless they know how the contagion's transmitted, and how to counteract it. Your own colonists turned back. These men wouldn't have landed if they hadn't known they were safe!"

There was silence.

"If the plague is an intended crime," added Calhoun, "you are the witnesses to it. You've got to be gotten rid of before colonists from somewhere other than Dettra arrive here."

The dark-bearded man growled, "Monstrous! Monstrous!"

"Agreed," said Calhoun. "But there's no interstellar government now, any more than there was a planetary government in the old days back on Earth. So if somebody pirates a colony ready to be occupied, there's no authority able to throw them out. The only recourse would be war. And nobody is going to start an interplanetary war—not with the bombs that can be landed!

If the invaders can land a population here, they can keep the place." He paused, and said with irony, "Of course they could be persuaded that they were wrong."

But that was not even worth thinking about. In the computation of probabilities in human conduct, self-interest is a high-value factor. Children and barbarians have clear ideas of justice due *to* them, but no idea at all of justice due *from* them. And though human colonies spread toward the galaxy's rim, there was still a large part of every population which was civilized only in that it could use tools. Most people still remained comfortably barbaric or childish in their emotional lives. It was a fact that had to be considered in Calhoun's profession. It bore remarkably on matters of contagion, and health, and life itself.

"You'll have to hide. Perhaps permanently," he told them. "It depends partly on what happens to me, however. I have to go to the city. There's a very serious health problem there."

Kim said with irony, "In the city? Everybody's healthy there. They're so healthy that they come out to hunt us down for sport!"

"Considering that the city's thoroughly infected, their immunity is a health problem," said Calhoun. "But besides that, it looks like the original cause of the plague is there, too. I'd guess that the originator of this plague is technical director of the exterminating operation that's in progress on this planet. I'd guess he's in the ship that brought the butcher-invaders. I'd be willing to bet that he's got a very fine laboratory on the ship."

Kim stared at him. He clenched and unclenched his hands.

"And I'd say it ought to be quite useless to fight this plague before that man and that laboratory were taken care of," said Calhoun. "You people are probably all right. I think you'll wake up feeling better. You may be well. But if the plague is artificial, if it was developed to make a colony planet useless to the world that built it, but healthy for people who want to seize it . . ."

"What?"

"It may be the best plague that was developed for the purpose, but you can be sure it's not the only one. Dozens of strains of deadly bugs would have to be developed to be sure of getting the deadliest. Different kinds of concealment would have to be tried, in case somebody guessed the synergy trick, as I did, and could do something about the first plague used. There'd have to be a second and third and fourth plague available. You see?"

Kim nodded, speechless.

"A setup like that is a real health hazard," said Calhoun. "As a Med Service man, I have to deal with it. It's much more important than your life or mine or Murgatroyd's. So I have to go into the city to do what can be done. Meanwhile, you'd better lie down now. Give Murgatroyd's antibodies a chance to work."

Kim started to move away. Then he said, "You've been exposed. Have you protected yourself?"

"Give me a quarter-cc shot," said Calhoun. "That should do."

He handed the injector to the gaunt young man. He noted the deftness with which Kim handled it. Then he helped get the survivors of the original group—there were six of them now—to the leafy beds under the shelters. They were very quiet, even more quiet than their illness demanded. They were very polite. The old man and woman who'd struggled back to the glade together made a special effort to bid Calhoun good night with the courtesy appropriate to city folk of tradition.

Calhoun settled down to keep watch through the night. Murgatroyd snuggled confidingly close to him. There was silence.

But not complete silence. The night of Maris III was filled with tiny noises, and some not so faint. There were little squeaks which seemed to come from all directions, including overhead. There were chirpings which were definitely at ground level. There was a sound like effortful grunting in the direction of the hills. In the lowlands there was a rumbling which moved very slowly from one place to another. By its rate of motion, Calhoun guessed that a pack or herd of small animals was making a night journey and uttering deep-bass noises as it traveled.

He debated certain grim possibilities. The man he'd killed had had a ground-car key in his pocket. He'd probably come out in a powered vehicle. He might have had a companion, and the method of hunting down fugitives—successful, in his case—was probably well established. That companion might come looking for him, so watchfulness was necessary.

Meanwhile, there was the plague. The idea of synergy was still most plausible. Suppose the toxins—the poisonous metabolic products—of two separate kinds of bacteria combined to lessen the ability of the blood to carry oxygen and scavenge away carbon dioxide? It would be extremely difficult to identify the pair, and the symptoms would be accounted for. No pure culture of any organism to be found would give the plague. Each, by itself, would be harmless. Only a combination of the two would be injurious. And if so much was assumed, and the blood lost its capacity to carry oxygen, mental listlessness would be the first symptom of all. The brain requires a high oxygen level in its blood supply if it is to work properly. Let a man's brain be gradually, slowly, starved of oxygen and all the noted effects would follow. His other organs would slow down, but at a lesser rate. He would not remember to eat. His blood would still digest food and burn away its own fat—though more and more sluggishly, while his brain worked only foggily. He would become only semiconscious, and then there would come a time of coma when unconsciousness claimed him and his body lived on only as an idling machine, until it ran out of fuel and died.

Calhoun tried urgently to figure out a synergic combination which might make a man's blood cease to do its work. Perhaps only minute quantities of the dual poison might be needed. It might work as an antivitamin or an antienzyme, or—

The invaders of the city were immune, though. Quite

possibly the same antibodies Murgatroyd had produced were responsible for their safety. Somewhere, somebody had very horribly used the science of medicine to commit a monstrous crime. But medicine was still a science. It was still a body of knowledge of natural law. And natural laws are consistent and work together toward that purpose for which the universe was made.

He heard a movement across the clearing. He reached for his blaster. Then he saw what the motion was. It was Kim Walpole, intolerably weary, trudging with infinite effort to where Helen Jons lay. Calhoun heard him ask heavily, "You're all right?"

"Yes, Kim," said the girl softly. "I couldn't sleep. I'm wondering if we can hope."

Kim did not answer.

"If we live . . ." said the girl yearningly. She stopped.

Calhoun felt that he ought to put his fingers in his ears. The conversation was strictly private. But he needed to be on guard, so he coughed, to give notice that he heard. Kim called to him, "Calhoun?"

"Yes," said Calhoun. "If you two talk, I suggest that you do it in whispers. I'm going to watch in case the man I killed had a companion who might come looking for him. One question, though. If the plague is artificial, it had to be started. Did a ship land here two weeks or a month before your workmen began to be ill? It could have come from anywhere."

"There was no landing of any ship," said Kim. "No."

Calhoun frowned. His reasoning seemed airtight. The plague must have been introduced here from somewhere else!

"There had to be," he insisted. "Any kind of ship! From anywhere!"

"There wasn't," repeated Kim. "We had no off-planet communication for three months before the plague appeared. There's been no ship here at all except from Dettra, with supplies and workmen and that sort of thing."

Calhoun scowled. This was impossible. Then Helen's

voice sounded very faintly. Kim made a murmurous response. Then he said, "Helen reminds me that there was a queer roll of thunder one night not long before the plague began. She's not sure it means anything, but in the middle of the night, with all the stars shining, thunder rolled back and forth across the sky above the city. This was a week or two before the plague. It waked everybody. Then it rolled away to the horizon and beyond. The weather people had no explanation for it."

Calhoun considered. Murgatroyd nestled still closer to him. He snapped his fingers suddenly.

"That was it!" he said savagely. "That's the trick! I haven't all the answers, but I know some very fine questions to ask now. And I think I know where to ask them."

He settled back. Murgatroyd slept. There was the faintest possible murmur of voices where Kim Walpole and the girl Helen talked wistfully of the possibility of hope.

Calhoun contemplated the problem before him. There were very, very few survivors of the people who belonged in the city. There was a shipload of murderers—butchers!—who had landed to see that the last of them were destroyed. Undoubtedly there was a highly trained and probably brilliant microbiologist in the invaders' expedition. One would be needed, to make sure of the success of the plague and to verify the absolute protection of the butchers, so that other colonists could come here to take over and use the planet. There could be no failure of protection for the people *not* of Dettra who expected to inhabit this world. There would have to be completely competent supervision of this almost unthinkable, this monstrous stealing of a world.

"The plague would probably be a virus pair," muttered Calhoun. "Probably introduced and scattered by a ship with wings *and* rockets. It'd have wings because it wouldn't want to land, but did want to sweep back and forth over the city. It'd drop frozen pellets of the double virus culture. They'd drop down toward the ground, melting and evaporating as they fell, and they'd flow

over the city as an invisible, descending blanket of contagion coating everything. Then the ship would head
away over the horizon and out to space on its rockets.
Its wings wouldn't matter out of atmosphere and it'd go
into overdrive and go back home to wait . . ."

He felt an icy anger, more savage than any rage could
be. With this technique, a confederation of human
beings utterly without pity could become parasitic on
other worlds. They could take over any world by
destroying its people, and no other people could make
any effective protest, because the stolen world would be
useless except to the murderers who had taken it over.
This affair on Maris III might be merely a test of the
new ruthlessness. The murderer planet could spread its
ghastly culture like a cancer through the galaxy.

But there were two other things involved beside a
practice of conquest through murder by artificial
plagues. One was what would happen to the people—
the ordinary, commonplace citizens—of a civilization
which spread and subsisted by such means. It would not
be good for them. In the aggregate, they'd be worse off
than the people who died.

The other?

"They might make a field test of their system," said
Calhoun very coldly, "without doing anything more
serious to the Med Service than killing one man—me—
and destroying one small Med Ship. But they couldn't
adopt this system on any sort of scale without destroying the Med Service first. I'm beginning to dislike this
business excessively!"

V

"Very much of physical science is merely the comprehension of long-observed facts. In human conduct there is a long tradition of observation, but a very brief record of comprehension. For example, human lives in contact with other human lives follow the rules of other ecological systems. All too often, however, a man imagines that an ecological system is composed only of things, whereas such a system operates through the actions of things. It is not possible for any part of an ecological complex to act upon the other parts without being acted upon in its turn. So that it follows that it is singularly stupid—but amazingly common—for an individual to assume human society to be passive and unreactive. He may assume that he can do what he pleases, but inevitably there is a reaction as energetic as his action, and as well-directed. Moreover, probability . . ."

Probability and Human Conduct—Fitzgerald

AN HOUR AFTER sunrise Calhoun's shoulder pack was empty of food. The refugees arose, and they were weak and ravenous. Their respiration had slowed to normal. Their pulses no longer pounded. Their eyes were no longer dull, but very bright. But they were in advanced states of malnutrition, and now were aware of it. Their brains were again receiving adequate oxygen and their metabolism was at normal level—and they knew they were starving.

Calhoun served as cook. He trudged to the spring that Helen described. He brought back water. While they sucked on sweet tablets from his rations and watched with hungry eyes, he made soup from the dehydrated rations he'd carried for Murgatroyd and himself. He gave it to them as the first thing their stomachs were likely to digest.

He watched as they fed themselves. The elderly man and woman sipped delicately, looking at each other. The man with the broad dark beard ate with tremendous self-restraint. Helen fed the weakest, oldest man, between spoonsful for herself, and Kim Walpole ate slowly, brooding.

Calhoun kept them going, slowly providing them with food, until he had no more to offer. By then they had made highly satisfying gains in strength. But it was then late morning.

He drew Kim aside.

"During the night," he said, "I got another lot of serum ready. I'm leaving it with you, with an injector. You'll find other fugitives. I gave you massive doses. You'd better be stingy. Try half-cc shots. Maybe you can skimp that."

"What about you?" demanded Kim.

Calhoun shrugged.

"I've got an awful lot of authority, if I can make it stick," he said drily. "As a Med Ship man I've power to take complete charge of any health emergency. You people have a plague here. That's one emergency. It's artificial. That's another. The people who've spread it here have reason, in their success to date on this planet, to think they can take over any other world they choose. And, human nature being what it is, that's the biggest health hazard in history. I've got to get to work on it."

"There's a shipload of armed murderers here," said Kim.

"I'm not much interested in them," admitted Calhoun. "I want to get at the man who's at the head of this thing. As I told you, he should have other plagues in stock. It's entirely possible that the operation here is no more than a small-scale field test of a new technique for conquest."

"If those butchers find you, you'll be killed."

"True," admitted Calhoun. "But the number of chance happenings that could favor me is much greater than the number that could favor them. I'm working with nature, and they're working against it. Anyhow, as a Med Service man, I should prevent the landing of anybody—anybody at all—on a plague-stricken planet like this. And I suspect that there are plans for landings. I should set up an effective quarantine."

His tone was dry. Kim Walpole stared. "You mean you'll try to stop them?"

"I shall try," said Calhoun, "to implement the authority vested in me by the Med Service for such cases as this. The rules about quarantine are rather strict."

"You'll be killed," said Kim again.

Calhoun ignored the repeated prediction.

"That invader found you," he observed, "because he knew that you'd have to drink. So he found a brook and followed it up, looking for signs of humans drinking from it. He found footprints about the spring. I found his footprints there, too. That's the trick you'll use to find other fugitives. But pass on the word not to leave tracks hereafter. For the other advice, I advise you to get all the weapons you can. Modern ones, of course. You've got the blaster from the man I killed."

"I think," said Kim between his teeth, "that I'll get some more. If hunters from the city do track us to our drinking places, I'll know how to get more weapons!"

"Yes," agreed Calhoun. "Now. Murgatroyd made the antibodies that cured you. As a general rule, you can expect antibody production in your own bodies once an infection begins to be licked. In case of extreme emergency, each of you can probably supply antibodies for a fair number of other plague victims. You might try serum from blisters you produce on your skin. Quite often antibodies turn up there. I don't guarantee it, but sometimes it works."

He paused. Kim Walpole said harshly, "But you!

Isn't there anything we can do for you?''

"I was going to ask you something," said Calhoun. He produced the telephoto films of the city as photographed from space. "There's a laboratory in the city. A biochemistry lab. Show me where to look for it.''

Walpole gave explicit directions, pointing out the spot on the photo. Calhoun nodded. Then Kim said fiercely, "But tell us something we can do! We'll be strong, presently, and we'll have weapons. We'll track downstream to where hunters leave their ground-cars and be equipped with them. We can help you!''

Calhoun nodded approvingly.

"Right. If you see the smoke of a good-sized fire in the city, and if you've got a fair number of fairly strong men with you, and if you've got ground-cars, you might investigate. But be cagey about it. Very cagey!''

"If you signal we'll come," said Kim Walpole grimly, "no matter how few we are.''

"Fine," said Calhoun. He had no intention of calling on these weakened, starving people for help.

He swung his depleted pack on his back again and slipped away from the glade. He made his way to the spring, which flowed up clear and cool from unseen depths. He headed down the little brook which flowed away from it. Murgatroyd raced along its banks. He hated to get his paws wet. Presently, where the underbrush grew thickly close to the water's edge, Murgatroyd wailed, *"Chee! Chee!"* Calhoun plucked him from the ground and set him on his shoulder. Murgatroyd clung blissfully there as Calhoun followed down the stream bed. He adored being carried.

Two miles down, there was another cultivated field. This one was planted with an outsized root crop, and Calhoun walked past shoulder-high bushes with four-inch blue-and-white flowers. He recognized the plant as one of the family Solanaceae—belladona was still used in medicine—but he couldn't identify it until he dug up a root and found a tuber. But the six-pound specimen he uncovered was still too young and green to be eaten.

Murgatroyd refused to touch it.

Calhoun was ruefully considering the limitations of specialized training when he came to the end of the cultivated field. There was a highway. It was new, of course. City, fields, highways, and all the physical aspects of civilized life had been built on this planet before the arrival of the colonists who were to inhabit it. It was extraordinary to see such preparations for a population not yet on hand. But Calhoun was much more interested in the ground-car he found waiting on the highway, hard by a tiny bridge under which a small brook flowed.

The key he'd taken from the dead invader fitted. He got in the car and beckoned Murgatroyd to the seat beside him.

"Characters like the man I killed, Murgatroyd," he observed, "aren't very important. They're mere butchers—killers. That sort of character likes to loot. There's nothing here for them to loot. They're bound to be bored. They're bound to be restless. We won't have much trouble with them. I'm worrying about the man who possibly designed and is certainly supervising the action of the plague. I look for trouble with him."

The ground-car was in motion then, toward the city. He drove on.

It was a good twenty miles, but he did not encounter a single other vehicle. Presently the city lay spread out before him. He surveyed it thoughtfully. It was very beautiful. Fifty generations of architects on many worlds had played with stone and steel, groping for perfection. This city was a close approach. There were towers which glittered whitely, and low buildings which seemed to nestle on the vegetation-covered ground. There were soaring bridges and gracefully curving highways, and park areas laid out and ready. There was no monotony anywhere.

The only exception to gracefulness was the massive landing grid, half a mile and a mile across, which was a lacework of monster steel girders with spider-thin wires of copper woven about them in the complex curves its operation required. Inside it, Calhoun could see the ship of the invaders. It had landed in the grid enclosure, and later Calhoun had blown out the transformers of the grid. They were probably in process of repair now. But the ship stood sturdily on the ground inside the great structure which dwarfed it.

"The man we're after will be in that ship, Murgatroyd," said Calhoun. "He'll have inner and outer lock-doors fastened, and he'll be inside a six-inch beryllium-steel wall. Rather difficult to break in upon. And he'll be uneasy. An intellectual type gone wrong doesn't feel at ease with the kind of butchers he has to associate with. I think the problem is to get him to invite us into his parlor. But it may not be simple."

"Chee," said Murgatroyd doubtfully.

"Oh, we'll manage," Calhoun assured him. "Somehow!"

He spread out his photographs. Kim Walpole had marked where he should go and a route to it. Having been in the city while it was being built, he knew even the service lanes which, being sunken, were not a part of the city's good looks.

"But the invaders," explained Calhoun, "won't deign to use grubby service lanes. They consider themselves aristocrats because they were sent to be conquerors, though the work required of them was simple butchery. I wonder what sort of swine run the world they came from!"

He put away the photos and headed for the city again. He branched off the main highway, near the city. A turn-off descended into a cut. The road in the cut was intended for loads of agricultural produce entering the city. It was strictly utilitarian. It ran below the surface of the park areas, and entered the city without pride. When among the buildings it ran between rows of undecorated gates, behind which waste matter was destined to be collected to be carted away as fertilizer for the fields. The city was very well designed.

Rolling through the echoing sunken road, Calhoun saw, just once, a ground-car in motion on a far-flung, cobwebby bridge between two tall towers. It was high overhead. Nobody in it would be watching grubby commerce roads.

The whole affair was very simple indeed. Calhoun brought the car to a stop beneath the overhang of a balconied building many stories high. He got out and opened the gate. He drove the car into the cavernous, so-far-unused lower part of the building. He closed the gate behind him. He was in the center of the city, and his presence was unknown. This was at three or later in the afternoon.

He climbed a clean new flight of steps and came to the sections the public would use. There were glassy walls which changed their look as one moved between them. There were the lifts. Calhoun did not try to use them. He led Murgatroyd up the circular ramps which led upward in case of unthinkable emergency. He and Murgatroyd plodded up and up. Calhoun kept count.

On the fifth level there were signs of use, while all the others had that dusty cleanness of a structure which has been completed but not yet occupied.

"Here we are," said Calhoun cheerfully.

But he had his blaster in his hand when he opened the door of the laboratory. It was empty. He looked approvingly about as he hunted for the storeroom. It was a perfectly equipped biological laboratory, and it had been in use. Here the few doomed physicians awaiting the city's population had worked desperately against the plague. Calhoun saw the trays of cultures they'd made, dried up and dead now. Somebody had turned over a chair. Probably when the laboratory was searched by the invaders, in case someone not of their kind still remained alive in it.

He found the storeroom. Murgatroyd watched with bright eyes as he rummaged.

"Here we have the things men use to cure each other," said Calhoun oracularly. "Practically every one a poison save for its special use! Here's an assortment of spores—pathogenic organisms, Murgatroyd. They have their uses. And here are drugs which are synthesized nowadays, but are descended from the poisons found on the spears of savages. Great helps in medicine. And here are the anesthetics—poisons too. These are what I am counting on."

He chose, very painstakingly. Dextrethyl. Polysulfate. The one marked inflammable and dangerous. The other with the maximum permissible dose on its label, and the names of counteracting substances which would neutralize it. He burdened himself. Murgatroyd reached up a paw. Since Calhoun was carrying something, he wanted to carry something, too.

They went down the circular ramp again as sunset drew near. Calhoun searched once more in the below-surface levels of the buildings. He found what he wanted—a painter's vortex-gun which would throw "smoke rings" of tiny paint droplets at a wall or object to be painted. One could vary the size of the ring at impact from a bare inch to a three-foot spread.

Calhoun cleaned the paint-gun. He was meticulous about it. He filled its tank with dextrethyl brought down from the laboratory. He piled the empty containers out of sight.

"This trick," he observed, as he picked up the paint-gun again, "was devised to be used on a poor devil of a lunatic who carried a bomb in his pocket for protection against imaginary assassins. It would have devastated a quarter-mile circle, so he had to be handled gently."

He patted his pockets. He nodded.

"Now we go hunting—with an oversized atomizer loaded with dextrethyl. I've polysulfate and an injector to secure each specimen I knock over. Not too good, eh? But if I have to use a blaster I'll have failed."

He looked out a window at the sky. It was now late dusk. He went back to the gate to the service road. He went out and carefully closed it behind him. On foot, with many references to the photomaps, he began to find his way toward the landing grid. It ought to be something like the center of the invaders' location.

It was dark when he climbed other service stairs from the cellar of another building. This was the communications building of the city. It had been the key to the mopping-up process the invaders began on landing. Its callboard would show which apartments had communicators in use. When such a call showed, a murder party could be sent to take care of the caller. Even after the first night, some individual, isolated folk might remain, unaware of what was happening. So there would be somebody on watch, just in case a dying man called for the solace of a human voice while still he lived.

There was a man on watch. Calhoun saw a lighted room. Paint-gun ready, he moved very silently toward it. Murgatroyd padded faithfully behind him.

Outside the door, Calhoun adjusted his curious weapon. He entered. The man nodded in a chair before the lifeless board. When Calhoun entered he raised his head and yawned. He turned.

Calhoun sprayed him with smoke rings—vortex rings. But the rings were spinning missiles of vaporized dextrethyl, that anesthetic developed from ethyl chloride some two hundred years before, and not yet bettered for its special uses. One of its properties was that the faintest whiff of its vapor produced a reflex to gasp. A second property was that, like the ancient ethyl chloride, it was the quickest-acting anesthetic known.

The man by the callboard saw Calhoun. His nostrils caught the odor of dextrethyl. He gasped.

He fell unconscious.

Calhoun waited patiently until the dextrethyl was out of the way. It was almost unique among vapors in that at room temperature it was lighter than air. It rose toward the ceiling. Presently Calhoun moved forward and brought out the polysulfate injector. He bent over the unconscious man. He did not touch him otherwise.

He turned and walked out of the room with Murgatroyd piously marching behind him.

Outside, Calhoun said, ''As one medical man to another, perhaps I shouldn't have done that. But I'm dealing with a health hazard, a plague. Sometimes one has to use psychology to supplement standard measures.

I consider that the case here. Anyhow this man should be missed sooner than most. He has a job where his failure to act should be noticed."

"Chee?" asked Murgatroyd zestfully.

"No," said Calhoun. "He won't die. He wouldn't be so unkind."

It was dark outdoors now. When Calhoun stepped out into the street—he'd touched nothing in the callboard office to show that he'd entered it—nightfall was complete. Stars shone brightly, but the empty, unlighted ways of the city were black. There seemed to be a formless menace in the air. When Calhoun moved down the street, Murgatroyd, who hated the dark, reached up a furry paw and held on to Calhoun's hand for reassurance.

Calhoun moved silently and Murgatroyd's footfalls were inaudible. The feel of the never-lived-in city was appalling. A sleeping city seems ghostly and strange, even with lighted streets. An abandoned city is intolerably desolate, with all its inhabitants gone or dead. But a city which has never lived, which lies lifeless under a night sky because its people never came to occupy it—that city has the worst feeling of all. It seems unnatural. It seems insane. It is like a corpse which could have lived but never acquired a soul, and now waits horribly for something demoniac to enter it and give it a seeming of life too horrifying to imagine.

The invaders unquestionably felt that creeping atmosphere of horror. Presently there was proof. Calhoun heard small, drunken noises in the street. He tracked them cautiously. He found the place—one lighted ground-floor window on a long street lined on both sides with towering structures reaching for the sky. The sheer walls were utterly dark. The narrow lane of stars that could be seen overhead seemed utterly remote. The street itself was empty and dark, and murmurous with echoes of sounds that had not ever really been made. And here there were no natural sounds at all. Building walls cut off the normal night-sounds of the open country. There was a dead and muffled and murmurous stillness fit to crack one's eardrums.

Except for the drunken singing. Men drank together in an unnecessarily small room, which they had lighted very brightly to try to make it seem alive. All about them was deadness and stillness, so they made supposedly festive noises, priming themselves to cheerfulness with many bottles. With enough to drink, perhaps the illusion could be believed in. But it was a pitifully tiny thread of sound in a dark and empty city. Outside, where Calhoun and Murgatroyd paused to listen, the noise of drunken singing had a quality of biting irony.

Calhoun grunted, and the sound echoed endlessly between the stark walls around and above.

"We could use those characters," he said coldly, "only there are too many of them."

He and Murgatroyd went on. He'd familiarized himself with the stars, earlier, and knew that he moved in the direction of the landing grid. He'd arranged for one man on duty—at the callboard—to fail to do his work. The process was carefully chosen. He'd knocked out the invader with vortex rings of dextrethyl vapor, and then had given him a shot of polysulphate. The combination was standard, like magnesium sulphate and ether, centuries before. Polysulphate was an assisting anesthetic, never used alone because a man who was knocked out by it stayed out for days. In surgery it was used in a quantity which seemed not to affect a man at all, yet the least whiff of dextrethyl would then put him under for an operation, while he could instantly be revived. It was safer and under better control than any other kind of anesthesia.

But Calhoun had reversed the process. He'd put the callboard operator under with vapor, and then given polysulphate to keep him under for sixty hours or more. And then he'd left him. When the invader was found unconscious, it would bother the other butchers very much. They'd never suspect his condition to be the result of enemy action. They'd consider him in a coma. A coma was the last effect of the plague that had pre-

sented them with a planet. They'd believe their fellow to
be dying of the plague they were supposed to be immune
to. They would panic, expecting immediate death for
themselves. But more than one man in a comalike state
would be more effective in producing complete dis-
organization and despair.

A door banged, back by the lighted window in the
desolate black street. Someone came out. Someone else.
A third man. They moved along the street, singing
hoarsely and untunefully and with words as slurred and
uncertain as their footsteps. Echoes resounded between
the high building walls. The effect was eerie.

Calhoun moved into a doorway. He waited. When
the three men were opposite him, they linked arms to
steady themselves. One man roared out quite unprintable verses of a song in which another joined uncertainly from time to time. The third protested
aggrievedly. He halted, and the three of them argued
solemnly about something indefinable, swaying as they
talked with owlish, drunken gravity.

Calhoun lifted the paint-gun. He held down the
trigger. Invisible rings of dextrethyl vapor whisked
toward the trio. They gasped. They collapsed. Calhoun
took his measures.

Presently one man lay unconscious on the street in a
coma which imitated perfectly, except for the emaciation, the terminal coma of the fugitives from the city.
Some distance away Calhoun plodded on toward the
landing grid with a second man, also unconscious, over
his shoulder. Murgatroyd followed closely. The third
man, stripped to his underwear, waited where he might
be found within the next day or two.

VI

"It is improper to use the term 'gambler' of a man who uses actuarial tables or tables of probability to make wages which ensure him a favorable percentage of returns. Still less is it proper to call a man who cheats a gambler. He eliminates chance from his operations by his cheating. He does not gamble at all.

"The only true gambler is one who takes risks without considering chance; who acts upon reason or intuition or hunch or superstition without advertising to probability. He ignores the fact that chance as well as thought has a share in determining the outcome of any action. In this sense, the criminal is the true gambler. He is always confident that probability will not interfere; that no random happening will occur. To date, however, there has been no statistical analysis of a crime which has proved it an action which a reasonably prudent man would risk. The effects of pure, random happen-chance can be so overwhelming . . ."

Probability and Human Conduct—Fitzgerald

THE NIGHT NOISES of the planet Maris III came from all the open space beyond the city itself. From the buildings themselves, of course, there was only silence. There were park areas left between them here and there, and green spaces bordered all the highways. But only small chirping sounds came from the city. The open country sang to the stars.

Calhoun settled himself, with an unconscious burden

and Murgatroyd. He could not know how long it would be before the callboard operator would be missed and checked on. He was sure, though, that the appearance of terminal coma in a man who should be immune to the plague would produce results. The callboard man would be brought to the microbiologist who must be in charge of this murder operation. There had to be such a man. He had to know all about the plague. He had to be able to meet any peculiarity that came up. At a guess, only the best qualified of all the men who'd worked to develop the plague would be trusted with its first field test. He might even be the man who himself had devised the synergic combination. He'd be on hand. He'd have every possible bit of equipment he could need, in a superlatively arranged laboratory on the ship. And the callboard man would be brought to him.

Calhoun waited. He had another man in seeming coma, ready for use when the time came. Now he rested in the deep star-shadow of one of the landing grid's massive supports. Murgatroyd stayed close to him. The *tormal* was normally active by day. Darkness daunted him. He tended to whimper if he could not be close to Calhoun.

Overhead loomed the soaring, heavy arches of the landing grid. The grid could handle twenty-thousand-ton liners, and heavier ones too. It was designed to conduct the interstellar business of a world. Beyond it, the city reared up against the stars. The control building, from which the grid was operated, sprawled over half an acre, not far from where Calhoun lay in wait. His eyes were adjusted to the darkness, and he could see faint glows as if there were lighted windows facing away from him. He was within a hundred yards of the giant, globular ship which had brought the invaders here to do their work of butchery.

There was quiet save for the chorus of myriads of small voices which serenaded the heavens. It was a remarkable total sound. Now and again Calhoun heard sustained deep-bass notes, like the lowest possible tones of a great organ. Then there were liquid trillings, which might come from any kind of bird or beast or reptile. In between came chirpings and abrupt paeans of music, like woodwinds essaying tentative melodic runs.

It was easy for Calhoun to wait. The whole affair had added itself up in his mind. He felt that he not only knew what had happened on this world, but what might happen elsewhere if this particular enterprise proved profitable.

This world of Maris III was to have been a daughter-planet of the old, long-settled Dettra Two. There would have been a close linkage of interest and traditions between the two worlds. They would have had a common tradition, and common blood, and all the ties that can keep two civilizations akin. The older culture had built a city and farms and facilities for half a million of its more adventurous members. They would have come here and entered upon and possessed this world, and they would have zestfully begun its development in the image of the older planet. They would have proudly begun payment for what they had received, and even more proudly prepared to receive more and more and yet more of the senior world's crowded people.

All this was in accord with natural law, which not only determines the courses of worlds about their central suns, but dictates what is wise and fit and suitable for mankind. But men need not heed the laws of nature. They cannot be changed, but they can be broken. And somewhere there was a world, or at least the government of a world, which essayed to break the laws Calhoun knew were essential.

In the great cosmos even crime is matter-of-fact. Natural laws can be twisted to aid it. For example, a spaceship could be built with wings. In space they would not matter. Normally they would be useless. But if somebody wanted to commit a very great crime, a spaceship could be built with wings, and instead of entering atmosphere on rockets designed only to let it down gently in case of emergency, it could enter an unsuspecting planet's air and fly there on the wings it had brought through light-years of emptiness.

Such a winged spacecraft, flying by rocket power as an airplane, could dump out frozen pellets of contagion. It could choose a place for this dumping which was upwind from a city, and it could choose a height so that an area of many, many square miles would be saturated with invisible, deadly creators of disease. The ship could even fly away and up and up and up, and ultimately depend on its rockets alone in airlessness to take it up to where its space-drive could operate in unstressed space. It could return to its home in overdrive, and the only sign of its coming anywhere—the only sign that would be known—would be a memory of thunder rolling in a star-filled sky. But later there would be a plague.

Exactly this had happened here. The empty city had been drenched with virus particles so tiny that only electron microscopes could tell that they existed, and could not tell them from others closely kin to them. But they were deadly. Singly, no. Alone, each of two types might produce only the most trivial of infections. Combined, they produced a toxin which took from human blood its power to carry oxygen. In a sense, the effect was like that of carbon monoxide. More directly, they caused bodies to starve for oxygen.

And all this was unnatural. Men had devised the plague and the means of spreading it. They made use of it. On the world where thunder had rolled in a cloudless sky, men and women died. Presently a ship came to verify it, to make sure that everything went wrong on Maris III. They knew the plague could not harm them. They murdered the few survivors in the city that they could find. They hunted down the others in the open country.

They now waited for more of their own kind to come, to occupy the planet made ready for them. When ships came from Dettra Two, which had built the city and prepared the fields, the settlers then in occupation could refuse to let them land. Or they could let them land and then watch them die. Maris III was useless now to the world that had developed it. Only the world that had

murdered its first small population could have any
benefit from it at all. Because, of course, the emigrants
from the criminal world could be immunized to the
plague their rulers had sent before them. They could live
there freely, like the butchers who came first of all. It
might seem a very brilliant course of conduct.

But Calhoun ground his teeth. He could see other
angles to this affair. Men who could arrange this could
go further. Much further. What he'd imagined was
trivial compared to what could come next.

There was a light in motion in the city. Calhoun sat
up, all alertness, to watch it. It was a ground-car on a
highway, headlights glaring to light the way before it. It
vanished behind buildings. It reappeared. It crossed a
far-flung bridge and vanished again, and again reappeared. It was drawing closer, and presently its lights
glared in Calhoun's eyes as it sped furiously across the
landing grid's turf floor, headed for the sprawling
building where the transformers and the controls for the
grid were housed.

There it came to a swiftly braked stop. Its light stayed
on. Men jumped from it and ran into the control building. Calhoun heard no voices. The songs of the night
creatures would have blotted out human voices. In
minutes, though, more men came out of the building.
They clustered about the ground-car. After only seconds, the car was again in motion, jouncing and bounc-
ing over the turf toward the grounded spaceship.

It stopped within a hundred yards of where Calhoun
had concealed himself. The headlights glittered and
glistened against the bulging, silvery metal of the
spacecraft. A man shouted at it, "Open up! Open up!
Something's happened! A man's sick! It looks like the
plague!"

There was no sign. He shouted again. Another man
pounded on the thick metal of the airlock's outer door.

A voice spoke suddenly out of external loudspeakers.
"What's this? What's the matter?"

Many voices tried to babble, but a harsh voice si-
lenced them and barked statements, every one of which

Calhoun could have written down in advance. There'd been a man on watch in the city's communication center. He didn't put through calls from different places in use by the invaders. Someone went to find out why. The man at the callboard was unconscious. It looked like he had the plague. It looked like the shots he'd had to make him immune didn't work.

The voice coming over the loudspeakers said, *"Nonsense! Bring him in!"*

Seconds later the airlock door cracked open and descended outward, making a ramp from the ground to the cubbyhole which was the lock as now revealed. The men on the ground hauled a limp figure out of the ground-car. They half-carried and half-dragged it up the ramp into the lock. Calhoun saw the inner door open. They dragged the figure inside.

Then nothing happened, except that one man came out almost immediately, wiping his hands on his uniform as if hysterically afraid that by touching his unconscious companion he'd infected himself with the plague.

Presently another man came out. He trembled. Then the others. The harsh voice said savagely, "So he's got to find out what's the matter. It *can't* be the plague. We had shots against it. It's bound to be all right. Maybe he fainted or something. Stop acting like you're going to die! Go back on duty! I'll order a roll call, just in case."

Calhoun listened with satisfaction. The inner airlock door closed, but the outer one remained down as a ramp. The car trundled away, stopped and discharged some passengers at the control building, and went off into the distance. It disappeared on the highway where it had first appeared.

"The man I knocked out," he said dryly, to Murgatroyd, "impresses them unfavorably. They hope he's only an accident. We'll see. But that authoritative person is going to order a roll call. He ought to find something to bother them all, when that takes place."

"Chee," said Murgatroyd in a subdued tone.

There was again silence and stillness save for the open

country song to the stars. There seemed to be occasional drumbeats in that chorus now.

It was half an hour before light showed on the ground by the control building. It was as if invisible doors had been opened, and light streamed out of them. In minutes a traveling light appeared. It vanished and was again visible, like the lights of the first car.

"Ha!" said Calhoun, gratified. "Checking up, they found the invader we left in the street. They reported it by communicator. Maybe they reported two others missing—one of whom is beside you, Murgatroyd. They ought to feel slightly upset."

The car dashed across the landing grid's center and braked. Figures waited for it. With the briefest of pauses it came again to the ship with the opened airlock door. The harsh voice panted, "Here's another one! We're bringing him in."

The loudspeaker said, somehow vexedly, *"Very well. But the first man hasn't got the plague. His metabolic rate is normal. He has not got the plague!"*

"Here's another one, just the same!"

The figures struggled up the ramp with a second limp burden. Minutes later they emerged again.

"He didn't get that first man awake," said an uneasy voice. "That looks bad to me."

"He says it ain't the plague."

"If he says it's not," snapped the authoritative voice, "then it's not! He ought to know. He invented the plague!"

Calhoun, behind the giant support for the landing grid, said, "Ah!" very quietly to himself.

"But—look here," said a frightened voice. "There were doctors in the city when we got here. Maybe some of 'em got away. Maybe—maybe they had some kinda germ that they've turned loose to kill us . . ."

The authoritative voice snarled. All the voices broke into a squabbling babble. The invaders were worried. They were frightened. Normally it would never have occurred to them to suspect a disease deliberately introduced among them. But they were here to follow up just such a disease. They did not understand such menaces. They'd been willing enough to profit, so long as the matter was strictly one-sided. But now it looked like some disease was striking them down. It seemed very probable that it was the plague to which they had been assured that they were immune. Some of them already had the shakes.

The car went away from the grounded spaceship. It stopped for a long time before the control building. There was agitated argument there. Calhoun heard the faint squabbling sound above the voices of the night. The car went away again.

He allowed twenty minutes to pass. They seemed very long to him. Then he picked up the man he'd knocked out, outside the room with the noisy drinking party. He heaved him over his shoulder. He'd pulled the uniform of the third of his dark-street victims over his own, and that third man lay in an areaway in his underwear. He'd be found eventually.

"We'll ask for our invitation into the ship—and the laboratory, Murgatroyd. Come along!"

He moved toward the still and silent spaceship.

It swelled and loomed enormously as he approached it. The outside lock door still lay extended downward as a ramp. He tramped on the metal incline. He went into the lock. There he banged on the inner door and called, "Here's another one! Out like the others! What'll I do with him?"

There'd be microphones in the lock, as there were outside. But his voice wouldn't go so loudly to the control building. He could not plausibly moderate his tone. He made it agitated.

"Here's a third man, out like the others! What'll I do with him?"

A metallic voice said angrily, *"Wait!"*

Calhoun waited. Two unconscious men, brought separately by a group of men who were more frightened the second time than the first, made it extremely likely that a third unconscious man would not have a group of solicitous companions with him. One man to risk the supposed contagion was very much more likely.

He heard footsteps beyond the inner lock door. It opened. A voice rasped, "Bring him in!"

He turned his back, this man who had come down to the airlock to spring the catch of the inner door. Calhoun followed him inside the ship, with Murgatroyd trodding fearfully between his feet. The lock door clicked shut. The figure in the white lab coat went trudging on ahead. It was a small figure. It limped a little. It was not well shaped.

Calhoun, with an unconscious member of the invading party used as a drape to hide his paint-gun—so suitable a weapon, as it had turned out up to now—followed after him. He listened grimly for any sound which would indicate any other human being inside the spaceship. Now that he had seen—even from behind—the figure of the field director of the project to exterminate the proper inhabitants of Maris III, he coldly reasoned that there would probably not be even a laboratory assistant.

The queer figure moving before him fitted in a specific niche. There are people who, because they are physically unattractive, become personalities. All too many girls—and men, too—do not bother to become anything but good to look at. Some people who are not good to look at accept the situation courageously and become people who are good to know. But others rebel bitterly.

Knowing, as he did, that this man had used brains and skill and tedious labor to devise a method of mass murder, Calhoun felt almost able to write his biography. He had been grotesque. He hated those who found him grotesque. He dreamed grandiose dreams of gaining power so that he could punish those he envied and hated. He put into his schemes for revenge against a cosmos that gave him scorn all the furious energy that could have been used in other ways. He would develop an astounding patience and an incredible venom. He would scheme and scheme and scheme . . .

Calhoun had met people who could have chosen this

way. One of the great men at Sector Headquarters, whose praise was more valued than fine gold, was odd to look at when you first glimpsed him. But you never noticed it after five minutes. There was a planetary president in Cygnus, a teacher on Cetis Alpha, a musician . . . Calhoun could think of many. But the hobbling figure before him hadn't chosen to follow the natural law, which advises courage. He'd chosen hate instead, and frustration was inevitable.

Into the laboratory. Here Murgatroyd cheered. This place was brightly lighted. Gleaming instruments were familiar. Even the smells of a beautifully equipped biological laboratory were reassuring and homelike to Murgatroyd. He said happily, *"Chee-chee-chee!"*

The small figure whirled. Dark eyes widened and glared. Calhoun slipped his burden to the floor. His Med Service uniform appeared beneath the invaders' tunic as the downward-sliding body tugged at the cloth.

"I'm sorry," said Calhoun gently, "but I have to put you under arrest for violating the basic principles of public health. Contriving and spreading a lethal plague amounts to at least that."

The figure whirled. It snatched. Then it darted toward Calhoun, desperately trying to use a surgeon's scalpel, the only deadly weapon within reach.

Calhoun pressed the trigger of the vortex-ring apparatus which was designed to paint the walls of buildings. Only this one didn't have paint in it. It shot invisible vortex rings of dextrethyl vapor instead.

VII

"In one perfectly real sense, all motives and all satisfactions are subjective. After all, we do live in our own skulls. But a man can do something he wishes to do and then contemplate the consequences of his action with pleasure. This pleasure, to be sure, is subjective, but it is directly related to reality and to the objective cosmos about him. However, there is an ultrasubjective type of motivation and satisfaction which is of great importance in human conduct. Many persons find their greatest satisfaction in contemplating themselves in some particular context. Such people find apparently complete satisfaction in a dramatic gesture, in a finely stated aspiration, or simply in a mere pretense of significance or wisdom or worth. The objective results of such gestures or pretenses are rarely considered. Very often great hardship and suffering and even deaths have been brought about by some person who raptly contemplated the beautiful drama of his behavior, and did not even think of its consequences to someone else. . . ."

Probability and Human Conduct—Fitzgerald

CALHOUN MADE THE small man helpless with the invader's uniform he'd pulled over his own, and now tore it into strips. He was painstaking about the job. He tied his captive in a chair, and then encased him in a veritable cocoon of cloth strips. Then he examined the laboratory.

Murgatroyd strutted as Calhoun went over the equipment. Most of it was totally familiar. There were culture trays, visual and electron microscopes, autoclaves and irradiation apparatus, pipettes and instruments for microanalysis, thermostatic cabinets capable of keeping culture material within the hundredth of a degree of desired temperature. Murgatroyd was completely at home now.

Presently Calhoun heard a gasp. He turned and nodded to his prisoner.

"How-do," he said politely. "I've been very much interested in your work. I'm Med Service, by the way. I came here to do a routine planetary health check and somebody tried to kill me when I called for landing coordinates. They'd have done better to let me land and then blast me when I came out of my ship. The other was the more dramatic gesture, of course."

Dark, beady eyes regarded him. They changed remarkably from moment to moment. At one instant they were filled with a flaming fury which was practically madness. At another they seemed to grow cunning. Yet again they showed animal-like fear.

Calhoun said detachedly, "I doubt that there's any use in talking to you now. I'll wait until you have the situation figured out. I'm in the ship. There appears to be nobody else in a condition to start any trouble. The two men your—ah—mop-up party brought here are out for some days." He added explanatorily, "Polysulphate. An overdose. It's so simple I didn't think you'd guess it. I knocked them out so you'd be ready to let me in with a third specimen."

The mummylike bound figure made inarticulate noises. There was the sound of grinding teeth. There were bubbling sounds of crazy, frustrated rage.

"You're in a state of emotional shock," said Calhoun. "I guess that part is real and part is faked. I'll leave you alone to get over it. I want some information. I think you'll want to bargain. I'll leave you alone to work it out."

He went out of the laboratory. He felt an acute distaste for the man he'd captured. It was true that he believed the small man had received an acute emotional shock on finding himself captured and helpless. But a part of that shock would be rage so horrible as to threaten madness. Calhoun guessed coldly that anyone who had made the decision and lived the life he ascribed to the bound man—his guess, as it happened, was remarkably exact—could literally be goaded to death or madness, now that he was bound and could be taunted at will. It happened that he did not want to taunt his prisoner.

He went over the ship. He checked its type and design, verified the spaceyard in which it had been built, made an exact list in his own mind of what would be needed to make it into an inert hulk of no use to anybody, and then went back to the laboratory.

His prisoner panted, exhausted. There were very minor stretchings of the cloth strips which held him. Calhoun matter-of-factly made them tight again. His prisoner spat unspeakable, hysterical curses at him.

"Good," said Calhoun, unmoved. "Get the madness out of your system and we'll talk."

He moved to leave the laboratory again. A voice came out of a loudspeaker, and he instantly searched for and found the microphone by which it could be answered. He flicked it off as his prisoner tried to scream commands into it.

"Haven't you found out yet?" asked the loudspeaker apprehensively. *"Don't you know what's the matter with those men? There are two more missing on roll call. There's something like panic building up. The men are guessing that a native doctor's spreading a plague among us!"*

Calhoun shrugged. The voice came from outside. It had been an authoritative voice, not long since. Now it was a badly worried one. He did not answer its questions. It repeated them. It waited and asked again. It almost pleaded for a reply. With the microphone off, however, the authoritative voice, which must be that of the commander of the butchers, grew resentful at being ignored. It faded out, trembling, shaking a little, but whether with hatred or terror he could not be sure. It could be either.

"Your popularity's diminishing," said Calhoun. He put down the microphone, safely off. He noted a spacephone receiver alongside the speaker-amplifier. "Hm," he said. "Suspicious, eh? You didn't even trust the skipper. Had to do your own receiving. Typical!"

The trussed-up, wizened man spoke suddenly with absolute cold precision.

"What do you want?" he demanded.

"Information," said Calhoun.

"For yourself? What do you want? I can give it to you!" said the mouth beneath the half-mad dark eyes. "I can give you anything you can imagine! I can give you riches more than you can dream!"

Calhoun sat negligently on the arm of a chair.

"I'll listen," he observed. "But apparently you're only technical director of the operation here. It's not a very big operation. You had only a thousand people to kill. You're acting under orders. How could you give me anything important?"

"This—" His prisoner cursed. "This is a test—an experiment! Let me go, let it be finished, and I can give you a world to rule. I'll make you king of a planet! You'll have millions of slaves! You'll have women by the hundreds or thousands if you choose!"

Calhoun said detachedly, "You wouldn't expect me to believe that without the details."

The dark eyes flamed. Then, with an effort of will that was as violent as his rage had been, the small bound figure brought itself to composure. It was not calmness. Fury surged up when he attempted a persuasive gesture and could not move. Frustration maddened him to panting for breath. But between such moments, he talked with a terrifying plausibility, with a precision of detail that showed a scheme worked out with infinite care. It was *his* scheme. He had convinced a planetary government to try it. He was necessary to it. He would have power to spare and he could bribe Calhoun with everything that was rich and alluring and apparently irresistible. He set persuasively to work to bribe him.

It was quite horrible.

First there had to be an explanation, in such detail that a Med Service man could know that his bribes would infallibly be available and could not fail.

The taking-over of Maris III was, as Calhoun had more than guessed, a mere field trial of a new method for interplanetary war and conquest. Here was a new planet. It had a small caretaker population waiting for the hundreds of thousands of permanent inhabitants due to take over its ready-built city and roads and farms. It had been used for the testing of a new and irresistible kind of conquest. Plague! Plague had been rained upon its principal and, so far, only city. In the night. The people knew nothing about it. They began to die, and even then did not know why they died or what had caused it or when the cause of their deaths was introduced. They died!

Calhoun nodded. He was not impressed by the mysterious phrasing. It might have been imposing to somebody who had not worked out for himself how the plague had been introduced and what it was and how it had been designed to escape detection by ordinary microbiological methods.

His captive went on. His tone wheedled, and was strident, and in turn was utterly convincing and remarkably persuasive.

Once Maris III was occupied by colonists from the world that had sent the plague, nothing could be done. Dettra Two could never land its people in the city. They would die. Only the usurping population could survive there. For all time to come the world of Maris III must belong to the folk who had planted it with death. The permanent colonists here must be immunized like the members of the invading party themselves.

"Who," said Calhoun, "are not as happy as they used to be."

His captive licked his lips and went on, his eyes deadly and his tone reasonable and seductive and remarkably hypnotic.

But Maris III was only a test. Once the process was proved here, there were other worlds to be taken over.

Not only new colony-worlds like this. Old and established worlds would find themselves attacked by plagues their doctors would be helpless to combat. Then there would come ships from the world that had tried out its technique on Maris III. The ships would end the plagues. They would prove it. They would offer to sell life to all the citizens of the dying worlds—at a price.

"Unprofessional," said Calhoun, "but probably profitable."

The price, in effect, would be submission. It would amount to slavery. Those who would not accept the bargain would die.

"Of course," said Calhoun, "they might try to back out of such a bargain later."

His captive smiled a thin-lipped smile, while his eyes did not change at all. He explained convincingly that if there was a revolt, it would not matter. The countermeasure to a new defiance would always be a new plague. There were many plagues ready to use. They would build an interstellar empire in which rebellion would be a form of suicide. No world once taken over could ever free itself. No world once chosen could possibly resist. There would be worlds by tens and scores and hundreds to be ruled by men like Calhoun. He would rate a planet-kingdom of his own. His Med Service training entitled him to an empire! He would be absolute ruler and absolute master of millions of abject slaves who must please his most trivial whim or die!

"An objection," said Calhoun. "You haven't mentioned the Med Service. I don't think it would take kindly to such a system of planetary conquest."

Here was the highest test of the prisoner's ability to sway and persuade and convince and almost to hypnotize. He had a matter of minutes to make the Med Service ridiculous, and to point out the defenselessness of its Sector Headquarters, and then—without arousing ancient prejudices—to make it seem natural and inevitable and almost humorous that Med Service Sector Headquarters would receive special precautionary fusion-bomb treatment as soon as the Maris III task was finished. Calhoun stirred. His prisoner spoke even more urgently, more desperately. He pictured worlds on which every living being would be Calhoun's slave—

"That'll do," said Calhoun. "I've got the information I wanted."

"Then release me," said his prisoner eagerly. And then his burning eyes read Calhoun's no-longer-guarded expression.

"You accept," he cried fiercely. "You accept! You *can't* refuse! *You can't!*"

"Of course I can," said Calhoun annoyedly. "You've no idea! I wouldn't want a million slaves, or even one. I'm reasonably sane! And such a crazy scheme couldn't work anyhow. Sheer probability would throw in so many unfavorable chance happenings that it would be bound to go smash. I'm proof of it. I'm an unfavorable chance happening right here, the very first time you try the beastly business!"

His prisoner tried to talk more persuasively still. He tried to be more tempting still. He tried, but his throat clicked. He struggled to be more convincing and more alluring than it was possible to be. Suddenly he shrieked curses at Calhoun. They were horrible to listen to. He screamed—

Calhoun raised the paint-gun, his features twisted and wry. He sent a single small vortex ring.

In the sudden silence that fell, a tiny, tinny voice sounded from the spacephone receiver at one side of the laboratory.

"Calling ground," said a voice faintly. *"Ship from home with passengers calling ground on Maris III. Calling ground . . ."*

Calhoun jerked his head about and listened to the reiterated call. Then he bent to the necessary next thing to be done with his prisoner.

"Calling ground," said the voice patiently. *"We do not read you. If you are answering, we do not pick up your signal. We will go in orbit and continue to call. Calling ground . . ."*

Calhoun turned it off. Murgatroyd said inquiringly, "Chee?"

"That's a deadline," said Calhoun grimly. "For us.

It's a shipload of happy, immunized colonists, ready to land here. We blew the landing grid, Murgatroyd, when they tried to butter us over the inside of the Med Ship. Apparently we blew their spacephone at the same time. So the spacephone in this ship here is the only one working. And we have too much sense to answer that call. But it gives us a deadline, just the same. If they still don't raise their friends, the ship may stay in orbit, but somebody'll come down in a lifeboat to find out what's wrong. And that will shoot the works! We'll have a passenger ship full of enthusiasts ready to land and finish the mopping-up business—and us! There's just you and me, Murgatroyd, to take care of the situation. Let's get at it!''

But it was very close to dawn when he and Murgatroyd left the grounded ship. Calhoun grimaced when he saw the vast crimson glory of approaching sunrise in the sky to the east. He saw a ground-car before the building in which the landing grid controls were housed.

"Worked up like these characters are," said Calhoun, "and suspecting somebody of spreading plagues for them to catch, they won't be cordial to anybody who didn't come here with them. I don't like the idea of trying simply to walk away when there's all this daylight. I think we'd better try to take that car, Murgatroyd. Come along!''

He headed for the control building. Judging by the night before, the occupied rooms had no windows facing toward the landed spacecraft. But he moved cautiously from one great arch-foundation to the next. When he'd reached the last possible bit of shelter, however, the ground-car was still fifty yards away.

"We run for it," he told Murgatroyd.

He and the tiny *tormal* bolted through the rosy dawn light. They had covered thirty yards when someone came out of the control building. He moved toward the ground-car. He heard Calhoun's pelting footsteps on the turf. He turned. For one instant he stared. Calhoun was a stranger. There should be no living strangers on this planet—they should all be dead. Here was an explanation of two men found unconscious and probably dying, and two more missing. The invader roared. His blaster came out.

Calhoun fired first. The snarling rasp of a blaster is unmistakable. The invader's weapon burst thunderously.

"Run!" snapped Calhoun.

Voices. A man peered out a window. Calhoun was a stranger with a blaster in his hand. The sight of him was a challenge to murder. The man in the window yelled. As Calhoun snapped a shot at him he jerked inside and the window crackled and smoked where the blaster-charge hit.

Man and *tormal* reached the line of the ground-car and the building door. The door was open. Calhoun swung up the dextrethyl sprayer and pumped explosive dextrethyl vapor into the room in a steady stream of vortex rings. He backed toward the ground-car, with Murgatroyd dancing agitatedly about his feet.

There was a crash of glass. Somebody'd plunged out a window. There were rushing feet inside. They'd be racing toward the door, from inside. But the hallway, or whatever was immediately inside, would be filled with anesthetic gas. Men would gasp and fall.

A man did fall. Calhoun heard the crash of his body as it hit the floor. But another man came plunging around the building's corner, blaster out, searching for Calhoun. He had to sight his target though, and then aim for it. Calhoun had only to pull his trigger. He did.

More shouting inside the building. More rushing feet. More falls. Then there was the beginning of the rasping snarl of a blaster, and finally a cushioned, booming, roaring detonation which was the ignited dextrethyl vapor. The blast lifted part of the building's roof. It shattered partitions. It blew out windows.

Calhoun backed toward the ground-car. A blaster-bolt flashed past him. He deliberately traversed the building with his trigger held down. Smoke and flame leaped up. At least one more invader crumpled.

Calhoun heard a voice yelling, *"We're being attacked! The natives are throwing bombs! Rally! Rally! We need help!"*

It would be a broadcast call for assistance. Wherever men idled or loafed or tried desultorily to find something to loot, they would hear it. Even the crew working to repair the landing grid—and they would be close by—would hear it and swarm to help. Hunters would come. Men in cars—

Calhoun snatched Murgatroyd to the seat beside him. He turned the ignition key and tires screamed as he shot away.

VIII

"It has to be recognized that man is a social animal in the same sense, though in a different manner, that ants and bees are social creatures. For an ant city to prosper, there have to be natural laws to protect it against unfavorable actions on the part of its members. It is not enough to speak of instincts to prevent antisocial actions. There are mutations of instinct as well as of form, in ants as in other creatures. It is not enough even to speak of social pressure, which among ants would be an impulse to destroy deviant members of the community. There are natural laws to protect an ant city against the instinct-control which would destroy it, as well as against the abandonment of instincts or actions necessary to the ant city as a whole. There are, in short, natural laws and natural forces which protect societies against their own members. In human society . . ."

Probability and Human Conduct—Fitzgerald

THE HIGHWAYS WERE, of course, superb. The car raced forward, and its communicator began to chatter as somebody in the undamaged part of the grid-control building announced hysterically that a stranger had killed men and gotten away in a car. It described its course. It commanded that he be headed off. It shrilly demanded that he be killed, killed, killed!

Another voice took over. This voice was curt and coldly furious. It snapped precise instructions.

And Calhoun found himself on a gracefully curving,

rising road. It soared, and he was midway between towers when another car flashed toward him. He took his blaster in his left hand. In the split second during which the cars passed each other, he blasted it. There was a monstrous surge of smoke and flame as the stricken car's Duhanne cell shorted and vaporized half the metal of the car itself.

There came other voices. Somebody had sighted the explosion. The voice in the communicator roared for silence.

"You," he rasped. *"If you got him, report yourself!"*

"Chee-chee-chee!" chattered Murgatroyd excitedly.

But Calhoun did not report.

"He got one of us," raged the icy voice. *"Get ahead of him and blast him!"*

Calhoun's car went streaking down the far side of the traffic bridge. It rounded a curve on two wheels. It flashed between two gigantic empty buildings and came to a side road, and plunged into that, and came again to a division and took the left-hand turn, and next time took the right. But the muttering voices continued in the communicator. One of the invaders was ordered to the highest possible bridge from which he could watch all lower-level roadways. Others were to post themselves here and there—and to stay still! A group of four cars was coming out of the storage building. Blast any single car in motion. Blast it! And report, report, report!

"I suspect," said Calhoun to the agitated Murgatroyd beside him, "that this is what is known as military tactics. If they ring us in . . . There aren't but so many of them, though. The trick for us is to get out of the city. We need more choices for action. So—"

The communicator panted a report of his sighting from a cobweblike bridge at the highest point of the city. He was heading—

He changed his heading. He had so far seen but one of his pursuers' cars. Now he went racing along empty, curving highways, among untenanted towers and be-tween balconied walls with blank-eyed windows gazing at him everywhere.

It was nightmarish because of the magnificence and the emptiness of the city all about him. He plunged along graceful highways, across delicately arched bridges, through crazy ramifications of its lesser traffic arteries—and he saw no motion anywhere. The wind whistled past the car windows, and the tires sang a high-pitched whine, and the sun shone down and small clouds floated tranquilly in the sky. There were no signs of life or danger anywhere on the splendid highways or in the beautiful buildings. Only voices muttered in the communicator of the car. He'd been seen here, flashing around a steeply banked curve. He'd swerved from a waiting ambush by pure chance. He'd—

He saw green to the left. He dived down a sloping ramp toward one of the smaller park areas of the city.

And as he came from between the stone guard rails of the road, the top of the car exploded over his head. He swerved and roared into dense shrubbery, jerked Murgatroyd free despite the *tormal*'s clinging fast with all four paws and his tail, and dived into the underbrush. Somehow, instinctively, he clung to the vortex-gun.

He ran, with his free hand plucking solidified droplets of hot metal from his garments and his flesh. They hurt abominably. But the man who'd fired wouldn't believe he'd missed, followed as his blasting was by the instant wrecking of the car. That man would report success before he moved in to view the corpse of his supposed victim. But there'd be other cars coming. At the moment it was necessary for Calhoun to get elsewhere, fast.

He heard the rushing sound of arriving cars while he panted and sweated through the foliage of the park. He reached the far side and a road, and on beyond there was a low stone wall. He knew instantly what it was. Service highways ran in cuts, for the most part roofed over to hide them from sight, but now and again open to the sky for ventilation. He'd entered the city by one of them. Here was another. He swung himself over the wall and dropped. Murgatroyd recklessly and excitedly followed.

It was a long drop, and he staggered when he landed. He heard a soft rushing noise above. A car raced past. Instants later, another.

Limping, Calhoun ran to the nearest service gate. He entered and closed it. Scorched and aching, he climbed to the echoing upper stories of this building. Presently he looked out. His car had been wrecked in one of the smaller park areas of the city. Now there were other cars at two-hundred-yard intervals all about it. It was believed that he was in the brushwood somewhere. Besides the cars of the cordon, there were now twenty men on foot receiving orders from an authoritative figure in their midst.

They scattered. Twenty yards apart, they began to move across the park. Other men arrived and strengthened the cordon toward which he was supposed to be driven. A fly could not have escaped.

Those who marched across the park began methodically to burn it to ashes before them with their blasters.

Calhoun watched. Then he remembered something and was appalled. Two days before while he was among the fugitives in the glade, Kim Walpole had asked hungrily if they whose lives he had saved could not do something to help him. And he'd said that if they saw the smoke of a good-sized fire in the city they might investigate. He'd had not the faintest intention of calling on them. But they might see this cloud of smoke and believe he wanted them to come and help!

"Damn!" he said wryly to Murgatroyd. "After all, there's a limit to any one series of actions with probable favorable chance consequences. I'd better start a new one. We might have whittled the invaders down and made the rest run away, but I had to start using a car! And that led to the chance making of a fire! So now we start all over with a new policy."

He explored the building quickly. He prepared his measures. He went back to the window from which he'd looked. He cracked it open.

He opened fire with his blaster. The range was long, but with the beam cut down to minimum spread he'd knocked over a satisfying number of the men below before they swarmed toward the building, sending before them a barrage of blaster-fire that shattered the windows and had the stone façade smoking furiously.

"This," said Calhoun, "is an occasion where we have to change their advantage in numbers and weapons into an unfavorable circumstance for them. They'll be brave because they're many. Let's go!"

He met four ground-car loads of refugees with his arms in the air. He did not want to be shot down by mistake. He said hurriedly, when Kim and the other lean survivors gathered about him, "Everything's all right. We've a pack of prisoners but we won't bother to feed them intravenously for the moment. How'd you get the ground-cars?"

"Hunters," said Kim savagely. "We found them and killed them and took their cars. We found some other refugees, too, and I cured them—at least they will be cured soon. When we saw the smoke, we started for the city. Some of us still have the plague, but we've all had our serum shots. And half of us have arms now."

"All of us have arms," said Calhoun, "and to spare. The invaders are quite peacefully sleeping—just about all of them. I did knock over a few with long-range blaster-shots, and they won't wake up. Most of them, though, tried to storm a building from which I'd fired on them. I stood them off a fair length of time, and then ducked after dumping dextrethyl in the air-conditioning system. Murgatroyd and I waited a suitable time and then lengthened their slumber period with polysulphate. I doubt there'll be any more trouble with the butchers. But we've got to get to the spaceship they landed in. I fixed it so it couldn't possibly take off, but there are some calls coming in from space. The only working spacephone here is in the ship. The first load of immunized, enthusiastic colonists are in orbit now, giving the gang aground a little more time to answer. I want you people to talk to them."

"We'll bring their ship down," said the broad-bearded man hungrily, "and blast them as they come out of the port!"

Calhoun shook his head.

"To the contrary," he said mildly. "You'll put on the clothes of some of our prisoners, and you'll let yourselves be seen by the joyous newcomers in their spacephone screen. You'll pretend to be the characters we really have safely sleeping, and you'll say that the plague worked much too well. You'll say it wiped out the original inhabitants—that's you—and then changed into a dozen other plagues and wiped out all the little butcher-boys who came to mop up. You'll give details of the other kinds of plague that the real plague turned into. You'll be pathetic. You'll beg them to land and pick up you four or five dying, multiply diseased, highly contagious survivors. You'll tell them the plague has mutated until even the native animals are dying of it. Flying things fall dead from the air. Chirping things in the trees and grass are wiped out. You'll picture Maris III as a world on which no animal life can hope ever to live again—and you'll beg them to come down and pick you up and take you home with them."

The broad-bearded man stared. Then he said, "But they won't land."

"No," agreed Calhoun. "They won't. They'll go home. Unless the government has them all killed before they can talk, they'll tell their world what happened. They'll be half-dead with fear that the immunizing shots they received will mutate and turn them into the kind of plague victims you'll make yourself look like. And just what do you think will happen on the world they came from?"

Kim said hungrily, "They'll kill their rulers. They'll try to do it before they die of the plagues they'll imagine. They'll revolt! If a man has a belly-ache he'll go crazy with terror and try to kill a government official because his government has murdered him!"

Kim drew a deep breath. He smiled with no amusement at all.

"I like that," he said with a sort of deadly calm. "I like that very much."

"After all," observed Calhoun, "once an empire had been started, with the subjugated populations kept subdued by a threat of plague, how long would it be before the original population was enslaved by the same threat? Go and invent some interesting plagues and make yourselves look terrifying. Heaven knows you're lean enough! But you can make yourselves look worse. I said, once, that a medical man sometimes has to use psychology in addition to the regular measures against plague. The Med Service will check on that planet presently, but I think its ambition to be a health hazard to the rest of the galaxy will be ended."

"Yes," said Kim. He moved away. Then he stopped. "What about your prisoners? They're knocked out now. What about them?"

Calhoun shrugged.

"Oh, we'll let them sleep until we finish repairing the landing grid. I think I can be helpful with that."

"Every one of them is a murderer," growled the broad-bearded man.

"True," agreed Calhoun. "But lynching is bad business. It even offers the possibility of unfavorable chance consequences. Let's take care of the shipload of colonists first."

So they did. It was odd how they could take a sort of pleasure in the enactment of imagined disaster even greater than they had suffered. Their eyes gleamed happily as they went about their task.

The passenger ship went away. It did not have a pleasant journey. When it landed, its passengers burst tumultuously out of the spaceport to tell their story. Their home world went into a panic which was the more uncontrollable because the people had been very carefully told how deadly the tamed plagues would be to the inhabitants of worlds that they might want to take over. But now they believed the tamed plagues had turned upon them.

The deaths, especially among members of the ruling class, were approximately equal in number to those a deadly pandemic would have caused.

But back on Maris III things moved smoothly. Rather

more than eighty people, altogether, were found and treated and ultimately helped with the matter of the slumbering invaders. That was almost a labor of love. Certainly it gave great satisfaction. The landing grid was back in operation two days after the passenger ship left. They took the landed spaceship and smashed its drive and communicators, and they wrecked its Duhanne cells. They took out the breech-plugs of the rockets and dumped the rocket fuel, saving just enough for the little Med Ship. Naturally, they removed the lifeboats.

And then they revived the unconscious butcher-invaders and put them, one by one, into the spacecraft in which they had come. That craft was now a hulk. It could not drive or use rockets or even signal. Its vision screens were blind; the Med Ship used some of them.

And then they used the landing grid—Calhoun checking the figures—and they put their prisoners up in orbit to await the arrival of proper authority. They could feed themselves, but any attempt at escape would be pure and simple suicide. They could not attempt to escape.

"And now," said Calhoun, when the planet was clean of strangers again, "now I'll bring my ship to the grid. We'll recharge my Duhanne cells and replace my vision screens. I can make it here on rockets, but it's a long way to headquarters. So I'll report, and a field team will come here and check out the planet, artificial plagues included. They'll arrange, somehow, to take care of the prisoners up in orbit. That's not my affair. Maybe Dettra Two would like to have them. In the meantime, they can search their consciences."

Kim said, frowning, "You put something over on us! You kept us so busy we forgot one man. You said there'd be a microbiologist in the invaders' party. You said he'd probably be the man who had invented the plague. And he's up there in orbit with the rest—he'll get no more than they get! You put something over on us. He deserves some special treatment!"

Calhoun said very evenly, "Revenge is always apt to have unfavorable chance consequences. Let him alone.

You've no right to punish him. You've only a right to punish a child to correct it, or to punish a man to deter others from doing what he's done. Do you expect to correct the kind of man who'd invent the plague that flourished here, and meant to use it for the making of an empire of slaves? Do you think others need to be deterred from trying the same thing?''

Kim said thickly, ''But he's a murderer! All the murders were his! He deserves—''

''Condign punishment?'' asked Calhoun sharply. ''You've no right to administer it. Anyhow, think what he's up against!''

''He's—he's . . .'' Kim's face changed. ''He's up there in orbit, hopeless, with his butchers all around him and blaming him for the fix they're in. They've nothing to do but hate him. Nothing . . .''

''You didn't arrange that situation,'' said Calhoun coldly. ''He did. You simply put prisoners in a safe place because it would be impractical to guard them, otherwise. I suggest you forget him.''

Kim looked sickish. He shook his head to clear it. He tried to thrust the man who'd planned pure horror out of his mind. He said slowly, ''I wish we could do something for you.''

''Put up a statue,'' said Calhoun dryly, ''and in twenty years nobody will know what it was for. You and Helen are going to be married, aren't you?'' When Kim nodded, Calhoun said, ''In course of time, if you remember and think it worthwhile, you may inflict a child with my name. That child will wonder why, and ask, and so my memory will be kept green for a full generation.''

''Longer than that,'' insisted Kim. ''You'll never be forgotten here!''

Calhoun grinned at him.

Three days later, which was six days longer than he'd expected to be aground on Maris III, the landing grid heaved the little Med Ship out to space. The beautiful, nearly empty city dwindled as the grid field took the tiny spacecraft out to five planetary diameters and there released it. And Calhoun spun the Med Ship about and oriented it carefully for that place in the Cetis cluster where Med Service Headquarters was. He threw the overdrive switch.

The universe reeled. Calhoun's stomach seemed to turn over twice, and he had a sickish feeling of spiraling dizzily in what was somehow a cone. He swallowed. Murgatroyd made gulping noises. There was no longer a universe perceptible about the ship. There was dead silence. Then those small random noises began which have to be provided if a man is not to crack up in the dead stillness of a ship traveling at thirty times the speed of light.

Then there was nothing more to do. In overdrive travel there is never anything to do but pass the time away.

Murgatroyd took his right-hand whiskers in his right paw and licked them elaborately. He did the same to his left-hand whiskers. He contemplated the cabin, deciding upon a soft place in which to go to sleep.

"Murgatroyd," said Calhoun severely, "I have to have an argument with you. You imitate us humans too much! Kim Walpole caught you prowling around with an injector, starting to give our prisoners another shot of polysulfate. It might have killed them! Personally, I think it would have been a good idea, but in a medical man it would have been most unethical. We professional men have to curb our impulses! Understand?"

"*Chee!*" said Murgatroyd. He curled up and wrapped his tail meticulously about his nose, preparing to doze.

Calhoun settled himself comfortably in his bunk. He picked up a book. It was Fitzgerald on *Probability and Human Conduct*.

He began to read as the ship went on through emptiness.

PLAGUE
ON KRYDER II

■

AFTER CALHOUN and Murgatroyd the *tormal* were established on board, the Med Ship *Aesclipus Twenty* allowed itself to be lifted off from Med Service Headquarters and thrust swiftly out to space. The headquarters landing grid did the lifting. Some five planetary diameters out, the grid's force fields let go and Calhoun busied himself with aiming the ship for his destination, which was a very long way off. Presently he pushed a button. The result was exactly the one to be expected. The Med Ship did something equivalent to making a hole, crawling into it, and then pulling the hole in after itself. In fact, it went into overdrive.

There were the usual sensations of dizziness, nausea, and a contracting spiral fall. Then there was no cosmos, there was no galaxy, and there were no stars. The *Aesclipus Twenty* had formed a cocoon of highly stressed space about itself which was practically a private subcosmos. As long as it existed the Med Ship was completely independent of all creation outside. However, the cocoon was active. It went hurtling through emptiness at many times the speed of light. The *Aesclipus Twenty* rode inside it. When the overdrive field—the cocoon—collapsed and the ship returned to normal space, it would find itself very far from its starting point. For every hour spent in overdrive, the ship should break out somewhat more than a light-year of distance farther away from Med Service Headquarters.

On this occasion the Med Ship stayed in overdrive for

three long weeks, while the overdrive field hurtled toward the planet Kryder II. Calhoun was supposed to make a special public health visit there. Some cases of what the planetary government called a plague had turned up. The government was in a panic because plagues of similar type had appeared on two other worlds previously and done great damage. In both other cases a Med Ship man had arrived in time to check and stop the pestilence. In both cases the plague was not a new one, but a pestilence of familiar diseases. In both forerunners of this third plague, the arriving Med Ship's *tormal* had succumbed to the infection. So the government of Kryder II had called for help, and Calhoun and Murgatroyd answered the call. They were on the way to take charge.

Calhoun was singularly suspicious of this assignment. The report on the contagion was tricky. Typically, a patient was admitted to hospital with a case of—say—typhoid fever. It was a sporadic case, untraceable to any previous clinical one. The proper antibiotic was administered. With suitable promptness, the patient ceased to have typhoid fever. But he was weakened, and immediately developed another infectious disease. It might be meningitis. That yielded to treatment, but something else followed, perhaps a virus infection. The series went on until he died. Sometimes a patient survived a dozen such contagions, to die of a thirteenth. Sometimes he remained alive, emaciated and weak. No amount of care could prevent a succession of totally unrelated illnesses. Exposure or non-exposure seemed to make no difference. And the cause of this plague of plagues was undetectable.

It shouldn't be impossible to work out such a problem, of course. Both previous plagues had been checked. Calhoun read and reread the reports on them and wasn't satisfied. The Med Ship man who'd handled both plagues was reported dead, not of sickness, but because his ship had blown itself to bits on the Castor IV spaceport. Such things didn't happen. *Tormals* had died in each pestilence, and *tormals* did not die of infectious diseases.

Murgatroyd was the *tormal* member of the *Aesclipus Twenty*'s crew. During three weeks of overdrive travel he was his normal self. He was a furry, companionable small animal who adored Calhoun, coffee, and pretending to be human, in that order. Calhoun traveled among the stars on professional errands, and Murgatroyd was perfectly happy to be with him. His tribe had been discovered on one of the Deneb planets; their charming personalities made them prized as pets. A long while ago it had been noticed that they were never sick. Then it developed that if they were exposed to any specific disease, they instantly manufactured overwhelming quantities of antibody for that infection. Now it was standard Med Service procedure to call on them for this special gift. When a new strain or a novel variety of disease-producing germ appeared, a *tormal* was exposed to it. They immediately made a suitable antibody, the Med Service isolated it, analyzed its molecular structure, and synthesized it. So far there hadn't been a single failure. So *tormals* were highly valued members of Med Ship crews.

Now two of them had died in epidemics of the kind now reported from Kryder II. Calhoun was suspicious and somehow resentful of the fact. The official reports didn't explain it. They dodged it. Calhoun fumbled irritably with it. One report was from the Med Service man now dead. He should have explained! The other was from doctors on Castor II after the Med Ship blew up. Nothing explained the explosion of the ship and nothing explained how *tormals* could die of an infection.

Perhaps Calhoun disliked the idea that Murgatroyd could be called on to give his life for Med Service. Murgatroyd worshiped him. Murgatroyd was a *tormal*, but he was also a friend.

So Calhoun studied the reports and tried to make sense of them while the *Aesclipus Twenty* traveled at a very high multiple of the speed of light. Its cocoon made it utterly safe. It required no attention. There was a control-central unit below decks which competently ran it, which monitored all instruments and kept track of their functioning. It labored conscientiously for three full weeks and a few hours over. Then it notified Calhoun that breakout from overdrive was just one hour away.

He doggedly continued his studies. He still had the reports of the earlier plagues on his desk when the control-central speaker said briskly, *"When the gong sounds, breakout will be five seconds off."*

There followed a solemn tick, tock, tick, tock like a slow swaying metronome. Calhoun tucked the reports under a paperweight and went to the pilot's chair. He strapped himself in. Murgatroyd recognized the action. He went padding under another chair and prepared to hold fast to its rungs with all four paws and prehensile tail. The gong sounded. The voice said, *"Five—four—three—two—one."*

The ship came out of overdrive. There was a sensation of intense dizziness, a desire to upchuck which vanished before one could act on it. Calhoun held onto his chair during that unhappy final sensation of falling in a narrowing spiral. Then the Med Ship was back in normal space. Its vision screens swirled.

They should have cleared to picture ten thousand myriads of suns of every imaginable tint and degree of brilliance, from faint phosphorescence to glaring stars of first magnitude or greater. There should have been no familiar constellations, of course. The Milky Way should be recognizable though subtly changed. The Horse's Head and Coalsack dark nebulas should have been visible with their outlines modified by the new angle from which they were seen. There should have been a Sol-type sun relatively near, probably with a perceptible disk. It ought to be the sun Kryder, from whose second planet had come a frightened demand for help. The *Aesclipus Twenty* ought to be near enough to pick out Kryder's planets with an electron telescope. Normally well conducted journeys in overdrive ended like that. Calhoun had made hundreds of such sun-falls. Murgatroyd had seen almost as many.

But there was never a breakout like this!

The Med Ship was back in normal space. Certainly. It

was light-centuries from its starting point. Positively. Somehow, there were no stars. There was no Milky Way. There were no nebulas, dark or otherwise. There was absolutely nothing of any other kind to match up with reasonable expectations, considering what had led up to this moment.

The screens showed the Med Ship surrounded by buildings on a planet's surface, with a blue and sunlit sky overhead. The screens, in fact, showed the buildings of the Interstellar Medical Service as surrounding the Med Ship. They said that Calhoun had traveled three weeks in overdrive and landed exactly back at the spot from which he'd been lifted to begin his journey.

Murgatroyd, also, saw the buildings on the vision screens. It is not likely that he recognized them, but when the *Aesclipus Twenty* landed, it was the custom for Calhoun to go about his business and for Murgatroyd to be admired, petted, and stuffed to repletion with sweets and coffee by the local population. He approved of the practice.

Therefore when he saw buildings on the vision screens he said, *"Chee!"* in a tone of vast satisfaction. He waited for Calhoun to take him aground and introduce him to people who would spoil him.

Calhoun sat perfectly still, staring. He gazed unbelievingly at the screens. They said, uncompromisingly, that the Med Ship was aground inside the Med Service Headquarters landing grid. The buildings were outside it. The screens showed the sky, with clouds. They showed trees. They showed everything that should be visible to a ship aground where ships receive their final checkover before being lifted out to space.

Murgatroyd said, *"Chee-chee!"* with a pleased urgency in his tone. He was impatient for the social success that came to him on every land-on planet. Calhoun turned his eyes to the outside pressure dial. It said there was seven hundred thirty millimeters of gas-pressure —air-pressure—outside. This was complete agreement with the screens.

"The devil!" said Calhoun.

The logical thing to do, of course, would be to go to

the air-lock, enter it, and then open the outer door to demand hotly what the hell was going on. Calhoun stirred in the pilot's chair to do exactly that. Then he clamped his jaws tightly.

He checked the nearest-object meter. Its reading was what it should be if the Med Ship were aground at headquarters. He checked the hull temperature. Its reading was just what it should be if the ship had been aground for a long time. He checked the screens again. He checked the magnetometer, which gave rather unlikely indications in overdrive, but in normal empty space recorded only the Med Ship's own magnetic field. It now registered a plausible Gauss-strength for a planet like the one on which headquarters was built.

He swore. Absurdly enough, he flipped the switch for the electron telescope. It filled a screen with dazzle, as if there were too much light. He could not use it.

Murgatroyd said impatiently, *"Chee! Chee! Chee!"*

Calhoun snapped at him. This was completely impossible: It simply could not be! A little while ago, he'd known the sensations of breakout from overdrive. He'd been dizzy, he'd been nauseated, he'd felt the usual horrible sensation of falling in a tightening spiral. That experience was real. There could be no doubt about it.

Instruments could be gimmicked to give false reports. In the course of a Med Ship man's training, he went through training voyages in ships which never left ground, but whose instruments meticulously reacted as they would in a real voyage. In such training exercises, vision screens showed blackness when the mock-up ship was theoretically in overdrive, and star-systems when it theoretically came out. A student Med Ship man went through illusory "voyages" that included even contact with theoretic planets; everything that could happen in a spaceship, including emergencies, was included in such mock-up trips. No training unit could simulate the sensation of going into overdrive or coming out of it, and he'd felt them. This was no mock-up trip.

Growling a little, Calhoun threw the communicator-switch. The speaker gave out the confused murmur of ground level signals, like those a space-type communicator picks up in atmosphere. Through it, vaguely, he could hear the whispering, faintly crackling Jansky radiation which can be received absolutely anywhere. He stared again at the vision screens. Their images were infinitely convincing. Overwhelming evidence insisted that he should go to the air-lock and out of it and hunt up somebody to explain this absurdity. It was inconceivable that a ship should travel for three weeks vastly faster than light and then find itself peacefully aground in its home port. It couldn't happen!

Murgatroyd said impatiently, *"Chee!"*

Calhoun slowly unbuckled the seat-belt intended to help him meet any possible emergency at breakout, but a seat-belt wouldn't help him decide what was reality. He got cagily to his feet. He moved toward the air-lock's inner door. Murgatroyd padded zestfully with him. Calhoun didn't go into the lock. He checked the dials, and from inside the ship he opened the outside lock door. From inside the ship he closed it again. Then he opened the inner lock door.

He heard a hissing that rose to a shout, and stopped.

He swore violently. Every instrument said the ship was aground, in atmosphere, at Interstellar Medical Service Headquarters, but he opened the outer lock door. If there was air there, nothing would happen. If there was no air outside, the air in the lock would escape and leave a vacuum behind it. He'd closed the outer door and opened the inner one. If there was air inside the lock, nothing could happen, but air had rushed into it with a noise like a shout.

So there'd been a vacuum inside the air-lock; so there was emptiness outside. So the *Aesclipus Twenty* was not back at home. It was not aground. Hence, the appearance of Med Service Headquarters outside was illusion and the sound of ground-level communication signals was deception.

The Med Ship *Aesclipus Twenty* was lying to the man it had been built to serve. It had tried to lure him into walking out of an air-lock to empty space. It was trying to kill him.

II

ACTUALLY, OUTSIDE THE ship there was nothing even faintly corresponding to the look of things from within. The small vessel of space actually floated in nothingness. Its hull glittered with that total reflection coating which was so nearly a non-radiating surface and was therefore so effective in conserving the heat supply of the ship. There was a glaring yellow star before the ship's nose. There were other white-hot stars off to port and starboard. There were blue and pink and greenish flecks of light elsewhere, and all the universe was specked with uncountable suns of every conceivable shade. Askew against the firmament, the Milky Way seemed to meander across a strictly spherical sky. From outside the Med Ship, its nature was self-evident. Everywhere, suns shone steadily, becoming more and more remote until they were no longer resolvable into stars but were only luminosity. That luminosity was many times brighter where the Milky Way shone. It was the Milky Way.

Minutes went by. The *Aesclipus Twenty* continued to float in emptiness. Then, after a certain interval, the outside airlock door swung open again and remained that way. Then a radiated signal spread again through the vacancy all about. It had begun before, when the outer door was opened, and cut off when it shut. Now it began to fill a vast spherical space with a message. It traveled, of course, no faster than the speed of light, but in one minute its outermost parts were eleven million miles away. In an hour, they would fill a globe two light-hours in diameter—sixty times as big. In four or five hours, it should be detectable on the planets of that nearby yellow star.

Calhoun regarded the light on the ship's control-board which said that a signal was being transmitted. He hadn't sent it. He hadn't ordered it. The ship had sent it off itself, as of itself, it had tried to lure him out to the vacuum beyond the air-lock.

But the ship was not alive. It could not plan anything. It could not want anything. It had been given orders to lie to him, and the lies should have caused his death. But a man would have had to invent the lies. Calhoun could even estimate exactly how the orders had been given—but not by whom—and where they'd been stored until this instant and how they'd been brought into action. He had no idea why.

The Med Ship was inevitably a highly complex assemblage of devices. It was impractical for one man to monitor all of them, so that task was given to another device to carry out. It was the control-central unit, in substance a specialized computer to which innumerable reports were routed, and from which routine orders issued.

Calhoun did not need, for example, to read off the CO_2 content in the ship's air, the rate of air-renewal, the ionization constant, the barometric pressure and the humidity and temperature to know that the air of the ship was right. The control-central unit issued orders to keep it right, and informed him when it was, and would order a warning if it went wrong. Then he could check the different instruments and find out what was the trouble. However, the control-central made no decisions. It only observed and gave routine orders. The orders that were routine could be changed.

Somebody had changed them; very probably a new and extra control-central unit had been plugged into the ship and the original one cut off. The extra one had orders that when the ship came out of overdrive it was to present pictures of Med Service Headquarters and report other data to match. It could not question these orders. It was only a machine, and it would carry them out blindly and without evaluation.

So now Calhoun ought to be floating in emptiness, his body an unrecognizable object whose outer surface had exploded and whose inner parts were ice. The ship had carried out its orders. Now, undoubtedly, there was something scheduled to happen next. Calhoun hadn't started the signal. It would not be transmitted—it would not have been planned—unless there would be something listening for it, another ship, almost certainly.

Another item. This had been most painstakingly contrived. There must be orders to take effect if the first part did not dispose of Calhoun. The ship had been a deadfall trap, which he'd evaded. It might now be a booby trap, just in case the deadfall failed to work. Yes. A man who orders a machine to commit murder will have given it other orders in case its first attempt fails. If Calhoun went down to verify his suspicion of an extra control-central, that might be the trigger that would blast the whole ship; that in any event would try to kill him again.

Murgatroyd said, *"Chee! Chee!"* The vision screens meant to him that there must be people waiting outside to give him sweet cakes and coffee. He began to be impatient. He added in a fretful tone, *"Chee!"*

"I don't like it either, Murgatroyd," said Calhoun wryly. "Somebody's tried to kill us—at any rate me—and he must think he had some reason, but I can't guess what it is! I can't even guess how anybody could get to a Med Ship at headquarters to gimmick it if they wanted to slaughter innocent people like you and me! Somebody must have done it!"

"Chee-chee!" said Murgatroyd, urgently.

"You may have a point there," said Calhoun slowly. "We, or at least I, should be dead. We are expected to be dead. There may be arrangements to make certain we don't disappoint somebody. Maybe we'd better play dead and find out. It's probably wiser than trying to find out and getting killed."

A man who has detected one booby trap or deadfall designed for him is likely to suspect more. Calhoun was inclined to go over his ship with a fine-toothed comb and look for them. A setter of booby traps would be likely to anticipate exactly that and prepare for it. Lethally.

Calhoun looked at the pilot's chair. It might not be wise to sit there. Anybody who received the ship's self-sent call would receive with it an image of that chair and whoever sat in it. To play dead, he shouldn't do anything a dead man couldn't do. So he shrugged. He sat down on the floor.

Murgatroyd looked at him in surprise. The signal going-out light burned steadily. That signal now filled a sphere two hundred million miles across. If there was a ship waiting to pick it up—and there'd be no reason for the call otherwise—it might be one or two or ten light-hours away. Nobody could tell within light-hours where a ship would break out of overdrive after three weeks in it.

Calhoun began to rack his brains. He couldn't guess the purpose of his intended murder, but he didn't mean to underestimate the man who intended it.

Murgatroyd went to sleep, curled up against Calhoun's body. There were the random noises a ship tape makes for human need. Absolute silence is unendurable. So there were small sounds released in the ship. Little, meaningless noises. Faint traffic. Faint conversation. Very faint music. Rain, and wind, and thunder as heard from a snug, tight house. It had no significance, so one did not listen to it, but its absence would have been unendurable.

The air apparatus came on and hummed busily, and presently shut off. The separate astrogation unit seemed to cough, somewhere. It was keeping track of the position of the ship, adding all accelerations and their durations—even in overdrive—ending with amazingly exact data on where the ship might be.

Presently Murgatroyd took a deep breath and woke up. He regarded Calhoun with a sort of jocular interest. For Calhoun to sit on the floor was unusual. Murgatroyd realized it.

It was at just this moment, but it was hours after breakout, that the space communicator speaker said metallically, *"Calling ship in distress! Calling ship in distress! What's the trouble?"*

This was not a normal reply to any normal call. A ship answering any call whatever should identify the caller and itself. This wasn't normal. Calhoun did not stir from where he sat on the floor. From there, he wouldn't be visible to whoever saw a picture of the pilot's chair. The call came again.

"Calling ship in distress! Calling ship in distress! What's your trouble? We read your call! What's the trouble?"

Murgatroyd knew that voices from the communicator should be answered. He said, *"Chee?"* and when Calhoun did not move he spoke more urgently, *"Chee-chee-chee!"*

Calhoun lifted him to his feet and gave him a pat in the direction of the pilot's chair. Murgatroyd looked puzzled. Like all *tormals*, he liked to imitate the actions of men. He was disturbed by breaks in what he'd considered unchangeable routine. Calhoun pushed him. Murgatroyd considered the push a license. He padded to the pilot's chair and swarmed into it. He faced the communicator screen.

"Chee!" he observed. *"Chee! Chee-chee! Chee!"*

He probably considered that he was explaining that for some reason Calhoun was not taking calls today, and that he was substituting for the Med Ship man. However, it wouldn't give that impression at the other end of the communication link-up. It would be some time before his words reached whoever was calling, but Murgatroyd said zestfully, *"Chee-chee!"* and then grandly, *"Chee!"* and then in a confidential tone he added, *"Chee-chee-chee-chee!"*

Anybody who heard him would be bound to consider

that he was the *tormal* member of the Med Ship's crew, that her human crew member was somehow missing, and that Murgatroyd was trying to convey that information.

There came no further calls. Murgatroyd turned disappointedly away. Calhoun nodded rather grimly to himself; somewhere there would be a ship homing on the call the Med Ship was sending without orders from him. Undoubtedly somebody in that other ship watched, and had seen Murgatroyd or would see him. It would be making a very brief overdrive hop toward the Med Ship. Then it would check the line again, and another hop. It would verify everything. The care taken in the call just made was proof that somebody was cagey. At the next call, if they saw Murgatroyd again, they would be sure that Calhoun was gone from the Med Ship. Nobody would suspect a furry small animal with long whiskers and a prehensile tail of deception.

Murgatroyd came back to Calhoun, who still sat on the floor lest any normal chair be part of a booby trap to check on the success of the air-lock device.

Time passed. Murgatroyd went back to the communicator and chattered at it. He orated in its direction. He was disappointed that there was no reply.

A long time later the communicator spoke briskly—the automatic volume control did not work, until the first syllable was halfway spoken. It had to be very neat indeed.

"Calling distressed ship! Calling distressed ship! We are close to you. Get a line on this call and give us coordinates."

The voice stopped and Calhoun grimaced. While the distress call—if it was a distress call—went out from the Med Ship there was no need for better guidance. Normally, a ship legitimately answering a call will write its own identification on the spreading waves of its communicator. However, this voice didn't name *Aesclipus Twenty*. It didn't name itself. If these messages were picked up some light-hours away on a planet of the sun Kryder, nobody could realize that a Med Ship was one of the two ships involved, or gain any idea who or what the other ship might be. It was concealment. It was trickiness. It fitted into the pattern of the false images still apparent on the Med Ship's screens and the deceptive data given by its instruments.

The voice from outside the ship boomed once more and then was silent. Murgatroyd went back to the screen. He made oratorical gestures, shrilled, *"Chee-chees,"* and then moved away as if very busy about some other matter.

Again a long, long wait before anything happened. Then there was a loud, distinct clanking against the Med Ship's hull. Calhoun moved quickly. He couldn't have been seen from the communicator before, and he'd wanted to hear anything that came to the Med Ship. Now it would probably be boarded, but he did not want to be seen until he had more information.

He went into the sleeping cabin and closed the door behind him. He stopped at a very small cupboard and put something in his pocket. He entered a tall closet where his uniforms hung stiffly. He closed that door. He waited.

More clankings. At least two spacesuited figures had landed on the Med Ship's hull-plating. They'd still have long, slender space ropes leading back to their own ship. They clanked their way along the hull to the open air-lock door. Calhoun heard the changed sound of their magnetic shoe soles as they entered the air-lock. They'd loosen the space ropes now and close the door. They did. He heard the sound of the outer door sealing itself. There was the hissing of air going into the lock.

Then the inner door opened. Two figures came out. They'd be carrying blasters at the ready as they emerged. Then he heard Murgatroyd.

"Chee-chee-chee! Chee!"

He wouldn't know exactly how to act. He normally took his cue from Calhoun. He was a friendly little animal. He had never received anything but friendliness from humans, and of course he couldn't imagine anything else. So he performed the honors of the ship with a grand air. He welcomed the newcomers. He practically made a speech of cordial greeting.

Then he waited hopefully to see if they'd brought him any sweet cakes or coffee. He didn't really expect it, but a *tormal* can always dream.

They hadn't brought gifts for Murgatroyd. They didn't even respond to his greeting. A *tormal* was standard on a Med Ship. They ignored him. Calhoun heard the clickings as spacesuit faceplates opened.

"Evidently," said a rumbling voice, "he's gone. Very neat. Nothing to clean up. Not even anything unpleasant to remember."

A second voice said curtly, "It'll be unpleasant if I don't cut off the rest of it!"

There was a snapping sound, as if a wire had forcibly been torn free from something. It was probably a cable to the control-board which, in the place of a rarely or never used switch, had connected something not originally intended, but which if the cable were broken could not act. Most likely the snapping of this wire should return the ship to a proper control-central system's guidance and operation. It did.

"Hm," said the first voice, "there's Kryder on the screens, and there's our ship. Everything's set."

"Wait!" commanded the curt voice. "I take no chances, I'm going to cut that thing off down below!"

Someone moved away. He wore a spacesuit. The faint creaking of its constant volume joints were audible. He left the control-room. His magnetic shoes clanked on uncarpeted metal steps leading down. He was evidently headed for the mechanical and electronic section of the ship. Calhoun guessed that he meant to cut completely loose the extra, gimmicked control-central unit that had operated the ship through the stages that should have led to his death. Apparently it could still destroy itself and the Med Ship.

The other man moved about the cabin. Calhoun heard Murgatroyd say, *"Chee-chee!"* in a cordial tone of voice. The man didn't answer. There are people to whom all animals, and even *tormals* are merely animate objects. There was suddenly the rustling of paper. He'd found the data sheets Calhoun had been studying to the very last instant before breakout.

Clankings. The man with the curt voice came back from below.

"I fixed it," he said shortly. "It can't blow now!"

"Look here!" said the rumbling voice, amused. "He had reports about your Med Ship on Castor IV!" He quoted sardonically, "It has to be assumed that a blaster was fired inside the ship. In any event the ship's fuel stores blew and shattered it to atoms. There is no possibility for more than guesses as to the actual cause of the disaster. The Med Ship's doctor was evidently killed, and there was some panic. The destruction of a large sum in currency, which the Med Ship was to have left off at a nearby planet to secure the shipment of un-contaminated foodstuffs to Castor IV, caused some delay in the restoration of normal health and nourish-ment on the planet. However—" The rumbling voice chuckled. "That's Kelo! Kelo wrote this report!"

The curt voice said, "I'm going to check things."

Calhoun heard the sounds of a thorough checkover, from air apparatus to space communicator. Then the ship was swung about, interplanetary drive went on and off and somebody who knew Med Ships made sure that the *Aesclipus Twenty* responded properly to all con-trols. Then the curt voice said, "All right. You can go now."

One man went to the air-lock and entered it. The lock-pumps boomed and stopped. The outer lock door opened and closed. The man left behind evidently got out of his spacesuit. He carried it below. He left it. He returned as the rumbling voice came out of a speaker, "I'm back on our ship. You can go now."

"Thanks," said the curt voice, sarcastically.

Calhoun knew that the newcomer to the ship had seated himself at the control-board. He heard Murga-troyd say, almost incredulously, *"Chee? Chee?"*

"Out of my way!" snapped the curt voice.

Then the little Med Ship swung, and seemed to teeter

very delicately as it was aimed with very great care close to the nearby yellow star. Before, the ship's screens had untruthfully insisted that Med Service Headquarters surrounded the ship. Now they worked properly. There were stars by myriads of myriads, and they looked as if they might be very close. Yet the bright yellow sun would be the nearest, and it was light-hours away. A light-hour is the distance a ray of light will travel, at a hundred eighty-odd thousand miles per second, during thirty-six hundred of them.

There was a sensation of shocking dizziness and intolerable nausea, swiftly repeated as the Med Ship made an overdrive hop to carry it only a few light-hours. Then there was that appalling feeling of contracting spiral fall. Murgatroyd said protestingly, *"Chee!"*

Then Calhoun moved quietly out of the closet into the sleeping cabin, and then out of that. He was more than halfway to the control-board before the man seated there turned his head. Then Calhoun leaped ferociously. He had a pocket blaster in his hand, but he didn't want to use it if it could be helped.

It was just as effective as a set of brass knuckles would have been, though. Before the other man regained consciousness, Calhoun had him very tidily bound and was looking interestedly over the contents of his pockets. They were curious. Taken literally, they seemed to prove that the man now lying unconscious on the floor was a Med Ship man on professional assignment, and that he was entitled to exercise all the authority of the Med Service itself.

On the word of his documents, he was considerably more of a Med Ship man than Calhoun himself.

"Curiouser and curiouser!" observed Calhoun to Murgatroyd. "I'd say that this is one of those tangled webs we weave when first we practice to deceive. But what's going on?"

The *Aesclipus Twenty* hovered, using emergency rocket fuel lavishly while her motion relative to the ground below her carried her past a ridge of high, snow clad mountains and then over a shoreline with pack ice piled against its beaches.

This was not the planet from which a call had been sent and which Calhoun was answering. There was no sign of habitation anywhere. Cold blue sea swept past below. There were some small ice cakes here and there, but as the shore was left behind they dwindled in number and the water surface became unbroken save by waves. The mountains sank to the horizon, and then ahead—in the direction of the Med Ship's motion—an island appeared. It was small and rocky and almost entirely snow-covered. There was no vegetation. It was entirely what Calhoun had expected from his examination by electron telescope from space.

This was approximately the equator of the planet Kryder III, which was one planetary orbit farther out than the world which was Calhoun's proper destination. This was an almost frozen planet. It would be of very little use to the inhabitants of Kryder II. There might be mineral deposits worth the working, but for colonization it would be useless.

Calhoun very painstakingly brought the little space-ship down on the nearest possible approach to bare flat stone. Ragged, precipitous peaks rose up on either hand as the ship descended. Miniature glaciers and waterfalls of ice appeared. Once there was a sudden tumult and a swarm of furry—not feathered—creatures poured out of some crevice and swarmed skyward, doubtless making a great outcry because of having been disturbed.

Then the rocket flames touched ice and stone. Steam floated in clouds about the ship. It appeared on the vision screens as an opaque whiteness. Then the Med Ship tapped stone, and tapped again, and then settled only very slightly askew on what would have to be fairly solid rock. Writhing steam tendrils blotted out parts of all the outside world for long minutes afterward. At last, though, it cleared.

Murgatroyd looked at the snowscape. He saw a place of cold and ice and desolation. He seemed to reach a conclusion.

"Chee!" he said with decision.

He went back to his private cubbyhole. He'd have none of such a landing place. He preferred to touch ground where there were people to stuff him with assorted edibles.

Calhoun waited alertly until it was certain that the ship's landing-fins had complete solidity under them. Then he pushed himself away from the control-board and nodded to his prisoner.

"Here we are," he observed. "This is Kryder III. You didn't intend to land here. Neither did I. We both expected to touch ground on Kryder II, which is inhabited. This world isn't. According to the Directory, the average daytime temperature here is two degrees Centigrade. We've landed on an island which is forty miles away from a continental landmass. Since you aren't inclined to be cooperative, I'm going to leave you here, with such food as I can spare and reasonable equipment for survival. If I can, I'll come back here for you. If I can't, I won't. I suggest that while I get things ready for you to go aground, that you think over your situation. If you give me information that will make it more likely I can come back, it'll be all to the good for you. Anything you hold out will lessen my chances and therefore yours. I'm not going to argue about it. I'm not threatening you. I'm simply stating the facts. Think it over.''

He left the control-room to go down into the storage compartments of the ship. It was in no sense a cargo-carrier, but it had to be prepared for highly varied situations its occupant might have to meet. Calhoun began to gather divers items. To gather them he had to put carefully away two objects he'd sealed quite airtight in plastic bags. One was a duplicate of the control-central device that had tried to get him out the air-lock. It was sealed up so no trace of odor could escape, or slowly evaporating oil—such as make fingerprints—or of any of those infinitesimal traces of one's identity every man leaves on anything he handles. The other was the spacesuit the prisoner had worn when he boarded the Med Ship. It was similarly sealed in. The technicians back at Headquarters could make an absolute, recorded analysis of such identifying items, and could prove who'd handled the one device or worn the other.

He came back to the control-room. He carried bundles. He adjusted the lock so both inner and outer doors could be open at the same time. A cold and daunt-ing wind came in as the doors spread wide. Calhoun went down to ground. His breath was like white smoke when he returned.

"Tent and sleeping bag," he commented. "It's chilly!"

He went down to the storage compartments again. He came up with another burden.

"Food and a heater, of sorts," he said.

He went out. He came back. He went below again. He was definitely generous in the food supply he piled about the first two loads of equipment. When he'd finished, he checked on his fingers. Then he shook his head and went below for cold-climate garments. He brought them up and put them with the rest.

"Anything you want to say?" he asked pleasantly when he returned. "Anything to help me survive and get back here to pick you up again?"

The bound man ground his teeth.

"You won't get away with turning up in my place!"

Calhoun raised his eyebrows.

"How bad's the plague?"

"Go to the devil!" snapped the bound man.

"You were going to land as a Med Ship man," observed Calhoun. "Judging by two previous operations like this, you were going to check the plague. You did that on Castor IV."

The bound man cursed him.

"I suspect," said Calhoun, "that since you blamed the first plague on contaminated grain, and it did stop when all the grain on the planet was burned and fresh supplies brought in from elsewhere, *and* since the same thing happened with the blame on meats on Castor IV, my guess is also contaminated food on Kryder II. Criminals rarely change their method of operation as long as it works well. But there are two things wrong with this one. One is that no bacterium or virus was ever identified as the cause of the plagues. The other is that two *tormals* died. *Tormals* don't die of plagues. They can't catch them. It's impossible. I'm confident that I can keep Murgatroyd from dying of the plague on Kryder II."

The bound man did not speak, this time.

"And," said Calhoun thoughtfully, "there's the very curious coincident that somebody stole the money to buy uncontaminated grain, in the first plague, and the money to buy meat for Castor IV was destroyed when your Med Ship blew up in the spaceport. It was your Med Ship, wasn't it? And you were reported killed. Something had gone around—had, I said—which was about as lethal as the toxin made by *clostridium botulinum*. Only it wasn't a germ caused toxin, because there wasn't any germ, or virus either. Are you sure you don't want to talk?"

The man on the floor spat at him. Then he cursed horribly. Calhoun shrugged. He picked up his prisoner and carried him to the lock door. He took him out. He laid him on the pile of stores and survival equipment.

He carefully unknotted some of the cords that bound his prisoner's hands.

"You can get loose in five minutes or so," he observed. "By the sunset line when we came in, night is due to fall before long. I'll give you until dark to improve your chances of living by improving mine, then . . ."

He went back to the Med Ship. He entered it and closed the lock doors. Murgatroyd looked inquisitively at him. He'd watched out the lock while Calhoun was aground. If he'd moved out of sight, the little *tormal* would have tried to follow him. Now he said reproachfully, *"Chee! Chee!"*

"You're probably right," said Calhoun dourly. "I couldn't get anywhere by arguing with him, and I wasn't more successful with threats. I don't think he'll talk even now. He doesn't believe I'll leave him here. But I'll have to!"

Murgatroyd said, *"Chee!"*

Calhoun did not answer. He looked at the vision screen. It was close to sunset outside. His captive writhed on top of the mass of cloth and stores. Calhoun grunted impatiently, "He's not too good at loosening knots! The sun's setting and he needs light to get the tent up and the heater going. He'd better hurry!"

He paced up and down the control-room. There were small, unobtrusive sounds within the Med Ship. They were little, meaningless noises. Remote traffic sounds. Snatches of talk, which were only murmurings. Almost infinitely faint tinklings of music not loud enough to identify. In the utter soundlessness of empty space, a ship would be maddeningly silent except for such wisps of things to hear. They kept him from feeling maddeningly alone. They kept him reminded that there were worlds on which people moved and lived. They were links to the rest of humanity and they prevented the psychosis of solitude—with, of course, the help of a companionable small animal who adored being noticed by a man.

He went back to the screens. The sun was actually setting, now, and the twilight would be brief, because despite the ice and snow about, this was the equator of this particular world. The prisoner outside still struggled to free himself. He had moved, in his writhing, until he was almost off the pile of dark stuff on the snow. Calhoun scowled. He needed information. This man, who'd shared in a trick designed to kill him, could give it to him. He'd tried to persuade the man to talk. He'd tried to trap him into it. He'd tried everything but physical torture to get a clear picture of what was going on, on Kryder II. A plague which had no bacterium or virus as its cause was unreasonable. The scheduling of a fake Med Ship man's arrival—at the cost of a very neat trick to secure the death of the real one—and the coordination of a human scheme with the progress of a pestilence, this was not reasonable either. Though Calhoun had irritated his prisoner into fury after persuasion failed, the man had given no information. He'd cursed Calhoun. He'd raged foully. But he'd given no plausible information at all.

It became dark outside. Calhoun adjusted the screens to a higher light-gain. There was only starlight and even with the screens turned up he could see only convulsive struggling movements of a dark figure upon a dark patch of equipment.

He swore.

"The clumsy idiot!" he snapped. "He ought to be able to get loose! Maybe he'll think I mean just to scare him. . . ."

He took a hand lamp and opened the air-lock doors again. He cast the light ahead and down. His captive now lay face-down, struggling.

Growling, Calhoun descended to the snow, leaving the air-lock doors open. He went over to his prisoner. Innumerable stars glittered in the sky, but he was accustomed to the sight of space itself. He was unimpressed by the firmament. He bent over the squirming, panting figure of the man he'd apparently not helped enough toward freedom.

But at the last instant the hand lamp showed the

former prisoner free and leaping from a crouched position with his hands plunging fiercely for Calhoun's throat. Then the two bodies came together with an audible impact. Calhoun found himself raging at his own stupidity in being fooled like this. The man now grappling him had been full party to one attempt to kill him by a trick. Now he tried less cleverly but more desperately to kill him with his bare hands.

He fought like a madman, which at that moment he very possibly was. Calhoun had been trained in unarmed combat, but so had his antagonist. Once Calhoun tripped, and the two of them rolled in powdery snow with uneven ice beneath it. In that wrenching struggle, Calhoun's foot hit against something solid. It was a landing-fin of the *Aesclipus Twenty*. He kicked violently against it, propelling himself and his antagonist away. The jerk should have given Calhoun a momentary advantage. It didn't. It threw the two of them suddenly away from the ship, but onto a place where the stone under the snow slanted down. They rolled. They slid, and they went together over a stony ledge and fell, still battling, down into a crevasse.

Murgatroyd peered anxiously from the air-lock door. There was no light save what poured out from behind him. He fairly danced in agitation, a small, spidery, furry creature silhouetted in the air-lock door. He was scared and solicitous. He was panicky. He made shrill cries for Calhoun to come back. *"Chee!"* he cried desperately. *"Chee-chee! Chee-chee-chee-chee! . . ."*

He listened. There was the keening sound of wind. There was a vast, vast emptiness all around. This was a world of ice and dreariness, its continents were white and silent, and its beaches were lined with pack ice, there was nothing to be heard anywhere except cold and senseless sounds of desolation. Murgatroyd wailed heartbrokenly.

But after a long, long time there were scratching sounds. Still later, pantings. Then Calhoun's head came up, snow-covered, over the edge of the crevasse into which he'd tumbled. He rested, panting. Then, desperately, he managed to crawl to where snow was waist-deep but the ground proven solid by his previous footprints. He staggered upright. He stumbled to the ship. Very, very wearily, he climbed to the lock door. Murgatroyd embraced his legs, making a clamor of reproachful rejoicing that after going away he had come back.

"Quit it, Murgatroyd," said Calhoun wearily. "I'm back, and I'm all right. He's not. He was underneath when we landed, thirty feet down. I heard his skull crack when we hit. He's dead. If he hadn't been, how I'd have gotten him up again I don't know, but he was dead. No question."

Murgatroyd said agitatedly, *"Chee! Chee-chee!"*

Calhoun closed the lock doors. There was a nasty rock scrape across his forehead. He looked like a man of snow. Then he said heavily, "He could have told me what I need to know! He could have told me how they make the plagues work! He could have helped me finish the whole business in a hurry, when there are men dying of it. But he didn't believe I'd actually do anything to him. Stupid! It's insane!"

He began to brush snow off of himself, with an expression of such sickish bitterness on his face as was normal for a Med Ship man—whose business it is to keep people from dying—when he realized that he had killed a man.

Murgatroyd went padding across the control-room. He swarmed up to where Calhoun kept the crockery. He jumped down to the floor again. He pressed his private, tiny coffee cup upon Calhoun.

"Chee!" said Murgatroyd agitatedly. *"Chee-chee! Chee!"*

He seemed to feel that if Calhoun made coffee, that all matters would be returned to normal and distressing memories could be cast aside. Calhoun grimaced.

"If I died you'd have no coffee, eh? All right, as soon as we're on course for Kryder II I'll make you some. But I think I've blundered. I tried to act like a detective instead of a medical men because it should have been quicker. I'll make some coffee in a little while.''

He seated himself in the pilot's chair, glanced over the instrument readings, and presently pressed a button.

The *Aesclipus Twenty* lifted from her landing place, her rockets lighting the icy stone spires of the island with an unearthly blue-white flame. The speed of her rising increased. A little later, there was only a dwindling streak of rocket fire ascending to the stars.

IV

THE CRESCENT WHICH was the planet Kryder II enlarged gradually, with the sun many millions of miles beyond it. The *Aesclipus Twenty* swung in its course, pointing at a right angle to the line along which it had been moving. Its drive-baffles glowed faintly as the Lawlor interplanetary drive gave it a new impetus, changing its line of motion by adding velocity in a new direction to the sum of all the other velocities it had acquired. Then the ship swung back, not quite to its former bearing but along the line of its new course.

Inside the ship, Calhoun again aimed the ship. He used the sighting circle at the very center of the dead-ahead vision screen. He centered a moderately bright star in that glowing circle. The star was a certain number of seconds of arc from the planet's sunlit edge. Calhoun watched. All about, in every direction, multitudes of shining specks—actually suns—floated in space. Many or most of them warmed their families of planets with the solicitude of brooding hens. Some circled each other in stately, solemn sarabands. There were some, the Cepheids, which seemed to do neither but merely to lie in emptiness, thin and gaseous, pulsating slowly as if breathing.

Calhoun relaxed, satisfied. The guide star remained at exactly the same distance from the crescent planet, while the Med Ship hurtled toward it. This arrangement was a standard astrogational process. If the moving planet and the sighting star remained relatively motionless, the total motion of the Med Ship was exactly adjusted for approach. Of course, when close enough the relationship would change, but if the ship's original line was accurate, the process remained a sound rule-of-thumb method for approaching a planet.

The Med Ship sped on. Calhoun, watching, said over his shoulder to Murgatroyd, "We're pretty much in the dark about what's going on, Murgatroyd, not in the matter of the plague, of course. That's set up to be ended by somebody arriving in a Med Ship, as in two cases before this one. But if they can end it, they needn't have started it. I don't like the idea of anything like this being unpunished."

Murgatroyd scratched reflectively. He could see the vision screens. He could have recognized buildings as such, though probably not as individual ones. On the screens, save for the sun and one crescent planet, there were only dots of brightness of innumerable colorings. To Murgatroyd, who spent so much of his life in space travel, the stars had no meaning whatever.

"Technically," observed Calhoun, "since medicine has become a science, people no longer believe in plague-spreaders. Which makes spreading plagues a possible profession."*

Murgatroyd began to clean his whiskers, elaborately licking first the right-hand and then the left-hand ones.

* In June of 1630 (standard) one Guglielmo Piazza, who was commissioner of health of the city of Milan, was seen to wipe ink off his fingers against a building wall. He was immediately accused of wiping the walls with matter to produce bubonic plague. Put to the torture, he finally confessed; when pressed for confederates he despairingly named a barber named Mora. The barber, under torture, named a Don Juan de Padilla as another confederate in the dissemination of bubonic plague. They were not asked to name others, but were executed in the utterly barbarous methods of the period and a "column of infamy" erected to warn others against this crime. This is but one example. See *"Devils, Drugs and Doctors,"* Haggard, Harper and Bro., N.Y., 1929.

Calhoun again checked the relative position of the sighting star and Kryder II. He brought out a microfilm reel and ran it through. It was a resume of the history of toxicology. He hunted busily for items having to do with the simulation of bacterial toxins by inorganic compounds. He made notes, not many. He consulted another reel. It dealt with antigens and antibodies. He made more notes and consulted a third reel.

He worked carefully with pencil and paper and then, with his memos at hand, he punched the keys of the very small computer which acted as a reference library. It was a very remarkable library. It was packed in a number of cubic feet of microfiles which stored tens of thousands of items of information in a cubic inch of substance. The little computer could search them all—all the millions of millions of facts—in a matter of minutes and make its discoveries into a report. Calhoun set it to find the known compounds with such-and-such properties, a boiling point above so-and-so, with an inhibitive effect upon the formation of certain other compounds.

The little device accepted his command. It could do what Calhoun could not, in the speed and precision of its search. But he could take the information it provided and do what no computer could imaginably try. Calhoun could set up his own problem. No computer can do that. Calhoun could devise a way to solve it. No computer can do anything so original. Calhoun could think.

He went back to the pilot's chair. The crescent world was noticeably nearer and larger. Calhoun became absorbed in the delicate task of putting the Med Ship in suitable orbit around Kryder II. The ship obeyed him. It swung around to the green world's sunlit hemisphere. He addressed the communicator microphone:

"Med Ship Aesclipus Twenty *calling ground to report arrival and ask coordinates for landing. Our mass if fifty standard tons. Repeat, five-oh tons. Purpose of landing . . . response to planetary health department request for services."*

Behind him, the small computer stuttered and extruded a six-inch strip of paper tape, on which there was new printing. Calhoun heard, but did not heed it. He watched as more of the surface of the nearing planet came into view with the Med Ship's swing around it. There were bright green continents, showing irregular streaks of white glaciation where mountain ranges rose. There were seas and oceans and cloud masses and that filmy blue haze at the horizon which so much surprised the first explorers of space.

"*Med Ship* Aesclipus—" Calhoun's recorded voice repeated the call. Murgatroyd popped his head out of his personal cubbyhole. When Calhoun talked, but not to him, it meant that presently there would be other people around. And people did not long remain strangers to Murgatroyd. He made friends with ease and zest. Except for Calhoun, Murgatroyd defined friends as people who gave him sweet cakes and coffee.

The communicator speaker said, "*Calling Med Ship! Ground calling Med Ship! Coordinates are . . .*" The voice named them. It sounded warm and even rejoicing through the speaker, as if the landing-grid operator had a personal interest in the arrival of a man sent by the Interstellar Medical Service. "*We're plenty glad you've come, sir! Plenty glad! Did you get the coordinates? They're . . .*"

"*Chee!*" said Murgatroyd zestfully.

He clambered down to the control-room floor and looked at the screen. When Calhoun spoke again to the grid operator, Murgatroyd strutted. He would land, and he would be the center of attention everywhere so long as the Med Ship was aground. He practically crooned his delight.

"*Yes, sir!*" said the voice from the ground. "*Things were looking pretty bad! There's a Doctor Kelo here, sir. He was on Castor IV when they had a plague there. He says the Med Service man that came there got it licked right off. Excuse me, sir. I'm going to report you're coming in.*"

The voice stopped. Calhoun glanced at the coordinates he'd written down and made adjustments for the

Med Ship's needed change of course. It was never necessary to be too precise in making a rendezvous with a landing grid. A ship had to be several planetary diameters out from ground to have even its interplanetary drive work. But a grid's force fields at so many thousands of miles distance were at first widely spread and tenuous. They reported to ground when they first touched the incoming ship. Then they gathered together and focused on the spacecraft, and then they tightened and grew strong. After that they pulled the ship down gently out of emptiness to the center of that half-mile high circle of steel girders and copper cable which was the landing grid. It took time to pull a ship down some thousands of miles. Too violent a pull could be disastrous to the crew, but ordinarily it was marvelously effective and totally safe.

The communicator screen swirled suddenly and then presented a very clear picture of the grid-control office. It showed the operator. He gazed admiringly at Calhoun.

"I've reported, sir," he said warmly, *"and Doctor Kelo's coming right now! He was at the big hospital, where they've been working on what the plague can be. He's coming by copter . . . won't be long."*

Calhoun reflected. According to his data, Doctor Kelo had been a prominent physician on Castor IV when the Med Ship man there had presumably been killed in the detonation of the ship. Doctor Kelo had made a report on that matter. The two men who'd come to take over the Med Ship at its breakout point, not an untold number of hours ago, had read his report with seeming amusement. They'd noted Doctor Kelo's name. It was at least interesting that this same Doctor Kelo was here, where there also was a plague. However, the Med Ship man he expected wasn't Calhoun. Calhoun was supposed to be floating somewhere in emptiness, lighthours away from here.

The grid operator watched his dials. He said, pleased, *"Got it, sir! Fifty tons, you said. I'll lock on."*

Calhoun felt the curious fumbling sensation the grid's

force fields produced when they touched and gathered
around the ship, and then the cushiony thrustings and
pushings when the fields focused and intensified. The
Aesclipus Twenty began its descent.

"I'll bring you down now, sir," said the operator of
the grid, very happily. *"I'll make it as quick as I can,
but you're a long way out!"*

Landing was bound to be a lengthy process, much
longer than lifting off. One could not snatch a ship from
space. It had to be brought down with no more acceleration planetward than a ship's company could endure. Eventually the downward speed had to be checked
so the contact with the ground would be a gentle one. A
grid could smash a ship to atoms by bringing it down on
the spaceport tarmac with a velocity of miles per
second. This was why interplanetary wars were impossible. A landing grid could smash any ship in space if
it approached a planet with hostile intentions.

"I suppose," said Calhoun, "there's a lot of concern
about the—epidemic. The planetary health department
asked for me."

*"Yes, sir! It's real bad! Started three months ago.
There were half a dozen cases of pneumonia. Nobody
thought much about it. They were treated, and stopped
having pneumonia, but they weren't well. They had
something else, not the same thing, either. There was
typhoid and meningitis and so on. This is what the
newscasts say. Then other cases turned up. A child
would have measles, and it would turn to tetanus, and
that to pneumonia, and that to scarlet fever. . . . It
couldn't happen, the doctors said, but it was happening! The hospitals filled up. More came in all the
time, and none of them could leave. They could keep
most of the cases alive, but they had to cure 'em of
something else all the time. They had to turn schools
and churches into hospitals. One person in ten is sick
already. More are taken down every minute. Presently,
there won't be doctors enough to diagnose the diseases
patients contract continually. They figure that a quarter
of the whole population will be down inside of two*

weeks more, and then they'll start dying faster than they do now, because there won't be enough well people to take care of 'em. They figure there won't be anybody on his feet in a month and a half from now and that'll be the end for everybody.''

Calhoun clamped his jaws together.

"They've stopped giving it out," said the grid operator. He added professionally, *"I've got you coming down at four hundred feet a second, but I'm going to pull a lot harder! You're needed down here in a hurry! I'll put on the brakes at a thousand miles, and you'll touch ground like a feather.''*

Calhoun ground his teeth. Strictly speaking, he should discuss the plague only with qualified medical men. But the public attitude toward a disease has to be considered in its treatment. This, however, was plainly not a disease. A given bacterium or virus can produce one disease only. Its activity may vary in virulence, but not in kind. Viruses do not change to bacteria. Cocci do not change to spirochetes. Each pathogenic organism that exists remains itself. It may change in viciousness, but never in form. The plague as described could not be a plague! It could not be!

Immediately one ceased to think of it as a natural plague; immediately one considered it artificial, it made sense. It tended to spread toward a total, cent-percent matching of number of cases to the number of people on the planet. Normal pestilences do not. It was planned that a fake Med Ship man should arrive at a certain time and end it. This would be absurd if the plague were a natural one. It was the third of its kind, and the first two had killed *tormals*—which pestilences could not—and in each case large sums of money had disappeared.

"Doctor Kelo, sir," said the grid operator, *"said he was sure that if a Med Ship man could get here with his—what's that little creature? A* tormal? *Once a Med Ship man got here with his* tormal, *the plague was as good as licked.''* He stopped and listened. *"Doctor Kelo must be here now. There's a copter landing outside.''*

Then the grid man said with a rather twisted grin, *"I*

tell you, everybody's glad you're here! I've got a wife and kids. They haven't got the plague yet, but . . ."

He stood up. He said joyously, *"Doctor Kelo! Here he is! Right here on the screen! We've been talkin'. He's comin' down fast, and I'll have him aground in a hurry!"*

A voice said, *"Ah, yes! I am most pleased. Thank you for notifying me."*

Then a new figure appeared on the vision screen. It was dignified. It was bearded. It was imposing in the manner of the most calmly confident of medical men. One could not look at Doctor Kelo without feeling confidence in him. He seemed benign. He beamed at the grid man and turned to the vision screen.

He saw Calhoun. Calhoun regarded him grimly. Doctor Kelo stared at him. Calhoun was not the man who'd been put aboard the Med Ship at first breakout point. He wasn't the man who'd handled the Castor IV epidemic, or the one before that. He wasn't the man who was supposed to have been killed when a Med Ship blew up in the Castor IV spaceport. He wasn't . . .

"How do you do?" said Calhoun evenly. "I gather we are to work together—again, Doctor Kelo."

Doctor Kelo's mouth opened, and shut. His face went gray. He made an inarticulate sound. He stared at Calhoun in absolute stupefaction. Murgatroyd squirmed past Calhoun's body to look into the communicator screen. He saw a man, and to Murgatroyd that meant that shortly he would be aground among people who admired him adoringly and would therefore stuff him with all the things he liked to eat and drink.

"Chee!" said Murgatroyd cordially. *"Chee-chee!"*

The stark incredulity of the bearded face changed to shock. That expression became purest desperation. One of Doctor Kelo's beautifully manicured hands disappeared. It appeared again. There was a tiny snapping sound and the grid operator became suddenly boneless. He seemed to bend limply in all his joints and almost to pour downward to the floor.

Doctor Kelo turned swiftly to the dials of the landing-grid control-board. He surveyed them, panting suddenly. Of course, a landing grid can do its work in many different fashions. It can use the processes of normal space commerce to make space war impossible. Because it can be deadly.

Doctor Kelo reached out. Calhoun could not see exactly what he did, but he could guess its purpose. Immediately, he felt a surging of the Med Ship which told him exactly what had been done. It was an increased downward velocity of the ship, which had to be brought down rapidly for most of its descent, or otherwise the grid would swing around to the night side of this world where, with a planet's bulk between, it could not do anything with the Med Ship at all. However, high acceleration toward the ground could be used to a certain point only. Below a critical distance the ship couldn't be stopped. It would be bound to crash to flaming destruction against the world it had meant to land on.

The ship surged again. It plunged planetward with doubled acceleration. In the grip of the landing grid's force fields, it built up to a velocity far beyond any at which it could be slowed for a safe landing. It was building up toward the speed of shooting stars, which consume themselves when they touch atmosphere. It was still thousands of miles out in emptiness, still speeding crazily to inevitable destruction.

V

CALHOUN SAID COLDLY, "I've got to learn how a murderer thinks, Murgatroyd. While I'm thinking there's a situation they have to meet, these characters work out a way to kill me, as if that was bound to settle everything. I can't anticipate the ideas they get automatically!"

He placed his hands on the control-board where he could act in an infinitesimal fraction of a second. He waited. The Med Ship was in the grip of an immaterial field of force which was capable of handling a merchant ship of space, whereas the *Aesclipus Twenty* was as small as a ship could be and still perform a Med Ship's functions.

The fact that a field of force is not a solid object has its consequences. A solid object can exert a thrust in three dimensions. If it is rigid, it can resist or impose thrusts in any direction, up or down, right or left, and away from or toward itself. However, a field of force can only act in one: toward or away from, or up or down, or left or right. It cannot push in one direction while resisting a thrust from another. So a grid field could pull a ship downward with terrific force, but it could not pull the ship sidewise at the same moment, and that happened to be what was necessary.

There is a certain principle known as the conservation of angular momentum. A ship approaching a planet has always some velocity relative to the planet's surface.

Within a wide range of speeds, that angular velocity will make a ship take up an orbit at a distance appropriate to its speed. The greater the speed, the lower the orbit. It is like a weight on a string, twirled around one's finger. As the string winds up, the weight spins faster. It is like a figure skater spinning in one spot on the ice with arms outstretched, who spins more and more rapidly as he brings his arms closer to his body. The *Aesclipus Twenty* had such orbital, angular momentum. It could not descend vertically without losing its velocity. If it was to land safely, it would have to lose its velocity and at the moment it touched ground it must have exactly the motion of the ground it touched, for exactly the same reason that one stops a ground-car before stepping out of it.

But a grid field could only push or pull in one direction at a time. To land a ship it must cease to pull planetward from time to time, and push the ship sidewise to match its speed to that of the ground. If it didn't, the ship would go on beyond the horizon—or seem to.

So Calhoun waited. Grimly. The ship, plunging vertically, still retained its lateral speed. That speed drove it toward the horizon. It was necessary to pull it back to pull it down. So the bearded man, cursing as the ship swung away from the vertical, fumbled to pull it back.

An extremely skilled operator might well have done so, even against Calhoun's resistance. The shift of directional pull—or thrust—could have been made so swiftly that the ship would be actually free of all fields for less than the hundredth of a second. However, such fine work required practice.

Calhoun felt the ship shiver for the fraction of an instant. For that minute portion of a heartbeat, the downward pull had to be cut off so the sidewise push could be applied. But in that instant Calhoun jammed down the emergency rockets' control to maximum possible thrust. He was flung back into the pilot's chair. The weight of his chest forced air explosively out of his lungs. Murgatroyd went skittering across the floor. He caught an anchored chair leg with a wide sweep of his spidery arms and clung there desperately, gasping.

Three. Four. Five seconds. Calhoun swung the ship's nose and went on. Seven. Eight. Nine. Ten.

He cut the rocket-blast at the last instant before he would have blacked out. He panted. Murgatroyd said indignantly, *"Chee! Chee! Chee!"*

Calhoun said with some difficulty, "Right! I did you a dirty trick, but it had to be done! Now if we can keep him from getting his field locked on us—again . . ."

He sat alertly in the pilot's chair, recovering from the strain of such violent acceleration for even so brief a period. A long time later there was a faint, fumbling sensation as if a force field, groping, touched the ship. He blasted off at an angle at high acceleration again.

Then the ship was clear. It reached a spot where the landing grid, on the curved surface of Kryder II, was below the horizon. The Med Ship had orbital velocity. Calhoun made certain of it when he looked at the nearest-object indicator. He was then very close to atmosphere but the planet now below him curved downward and away from his line of flight. The ship was actually rising from the planetary surface. Calhoun had escaped a collision with Kryder II by speeding up across its face. One can sometimes avoid a collision in traffic by speeding up, but it is not the safest thing for either ground-cars or spaceships to do.

Murgatroyd made querulous noises to himself. Calhoun got out the data on the planet Kryder II. There were continents and highways and mountain ranges and cities. He studied the maps and a view of the actual surface beneath him. The communicator screen was blank, and had been since the horizon rose between the grid and the fleeing ship. He flipped it off. At the sunset line there was a city. He located himself.

Murgatroyd said, *"Chee!"* in an apprehensive tone as the emergency rockets roared again.

"No," said Calhoun. "No more full-force rocketeering, Murgatroyd. And I'm not going to take the chance of being outwitted again. I've been fooled twice by not knowing how a murderer's mind works. I'm going to operate out of contact with such characters for a while. I'm going to land and do a burglary and get back out to space again."

He checked on maps. He glanced frequently at the nearest-object dial. He swung the ship and blasted his rockets again, and watched the dial, and used the rockets still again. The Med Ship was slowing. It curved downward. Presently, the needle of the nearest-object dial quivered. The Med Ship, still out of atmosphere, was passing above mountains.

"Now, if we can land beyond, here . . ." said Calhoun.

Murgatroyd was not reassured. He watched. He grew uneasy as Calhoun went through the elaborate, tricky, and definitely dangerous operation of landing the Med Ship in the dark, on unknown terrain, and by instruments only except for the last few minutes. During those last few minutes the screens showed forests below the hovering Med Ship, lighted in unearthly fashion by the rocket flames. With that improbable light he finished the landing. He remained alert until sure that the ship was steady on her landing-fins. He cut off the rockets. He listened to the outside microphones' report. There were only the night sounds of a long colonized planet, where a Terran ecological system had been established and there were birds and insects of totally familiar varieties.

He nodded to himself. He turned on the planetary communications receiver. He listened for a long time. He heard news broadcasts. There was no mention of the Med Ship reported as arriving. There was resolutely hopeful news of the plague. It had broken out in a new area, but there was great hope that it could be contained. The use of combined antibiotics seemed to promise much. The death rate was said to be down slightly. There was no mention of the fact that the real percentage of deaths might be obscured by a large increase of new patients who wouldn't normally die just yet.

Calhoun listened. At last, he stirred. His eyes fell upon the small computer which had searched in the ship's microfiles for data on compounds with boiling points below such-and-such, with absorption coefficients in certain ranges, which had an inhibitive effect upon the formation of certain other substances.

Projecting from the answer slot there was a six-inch strip of newly printed paper, waiting to give him the information he'd asked for. He read it. He looked pleased.

"Not bad," he told Murgatroyd. "The broadcasts say the plague is prevalent in this area, and this says we want some groceries and ditch water. I've the crudes to make up these prescriptions."

He made ready to go aground. He was armed. He took a compass. He took certain highly odorous pellets. Murgatroyd zestfully made ready to accompany him.

"No," said Calhoun. "Not this time, Murgatroyd! You have many gifts, but burglary isn't one of them. I couldn't even depend on you to be a properly suspicious lookout."

Murgatroyd could not understand. He was bewildered when Calhoun left him in the Med Ship with water and food at hand. When Calhoun closed the inner air-lock door, he could still hear Murgatroyd arguing desperately, *"Chee! Chee-chee!"*

Calhoun dropped an odorous pellet on the ground and moved away on a compass course. He had a hand lamp, which he used sparingly. There were tree trunks to run into and roots to stumble over and much brushwood to be thrust through. Ultimately he came upon a highway. He deposited a pellet. With his hand lamp off, he searched as much of the sky as he could. He concluded that there was a faint glow in the sky to southward. He set out along the highway toward it.

It was not less than four miles away, and then there was a small town, and it seemed lifeless. Street lights burned, but there were no lighted windows anywhere. There was no motion.

He moved cautiously among its streets. Here and

there he saw a sign, *"Quarantine."* He nodded. Things had gotten really bad! Normal sanitary measures would prevent the spread of contagion of a normal kind. When infections led to the quarantine of every house where plague appeared, it meant that doctors were getting panicky and old-fashioned. However, the ideas of the causes of pestilences would remain modern. Nobody would suspect an epidemic of being actually a crime.

He found a merchandise center. He found a food shop. All the night was dark and silent. He listened for a long, long time, and then committed burglary.

With his hand lamp turned down to the faintest of glimmers, he began to accumulate parcels. There was plague in this area and this town. Therefore, he painstakingly picked out parcels of every variety of foodstuff in the food shop's stock. He stuffed his loot into a bag. He carried everything, even salt and sugar and coffee, meat, bread, and vegetables in their transparent coverings. He took a sample—the smallest possible—of everything he could find.

He piously laid an interstellar currency note on the checkout desk. He left. He went back to the highway by which he'd arrived. He trudged four miles to where a pellet designed for something else made a distinctive patch of unpleasant smell. He turned and traveled by compass until he found another evil-smelling spot. Again by compass . . . and he arrived back at the Med Ship. He went in.

Murgatroyd greeted him with inarticulate cries, embracing his legs and protesting vehemently of his sufferings during Calhoun's absence. To keep from stepping on him, Calhoun tripped. The bag of his burglarized acquisitions fell. It broke. Something smashed.

"Stop it!" commanded Calhoun firmly. "I missed you too. But I've got work to do, and I didn't run across any ditch water. I've got to go out again."

He forcibly prevented Murgatroyd from going with him, and he spent an hour fumbling for a swampy spot in the dark forest. In the end he packed up damp and half-rotted woods-mold. He carried that back to the ship. Then he began to collect the grocery packages he'd dropped. A package of coffeebeans had broken.

"Damn!" said Calhoun.

He gathered up the spilled beans. Murgatroyd assisted. Murgatroyd adored coffee. Calhoun found him popping the beans into his mouth and chewing in high delight.

He went about the essential, mundane labor he'd envisioned. He prepared what a physician of much older times would have called a decoction of rotted leaves. He examined it with a microscope. It was admirable! There were paramecia and rotifers and all sorts of agile microscopic creatures floating, swimming, squirming and darting about in the faintly brownish solution.

"Now," said Calhoun, "we will see if we see anything."

He put the fraction of a drop of a standard and extremely mild antiseptic on the microscope slide. The rotifers and the paramecia and the fauna of the ditch water died. Which, of course, was to be expected. Single-celled animals are killed by concentrations of poison which are harmless to greater animals. Antiseptics are poisons and poisons are antiseptics, but antiseptics are poisons only in massive doses. But to a rotifer or to paramecia all doses are massive.

"Therefore," explained Calhoun to a watching and inquisitive Murgatroyd, "I act more like an alchemist than a sane man. I feel apologetic, Murgatroyd. I am embarrassed to make decoctions and to mix them with synthesized ditch water. But what else can I do? I have to identify the cause of the plague here, without having contact with a single patient because Doctor Kelo . . ."

He shrugged and continued his activities. He was making solutions, decoctions, infusions of every kind of foodstuff the food shop he'd burglarized contained. The plague was not caused by an agent itself in infections. It was caused by something which allowed infections to thrive unhindered in human bodies. So Calhoun made soups of meat, all the kinds of meat, of grain and grain products, and vegetables taken from their transparent coverings. Even such items as sugar, salt, pepper and coffee were included.

Those solutions went upon microscope slides, one by one. With each, in turn, Calhoun mingled the decoction of rotting vegetation which was, apparently, as well-suited for his research as stagnant water from a scummy pond. The animalcules of the decoction appreciated their diverse food supplies. They fed. They throve. Given time, they would have multiplied prodigiously.

Eventually Calhoun came to the solution of coffee. He mixed it with his experimental microscopic-animal zoo, and the paramecia died. Rotifers ceased to whirl and dart about upon their sub-miniature affairs. When an infusion of coffee from the food shop was added to the liquid environment of one-celled animals, they died.

Calhoun checked. It was so. He made an infusion of coffee from the Med Ship's stores. It was not so. Coffee from the ship was not fatal to paramecia. Coffee from the shop was. But it would not follow that coffee from the shop would be fatal to humans. The alcoholic content of beer is fatal to paramecia. Wine is a fair antiseptic. No! The food store coffee could very well be far less toxic than the wildest of mouthwashes, and still kill the contents of Calhoun's ditch-water zoo.

However, the point was that something existed which allowed infections to thrive unhindered in human bodies. Something destroyed the body's defenses against infections. Nothing more would be needed to make the appearance of a plague. Every human being carries with him the seeds of infection, from oral bacteria to intestinal flora, and even often streptococci in the hair follicles of the skin. Destroy the body's means of defense and anyone was bound to develop one of the diseases whose sample bacteria he carries about with him.

Instantly one ceased to think of the plague on Kryder II—and Castor IV before it—instantly one ceased to think of the epidemic as an infection miraculously spreading without any germ or bacterium or virus to carry it, instantly one thought of it as a toxin only, a poison only, a compound as monstrously fatal as the toxin of—say—the bacillus *clostridium botulinum*. Immediately everything fell into place. The toxin that could simulate a plague could be distributed on a food-stuff: grain or meat or neatly packaged coffee. It would be distributed in such dilution that it was harmless. It would not be detected by any culture-medium process. In such concentration as humans would receive, it would have one effect, and one effect only. It would hinder the body's formation of antibodies. It would prevent the production of those compounds which destroy infective agents to which human beings are exposed. It would simply make certain that no infection would be fought. Antibodies introduced from outside could cure a disease the body could not resist, but there would always be other diseases. . . . Yet, in a concentration greater than body fluids could contain, it killed the creatures that thrived in ditch water.

Calhoun consulted the slip of paper the computer had printed out for him. He went down to the ship's stores. A Med Ship carries an odd assortment of supplies. Here were the basic compounds from which an unlimited number of other compounds could be synthesized. With the computer-slip for a prescription form, he picked out certain ones. He went back to the ditch-water samples presently. He worked very painstakingly. Presently, he had a whitish powder. He made a dilute—a very dilute solution of it. He added that solution to ditch water. The paramecia and rotifers and other tiny creatures swam about in bland indifference. He put in a trace of coffee decoction. Presently, he was trying to find out how small a quantity of his new solution, added to the coffee infusion, made it harmless to paramecia.

It was not an antidote to the substance the coffee contained. It did not counter the effects of that monstrously toxic substance, but it combined with that substance. It destroyed it; it was the answer to the plague on Kryder II.

It was broad daylight when he'd finished the horribly

tedious detail work the problem had required. In fact, it was close to sundown. He said tiredly to Murgatroyd, "Well, we've got it!"

Murgatroyd did not answer. Calhoun did not notice for a moment or so. Then he jerked his head about.

Murgatroyd lay on the Med Ship floor, his eyes half-closed. His breath came in quick, shallow pantings.

He'd eaten coffeebeans when they fell on the floor of the control-room. Calhoun picked him up, his lips angrily compressed. Murgatroyd neither resisted nor noticed. Calhoun examined him with a raging, painstaking care.

Murgatroyd was ill. He came of a tribe which was never sick of any infectious disease; they reacted with explosive promptness to any trace of contagion and produced antibodies which would destroy any invading pathogen. His digestive system was normally no less efficient, rejecting any substance which was unwholesome. But the toxic compound which caused the plague on Kryder II was not unwholesome in any direct sense. It did not kill anybody, by itself. It simply inhibited, it prevented, the formation of those antibodies which are a creature's defense against disease.

Murgatroyd had a fully developed case of pneumonia. It had developed faster in him than in a human being. It was horribly more severe. He'd developed it from some single *diplococcus pneumonia* upon his fur, or perhaps on Calhoun's garments, or possibly from the floor or wall of the Med Ship. Such microorganisms are everywhere. Humans and animals are normally immune to any but massive infection. But Murgatroyd was at the very point of death from a disease his tribe normally could not—could not!—contract.

Calhoun made the tests required to make him absolutely certain. Then he took his new solution and prepared to make use of it.

"Fortunately, Murgatroyd," he said grimly, "we've something to try for this situation. Hold still!"

VI

MURGATROYD SIPPED A cup of coffee with infinite relish. He finished it. He licked the last drop. He offered it to Calhoun and said inquiringly, *"Chee?"*

"It probably won't hurt you to have one more cup," said Calhoun. He added irrelevantly, "I'm very glad you're well, Murgatroyd!"

Murgatroyd said complacently, *"Chee-chee!"*

Then the space communicator said metallically, *"Calling Med Ship! Calling Med Ship! Calling Med Ship Aesclipus Twenty! Ground calling Aesclipus Twenty!"*

The Med Ship was then in orbit around Kryder II. It was a sound, high orbit, comfortably beyond atmosphere. Calhoun was officially waiting for word of how his communication and instruction to the authorities aground had turned out. He said, "Well?"

"I'm the Planetary Health Minister," said a voice. Somehow it sounded infinitely relieved. *"I've just had reports from six of our hospitals. They check with what you told us. The paramecia test works. There were a number of different foods—ah—contaminated at their packaging points, so that even if someone had identified one food as the cause of the plague in one place, in another area it wouldn't be true. It was clever! It was damnably clever! And of course we've synthesized your reagent and tried it on laboratory animals we were able—by your instructions—to give the plague."*

"I hope," said Calhoun politely, "that the results were satisfactory."

The other man's voice broke suddenly.

"One of my children . . . he will probably recover, now. He's weak. He's terribly weak! But he'll almost certainly live, now that we can protect him from reinfection. We've started planet-wide use of your reagent."

"Correction," said Calhoun. "It's not my reagent. It is a perfectly well-known chemical compound. It's not often used, and perhaps this is its first use medically, but it's been known for half a century. You'll find it mentioned . . ."

The voice at the other end of the communication link said fiercely, *"You will excuse me if I say nonsense! I wanted to report that everything you've told us has proved true. We have very many desperately ill, but new patients have already responded to medication to counter the—contamination of food they'd taken. They've gotten thoroughly well of normal disease and haven't developed others. Our doctors are elated. They are convinced. You can't have any idea how relieved . . ."*

Calhoun glanced at Murgatroyd and said dryly, "I've reason to be pleased myself. How about Doctor Kelo and his friends?"

"We'll get him! He can't get off the planet, and we'll find him! There's only one ship aground at the spaceport; it came in two days ago. It's stayed in port under self-quarantine at our request. We've instructed it not to take anyone aboard. We're chartering it to go to other planets and buy foodstuffs to replace the ones we're testing and destroying."

Calhoun, stroking Murgatroyd, said more dryly than before, "I wouldn't. You'd have to send currency to pay for the stuff you want to import. On two previous occasions very, very large sums gathered for that purpose have disappeared. I'm no policeman but that *could* be the reason for the plague. There are some people who might start a plague for the express purpose of being entrusted with some scores of millions of credits. . . ."

There was silence at the other end of the conversation. Then a man's voice, raging, *"If that's it!"*

Calhoun broke in.

"In my orbit I'll be below your horizon in minutes. I'll call back. My orbit's very close to two hours duration."

"If that's it," repeated the voice, raging, *"We'll . . ."*

There was silence. Calhoun said very cheerfully, "Murgatroyd, I'm good at guessing the way a relatively honest man's mind works. If I'd told them earlier that the plague victims were murdered, they'd have discounted the rest of what I had to say. But I'm learning the way a criminal's mind works too! It takes a criminal to think of burning down a house to cover up the fact that he robbed it. It takes a criminal to think of killing a man for what he may carry in his pockets. It would take a criminal to start a plague so he can gather money to steal, under the pretense that he's going to use it to buy unpoisoned food to replace the food he's poisoned. I had trouble understanding that!"

Murgatroyd said, *"Chee!"*

He got up. He walked in a rather wobbly fashion as if testing his strength. He came back and nestled against Calhoun. Calhoun petted him. Murgatroyd yawned. He'd been weakened by his illness. He still didn't understand it. *Tormals* are not accustomed to being ill.

"Now," said Calhoun reflectively, "I make a guess at how certain criminal minds will work if they eavesdropped just then. We've spoiled their crime on Kryder II. They'd put a lot of time and trouble into committing it. Now they've had their trouble and committed their murders for nothing. I think, I *think* they'll be angry. With me."

He settled Murgatroyd comfortably. He went about the ship stowing things away. The samples of ditch water and of foodstuffs he placed so no shock or sudden acceleration could spill them. He made sure there were no loose objects about the control-room. He went down below and made especially sure that the extra plastic-sealed control-central unit was properly stowed, and that the spacesuit worn by one of the two men to board the Med Ship at breakout was suitably held fast. They'd be turned over to the laboratories at headquarters. If carefully disassembled the control-central unit would give positive proof that a certain man in the headquarters technical staff had installed it. Suitable measures would be taken. The spacesuit would identify the man now at the bottom of a rocky crevasse on an icy, uninhabited world.

By the time Calhoun's preparations were finished, the ship had nearly completed its orbital round. Calhoun put Murgatroyd in his cubbyhole. He fastened the door so the little animal couldn't be thrown out. He went to the pilot's chair and strapped in.

Presently he called, *"Med Ship* Aesclipus Twenty *calling ground! Med Ship calling ground!"*

An enraged voice answered immediately.

"Ground to Med Ship! You were right! The ship in the spaceport lifted off on emergency rockets before we could stop it! It must have listened in when you talked to us before! It got below the horizon before we could lock on!"

"Ah!" said Calhoun comfortably. "And did Doctor Kelo get aboard?"

"He did!" raged the voice. *"He did! It's inexcusable! It's unbelievable! He did get aboard and we moved to seize the ship and its rockets flamed and it got away!"*

"Ah!" said Calhoun, again comfortably. "Then give me coordinates for landing."

He had them repeated. Of course, if someone were eavesdropping . . . but he shifted the Med Ship's orbit to bring him to rendezvous at a certain spot at a certain time, a certain very considerable distance out from the planet.

"Now," he said to Murgatroyd, "we'll see if I understand the psychology of the criminal classes, in fact . . ."

Then he remembered that Murgatroyd was locked in his cubbyhole. He shrugged. He sat very alertly in the pilot's chair while the planet Kryder II revolved beneath him.

There was silence except for those minute noises a

ship has to make to keep from seeming like the inside of a tomb. Murmurings. Musical notes. The sound of traffic. All very faint but infinitely companionable.

The needle of the nearest-object dial stirred from where it had indicated the distance to the planet's surface. Something else was nearer. It continued to approach. Calhoun found it and swung the Med Ship to face it, but he waited. Presently, he saw an infinitesimal sliver of reflected sunlight against the background of distant stars. He mentally balanced this fact against that, this possibility against that.

He flicked on the electron telescope. Yes. There were minute objects following the other ship. More of them appeared, and still more. They were left behind by the other ship's acceleration, but they spread out like a cone of tiny, deadly, murderous missiles. They were. If any one crashed into the Med Ship it could go clear through from end to end.

This was obviously the ship that had placed a man aboard the Med Ship to impersonate Calhoun aground. It was the ship whose company was ultimately responsible for the plague on Kryder II, and before that on Castor IV, and for another before that. It had been aground to receive, at a suitable moment, very many millions of credits in currency to pay for unpoisoned foodstuffs for Kryder II. Through Calhoun, it had had all its trouble for nothing. It came to destroy the Med Ship as merited if inadequate punishment.

However, Calhoun found himself beautifully confident in his own competence. He was headed, of course, for a ship that meant to destroy him. It tossed out missiles to accomplish that purpose. Dropping behind as they did, the effect was of the other ship towing a cone-shaped net of destruction.

So Calhoun jammed down his rocket-controls to maximum acceleration and plunged toward it. It was a ship guided by criminals, with criminal psychology. They couldn't understand and at first couldn't believe that Calhoun—who should be their victim—would think of anything but attempts to escape. But presently it was borne upon them that he seemed to intend to ram them in mid-space.

The other ship swerved. Calhoun changed course to match. The other ship wavered. Its pilot couldn't understand. He'd lost the initiative. The Med Ship plunged for the very nose of the other vessel. They moved toward each other with vastly more than the speed of rifle bullets. At the last instant the other ship tried crazily to sheer off. At that precise moment Calhoun swung the Med Ship into a quarter-turn. He cut his rockets and the *Aesclipus Twenty* plunged ahead, moving sidewise, and then Calhoun cut in his rockets again. Their white-hot flames, glittering through a quarter-mile of space, splashed upon the other ship. They penetrated. They sliced the other ship into two ragged and uneven halves, and those two halves wallowed onward.

The communicator chattered, *"Calling Med Ship! Calling Med Ship! What's happened?"*

At that time Calhoun was too busy to reply. The Med Ship was gaining momentum away from the line of the other ship's course, around which very many hurtling objects also moved. They would sweep through the space in which the other ship had died. Calhoun had to get away from them.

He did. Minutes later he answered the still-chattering call from the ground.

"There was a ship," he said evenly, "some ship which tried to smash me out here. But something seems to have happened to it. It's in two parts now, and it will probably crash in two pieces somewhere aground. I don't think there will be any survivors. I think Doctor Kelo was aboard."

The voice aground conferred agitatedly with others. Then it urgently requested Calhoun to land and receive the gratitude of people already recovering from the virulent pestilence. Calhoun said politely, "My *tormal* has been ill. It's unprecedented. I need to take him back to headquarters. I think I'm through here, anyhow."

He aimed the Med Ship, while voices made urgent official noises from the planet. He aimed very carefully for the sun around which the planet which was the Med Service Headquarters revolved. Presently he pushed a button, and the Med Ship did something equivalent to making a hole, crawling into it, and pulling the hole in after itself. In fact, it went into overdrive. It sped on toward headquarters at many times the speed of light, nestled in that cocoon of stressed space which was like a private sub-cosmos of its own.

Calhoun said severely, when matters settled down, "Three weeks of peace and quiet in overdrive, Murgatroyd, will be much better for you than landing on Kryder II and being fed to bursting with sweet cakes and coffee! I tell you so as your physician!"

"Chee," said Murgatroyd dolefully. *"Chee-chee-chee!"*

The Med Ship drove on.

RIBBON
IN THE SKY

I

"An error is a denial of reality, but mistakes are mere mental malfunctionings. In an emergency, a mistake may be made because of the need for precipitate action. There is no time to choose the best course; something must be done at once. Most mistakes, however, are made without any such exterior pressure. One accepts the first-imagined solution without examining it, either out of an urgent desire to avoid the labor of thinking, or out of impassioned reluctance to think about the matter at hand when prettier or more pleasurable other things can be contemplated. . . ."

The Practice of Thinking—Fitzgerald

IT TURNED OUT that somebody had punched the wrong button in a computer. It was in a matter in which mistakes are not permissable, but just as nothing can be manufactured without an ordinary hammer figuring somewhere in the making or the making-ready-to-make, so nothing can be done without a fallible human operator at some stage of the proceedings. And humans make mistakes casually, offhandedly, with impartial lack of either malice or predictability, so . . .

Calhoun heard the tape-speaker say, *"When the gong sounds, breakout will follow in five seconds."* Then it made solemn ticking noises while Calhoun yawned and put aside the book, *The Practice of Thinking*. He'd been studying. Study was a necessity in his profession.

Besides, it helped to pass the time in overdrive. He went to the control-desk and strapped in. Murgatroyd the *tormal* uncoiled his tail from about his nose and stood up from where he was catching twenty winks. He padded to the place under Calhoun's chair where there were things to grab hold of, if necessary, with one's four black paws and prehensile tail.

"*Chee,*" said Murgatroyd conversationally, in his shrill treble.

"I agree," Calhoun told him gravely. "Stone walls do not a prison make, nor Med Ship hulls a cage. But it will be good to get outside for a change."

The tape-speaker ticked and tocked and ticked and tocked. There was the sound of a gong. A voice said measuredly, "*Five—four—three—two—one.*"

The ship came out of overdrive. Calhoun winced and swallowed. Nobody ever gets used to going into overdrive or coming out of it. One is hideously dizzy for an instant, and his stomach has a brief but violent urge to upchuck, and no matter how often one has experienced it, it is necessary to fight a flash of irrational panic caused by the two sensations together.

After an instant Calhoun stared about him as the vision screens came to life. They showed the cosmos outside the Med Ship. It was a perfectly normal cosmos—not at all the cosmos of overdrive—but it looked extremely wrong to Calhoun. He and Murgatroyd and the Med Ship were in emptiness. There were stars on every hand, and they were of every conceivable color and degree of brightness. But every one of them was a point of light, and a point only.

This, obviously, was not what he'd expected. These days ships do not stop to view the universe from the monstrous loneliness which is between-the-stars. All ships go into overdrive as near their port of departure as they can. Usually, it is something like five or six planetary diameters out from the local spaceport. All ships come out of overdrive as near their destinations as computation makes possible. They do not stop to look at scenery on the way. It isn't good for humans to look

at stars when there are only stars to see. The sight
has a tendency to make them feel small—too small. Men
have been known to come out of such an experience
gibbering.

Calhoun scowled at the sight of between-the-stars.
This was not good. But he wasn't frightened—not yet.
There should have been a flaming sun somewhere nearby, and there should have been bright crescents or half-
disks or mottled cloudy planets swimming within view.
The sun should have been the star Merida, and Calhoun
should land in commonplace fashion on Merida II and
make a routine planetary health check on a settled, com-
placent population, and presently he should head back
to Med Headquarters with a report containing absolutely nothing of importance. However, he couldn't
do any of these things. He was in purely empty space. It
was appalling.

Murgatroyd jumped up to the arm of the control-
chair, to gaze wisely at the screens. Calhoun continued
to scowl. Murgatroyd imitated him with a *tormal's* fine
satisfaction in duplicating a man's actions. What he saw
meant nothing to him, of course. But he was moved to
comment.

"Chee," he said shrilly.

"To be sure," agreed Calhoun distastefully. "That is
a very sage observation, Murgatroyd. Though I deplore
the situation that calls for it. Somebody's bilged on us."

Murgatroyd liked to think that he was carrying on a
conversation. He said zestfully, *"Chee-chee! Chee-
chee-chee!"*

"No doubt," conceded Calhoun. "But this is a mess!
Hop down and let me try to get out of it."

Murgatroyd disappointedly hopped to the floor. He
watched with bright eyes as Calhoun annoyedly went to
the emergency equipment locker and brought out the
apparatus designed to take care of problems like this.
If the situation wasn't too bad, correcting it should be
simple enough. If it was too bad, it could be fatal.

The average separation of stars throughout the
galaxy, of course, is something like four or five light-

years. The distance between Sol-type stars is on an average very much higher, and with certain specific exceptions habitable planets are satellites of Sol-type suns. But only a fraction of the habitable planets are colonized, and when a ship has traveled blind, in overdrive, for two months or more, its pilot cannot simply look astern and recognize his point of departure. There's too much scenery in between. Further, nobody can locate himself by the use of star-maps unless he knows where something on the star-map is with reference to himself. This makes a star-map not always useful.

The present blunder might not be serious. If the Med Ship had come out into normal space no more than eight to ten light-years from Merida, Calhoun might identify that sun by producing parallax. He could detect relative distances for a much greater range. However, it was to be hoped that his present blunder was small.

He got out the camera with its six lenses for the six vision screens which showed space in all directions. He clamped it in place and painstakingly snapped a plate. In seconds he had everything above third magnitude faithfully recorded in its own color, and with relative brightnesses expressed in the size of the dots of tint. He put the plate aside and said, "Overdrive coming, Murgatroyd."

He pressed the short-hop button and there was dizziness and nausea and a flash of fear—all three sensations momentary. Murgatroyd said, *"Chee,"* in a protesting tone, but Calhoun held down the button for an accurate five minutes. He and Murgatroyd gulped together when he let up the button again and all space whirled and nausea hit as before. He took another plate of all the heavens, made into one by the six-lensed camera. He swung the ship by ninety degrees and pressed the short-hop button a second time; more dizziness, panic and digestive revolt followed. In five minutes it was repeated as the ship came out to normal space yet again.

"Chee-chee!" protested Murgatroyd. His furry paws held his round little belly against further insult.

"I agree," said Calhoun. He exposed a third film. "I don't like it either. But I want to know where we are, if anywhere."

He set up the comparator and inserted the three plates. Each had images of each of the six vision screens. When the instrument whirled, each of the plates in turn was visible for part of a second. Extremely remote stars would not jiggle perceptibly—would not show parallax—but anything within twenty light-years should. The jiggling distance could be increased by taking the plates still farther apart. This time, though, there was one star which visibly wavered in the comparator. Calhoun regarded it suspiciously.

"We're Heaven knows where," he said dourly. "Somebody really messed us up! The only star that shows parallax isn't Merida. In fact, I don't believe in it at all. Two plates show it as a Sol-class sun and the third says it's a red dwarf!"

On the face of it, such a thing was impossible. A sun cannot be one color as seen from one spot, and another color seen from another. Especially when the shift of angle is small.

Calhoun made rough computations. He hand-set the overdrive for something over an hour's run in the direction of the one star-image which wabbled and thereby beckoned. He threw the switch. He gulped, and Murgatroyd acted for a moment as if he intended to yield unreservedly to the nausea of entering overdrive, but he refrained.

There was nothing to do but kill time for an hour. There was a microreel of starplates, showing the heavens as photographed with the same galactic coordinates from every visited Sol-class star in this sector of the galaxy. Fewer than one in forty had a colonized planet, but if the nearest had been visited before, and if the heavens had been photographed there, by matching the stars to the appropriate plate he could find out where he was. Then a star-map might begin to be of some use to him. But he had still to determine whether the error was in his astrogation unit, or in the data fed to it. If the first he'd be very bad off indeed. If the second he could still be in a fix. But there was no point in worrying while in overdrive. He lay down on his bunk and tried to concentrate again on the book he'd laid aside.

"Human error, moreover," he read, *"is never purely random. The mind tends to regard stored data as infallible and to disregard new data which contradicts it. . . ."* He yawned, and skipped. *". . . So each person has a personal factor of error which is not only quantitative but qualitative. . . ."*

He read on and on, only half absorbing what he read. A man who has reached the status of a Med Ship man in the Interstellar Medical Service hasn't finished learning. He's still a way down the ladder of rank. He has plenty of studying before him before he gets very far.

The tape-speaker said, *"When the gong sounds, breakout will be five seconds off."* It began to tick-tock, slowly and deliberately. Calhoun got into the control-seat and strapped in. Murgatroyd said peevishly, *"Chee!"* and went to position underneath the chair. The voice said, *"Five—four—three—two—one."*

The little Med Ship came out of overdrive, and instantly its emergency rockets kicked violently and Murgatroyd held desperately fast. Then the rockets went off. There'd been something unguessable nearby, perhaps cometary debris at the extremist outer limit of a highly eccentric orbit. Now there was a star-field and a sun within two light-hours. If Calhoun had stared, earlier, when there was no sun in sight at all, now he gazed blankly at the spectacle before him.

There was a sun off to starboard. It was a yellow sun, a Sol-type star with a barely perceptible disk. There were planets. Calhoun saw immediately one gas-giant near enough to be more than a point, and a sliver of light which was the crescent of another more nearly in line toward the sun. But he gazed at a belt, a band, a ribbon of shining stuff which was starkly out of all reason.

It was a thin curtain of luminosity circling this yellow star. It was not a ring from the break-up of a satellite within Roche's Limit. There were two quite solid planets inside it and nearer to the sun. It was a thin, wide, luminous golden ribbon which looked like something that needed a flat iron to smooth it out. It looked somewhat like an incandescent smoke ring. It was not smooth. It had lumps in it. There were corrugations in it. An unimaginable rocket with a flat exhaust could have made it while chasing its tail around the sun. But that couldn't have happened, either.

Calhoun stared for seconds.

"Now," he said, "now I've seen everything!" Then he grunted as realization came. "Mmmmh! We're all right, Murgatroyd! It's not our computers that went wrong. Somebody fed them wrong data. We arrived where we aimed for, and there'll be a colonized planet somewhere around."

He unlimbered the electron telescope and began a search; he couldn't resist a closer look at the ribbon in space. It had exactly the structure of a slightly wobbly wrinkled belt without beginning or end. It had to be a complex of solid particles, of course, and an organization of solid particles cannot exist in space without orbital motion. However, orbits would smooth out in the course of thousands of revolutions around a primary. This was not smoothed out. It was relatively new.

"It's sodium dust," said Calhoun appreciatively. "Or maybe potassium. Hung out there on purpose. Particles small enough to have terrific surface and reflective power, and big enough not to be pushed out of orbit by light-pressure. Clever, Murgatroyd! At a guess it'll have been put out to take care of the climate on a planet just inside it. Which would be—there! Let's go look!"

He was so absorbed in his admiration that the almost momentary overdrive-hop needed for approach went nearly unnoticed. He even realized—his appreciation increasing—that this cloud of tiny particles accounted for the red dwarf appearance on one of the plates he'd taken. Light passing through widely dispersed, very small particles turns red. From one position, he'd photographed moving through this dust cloud.

The ribbon was a magnificent idea, the more magnificent because of its simplicity. It would reflect back otherwise wasted sun-heat to a too-cold planet and make it warmer. There was probably only an infinitesimal actual mass of powder in the ring, at that. Tens of scores of tons in all, hardly more.

The planet for which it had been established was the third world out. As is usual with Sol-class systems, the third planet's distance from the sun was about a hundred twenty million miles. It had ice caps covering more than two-thirds of its surface. The sprawling white fingers of glaciation marked mountain chains and highlands nearly to the equator. There was some blue sea, and there was green vegetation in a narrow belt of tropicality.

Calhoun jockeyed the Med Ship to position for a landing call. This was not Merida II; there should be a colony here! That glowing ribbon had not been hung out for nothing.

"Med Ship *Aesclipus Twenty*," he said confidently into the space-phone mike. "Calling ground. Requesting coordinates for landing. My mass is fifty tons. Repeat, five-oh tons. Purpose of landing, to find out where I am and how to get where I belong."

There was a clicking. Calhoun repeated the call. He heard murmurings which were not directed into the transmitter on the planet. They were speaking in the transmitter room aground. He heard an agitated: *"How long since a ship landed?"* Another voice was saying fiercely, *"Even if he doesn't come from Two City or Three City, who knows what sickness . . ."* There was sudden silence, as if a hand had been clapped over the microphone below. Then a long pause. Calhoun made the standard call for the third time.

"Med Ship Aesclipus Twenty," said the space-phone speaker grudgingly, *"you will be allowed to land. Take position."* Calhoun blinked at the instructions he received. The coordinates were not the normal galactic ones. They gave the local time at the spaceport, and the

planetary latitude. He was to place himself overhead. He could do it, of course, but the instructions were unthinkable. Galactic coordinates had been used ever since Calhoun knew anything about such matters. But he acknowledged the instructions. Then the voice from the speaker said truculently: *"Don't hurry! We might change our minds! And we have to figure settings for an only fifty-ton ship, anyhow."*

Calhoun's mouth dropped open. A Med Ship was welcome everywhere, these days. The Interstellar Medical Service was one of those over-worked, understaffed, kicked-around organizations that are everywhere taken for granted. Like breathable air, nobody thought to be grateful for it, but nobody was suspicious of it, either.

The suspicion and the weird coordinates and the ribbon in space combined to give Calhoun a highly improbable suspicion. He looked forward with great interest to this landing. He had not been ordered to land here, but he suspected that a Med Ship landing was a long, long time overdue.

"I forgot to take star-pictures," he told Murgatroyd, "but a ribbon like this would have been talked about if it had been reported before. I doubt star-pictures would do us any good. The odds are that our only chance to find out where we are is to ask." Then he shrugged his shoulders. "Anyhow this won't be routine!"

"Chee!" agreed Murgatroyd profoundly.

II

> "An unsolvable but urgent problem may produce in a society, as in an individual, an uncontrollable emotional tantrum, an emotional denial of the problem's existence, or purposeful research for a solution. In olden days, the first reaction produced mass-tantrums then called "wars." The second produced dogmatic ideologies. The third produced modern civilization. All three reactions still appear in individuals. If the first two should return to societies, as such . . ."
>
> *The Practice of Thinking*—Fitzgerald

THE DESCENT, AT least, was not routine. It was nerve-racking. The force field from the planet's giant steel landing grid reached out into space and fumbled for the Med Ship. That was clumsily done. When it found the ship, it locked on, awkwardly. The rest was worse. Whoever handled the controls, aground, was hopelessly inept. Once the Med Ship's hull-temperature began to climb, and Calhoun had to throw on the space-phone and yelp for caution. He did not see as much of the nearing planet as he'd have liked.

At fifty miles of height, the last trace of blue sea vanished around the bulge of the world. At twenty miles, the mountain chains were clearly visible, with their tortured, winding ice rivers which were glaciers. At this height three patches of green were visible from aloft. One, directly below, was little more than a mile in diameter and the landing grid was its center and almost its circumference. Another was streaky and long, and there seemed to be heavy mist boiling about it and above it. The third was roughly triangular. They were many miles apart. Two of them vanished behind mountains as the ship descended.

There were no cities in view. There were no highways. This was an ice world with bare ground and open water at its equator only. The spaceport was placed in a snow ringed polar valley.

Near landing, Calhoun strapped in because of the awkwardness with which the ship was lowered. He took Murgatroyd on his lap. The small craft bounced and wabbled as unskilled hands let it down. Presently, Calhoun saw the angular girders of the landing grid's latticed top rise past the opened ports. Seconds later, the Med Ship bumped and slid and bounced heart-stoppingly. Then it struck ground with a violent jolt.

Calhoun got his breath back as the ship creaked and adjusted itself to rest on its landing-fins, after some months in space.

"Now," said the voice in the space-phone speaker—but it sounded as if it were trying to conceal relief—*"now stay in your ship. Our weapons are bearing on you. You may not come out until we've decided what to do about you."*

Calhoun raised his eyebrows. This was very unusual indeed. He glanced at the external-field indicator. The landing-grid field was off. So the operator bluffed. In case of need Calhoun could blast off on emergency rockets and probably escape close-range weapons any-how—if there were any—and he could certainly get around the bulge of the world before the amateur at the grid's controls could lock on to him again.

"Take your time," he said with irony. "I'll twiddle my fingers. I've nothing better to do!"

He freed himself from his chair and went to a port to see. He regarded the landscape about him with some-thing like disbelief.

The landing grid itself was a full mile across and half

as high. It was a vast, circular frame of steel beams reaching heavenward, with the curiously curving copper cables strung as they had to be to create the highly special force field which made space transportation practical. Normally, such gigantic structures rose in the centers of spaceport cities. They drew upon the planet's ionosphere for power to lift and land cargo ships from the stars, and between-times they supplied energy for manufactures and the operation of cities. They were built, necessarily, upon stable bed-rock formations, and for convenience were usually located where the cargoes to be shipped would require least surface transportation.

But here, there was no city. There was perhaps a thousand acres of greenness, a mere vague rim around the outside of the grid. There was a control-room building to one side, of course. It was solidly made of stone, but there had been an agglomeration of lean-tos added to it with slanting walls and roofs of thin stratified rock. There were cattle grazing on the green grass. The center of the grid was a pasture!

Save for the clutter about the grid-control building there were no structures, no dwellings, no houses or homes anywhere in view. There was no longer even a highway leading to the grid. Calhoun threw on the outside microphones and there was no sound except a thin keening of wind in the steelwork overhead. But presently one of the cattle made a mournful bellowing sound.

Calhoun whistled as he went from one port to another.

"Murgatroyd," he said meditatively on his second round, "you observe—if you observe—one of the consequences of human error. I still don't know where I am, because I doubt that starplates have ever been made from this solar system, and I didn't take one for comparison anyhow. But I can tell you that this planet formerly had a habitability rating of something like oh point oh, meaning that if somebody wanted to live here it would be possible but it wouldn't be sensible.

Although people did come here, and it was a mistake."

He stared at a human figure, far away. It was a woman, dressed in shapeless, badly draping garments. She moved toward a clump of dark-coated cattle and did something in their midst.

"The mistake looks pretty evident to me," added Calhoun. "I see some possibilities I don't like at all. There is such a thing as an isolation syndrome, Murgatroyd. A syndrome is a complex of pathological symptoms which occur together as a result of some morbid condition. To us humans, isolation is morbid. You help me to endure it, Murgatroyd, but I couldn't get along with only even your society—charming as it is—for but so long. A group of people can get along longer than a single man, but there is a limit for any small-sized group."

"*Chee,*" said Murgatroyd.

"In fact," said Calhoun, frowning, "there's a specific health problem involved, which the Med Service recognizes. There can be partial immunity, but there can be some tricky variations. If we're up against a really typical case we have a job on hand. And how did these people get that dust ring out in space? They surely didn't hang it out themselves!"

He sat down and scowled at his thoughts. Presently, he rose again and once more surveyed the icy landscape. The curious green pasture about the landing grid was highly improbable. He saw glaciers overhanging this valley. They were giant ice rivers which should continue to flow and overwhelm this relatively sheltered spot. They didn't. Why not?

It was more than an hour before the space-phone clattered. When Calhoun threw the switch again a new voice came out of it. This was also a male voice, but it was high-pitched as if from tension.

"*We've been talking about you,*" said the voice. It quivered with agitation which was quite out of reason. "*You say you're Med Service. All right. Suppose you prove it!*" The landed Med Ship should be proof enough for anybody. Calhoun said politely, "I have the regular identifications. If you'll go on vision I'll show you my credentials."

"Our screen's broken," said the voice, suspiciously. *"But we have a sick cow. It was dumped on us night before last. Cure her and we'll accept it as identification."*

Calhoun could hardly believe his ears. This was an emergency situation! The curing of a sick cow was considered more convincing than a Med Ship man's regular credentials! Such a scale of values hinted at more than a mere isolation syndrome. There were thousands of inhabited worlds, now, with splendid cities and technologies which most men accepted with the same bland confidence with which they looked for sunrise. The human race was civilized! Suspicion of a Med Ship was unheard of, but here was a world . . .

"Why—certainly," said Calhoun blankly. "I suppose I may go outside to—ah—visit the patient?"

"We'll drive her up to your ship," said the high, tense voice. *"And you stay close to it!"* Then it said darkly, *"Men from Two City sneaked past our sentries to dump it on us. They want to wipe out our herd! What kind of weapons have you got?"*

"This is a Med Ship!" protested Calhoun. "I've nothing more than I might need in an emergency!"

"We'll want them anyhow," said the voice. *"You said you need to find out where you are. We'll tell you, if you've got enough weapons to make it worthwhile."*

Calhoun drew a deep breath.

"We can argue that later," he said. "I'm just a trifle puzzled. But first things first. Drive your cow."

He held his head in his hands. He remembered to throw off the space-phone and said, "Murgatroyd, say something sensible! I never ran into anybody quite as close to coming apart at the seams as that! Not lately! Say something rational!"

Murgatroyd said, *"Chee?"* in an inquiring tone.

"Thanks," said Calhoun. "Thanks a lot."

He went back to the ports to watch. He saw men come out of the peculiar agglomeration of structures that had been piled around the grid's sturdy control-

building. They were clothed in cloth that was heavy and
very stiff, to judge by the way it shifted with its wearers'
movements. Calhoun wasn't familiar with it. The men
moved stolidly, on foot, across the incredible pasture
which had been a landing space for ships of space at
some time or other.

They reached a spot where a dark animal form rested
on the ground. Calhoun hadn't noticed it particularly.
Cattle, he knew, folded their legs and lay down and
chewed cuds. They existed nearly everywhere that
human colonies had been built. On some worlds there
were other domestic animals descended from those of
Earth. Of course, there were edible plants and some
wholesome animals which had no connection at all with
humanity's remote ancestral home, but from the beginning human beings had been adjusted to symbiosis with
the organic life of Earth. Foodstuffs of non-terrestrial
origin could only supplement Earth food, of course. In
some cases Earth foods were the supplements and local,
non-terrestrial foodstuffs the staples. However, human
beings did not thrive on a wholly un-Earthly diet.

The clump of slowly moving men reached the reclining cow. They pulled up stakes which surrounded
her, and coiled up wire or cordage which had made the
stakes into a fence. They prodded the animal. Presently,
it lurched to its feet and swung its head about foolishly.
They drove it toward the Med Ship.

Fifty yards away they stopped, and the outside
microphones brought the sound of their voices muttering. By then Calhoun had seen their faces. Four of
the six were bearded. The other two were young men.
On most worlds men prided themselves that they needed
to shave, but few of them omitted the practice.

These six moved hastily away, though the two
younger ones turned often to look back. The cow,
deserted, stumbled to a reclining position. It lay down,
staring stupidly about. It rested its head on the ground.

"I go out now, eh?" asked Calhoun mildly.

"*We're watching you!*" grated the space-phone
speaker.

Calhoun glanced at the outside temperature indicator

and added a garment. He put a blaster in his pocket. He went out the exit port.

The air was bitter cold, after two months in a heat-metered ship, but Calhoun did not feel cold. It took him seconds to understand why. It was that the ground was warm! Radiant heat kept him comfortable, though the air was icy. Heat elements underground must draw power from somewhere—the grid's tapping of the ionosphere and heating this pasture from underneath enables forage plants to grow here. They did. The cattle fed on them. There would be hydroponic gardens somewhere else, probably underground. They would supply vegetable food in greater quantity. In the nature of things human beings had to have animal food in a cold climate.

Calhoun went across the pasture with the frowning snowy mountains all about. He regarded the reclining beast with an almost humorous attention. He did not know anything about the special diseases of domestic animals. He had only the knowledge required of a Med Ship man, but that should be adequate. The tense voice had said that this beast had been "dumped," to "wipe out" the local herd. So there "was" infection and there would be some infective agent.

He painstakingly took samples of blood and saliva. In a ruminant, certainly, any digestive-tract infection should show up in the saliva. He reflected that he did not know the normal bovine temperature, so he couldn't check it, nor the respiration. The Interstellar Medical Service was not often called on to treat ailing cows.

Back in the ship he diluted his samples and put traces in the usual nutrient solutions. He sealed up droplets in those tiny slides which let a culture be examined as it grows. His microscope, of course, allowed for inspection under light of any wave-length desired, and so yielded information by the frequency of the light which gave clearest images of different features of the micro-organisms.

After five minutes of inspection he grunted and

hauled out his antibiotic stores. He added infinitesimal traces of cillin to the culture media. In the microscope, he watched the active microscopic creatures die. He checked with the other samples.

He went out to the listless, enfeebled animal. He made a wry guess at its body-weight. He used the injector. He went back to the Med Ship. He called on the space-phone.

"I think," he said politely, "that your beast will be all right in thirty hours or so. Now, how about telling me the name of this sun?"

The voice said sharply, *"There's a matter of weapons, too! Wait till we see how the cow does! Sunset will come in an hour. When day comes again, if the cow is better—we'll see!"*

There was a click. The space-phone cut off.

Calhoun pulled out the log-mike. There was already an audio record of all ship operations and communications. Now he added comments: a description of the ribbon in the sky, the appearance of the planet, and such conclusions as he'd come to. He ended: "The samples from the cow were full of a single coccus, which seemed to have no resistance to standard antibiotics. I pumped the beast full of cillin and called it a day. I'm concerned, though, because of the clear signs of an isolation syndrome here. They're idiotically suspicious of me and won't even promise a bargain, as if I could somehow overreach them because I'm a stranger. They've sentries out—they said somebody sneaked past them—against what I imagine must be Two City and Three City. I've an impression that the sentries are to enforce a quarantine rather than to put up a fight. It is probable that the other communities practice the same tactics, plus biological cold war if somebody did bring a sick cow here to infect and destroy the local herd. These people may have a landing grid, but they've an isolation syndrome and I'm afraid there's a classic Crusoe health problem in being. If that's so, it's going to be nasty!"

He cut off the log. The classic Crusoe problem would be extremely awkward if he'd run into it. There was a

legend about an individual back on old Earth who'd
been left isolated on an island by shipwreck for half a
lifetime. His name was given to the public-health diffi-
culties which occurred when accidental isolations occurred during the chaotic first centuries of galactic
migration. There was one shipwreck to which the name
was first applied. The ship was missing, and the de-
scendants of the crew and passengers were not contacted
until three generations had passed. Larger-scale and
worse cases occurred later, when colonies were established by entrepreneurs who grew rich in the establish-
ment of the new settlements, and had no interest in
maintaining them. Such events could hardly happen
now, of course, but even a Crusoe condition was still
possible in theory. It might exist here. Calhoun hoped
not.

It did not occur to him that the affair was not his
business because he hadn't been assigned to it. He
belonged to the Med Service, and the physical well being
of humans everywhere was the concern of that service.
If people lived by choice in an inhospitable environment, that was not a Med man's problem, but anything
which led to preventable deaths was. In a Crusoe colony
there were plenty of preventable deaths!

He cooked a meal to have something to occupy his
mind. Murgatroyd sat on his haunches and sniffed blissfully. Presently, Calhoun ate, and again presently darkness fell on this part of the world. There were new
noises, small ones. He went to look. The pasture inside
the landing grid was faintly lighted by the glowing ribbon in the sky. It looked like a many-times-brighter
Milky Way. The girders of the landing grid looked very
black against it.

He saw a dark figure plodding away until he vanished. Then he reappeared as a deeper black against the
snow beyond the pasture. He went on and on until he
disappeared again. A long time later another figure appeared where he'd gone out of sight. It plodded back
toward the grid. It was a different individual. Calhoun
had watched a changing of sentries. Suspicion, hostility,

the least attractive qualities of the human race, were brought out by isolation.

There could not be a large population here, since such suspicions existed. It was divided into—most likely—three, again, isolated communities. This one had the landing grid, which meant power, and a space-phone but no vision screen attached to it. The fact that there were hostile separate communities made the situation much more difficult, from a medical point of view. It multiplied the possible ghastly features which could exist.

Murgatroyd ate until his furry belly was round as a ball, and settled to stuffed slumber with his tail curled around his nose. Calhoun tried to read. But he was restless. His own time-cycle on the ship did not in the least agree with the time of daylight here on this planet. He was wakeful when there was utter quiet outside. Once one of the cattle made a dismal noise. Twice or three times he heard crackling sounds, like sharp detonations, from the mountains; they would be stirrings in the glaciers.

He tried to study, but painstaking analysis of the methods by which human brains defeated their own ends and came up with wrong answers was not appealing. He grew horribly restless.

It had been dark for hours when he heard rustling noises on the ground outside, through the microphones, of course. He turned up the amplification and made sure that it was a small party of men moving toward the Med Ship. From time to time they paused, as if in caution.

"Murgatroyd," he said dryly, "we're going to have visitors. They didn't give notice by space-phone, so they're unauthorized."

Murgatroyd blinked awake. He watched as Calhoun made sure of the blaster in his pocket and turned on the log-mike. He said, "All set, Murgatroyd?"

Murgatroyd said *"Chee"* in his small shrill voice just as a soft and urgent knock sounded on the exit-lock door. It was made with bare knuckles. Calhoun gri-

maced and went into the lock. He unbolted the door
and began to open it, when it was whipped from his
grasp and plunging figures pushed in. They swept him
back into the Med Ship's cabin. He heard the lock door
close softly. Then he faced five roughly, heavily clothed
men who wore cloaks and mittens and hoods, with cloth
stretched tightly across their faces below the eyes. He
saw knives, but no blasters.

A stocky figure with cold gray eyes appeared to be
spokesman.

"You're the man who got landed today," he said in a
deep voice and with an effect of curtness. "My name's
Hunt. Two City. You a Med Ship man?"

"That's right," said Calhoun. The eyes upon him
were more scared than threatening, all but the stocky
man named Hunt. "I landed to find out where I was,"
he added. "The data-card for my astrogator had been
punched wrong—what . . ."

"You know about sickness, eh?" demanded the
stocky man evenly. "How to cure it and stop it?"

"I'm a Med Ship man," admitted Calhoun. "For
whatever that may mean."

"You're needed in Two City," said the deep-voiced
Hunt. His manner was purest resolution. "We came to
get you. Get y'medicines. Dress warm. Load us down, if
you like, with what you want to take. We got a sledge
waiting."

Calhoun felt a momentary relief. This might make his
job vastly easier. When isolation and fear brings a
freezing of the mind against any novelty—even hope—a
medical man has his troubles. But if one community
welcomed him . . .

"Chee!" said Murgatroyd indignantly from overhead. Calhoun glanced up and Murgatroyd glared from
a paw-hold near the ceiling. He was a peaceable animal.
When there was scuffling he got out of the way. But
now he chattered angrily. The masked men looked at
him fearfully. Their deep-voiced leader growled at
them.

"Just an animal." He swung back to Calhoun. "We

got a need for you," he repeated. "We mean all right, and anything we got you can have if you want it. But you coming with us!"

"Are your good intentions," asked Calhoun, "proved by your wearing masks?"

"They're to keep from catchin' your sickness," said the deep voice impatiently. "Point to what you want us to take!"

Calhoun's feeling of encouragement vanished. He winced a little. The isolation syndrome was fully developed. It was a matter of faith that strangers were dangerous. All men were assumed to carry contagion. Once, they'd have been believed to carry bad luck. However, a regained primitiveness would still retain some trace of the culture from which it had fallen. If there were three settlements as the pasture lands seen from space suggested, they would not believe in magic, but they would believe in contagion. They might have, or once have had, good reason. Anyhow, they would fanatically refrain from contact with any but their own fellow citizens. Yet, there would always be troubles to excite their terrors. In groups of more than a very few there would always be an impulse against the isolation which seemed the only possible safety in a hostile world. The effectiveness of the counter-instinct would depend in part on communications, but the urge to exogamy can produce serious results in a small culture gone fanatic.

"I think," said Calhoun, "that I'd better come with you. But the people here have to know I've gone. I wouldn't like them to heave my ship out to space in pure panic because I didn't answer from inside it!"

"Leave a writing," said Hunt's deep voice, as impatiently as before. "I'll write it. Make them boil, they won't dare follow us!"

"No?"

"Think One City men," asked the stocky man scornfully, "think One City men will risk us toppling avalanches on them?"

Calhoun saw. Amid mountain country in a polar

zone, travel would be difficult at best. These intruders had risked much to come here for him; they were proud of their daring. They did not believe that the folk of lesser cities—tribes—groups other than theirs had courage like theirs. Calhoun recognized it as a part of that complex of symptoms which can begin with an epidemic and end with group-madness.

"I'll want this, and this, and that," said Calhoun. He wouldn't risk his microscope. Antibiotics might be useful. Antiseptics, definitely. His med-kit. . . . "That's all."

"Your blankets," said Hunt. "Y'want them too."

Calhoun shrugged. He clothed himself for the cold outside. He had a blaster in his pocket, but he casually and openly took down a blast-rifle. His captors offered no objection. He shrugged again and replaced it. Starting to take it was only a test. He made a guess that this stocky leader, Hunt, might have kept his community just a little more nearly sane than the group that had set him to the cure of a sick cow. He hoped so.

"Murgatroyd," he said to the *tormal* still clinging up near the control-room's top, "Murgatroyd, we have a professional call to make. You'd better come along. In fact, you must."

Murgatroyd came suspiciously down, and then leaped to Calhoun's shoulder. He clung there, gazing distrustfully about. Calhoun realized that his captors— callers—whatever they were—stayed huddled away from every object in the cabin. They fingered nothing. The scared eyes of most of them proved that it was not honesty which moved them to such meticulousness. It was fear. Of contagion.

"They're uncouth, eh?" said Calhoun sardonically. "But think, Murgatroyd, they may have hearts of gold! We physicians have to pretend to think so, in any case!"

"Chee!" said Murgatroyd resentfully as Calhoun moved toward the lock.

III

"Civilization is based upon rational thought applied to thinking. But there can be a deep and fundamental error about purposes. It is simply a fact that the purposes of human beings are not merely those of rational animals. It is the profoundest of errors to believe otherwise, to consider, for example, that prosperity or pleasure or even survival cannot be priced so high that their purchase is a mistake."

The Practice of Thinking—Fitzgerald

THERE WAS A sheet of paper fastened outside the combination lock of the Med Ship's exit port. It said that Calhoun had been taken away by men of Two City, to tend some sick person. It said that he would be returned. The latter part might not be believed, but the Med Ship might not be destroyed. The colony of the landing grid might try to break into it, but success was unlikely.

Meanwhile, it was an odd feeling to cross the grassy pasture land with hoar-frost crunching underfoot. The grid's steel girders made harsh lace of blackness against the sky, with its shining ribbon slashing across it. Calhoun found himself reflecting that the underground heat applied to the thousand-acre pasture had been regulated with discretion. There was surely power enough available from the grid to turn the area into a place of tropic warmth, in which only lush and thick-leaved vegetation could thrive. However, a storm from the frigid mountains would destroy such plants. Hardy, low-growing, semi-arctic grass was the only suitable ground cover. The iciest of winds could not freeze it so long as the ground was warmed.

Tonight's wind was biting. Calhoun had donned a parka of synthetic fur on which frost would not congeal at any temperature, but he was forced to draw fur before his face and adjust heated goggles before his eyes would stop watering. Yet in the three-quarter-mile trudge to the edge of the snow, his feet became almost uncomfortably warm.

That, though, ended where a sledge waited at the edge of the snow. Five men had forced themselves inside the Med Ship. A sixth was on guard beside the sledge. There had been no alarm. Now the stocky man, Hunt, urged him to a seat upon the sledge.

"I'm reasonably able-bodied," said Calhoun mildly.

"You don't know where we're going, or how," growled Hunt.

Calhoun got on the sledge. The runners were extraordinarily long. He could not see small details, but it appeared that the sledge had been made of extreme length to bridge crevasses in a glacier. There were long thin metal tubes to help. At the same time, it looked as if it could be made flexible to twist and turn in a narrow or obstacle-strewn path.

The six clumsily clad men pushed it a long way, while Calhoun frowned at riding. Then Murgatroyd shivered, and Calhoun thrust him inside the parka. There Murgatroyd wriggled until his nose went up past Calhoun's chin and he could sniff the outside air. From time to time he withdrew his nose—perhaps with frost-crystals on it. But always he poked his small black snout to sniff again. His whiskers tickled.

Two miles from the pastureland, the sledge stopped. One man fumbled somewhere behind Calhoun's seat and a roaring noise began. All six piled upon the long, slender snow-vehicle. It began to move. A man swore. Then, suddenly, the sledge darted forward and went gliding up a steep incline. It gathered speed. Twin arcs of disturbed snow rose up on either side, like bow-waves from a speeding water-skimmer. The sledge darted into a great ravine of purest white and the roaring sound was multiplied by echoes.

For better than half an hour, then, Calhoun experienced a ride which for thrills and beauty and hair-raising suspense made mere space-travel the stodgiest of transportation. Once the sledge shot out from beetling cliffs—all icy and glittering in the light from the sky—and hurtled down a slope of snow so swiftly that the wind literally whistled about the bodies of its occupants. Then the drive roared more loudly, and there was heavy deceleration, and abruptly the sledge barely crawled. The flexibility of the thing came into operation. Four of the crew, each controlling one segment of the vehicle, caused it to twist and writhe over the surface of a glacier, where pressure-ridges abounded and pinnacles of shattered, squeezed-up ice were not uncommon.

Once they stopped short and slender rods reached out and touched, and the sledge slid delicately over them and was itself a bridge across a crevasse in the ice that went down an unguessable distance. Then it went on and the rods were retrieved. Minutes later, the sledge-motor was roaring loudly, but it barely crawled up to what appeared to be a mountain crest—there were ranges of mountains extending beyond sight in the weird blue and golden skylight—and then there was a breathtaking dash and a plunge into what was incredibly a natural tunnel beside the course of an ice river; abruptly, there was a vast valley below.

This was their destination. Some thousands of feet down in the very valley bottom there was a strange, two-mile-long patch of darkness. The blue-gold light showed no color there, but it was actually an artificially warmed pasture land like that within and about the landing grid. From this dark patch vapors ascended, and rolled, and gathered to form a misty roof, which was swept away and torn to tatters by an unseen wind.

The sledge slowed and stopped beside a precipitous

upcrop of stone while still high above the valley bottom.
A voice called sharply.

"It's us," growled Hunt's deep voice. "We got him.
Everything all right?"

". . . No!" rasped the invisible voice. "They broke
out—he broke out and got her loose, and they run off
again. We shoulda killed 'em and had done with it!"

Everything stopped. The man on the sledge seemed to
become still in the shock of pure disaster, pure
frustration. Calhoun waited. Hunt was motionless.
Then one of the men on the sledge spat elaborately.
Then another stirred.

"Had your work for nothing," rasped the voice from
the shadow. "The trouble that's started goes for
nothing, too!"

Calhoun asked crisply, "What's this? My special
patients ran away?"

"That the Med man we heard about?" The invisible
speaker was almost derisive with anger. "Sure! They've
run off, all right . . . man and girl together. After we
made trouble with Three City by not killin' 'em and
with One City by sneakin' over to get you! Three City
men'll come boiling over. . . ." The voice raised
in pitch, expressing scorn and fury. "Because they fell
in love! We shoulda killed 'em right off or let 'em die in
the snow like they wanted in the first place!"

Calhoun nodded almost imperceptibly to himself.
When there is a syndrome forbidding association between societies, it is a part of the society's interior struggle against morbidity that there shall be forbidden
romances. The practice of exogamy is necessary for
racial health, hence there is an instinct for it. The more
sternly a small population restricts its human contacts to
its own members, the more repressed the exogamic impulse becomes. It is never consciously recognized for
what it is. But especially when repressed, other-than-
customary contacts trigger it explosively. The romantic
appeal of a stranger is at once a wise provision of nature
and a cause of incredible furies and disasters. It is
notorious that spaceship crews are inordinately popular

where colonies are small and strangers infrequent. It is no less notorious that a girl may be destitute of suitors on her own world, but has nearly her choice of husbands if she merely saves the ship-fare to another.

Calhoun could have predicted defiances of tradition and law and quarantine alike, as soon as he began to learn the state of things here. The frenzied rage produced by this specific case was normal. Some young girl must have loved terribly, and some young man been no less impassioned, to accept expulsion from society on a world where there was no food except in hydroponic gardens and artificially warmed pastures. It was no less than suicide for those who loved. It was no less than a cause for battle among those who did not.

The deep-voiced Hunt said now, in leaden, heavy tones, "Cap it. This is my doing. It was my daughter I did it for. I wanted to keep her from dying. I'll pay for trying. They'll be satisfied in Three City and in One alike if you tell 'em it's my fault and I've been drove out for troublemaking."

Calhoun said sharply, "What's that? What's going on now?"

The man in the shadows answered, by his tone as much to express disgust as to give information. "His daughter Nym was on sentry duty against Three City sneaks. They had a sentry against us. The two of 'em talked across the valley between 'em. They had walkies to report with. They used 'em to talk. Presently, she sneaked a vision screen out of store. He prob'ly did, too. So presently they figured it was worth dyin' to die together. They run off for the hotlands. No chance to make it, o'course!"

The hotlands could hardly be anything but the warm equatorial belt of the planet.

"We should've let them go on and die," said the stocky Hunt, drearily. "But I persuaded men to help me bring 'em back. We were careful against sickness! We—I—locked them separate and I—I hoped my daughter mightn't die of the Three City sickness. I even hoped that young man wouldn't die of the sickness they say we have that we don't notice and they die of. Then we heard your call to One City. We couldn't answer it, but we heard all you said, even to the bargain about the cow. And—we'd heard of Med men who cured sickness. I hoped you could save Nym from dying of the Three City sickness or passing it in our city. My friends risked much to bring you here. However my daughter and the man have fled again.''

"And nobody's goin' to risk any more!" rasped the voice from the shadow of the cliff. "We held a council! It's decided! They gone and we got to burn out the places they was in! No more! You don't head the Council any more, either! We decided that, too. And no Med man! The Council ruled it!"

Calhoun nodded yet again. It is a part of fear, elaborately to ignore everything that can be denied about the thing feared. Which includes rational measures against it. This was a symptom of the state of things which constituted a Med Service emergency, because it caused needless deaths.

Hunt made a gesture which was at once commanding and filled with despair.

"I'll take the Med Man back so One City can use him if they dare and not blame you for me taking him. I'll have to take the sledge, but he's used it so it'd have to be burned anyhow. You men be sure to burn your clothes. Three City'll be satisfied because I'm lost to balance for their man lost. The Med Man will tell One City I'm drove out. You've lost me and my daughter too, and Three City's lost a man. One City'll growl and threaten, but they win by this. They won't risk a showdown.''

Silence again. As if reluctantly, one man of the party that had abducted Calhoun moved away from the sledge and toward the abysmally deep shadow of the cliff. Hunt said harshly, "Don't forget to burn your clothes! You others, get off the sledge. I'm taking the Med man back and there's no need for a war because I made the mistake and I'm paying for it.''

The remaining men of the kidnapping party stepped off the sledge into the trampled snow, just here. One said clumsily, "Sorry, Hunt. 'Luck!"

"What luck could I have?" asked the stocky man, wearily.

The roaring of the sledge's drive, which had been a mere muffled throbbing, rose to a booming bellow. The snow-vehicle surged forward, heading downward into the valley with the dark area below. Half a mile down, it began to sweep in a great circle to return upon its former track. Calhoun twisted in his seat and shouted above the roar. He made violent gestures. The deep-voiced Hunt, driving from a standing position behind the seat, slowed the sledge. It came nearly to a stop and hissing noises from snow passing beneath it could be heard.

"What's the matter?" His tone was lifeless. "What d'you want?"

"Two people have run away," said Calhoun vexedly, "your daughter Nym and a man from Three City, whatever that is. You're driven out to prevent fighting between the cities."

"Yes," said Hunt, without expression.

"Then let's go get the runaways," said Calhoun irritably, "before they die in the snow! After all, you got me to have me save them! And there's no need for anybody to die unless they have to!"

Hunt said without any expression at all, "They're heading for the hotlands, where they'd never get. It's my meaning to take you back to your ship, and then find them and give them the sledge so's they'll—so Nym will keep on living a while longer."

He moved to shift the controls and set the sledge again in motion. His state of mind was familiar enough to Calhoun, shock or despair so great that he could feel no other emotion. He would not react to argument. He could not weigh it. He'd made a despairing conclusion and he was lost to all thought beyond carrying it out. His intention was not simply a violent reaction to a single event, such as an elopement. He intended desperate means by which a complex situation could be kept from becoming a catastrophe to others. Three City had to be dealt with in this fashion, and One City in that, and it was requisite that he die, himself. Not only for his daughter but for his community. He

had resolved to go to his death for good and suffi-
cient reasons. To get his attention to anything else, he
would have to be shocked into something other than
despair.

Calhoun brought his hand out of its pocket. He held
the blaster. He'd pocketed the weapon before he went to
examine the cow. He'd had the power to stop his own
abduction at any instant. But a medical man does not
refuse a call for professional service.

Now he pointed the blaster to one side and pressed the
stud. A half-acre of snow burst into steam. It bellowed
upward and went writhing away in the peculiar blue-
gold glow of this world at night.

"I don't want to be taken back to my ship," said
Calhoun firmly. "I want to catch those runaways and
do whatever's necessary so they won't die at all. The
situation here has been thrown into my lap. It's a Med
Service obligation to intervene in problems of public
health, and there's surely a public health problem
here!"

Murgatroyd wriggled vigorously under Calhoun's
parka. He'd heard the spitting of the blaster and the
roaring of exploded steam. He was disturbed. The
stocky man stared.

"What's that?" he demanded blankly. "You pick
up . . ."

"We're going to pick up your daughter and the man
she's with," Calhoun told him crossly. "Dammit,
there's an isolation syndrome from what looks like a
Crusoe health problem here! It's got to be dealt with!
As a matter of public health!"

The stocky Hunt stared at him. Calhoun's intentions
were unimaginable to him. He floundered among incredible ideas.

"We medics," said Calhoun, "made it necessary for
men to invent interplanetary travel because we kept
people from dying and the population on old Earth got
too large. Then we made interstellar travel necessary
because we continued to keep people from dying and
one solar system wasn't big enough. We're responsible
for nine-tenths of civilization as it exists today, because

we produced the conditions that make civilization necessary! And since on this planet civilization is going downhill and people are dying without necessity, I have the plain obligation to stop it! So let's go pick up your daughter Nym and this sweetheart of hers, and keep them from dying and get civilization on the up-grade again!"

The former leader of the kidnappers said hoarsely, "You mean . . ." Then he stammered, "Th-th-they're heading for the hotlands. No other way to go. Watch for their tracks!"

The drive-engine bellowed. The sledge raced ahead. And now it did not complete the circle that had been begun, to head back to the landing grid. Now it straightened and rushed in a splendid roaring fierceness down between the sides of the valley. It left behind the dark patch with its whirling mists. It flung aside bow-waves of fine snow, which made rainbows in the half-light which was darkness here. It rushed and rushed and rushed, leaving behind a depression which was a singular permanent proof of its passage.

Calhoun cringed a little against the wind. He could see little or nothing of what was ahead. The sprayed wings of upflung snow prevented it. Hunt, standing erect, could do better. Murgatroyd, inside the parka, again wriggled his nose out into the stinging wind and withdrew it precipitantly.

Hunt drove as if confident of where to go. Calhoun dourly began to fit things into the standard pattern of how such things went. There were evidently three cities or colonies on this planet. They'd been named and he'd seen three patches of pasture from the stratosphere. One was plainly warmed by power applied underground, electric power from the landing grid's output. The one now falling behind was less likely to be electrically heated. Steam seemed more probable because of the vapor-veil above it. This sledge was surely fuel-powered. At a guess, a ram-jet drove it. Such motors were simple enough to make, once the principle of air inflow at low speeds was known. Two City—somewhere to the rear—might operate on a fuel technology which

could be based on fossil oil or gas. The power source for
Three City could not now be guessed.

Calhoun scowled as he tried to fill in the picture. His
factual data was still limited. There was the misty
golden ribbon in space. It was assuredly beyond the
technical capacity of cities suffering from an isolation
syndrome. He'd guessed at underground hydroponic
gardens. There was surely no surface city near the landing grid and the city entrance they'd just left was in the
face of a cliff. Such items pointed to a limited technical
capacity. Both, also, suggested mining as the original
purpose of the human colony or colonies here.

Only mining would make a colony self-supporting in
an arctic climate. This world could have been colonized
to secure rare metals from it. There could be a pipeline
from an oil field or from a gas well field near a landing
grid. Local technological use of gas or oil to process
ores might produce ingots of rare metal worth interstellar freight charges. One could even guess that metal
reduced by heat-chemistry could be transported in oil
suspension over terrain and under conditions when
other forms of surface transportation were impractical.

If the colony began as a unit of that sort, it would require only very occasional visits of spacecraft to carry
away its products. It could be a company planet, colonized and maintained by a single interstellar cor-
poration. It could have been established a hundred and
fifty or two hundred years before, when the interstellar
service organizations were in their infancy and only
operated where they were asked to serve. Such a colony
might not even be on record in the Medical Service files.

That would account for everything. When for some
reason the mines became unprofitable, this colony
would not be maintained. The people who wished to
leave would be taken off, of course. However, some
would elect to stay behind in the warmed, familiar cities
they and their fathers had been born in. They couldn't
imagine moving to a strange and unfamiliar world.

So much was normal reasoning. Now the strictly technical logic of the Med Service took over to explain the
current state of things. In one century or less an isolated

community could lose, absolutely, its defenses against diseases to which it was never exposed. Amerinds were without defense against smallpox, back on Earth. A brown race scattered among thousands of tiny islands was nearly wiped out by measles when it was introduced. Any contact between a long-isolated community and another—perhaps itself long isolated—would bring out violently any kind of contagion that might exist in either.

There was the mechanism of carriers. The real frequency of disease-carriers in the human race had been established less than two generations ago. But a very small, isolated population could easily contain a carrier or carriers of some infection. They could spread it so freely that every member of their group acquired immunity during infancy. A different isolated group might contain a carrier of a different infection and be immune to it but distributive of a second disease.

It was literally true that each of the three cities might have developed in their first century of isolation a separate immunity to one disease and a separate defenselessness against all others. A member of one community might be actually deadly to a member of either of the others whom he met face to face.

With icy wind blowing upon him as the sled rushed on, Calhoun wryly realized that all this was wholly familiar. It was taught, nowadays, that something of the sort had caused the ancient, primitive human belief that women were perilous to men and that a man must exercise great precaution to avoid evil *mana* emanating from his prospective bride. When wives were acquired by capture and all human communities were small and fiercely self-isolated—why each unsanitary tribal group might easily acquire a condition like that Calhoun now assumed in cities One, Two, and Three. The primitive suspicion of woman would have its basis in reality if the women of one tribe possessed immunity to some deadly microbe their skin or garments harbored, and if their successful abductors had no defense against it.

The speeding sledge swerved. It leaned inward against the turn. It swerved again, throwing monstrous sheets of snow aloft. Then the drive-jet lessened its roar. The shimmering bow-waves ceased. The sledge slowed to a mere headlong glide.

"Their trail!" Hunt cried in Calhoun's ear.

Calhoun saw depressions in the snow. There were two sets of pear-shaped dents in the otherwise virgin surface. Two human beings, wearing oblong frames on their feet, crisscrossed with cordage to support them atop the snow, had trudged ahead, here, through the gold-blue night.

Calhoun knew exactly what had happened. He could make the modifications the local situation imposed upon a standard pattern, and reconstitute a complete experience leading up to now.

A girl in heavy, clumsy garments had mounted guard in a Two City sentry post above a snow-filled mountain valley. There were long and bitter cold hours of watching, in which nothing whatever happened. Eternal snows seemed eternally the same, and there was little in life but monotony. She'd known that across the valley there was another lonely watcher from an alien city, the touch of whose hand or even whose breath would mean sickness and death. She'd have mused upon the strangeness that protected her in this loneliness, because her touch or her breath would be contagion to him, too. She'd have begun by feeling a vague dread of the other sentry. But presently, perhaps, there came a furtive call on the talkie frequency used by sentries for communication with their own cities.

Very probably she did not answer at first, but she might listen. She would hear a young man's voice, filled with curiosity about the sentry who watched as he did.

There'd come a day when she'd answer shyly. There would be relief and a certain fascination in talking to someone so much like herself but so alien and so deadly! Of course, there could be no harm in talking to someone who would flee from actual face-to-face contact as desperately as herself. They might come to joke about their mutual dangerousness. They might find it amusing that cities which dared not meet should hate. Then there'd come a vast curiosity to see each other. They'd discuss that frankly, because what possible evil could come of two persons who were deadly to each other should they actually approach?

Then there'd come a time when they looked at each other breathlessly in vision screens they'd secretly stolen from their separate cities' stores. There could be no harm. They were only curious! But she would see someone at once infinitely strange, utterly dear, and he would see someone lovely beyond the girls of his own city. Then they would regret the alienness which made them perilous to each other. Then they would resent it fiercely. They'd end by denying it.

So across the wide valley of eternal snow there would travel whispers of desperate rebellion, and then firmly resolute murmurings, and then what seemed the most obvious of truths, that it would be much more satisfactory to die together than to live apart. Insane plannings would follow, arrangements by which two trembling young folk would meet secretly and flee. Toward the hotlands, to be sure, but without any other belief than that the days before death, while they were together, would be more precious than the lifetimes they would give up to secure them.

Calhoun could see all this very clearly, and he assured himself that he regarded it with ironic detachment. He asserted in his own mind that it was merely the manifestation of that blind impulse to exogamy which makes spacemen romantic to girls in far spaceports. But it was something more. It was also that strange and unreasonable and solely human trait which causes one to rejoice selflessly that someone else exists, so that human life and happiness is put into its place of proper insignificance in the cosmos. It might begin in instinct, but it becomes an achievement only humans can encompass.

Hunt knew it, the stocky, deep-voiced despairing figure who looked hungrily for the daughter who had defied him and for whom he was an exile from all food and warmth.

He flung out a mittened hand.

"There!" he cried joyously. "It's them!"

There was a dark speck in the blue-gold night-glow. As the sledge crept close, there were two small figures who stood close together. They defiantly faced the approaching sledge. As its drive-motor stopped and it merely glided on, its runners whispering on the snow, the girl snatched away the cold-mask which all the inhabitants of this planet wore out-of-doors. She raised her face to the man. They kissed.

Then the young man desperately raised a knife. It glittered in the light of the ribbon in the sky—and . . .

Calhoun's blaster made its inadequate rasping noise. The knife-blade turned incandescent for two-thirds of its length. The young man dropped the suddenly searing handle. The knife sank hissing into the snow.

"It's always thrilling to be dramatic," said Calhoun severely, "but I assure you it's much more satisfying to be sane. The young lady's name is Nym, I believe. I do not know the gentleman. Nym's father and myself have come to put the technical resources of two civilizations at your disposal as a first step toward treatment of the pandemic isolation syndrome on this planet, which with the complications that have developed amounts to a Crusoe health problem."

Murgatroyd tried feverishly to get his head out of Calhoun's parka past his chin. He'd heard a blaster. He sensed excitement. His nose emerged, whiffing frantically. Calhoun pushed it back.

"Tell them, Hunt," he said irritably. "Tell them what we're here for and what you've done already!"

The girl's father told her unsteadily—almost humbly, for some reason—that the jet-sledge had come to take her and her sweetheart to the hotlands where at least they would not die of cold. Calhoun added that he believed there would even be food there, because of the ribbon in the sky.

Trembling and abashed, the fugitives got on the sledge. Its motor roared. It surged toward the hotlands under the golden glow of that ribbon, which had no rational explanation.

IV

"An action is normally the result of a thought. Since we cannot retract an action, we tend to feel that we cannot retract the thought which produced it. In effect, we cling desperately to our mistakes. In order to change our views we have commonly to be forced to act upon new thoughts, so urgent and so necessary that without disowning our former, mistaken ideas, we can abandon them tactfully without saying anything to anybody, even ourselves."

The Practice of Thinking—Fitzgerald

MURGATROYD CAME DOWN a tree with his cheek-pouches bulged with nuts. Calhoun inserted a finger, and Murgatroyd readily permitted him to remove and examine the results of his scramble aloft. Calhoun grunted. Murgatroyd did have other and more useful abilities in the service of public health, but right here and now his delicate digestion was extremely convenient. His stomach worked so much like a human's that anything Murgatroyd ate was safe for Calhoun to an incredible degree of probability, and Murgatroyd ate nothing that disagreed with him.

"Instead of 'physician, heal thyself,' " Calhoun observed, "it's amounted to 'physician, feed thyself' since we got past the frost line, Murgatroyd. I am gratified."

"*Chee!*" said Murgatroyd complacently.

"I expected," said Calhoun, "only to benefit by the

charm of your society in what I thought would be a routine check-trip to Merida Two. Instead, some unknown fumble-finger punched a wrong button and we wound up here—not exactly here, but near enough. I brought you from the Med Ship because there was nobody to stay around and feed you, and now you feed us, at least by pointing out edible things we might otherwise miss."

"Chee!" said Murgatroyd. He strutted.

"I wish," protested Calhoun, annoyed, "that you wouldn't imitate that Pat character from Three City! As a brand-new husband he's entitled to strut a little, but I object to your imitating him! You haven't anybody acting like Nym, gazing at you raptly as if you'd invented not only marriage but romance itself, and all the other desirable things back to night and morning!"

Murgatroyd said, *"Chee?"* and turned to face away from Calhoun.

The two of them, just then, stood on a leaf-covered patch of ground which slanted down to the singularly smooth and reflective water of a tiny bay. Behind and above them reared gigantic mountains. There was snow in blinding-white sheets overhead, but the snow line itself was safely three thousand feet above them. Beyond the bay was a wide estuary, with more mountains behind it, with more snow fields on their flanks. A series of leaping cascades jumped downward from somewhere aloft where a glacier-foot melted in the sun's heat. Everywhere that snow was not, green stuff shone in the sunlight.

Nym's father, Hunt, came hurriedly toward the pair. He'd abandoned the thick felt cloak and heavy boots of Two City. Now he was dressed nearly like a civilized man, but he carried a sharpened stick in one hand and in the other a string of authentic fish. He wore an expression of astonishment. It was becoming habitual.

"Murgatroyd," said Calhoun casually, "has found another kind of edible nut. Terrestrial, too, like half the living things we've seen. Only the stuff crowding the glaciers seems to be native. The rest originated on Earth and was brought here, some time or another."

Hunt nodded. He seemed to find some difficulty in speaking.

"I've been talking to Pat," he said at last.

"The son-in-law," observed Calhoun, "who has to thank you not only for your daughter and his life, but for your public career in Two City which qualified you to perform a marriage ceremony. I hope he was respectful."

Hunt made an impatient gesture.

"He says," he protested, "that you haven't done anything either to Nym or to him to keep them from dying."

Calhoun nodded.

"That's true."

"But—they should die! Nym should die of the Three City sickness! Three City people have always said that we had a sickness too, that did not harm us, but they died of!"

"Which," agreed Calhoun, "is undoubtedly historical fact. However, tempus fugit. Its current value is that of one factor in an isolation syndrome and consequently a complicating factor in the Crusoe health problem here. I've let Nym and Pat go untreated to prove it. I think there's only a sort of mass hypochondria based on strictly accurate tradition, which would be normal."

Hunt shook his head.

"I don't understand," he protested helplessly.

"Some day I'll draw a diagram," Calhoun told him. "It is complicated. Did you check with Pat on what Three City knows about the ribbon in the sky? I suspect it accounts for the terrestrial plants and animals here, indirectly. There wouldn't be an accidental planting of edible nuts and fish and squirrels and pigeons and rabbits and bumblebees! I suspect there was a mistake somewhere. What does Pat say?"

Hunt shrugged his shoulders.

"When I talk to him," added Calhoun, "he doesn't pay attention. He simply gazes at Nym and beams. The man's mad! But you're his father-in-law. He has to be polite to you!"

Hunt sat down abruptly. He rested his spear against a

tree and looked over his string of fish. He wasn't used to
the abundance of foodstuffs here, and the temperature
—Calhoun estimated it at fifty degrees—seemed to him
incredibly balmy. Now he thoughtfully separated one
fish from the rest and with a certain new skill began to
slice away two neatly boneless fillets. Calhoun had
showed him the trick the day after a lesson in fish-
spearing, which was two days after their arrival.

"Children in Three City," growled Hunt, "are taught
the same as in Two City. Men came to this planet to
work the mines. There was a Company which sent them,
and every so often it sent ships to take what the mines
yielded, and to bring things the people wanted. Men
lived well and happily. The Company hung the ribbon
in the sky so the hotlands could grow food for the men.
But presently the mines could not deliver what they
made to the ships when they came. The hotlands grew
bigger, the glaciers flowed faster, and the pipes between
the cities were broken and could not be kept repaired.
So the Company said that since the mine produce could
no longer be had, it could not send the ships. Those who
wanted to move to other worlds would be carried there.
Some men went, with their wives and children. However, the grandfathers of our fathers' grandfathers were
content here. They had homes and heat and food. They
would not go."

Hunt regarded the pinkish brook trout fillet he'd just
separated. He bit off a mouthful and chewed, thoughtfully.

"That really tastes better cooked," said Calhoun
mildly.

"But it is good this way also," said Hunt. He was
grizzled and stocky and somehow possessed dignity
which was not to be lost merely by eating raw fish. He
waved the remainder of the fillet. "Then the ships
ceased to come. Then sickness came. One City had a
sickness it gave to people of Two and Three when they
visited it. Two City had a sickness it gave to One and
Three. Three City . . ." He grunted. "Our children in
Two say only Two City people have no sickness. Three

City children are taught that only Three City is clean of sickness.''

Calhoun said nothing. Murgatroyd tried to gnaw open one of the nuts he'd brought down from the tree. Calhoun took it and another and struck them together. Both cracked. He gave them to Murgatroyd, who ate them with great satisfaction.

Hunt looked up suddenly.

"Pat did not give a Three City sickness to Nym," he observed, "so our thinking was wrong. And Nym has not given a Two City sickness to him. His thinking was wrong.''

Calhoun said meditatively, "It's tricky. But sickness can be kept by a carrier, just as you people have believed of other cities. A carrier has a sickness but does not know it. People around the carrier have the sickness on their bodies or their clothing from the carrier. They distribute it. Soon everybody in the city where there is a carrier—'' Calhoun had a moment's qualm because he used the word "city." To Hunt the idea conveyed was a bare few hundred people. "Soon everybody is used to the sickness. They are immune. They cannot know it. Somebody from another city can come, and they are not used to the sickness, and they become ill and die.''

Hunt considered shrewdly.

"Because the sickness is on clothing? From the carrier?''

Calhoun nodded.

"Different carriers have different sicknesses. So one carrier in One City might have one disease, and all the people in One City became used to it while they were babies, became immune. There could be another carrier with another sickness in Two City. A third in Three City. In each city they were used to their own sickness.''

"That is it," said Hunt, nodding. "But why is Pat not dying or Nym? Why do you do nothing to keep them alive?''

"Suppose," said Calhoun, "the carrier of a sickness dies. What happens?''

Hunt bit again, and chewed. Suddenly, he choked.

He sputtered, "There is no sickness to spread on the clothing! The people no longer have it to give to strangers who are not used to it! The babies do not get used to it while they are little! There is no longer a One City sickness or a Two City sickness or a Three!"

"There is," said Calhoun, "only a profound belief in them. You had it. Everybody else still has it. The cities are isolated and put out sentries because they believe in what used to be true. People like Nym and Pat run away in the snow and die of it. There is much death because of it. You would have died of it."

Hunt chewed and swallowed. Then he grinned.

"Now what?" His deep voice was quaintly respectful to Calhoun, so much younger than himself. "I like this! We were not fools to believe, because it was true. But we are fools if we still believe, because it is not true any-more. How do we make people understand, Calhoun? You tell me. I can handle people when they are not afraid. I can make them do what I think wise—when they are not afraid. But when they fear . . ."

"When they fear," said Calhoun dryly, "they want a stranger to tell them what to do. You came for me, remember? You are a stranger to One City and Three City. Pat is a stranger to Two City. If the cities become really afraid . . ."

Hunt grunted. He watched Calhoun intently, and Calhoun was peculiarly reminded of the elected president of a highly cultured planet, who had exactly that completely intent way of looking at one.

"Go on!" said Hunt. "How do we frighten them into—this?"

He waved his hand about. Calhoun, his tone very dry indeed, told him. Words would not be enough. Threats would not be enough. Promises would not be enough. Even rabbits and pigeons and squirrels and fish—fish that were frozen like other human food—and piles of edible nuts, would not be enough, by themselves, but . . .

"An isolation syndrome is a neurotic condition, and a Crusoe problem amounts to neurotic hypochondria. You can do it, you and Pat."

Hunt grimaced.

"I hate the cold, now. But I will do it. After all, if I am to have grandchildren there should be other children for them to play with! We will take you back to your ship?"

"You will," said Calhoun. "By the way, what is the name of this planet, anyhow?"

Hunt told him.

Calhoun slipped across the pasture inside the landing grid and examined the ship from the outside. There had been batterings, but the door had not been opened. In the light of the ribbon in the sky he could see, too, that the ground was trampled down but only at a respectful distance. One City was disturbed about the Med Ship, but it did not know what to do. So long as nothing happened from it. . . .

He was working the combination lock door when something hopped, low-down and near him. He jumped, and Murgatroyd said, *"Chee?"* Then Calhoun realized what had startled him. He finished the unlocking of the port. He went in and closed the port behind him. The air inside seemed curiously dead, after so long a time outside. He flipped on the outside microphones and heard tiny patterings. He heard mildly resentful cooings. He grinned.

When morning came, the people of One City would find their pasture land inhabited by small snowshoe rabbits and small and bush-tailed squirrels and fluttering pigeons. They would react as Two City and Three City had already done—with panic. The panic would inevitably call up the notion of the most feared thing in their lives. Sickness. The most feared thing is always a rare thing, of course. One cannot fear a frequent thing, because one either dies of it or comes to take it for granted. Fear is always of the rare or nonexistent. One City would be filled with fear of sickness.

Sickness would come. Hunt would call them, presently, on a walkie-talkie communicator. He would express deep concern because—so he'd say—new domestic animals intended for Two City had been dumped

on One City pasture land. He'd add that they were
highly infective, and One City was already inescapably
doomed to an epidemic which would begin with severe
headaches, and would continue with cramps and extreme nervous agitation. He would say that Calhoun
had left medicines at Two City with which that sickness
and all others could be cured, and if the sickness
described should appear in One City—why—its victims
would be cured if they traveled to Two City.

The sickness would appear. Inevitably. There was no
longer sickness in the three communities. Arctic
colonies, never visited by people from reservoirs of infection, become magnificently healthy by the operation
of purely natural causes, but an isolation syndrome . . .

The people of One City would presently travel,
groaning, to Two City. Their suffering would be real.
They would dread the breaking of their isolation. But
they'd dread sickness—even sickness they only imagined—still more. When they reached Two City they
would find themselves tended by Three City members,
and they would be appalled and terrified. But mock
medication by Hunt and Pat—and Nym for the
women—would reassure them. A Crusoe condition requires heroic treatment. This was it.

Calhoun cheerfully checked over the equipment of
the Med Ship. He'd have to take off on emergency
rockets. He'd have to be very, very careful in setting a
course back to headquarters to report before starting
out again for Merida II. He didn't want to make any
mistake. . . . Suddenly, he began to chuckle.

"Murgatroyd," he said amiably, "it's just occurred
to me that the mistakes we make, that we struggle so
hard to avoid, are part of the scheme of things."

"Chee?" said Murgatroyd inquiringly.

"The Company that settled this planet," said Calhoun, grinning, "set up that ribbon out in space as a
splendidly conservative investment to save money in
freight charges. It was a mistake, because it ruined their
mining business and they had to write the whole colony
off. They made another mistake by not reporting to

Med Service, because now they've abandoned the colony and would have to get a license to reoccupy, which
they'd never be granted against the population already
here. Somebody made a mistake that brought us here,
and One City made a mistake by not accepting us as
guests, and Two City made a mistake by sending Nym
on sentry duty, and Three City made a mistake . . ."

Murgatroyd yawned.

"You," said Calhoun severely, "make a mistake
in not paying attention!" He strapped himself in. He
stabbed an emergency rocket control-button. The little
ship shot heavenward on a pencil-thin stream of fire.
Below him, people of One City would come pouring out
of underground to learn what had happened, and they'd
find the pasture swarming with friendly squirrels and
inquisitive rabbits and cooing pigeons. They'd be scared
to death. Calhoun laughed. "I'll spend part of the time
in overdrive making a report on it. Since an isolation
syndrome is mostly psychological, and a Crusoe condition is wholly so, I managed sound medical treatment by
purely psychological means! I'll have fun with that!"

It was a mistake. He got back to headquarters, all
right, but when his report was read they made him ex-
pand it into a book, with footnotes, an index, and a
bibliography.

It was very much of a mistake!

QUARANTINE
WORLD

I

THERE WASN'T A thing he could put his finger on, but from the beginning Calhoun didn't feel comfortable about the public health situation on Lanke. There wasn't anything really wrong about it, not anything. Calhoun felt that it was just a little bit too good to be true. He and Murgatroyd the *tormal* had arrived in the little Med Ship *Aesclipus Twenty*. They'd been greeted with effusive cordiality. Health Department officials opened everything to Calhoun's examination, with a smoothness and speed that almost looked like the planetary authorities were anxious for him to finish his job and get away from there. The Health Minister practically jumped through hoops to provide all the information he could ask for. The communicable diseases appeared to be well in hand. The average age-at-death rate for the planet was the fraction of a decimal-point low, but it was accounted for by a microscopic rise in the accidental-death reports. Calhoun couldn't find a thing to justify the feeling that a cover-up job was being done. If it was, it was being done perfectly. He was a little bit irritated by his own suspicions.

Still, he went through the routine for three sunny days and evenings. He had some new developments in the art of medicine that Med Service Headquarters wanted to have spread about. He explained them to attentive listeners. In turn, he listened interestedly to what he was told, and the night before he was to lift off for his return to headquarters he attended a top-drawer medical society meeting in a high ceilinged lecture hall in the Health Department building.

The Health Minister introduced him in a typical speech in which he expressed the value of modern medical science in strictly businessman terms. He mentioned that absenteeism due to sickness was at the lowest figure ever known in the industries of Lanke, and the fact added not less than so many hundreds of millions of credits to the gross annual product of Lanke. The extension of hormone-balance checkups, with other preventive practices, had reduced the overall incidence of sickness requiring hospitalization to the point where in the past ten years so many thousands of hospital beds had ceased to be required. Which added so many other millions of credits every year to the prosperity of Lanke.

There was another item which nobody thought about, but was perhaps the most valuable of all the achievements of medical science. He referred to the fact that epidemics were now substantially impossible. It was not necessary to calculate what an actual epidemic might cost. One could think simply of what the danger might be to see what medical science added to the planetary wealth. In interstellar trade alone, the simple threat of a dangerous plague on Lanke would mean the quarantining of the planet, and that would mean a financial panic, the closing of factories whose products could not be sold, widespread unemployment, appalling drops in the values of securities, and it could mean runs on banks, the abandonment of construction projects and even curtailment of agricultural production! The wealth that modern medical science contributed to the economy was the true great achievement of the medical profession! Much of this achievement was due to Lanke physicians alone, but the Interstellar Medical Service had made its contributions too, and he was happy to present to them Doctor Calhoun of that Service, whom many of them had met and talked to in the past few days.

Calhoun's speech, of course, was anticlimactic. He said the normal thing for such occasions. It amounted to polite congratulations to the doctors of Lanke for doing what doctors were supposed to do. He did feel, definitely, that something was being hidden from him, but he hadn't the evidence to justify him in saying so. So he made a speech in no wise remarkable and sat down to wait for the end of the meeting.

He'd much rather have been aboard the Med Ship. Murgatroyd was much better company than the Health Minister beside him. Murgatroyd didn't think of every possible human activity in terms of the money it made or saved. Murgatroyd had enjoyed his stay on Lanke. Calhoun hadn't.

Murgatroyd didn't have to pretend interest while people made dull speeches. Murgatroyd was a small, furry, cordial animal who liked humans and was liked by them. Aground, in human society, he made friends and charmed people and managed to get much petting and quantities of the sweet cakes and coffee he adored. Murgatroyd had fun. There'd been no call for use of the special talent that only *tormals* in all the galaxy possess, and he'd had a happy time. Calhoun looked forward to the restfulness of being back in the Med Ship with him, unbothered by the conviction that something was being put over that he couldn't put a finger on.

Then, suddenly, there were shoutings in another part of the building. A blaster rasped savagely. More shouts, more blasters went off in a storm of fire. Then there was dead silence.

In the lecture hall there was absolute stillness, as startled men listened for more of those decidedly unusual sounds.

They didn't come, but a man in police uniform did enter the back of the hall. He wore a look of most unofficial terror on his face. He spoke to the first doctor he came to inside that door. The doctor's face went gray. He went unsteadily out. Someone asked a question of the policeman. He answered and went out also, as if reluctantly. Others at the meeting moved to ask what had happened and what the policeman said.

The news—whatever it was—went about the hall with extraordinary dispatch. As each man heard, he paled. Some seemed near to fainting. There began, immediately, a universal attempt to leave the lecture hall without attracting attention.

"Dear me!" said the Health Minister, sitting on the speakers' platform beside Calhoun. "What can be the matter? Wait here and I'll find out."

He moved away. He stopped someone and asked a question. He was startled. He asked more questions. He came back to Calhoun in something like panic.

"What was it?" asked Calhoun.

"A—a burglar," said the Health Minister. His teeth seemed to be trying to chatter. "Just a burglar. There've been—robberies. We try to keep down crime, you know. It's an economic waste—terrible! But this man was trying to commit a burglary in—this building. He was discovered and he—jumped or fell from a window." The Health Minister wiped beads of sweat from his forehead. "He's dead. A—a shocking thing, of course. But not important. Not important at all. Not worth mentioning. . . ."

Calhoun didn't believe him. The Health Minister was scared. There was no danger here! He was afraid of something a politician might be afraid of. It was that sort of terror. It wasn't too likely, but it might be linked to whatever had been covered up so Calhoun wouldn't discover it. The policeman who'd come in had been frightened too. Why? Then Calhoun looked at the medical society members in the lecture hall. The meeting had been ended by whatever word passed from man to man. The members of the society were leaving. They tried to be dignified, but also they tried to hurry. There was something puzzlingly wrong, and the Health Minister had lied about it. Obviously, more questions would only produce more lies. So Calhoun shrugged.

"Anyhow," he observed, "the meeting's over. It's breaking up. I'll get back to the spaceport."

His actual intentions were somewhat different.

"Yes. Yes. Of course," said the Health Minister, shivering. He didn't seem to think of escorting Calhoun out.

Calhoun joined those leaving the hall and the building. They crowded down the stairs, not waiting for a slower lift. Very many of them looked white and sick. Calhoun reached the outer air. Only yards from the exit there was a half-circle of burning flares, stuck in the ground. They bathed the ground and the side of the Health Department building with a pitiless glare.

There was a dead man on the ground. He'd obviously fallen from a height. None of the eminent physicians streaming out of the building so much as glanced at him. They hastened away in the darkness. Only Calhoun approached the flares. A policeman on watch— badly frightened—warned him back. Calhoun considered coldly. Then he stepped into the light past the protesting officer.

The dead man's mouth was open in a gruesome fashion. While the policeman continued to protest, Calhoun made a brisk, superficial examination. The dead man had lost teeth by dental caries, which was remarkable. He had other cavities filled with metal, a process abandoned for centuries. His garments were not made of normal materials, but of some fiber Calhoun did not recognize. There was a scar on his cheek. Calhoun, bending over, saw that tissues on either side of his nose were swollen and pigmented. The appearance was abnormal.

He picked up a bit of cloth, torn in the dead man's fall down the side of the building. As he examined it, a voice gasped, "Calhoun! What are you doing?" It was the Health Minister, leaving the building of his cabinet department. He trembled uncontrollably. "Stop it! Drop it!"

"I was looking at this man," said Calhoun. "It's queer...."

"Come away!" cried the Health Minister hysterically. "You don't know what you're—do . . ." He stopped. He mopped his face, shaking. Then he said, desperately attempting a normal tone, "I'm sorry. It would be a good idea for you to get back to your ship. This man was a criminal. There may be others of his confederates about. The police are going to make a thorough search. We—we civilians should get out of the way."

"But I'd like to look him over!" protested Calhoun. "There's scar tissue on his face! See it? Since when have doctors allowed scar tissue to form in healing wounds? He's lost some teeth and there's a cavity in one of his incisors! How often have you seen dental caries? They simply don't happen anymore!"

The Health Minister swallowed audibly.

"Yes. Yes . . . now that you point it out, I see what you mean. We'll have to do an autopsy. Yes. We'll do an autopsy in the morning. But right now, to cooperate with the police—"

Calhoun looked again at the limp, crumpled figure on the ground. Then he turned away. The last of the medical society members came out of the building. They melted away into the night. Calhoun could almost smell panic in the air.

The Health Minister vanished. Calhoun hailed a skimmer-cab and got into it. On the way to the spaceport he considered darkly. He'd evidently seen something he wasn't supposed to see. It might well be connected with what he hadn't been able to put a finger on. He'd told the Health Minister that he was going back to the spaceport, but that hadn't been his intention then. He'd meant to find a tavern and buy drinks for its habitues until somebody's tongue got loosened. News of a man killed by the police would set tongues wagging in certain kinds of society on any planet.

However, he'd changed his intention. He had a scrap of cloth in his pocket from the dead man's clothing. There was a bit of blood on it. It was extraordinary. The dead man was extraordinary. He'd frightened everybody who seemed to know something Calhoun was not supposed to discover. Considering all he did know, he planned to find out a few things more from that cloth sample.

The skimmer-cab reached the spaceport gate. The guards waved it on. It reached the Med Ship and settled to a stop. Calhoun paid the driver and went into the Med Ship, to be greeted with extravagant enthusiasm by Murgatroyd, who explained with many shrill *"Chee-chees"* that he did not like to be left alone when Calhoun went elsewhere. Calhoun said, "Hold it, Murgatroyd! Don't touch me!"

He put the sample of cloth with its few specks of blood into a sterile bottle. He snapped the elastic cover in place. Murgatroyd said, *"Chee?"*

"I've just seen a pack of thoroughly scared men," said Calhoun dryly, "and I've got to see if they were right to be scared."

He washed his hands with some care, and then extended his precautions—he felt absurd about it—to an entire change of clothing. The terror of the dead man puzzled and bothered him.

"Chee-chee-chee!" said Murgatroyd reproachfully.

"I know!" said Calhoun. "You want coffee. I'll make it. But I'm worried!"

Murgatroyd frisked. It was Calhoun's habit to talk to him as if he were a human being. He'd mentioned coffee, and Murgatroyd could recognize that word. He waited for the drink to be made and served. Frowning, Calhoun made it, thinking hard the while. Presently, he passed over the little cup that fitted Murgatroyd's tiny paws.

"There you are. Now listen!" Calhoun spoke vexedly. "I've felt all along that there was something wrong here, and tonight something happened. It could be told in a dozen words. It was, but not to me. A man died and it terrified two policemen; an entire medical society and the Health Minister of the planet. It wasn't the death of a man which did all this. It was something his death or his presence meant. But I wasn't told. I was lied to. Lied to! What did they want me to keep on not knowing?"

Murgatroyd sipped at his cup. He said profoundly, *"Chee?"*

"I suspect the same thing," said Calhoun, again with

vexation. "Generally speaking, facts are hidden only from people whose job it would be to act on them. Facts have been hidden from me. What sort of facts is it my job to act on, Murgatroyd?"

Murgatroyd seemed to consider. He sipped again, reflectively. Then he said with decision, *"Chee-chee!"*

"I'm very much afraid you're right," Calhoun told him. "The local medical profession has repressed it. . . . The Health Minister has a very vivid picture in his mind of what could happen to the economy and the prosperity of Lanke if even the suspicion of an epidemic went about. In short, Murgatroyd, it looks like a thing has been covered up so carefully that it shows. When as much terror as I saw just tonight is felt by everybody— I'd better get to work!"

He put part of the cloth sample—including the small bloodstains—in a culture medium. A fiber or two, though, he examined under a microscope. He shook his head.

"Odd! It's a natural fiber, Murgatroyd! It wasn't made. It grew! They certainly don't grow fibers on Lanke! This man isn't a native son of this planet! Quaint, eh?"

It was quaint. Synthetic fibers were better than natural ones. Nobody used natural fibers anymore. Nobody!

He waited impatiently on the culture from the cloth. While it was still too early to expect any specific results, his impatience got the best of him. He filled a vivo-slide for the culture microscope which would let him watch the behavior of living microorganisms as they grew. He was startled, when he looked at the microscope-screen. There were perfectly commonplace microbes in the culture broth even so early. However, there was one variety that was astonishing. A curious, dancing, spherical, pigmented organism leaped and darted madly. It visibly multiplied at a prodigious rate. When Calhoun added the Daflos reagent to the contents of the slide, certain highly specific color effects appeared. The Daflos pathogenicity test was not infallible, but it wasn't meaningless, either. It said that the dancing, spherical microbes should be highly toxic. They produced a toxin the reagent reacted to. The rate of reproduction was astounding. It should, then, be highly infectious and probably lethal.

Calhoun frowned over the facts. The implications were matters a businessman on Lanke would want hidden, suppressed. A businessman would lie about them, desperately, until the last possible instant. A businessman's government might very well demand of the medical profession that it take precautions without causing undue alarm, and . . . Calhoun knew why the medical men at the meeting looked scared and sick. From the clothing and the blood of a dead man Calhoun had extracted a microbe which was probably that of a deadly plague—so said the Daflos reagents—of enormous infectivity which the clothing, teeth, and scar tissue suggested had come from some other world. This was enough to worry anybody. On Lanke, any physician who caused the danger to be realized, the facts to be known, and a planetary quarantine slapped on Lanke, such a physician would instantly be discredited and subjected to merciless hostility by his government. He'd be ruined professionally, financially and socially, and his family would share in his disgrace and ruin. The terror of the doctors had reason. Until the dead man was found, they'd had no reason for unease. When he was found, they knew instantly what the culture microscope had just told Calhoun. The doctors of Lanke were in a very bad fix. The government would not—would definitely not—permit a planetary quarantine if they could help it. It would not be anything but the automatic assumption that a financial panic and an industrial collapse must be avoided, whatever else had to be allowed. It would be very bad!

Calhoun began to see this with a bitter clarity. A curious flicker of light behind him made him turn. The outside-field detector-light was glowing on the controlboard. Normally it lighted only to report that the force fields of a landing grid touched the Med Ship when the ship was to be brought to ground, or else when it was to be lifted off to a distance at which a Lawlor drive could be used. There was no reason for it to come on now!

Then the G.C.—general communication—speaker said:

"Calling Med Ship Aesclipus Twenty*! Calling Med Ship* Aesclipus Twenty*! Spaceport control office calling Med Ship* Aesclipus Twenty*!"*

Calhoun threw the answer switch.

"Aesclipus Twenty here," he said shortly. "What's the matter?"

"Checking, sir," said the voice detachedly. *"Are you sealed up?"*

Calhoun glanced at the air-lock. Aground, of course, it could be opened like the two sets of doors of a vestibule, with direct communication between the inside of the ship and the outside air. However, without thinking particularly about it, Calhoun had left the Med Ship with its own air-renewal system operating.

"Yes," said Calhoun. "I'm sealed up. Why?"

"Message for you, sir," said the voice.

There was immediately the voice of the Health Minister, racked and upset, coming out of the speaker.

"You are requested to leave Lanke at once," it said agitatedly. *"Complaint will be made to the Med Service that you attempted to interfere with police measures against crime. Your ship will be lifted off as of now, and you are forbidden to return."*

Calhoun said angrily, "The devil you say! I declare a quarantine—"

The communicator clicked. The Health Minister had cut off. The detached control-office voice said woodenly, *"I'm lifting you off, sir, as ordered. Lift-off coming. . . ."*

Calhoun's mouth opened, to swear. Instantly he saw very many more things it had not been the intention of the Health Minister to tell him. He clenched his hands. This wasn't good!

Then the Med Ship stirred, and instantly thereafter seemed to fall toward the sky. Calhoun angrily flipped on the outside vision-plates and his sensations and the statements of the control-office voice agreed. The Med Ship was being lifted off. Below it, the lights of the spaceport receded. Then the street lights of Lanke's capital city were coming into view from behind tall buildings. They winked into sight from farther toward the dark horizon. The small spaceship went up and up.

The smaller, fainter lights of another city appeared. A little while later, the lights of still another. The capital city's pattern of streets grew ever smaller. More other city-glows appeared and seemed at once to dwindle and to drift toward and under the rising Med Ship. There was nothing to be seen anywhere except those minute, diminishing speckles of light.

Presently, the ship went into cloud cover and for seconds the vision screens were blank. Then it reached clear air again and then there was nothing but the starlit cloud cover below, and ten thousand million stars above.

The Med Ship was being lifted by the spaceport's landing grid. Eventually, the stars crept downward, and seemed to draw together, and the world of Lanke became only a diminishing circular patch of darkness against the galaxy's all-surrounding suns. Then the communicator speaker spoke woodenly again.

"Calling Med Ship Aesclipus Twenty*! Calling* Aesclip . . ."

"*Aesclipus* here," said Calhoun coldly.

"You are now five diameters out," said the unemotional voice, *"And I am about to release you. Check?"*

"Check," said Calhoun sardonically.

He flipped off the G.C. transmitter. He felt the new freedom of the Med Ship. He spoke in an even more sardonic tone to Murgatroyd. "This is a first, Murgatroyd! It's the first time a Med Ship man has ever been thrown off a planet because he found out too much!" Then he added with a definite grimness, "It happens that throwing us off the planet verifies what I was only partly guessing and requires what I was hesitating to do."

His tone disturbed Murgatroyd, who of course could not understand what had happened. But he was upset because Calhoun was. Murgatroyd said shrilly, *"Chee-chee!"*

"We're going back to headquarters," said Calhoun sourly. "We can take our news there quicker than we can send it. Anyhow they'll need more than you and me on Lanke to handle a plague—especially if it's a bad one. But I don't like it!"

He was angry. But it wasn't unprecedented for planetary governments to try to cover up things that would be bad for business. There'd been attempts before now to conceal outbreaks of disease. Some had probably succeeded. Those that failed turned out very badly indeed. Minor epidemics had become major plagues when a prompt call for Med Service help would have kept them minor and wiped them out. The Med Service had big ships, half a mile long and longer, with laboratories and equipment and personnel that could handle emergencies of planetary size. But very, very many lives had been lost because of governments subordinating everything but business to business. They'd tried to prevent business crises and financial panics and industrial collapse. They'd only delayed them—at incalculable costs in lives.

There was another factor, too. If a planetary government once concealed an emergency of this sort, it would never dare admit it later. A certain world in Cygnus had concealed a serious epidemic in order to protect its interstellar trade. Later the fact was learned by Med Service. It made a check of the public health status of that reckless world, in view of its just-learned medical history. It discovered and announced an imminent second epidemic—a perfectly accurate statement of fact. The first epidemic had not been cleaned up properly by the local physicians. The epidemic was cyclic—with a normal period of high incidence after every so many years. So the Med Service quarantined that world—justly—and took stringent measures—wisely—and there was consequently no second plague. But there were many hard-boiled businessmen who fumed that the Med Service had no reason for its action; that it had been punishing the Cygnus world for violating a primary rule for galactic public health. The planet had concealed a disease that might but hadn't been passed on to its customers. Businessmen believed the quarantine a penalty.

So Calhoun knew grimly that if there'd been a hidden plague on Lanke in the past, it would never be admitted now. Never! And any doctor who revealed the historical fact . . . The reason for the silence of Lanke's doctors was abundantly clear.

But this situation wasn't as simple as the Cygnus affair. The dead man Calhoun had partly examined wasn't a native of Lanke. Yet the doctors of Lanke knew all about him and the plague of which he was dying when blaster bolts drove him to a quicker death. He didn't belong on Lanke. Worse, he didn't belong anywhere else. His state of civilization wasn't appropriate anywhere in the galaxy. But he was positively a man. Calhoun had seen drama tapes about lost colonies and villages of castaways, and even elaborate hiding places for refugees from the laws of planets. But he didn't believe them.

"Still," he said irritably, "where did he come from?"

He felt that there were too many questions already. But there was something definite to do. Several things. For the first of them he swung the Med Ship about and aimed it at the small, remote star cluster where Sector Headquarters was established. He punched the computer keys. He said, "Overdrive coming, Murgatroyd! Five . . . four . . . three . . . two . . . one . . ."

There was a sudden intolerable giddiness and an instant's insupportable nausea, and the sensation of a spiral fall to nowhere. Then, abruptly, everything was quite all right. The Med Ship was in overdrive, surrounded by a cocoon of stressed space which changed its own position many times faster than the speed of light, and carried the little Med Ship with it.

Calhoun paced up and down the control-room,

scowling. The background tape began to make its unobtrusive sounds. In overdrive, of course, the Med Ship was wholly isolated from the normal universe of galaxies and stars. There was, in theory, only one conceivable way in which it could be affected by anything outside its own overdrive field, and that had never happened yet. So there could have been a sepulchral, nerve-racking silence in the small spacecraft but for such sounds as the background tape provided.

They were trivial, those sounds. One had to pay close attention to hear them. There was the sound of rain, and of traffic, and of wind in treetops and voices too faint for the words to be distinguished, and almost inaudible music—and sometimes laughter. The background tape carried no information; only the assurance that there were still worlds with clouds and people and creatures moving about on them.

But sensory assurance of the existence of a real cosmos is as essential to a man's subjective health as hormones and enzymes to his body. Calhoun would have suffered from the lack of such noises if they'd stopped, but he paid no attention to them when they began.

"That man," said Calhoun abruptly, "wasn't a normal inhabitant of Lanke, Murgatroyd! He didn't grow up on it! He carried microscopic flora and fauna with him—as don't we all?—but they were very probably as alien to Lanke as the man himself! The doctors knew about it, and they were afraid. Afraid! But where did he come from?"

Murgatroyd had retreated to his little cubbyhole in the control-room. He was curled up there with his furry tail draped across his nose. He blinked at Calhoun. It is a characteristic of *tormals* that they imitate the actions of humans as parrots imitate human speech. When Calhoun talked conversationally, Murgatroyd adored pretending that he discussed abstruse subjects with him. But now Calhoun really talked to himself. Murgatroyd realized it. He said, *"Chee!"* and prepared to take a nap.

Presently, Calhoun began an angry, systematic search through the Med Ship's microfilm library. It was a remarkable storage system for facts. It reduced a page of text to the size of a printed period, and the *Aesclipus Twenty* was able to carry more reference material for a Med Service man's needs than most national libraries contained. The data-retrieval system was one of the great technical achievements of the previous century. Calhoun had at his fingertips more information on medical subjects then earlier times could have imagined.

The library had nothing to say about a plague which produced—doubtless among other symptoms—enlarged and stiffened, pigmented tissues on either side of a man's nose. Nor did it have any record of a microorganism exactly matching the one he'd gotten from the cloth of the dead man's garments—or the specks of blood included—and suspected of the water he'd washed in.

The really basic question remained, too. Where had the inexplicable man come from?

Calhoun checked the progress of his cultures. All thrived.

Calhoun set up an imaginary globe in space, with Lanke as its center. He set the data-retrieval unit to find a habitable world, not known to be colonized, in that volume of emptiness. An abortive attempt at colonization might have left some castaways behind. That would raise almost as many questions as it answered, but it seemed the most likely approach to the problem.

There was no habitable world in the Stellar Directory portion of the ship's microfilm records. He tried a larger volume of space. Then a still larger one. Nothing.

He tried for less than a habitability-one world. Individual survival might be possible where a colony could not live. He set the search-unit to work again. It found a world which was airless, a gas-giant world with intolerable gravity, another which had an equatorial temperature of minus sixty degrees at noon. Another . . .

Ultimately, one turned up which looked plausible. It was the third-orbit planet of a Type G sun. It was not

unduly remote from Lanke. It was listed under the name
Delhi. Shallow, marshy seas. A single continent. Temperature, not unbearable. Life-types not unduly dangerous. Atmosphere typical of third-orbit planets but with
.04% of a complex methane-derivative gas, apparently
harmless. This data had been sent up from an exploring
spaceboat, later lost. There were what was believed to
be the ruins of a human settlement, photographed from
space. Classed as habitability zero because no ship had
ever returned to its home spaceport after landing on it.
The inimical factor was assumed to exist in the atmosphere, but was not known.

Here was material for guesses, but nothing more. It
threw no light on where the dead man with bad teeth
had come from. Calhoun went over all the other reports. No other was even as promising as this.

He had been seven hours in overdrive when the pro-
jected letters of the microfilm material separated into
twins. Every letter doubled. The reading-matter became
unreadable. With one eye covered, reading was just
barely possible, but he could see nothing with real
clarity.

He took his temperature. He felt perfectly well, but
he had a high fever and his eyes grew progressively
worse. He said grimly to Murgatroyd, "I begin to see
some excuse for the doctors on Lanke. Whatever they
were afraid of getting, I've got! It's highly infectious, all
right!"

Ten hours out from Lanke, his vision cleared again.
He could fuse the images from both eyes. He continued
to feel perfectly well, but his temperature was half a
degree higher than three hours earlier.

"This," he told Murgatroyd, "is not according to the
rules! I may have to call on you as a member of the
medical profession!"

He gave himself as thorough a physical examination
as one can give himself. He used the amplifier-microscope on his saliva, his blood, on every body fluid. Each
of them showed a minute, perfectly spherical pigmented
microorganism in appalling numbers. As he regarded

them on the screen of the amplifier-microscope they broke into halves, became small spheres, grew swiftly and prepared to divide again. Meanwhile, they danced and darted and whirled frantically. The reaction to the Daflos reagents indicated the presence of a deadly toxin.

"And I took precautions!" Calhoun said rather dizzily. "I washed and showered. I could almost have operated with no more attempt at a sterile environment!" He shook his head. "I think I can go a little longer. That dead man was farther along than this. I've time enough to call on you, Murgatroyd."

He looked at himself in the mirror. The curious enlargement of the flesh beside his nose had appeared. He began to get out his equipment. Something occurred to him.

"The Health Minister," he said sardonically, "didn't quarantine me. He sent me off. He had no fear of my reporting anything to headquarters! I should be dead before breakout, and you couldn't run the ship to headquarters and it would never be found." Then he said, "Let's prevent such an unpleasant fate, Murgatroyd!"

He drew a small sample of blood from his arm. He injected it into Murgatroyd where a small patch of skin on the *tormal*'s flank had been desensitized almost as soon as he was born. Murgatroyd made no objection.

It was the remarkable talent of *tormals*—all *tormals* —that they could not be infected by any microorganism. They could not ordinarily contract any ailment at all. Their digestive systems rejected any substance that would impair their health, and they had a dynamic reaction to infective material. When their normal defenses were bypassed and pathogenic material was put into their bloodstream, they produced antibodies, their structure could be determined and they could be synthesized in any desired quantity. So whatever infection a new planet might offer, it could be brought under control.

Now Murgatroyd went back to his cubbyhole, yawning. He crawled in to doze. Calhoun made a mental note to check his pulse and breathing in half an hour. He, himself, felt feverish. His head seemed to rock a little. His eyes went bad again. He saw double. Murgatroyd dozed peacefully. Calhoun doggedly waited for him to react to the microscopic spheres. His heartbeat should go up four or five counts a minute. He might run a degree of fever. He would be sleepy for two hours, or three, or even four. Then he'd wake up and his blood would contain antibodies against the material with which he'd been inoculated. He'd be back in robust health, and able to share it with Calhoun.

It didn't work out that way. When Calhoun went to check his pulse-rate in half an hour, Murgatroyd came wide awake. He said, *"Chee!"* in an inquiring tone. He scrambled out of his nest, filled with vim and zest for whatever the hour might bring forth. His pulse was normal. His temperature was equally correct.

Calhoun stared at him. Murgatroyd couldn't have looked healthier. He showed no sign of having needed to produce antibodies.

He hadn't. There are some diseases, contagious among animals, to which human beings are immune. There are some from which humans suffer, to which animals are not subject. More than once medical research has been halted while a hunt was made for an experimental animal in which a particular strain of microbes or viruses could live.

The plague of which Lanke was terrified and Calhoun a victim happened to be a plague to which Murgatroyd did not need to form antibodies. He was immune to it by the simple normal chemistry of his body, and there was nothing that Calhoun could do about it. He considered that he would unquestionably die within a certain short number of days or hours. The Med Ship would drive on, to breakout somewhere within a light-year more or less of its destination. From there, it should make a shorter overdrive-hop to a matter of no more than a million miles or two, and then it should use Lawlor Drive within the solar system, on whose planet the Interstellar Medical Service had its headquarters.

But if Calhoun was dead nothing of the sort would

happen. The Med Ship would breakout. Murgatroyd might still be alive, but he could do nothing. Eventually he would die, bewildered. The Med Ship would never, never be found so long as time ran on, and Lanke . . .

"Murgatroyd," said Calhoun, "this is a bad business! And you're right in it! I know what I'm up against, but what am I going to do for you?"

Murgatroyd said confidently, *"Chee-chee-chee!"*

"I'm seeing better," said Calhoun suddenly. "It seems to come in waves of better and worse. Intermittent."

He put his hand to his face to feel the now-marked unresilient stiffened flesh beside his nose. Murgatroyd looked hopefully at the coffee pot. He said, *"Chee?"* There was nothing to indicate the possibility of anything, not anticipated. There was no reason for anything to happen.

Then, abruptly, everything changed. The *Aesclipus Twenty* was in overdrive and there was only one thing which even in theory could affect her from outside. It was said that if a ship were in overdrive and all the cosmos exploded, and everything in all the galaxies ceased to be, including the galaxies themselves, that people in a ship in overdrive would not know of the disaster and would not hear the last trumpet until breakout-time came.

But now, here at this moment, Calhoun felt a familiar and monstrous dizziness, and an equally familiar and intolerable nausea, and then all the sensations of a whirling, spinning fall toward nothingness. Simultaneously the little ship's vision screens lighted, the *Aesclipus Twenty* broke out of overdrive and lay floating in space surrounded by a myriad of stars, and a small but bright red light flashed luridly on the control-board.

II

Murgatroyd made the first comment. It was an indignant, protesting, *"Chee-chee! Chee-chee!"*

He was accustomed to the sensations of going into overdrive and out of it again. He didn't like them. Nobody did. Murgatroyd endured them for the sake of being where Calhoun was, being petted by Calhoun, drinking coffee with Calhoun, and on occasion engaging in long, leisurely discussions to which Murgatroyd contributed his shrill voice and stubborn conviction that he was actually conversing. Now, though, he protested. Before breakout there was normally an hour-off warning, then a five-minute warning, and then a solemn tick-tock-tick-tock until a gong sounded and then a voice counted down to zero. Murgatroyd had learned that this was the routine for breakout; but just now the extremely unpleasant sensations had happened with no warning whatever. It was upsetting. It was a violation of the accepted order of things. He said, *"Chee-chee! Chee-chee!"* even more indignantly.

Calhoun stared at the star-speckled screens. He was entirely incredulous. The red light on the control-board was notice of something solid nearby in space. But that was impossible! The Med Ship was in between-the-stars, light-years from Lanke. In between-the-stars there is nothing more solid than starlight. Solidity in this emptiness would be even more unlikely than a ship breaking out of overdrive strictly on its own decision. However, the limit of improbability was reached when not only a ship broke out of itself, but the near-object warning flashed simultaneously.

Calhoun stared at the screens. It didn't make sense, unless a highly theoretic happening had occurred. In theory, two overdrive fields might affect each other. Nothing else could. For extremely abstract reasons, it had been determined that *if* two ships passed close to each other, and *if* they were of nearly the same size, and *if* both overdrive-field units were nearly of the same strength, either or both fields could blow out. For this reason a circuit-breaker was included in all overdrive designs. The odds against such a thing were ten plus a handful of zeros to one. It had never before been known to happen. Now it had.

Calhoun slipped into the pilot's chair. He threw switches. Overdrive off. It had gone off by itself. Circuit-checker on. A special instrument verified all contacts and connections. This instrument stuttered for an instant and then flashed the signal, *"Go."* A circuit-breaker had operated, but it was now reset. It was the one in the overdrive circuit. Calhoun barely noticed that the G.C. speaker had come on also and now relayed the crackling and hissing noises that would-be poets call, "the small-talk of the stars." Calhoun found himself gazing unbelievingly at the screens.

A second-magnitude star winked out and back to brightness. A less brilliant nearby star followed. Calhoun swung the radar and looked incredulously at what it reported. There was something in between-the-stars no more than four hundred miles away. With hundreds of thousands of cubic light-years of space to move about in, something in overdrive had passed within four hundred miles of the *Aesclipus Twenty*. Two circuit-breakers had operated, and—there they were! The radar blip said the other object was a trifle smaller than the Med Ship, and it appeared to be practically motionless, moving only enough to occult two nearby stars within a few seconds.

Murgatroyd said yet again, and even more indignantly, *"Chee!! Chee!!!"*

"I didn't do it, Murgatroyd," said Calhoun abstractly. "Quiet for a minute!"

He threw another switch and the electron-telescope came on. He searched with it. He made fine adjustments for focus. Then his face expressed blank unbelief.

The telescope screen showed another ship floating in the starlight. It was not much like any other ship Calhoun had ever seen. At first it seemed a freak; not alien but eccentric, not of a non-human design, but like something made by men who'd never seen a real spaceship. There was a pipelike object sticking out of its bow.

He pressed the G.C. call-button; but first he cut off the lens that would transmit a picture of himself. He called.

"General Call!" he snapped, "General Call! Med Ship *Aesclipus Twenty* making general call! What ship's that?"

There was no answer. He frowned. Only minutes since he'd discovered himself very definitely condemned to death by an unfamiliar plague germ. A little earlier he'd been thrown off the planet Lanke for discovering too much. Before that he'd seen a dead man who couldn't come from anywhere. This extremely unusual ship couldn't come from anywhere, either.

He suddenly heard murmuring voices. There seemed to be several persons speaking in low tones near an open microphone. They were in disagreement. One voice raised itself above the others but the words were still indistinct.

"Hello!" said Calhoun sharply. "I hear your voices! Who the devil are you and what's going on?"

It occurred to him as odd that, with a plague on him and the end to all his responsibilities drawing near, he still spoke authoritatively as a Med Service man and a citizen of the galaxy to persons whose actions required to be explained. He repeated sternly, "What's going on?"

The other ship was incredible. It was patched with patches on top of patches. It was preposterous. The electron telescope could not give the finer details in mere starlight, but it was rusty and misshapen and no spaceport would ever lift it off the ground! Yet here it was.

A voice rasped from the G.C. speaker overhead, *"Look! What do you think you're doing?"* As Calhoun blinked, it said pugnaciously, *"What d'you think you're doing to us? You . . . know what I mean!"*

Calhoun said coldly, "This is Med Ship *Aesclipus Twenty*. Who are you?"

"Med Ship?" snapped the angry voice, *"wha—"*

The voice stopped abruptly, as if a hand had been clapped over someone's mouth. There were more murmurings.

Calhoun grimaced. He didn't understand this other ship. He'd cut off his own vision lens because he didn't want anybody to see him with the marks of the plague on him. Whoever spoke from the patched-up other spacecraft didn't want to be seen, either. The murmurings came to an end. The harsh voice snapped, *"Never mind that! What'd you do to us? We were going about our business when—whango! Something hit us. And we're here instead of where we were going! What'd you do?"*

Calhoun saw a stirring of the radar blip. The other craft was moving toward the Med Ship. Then he felt the edges of everything becoming twinned. His eyes were going bad again. No, he didn't want to mention his own situation. Nothing could be done for him, and dying is a strictly private matter. He felt concern for Murgatroyd, but he was a Med Ship man and there was a certain way he should act. He was impatient. Whoever was piloting the other ship knew nothing about his work. Calhoun felt the indignation of a professional with an inept amateur.

The rasping voice said truculently, *"I'm asking what you did!"*

"We did something to each other," said Calhoun coldly. "We came too close to each other. Our overdrive units got overloaded. Our circuit-breakers cut them off. Do you want more information than that?"

"What other information have you got?" demanded
the voice.

Calhoun felt feverish. The symptoms of this plague
were evidently intermittent. They came and they went.
They'd probably grow more and more severe until he
died of them—but . . .

"I take it," he said coldly, "that you don't know
what you're doing or why, because you don't know
what's happened. Do you know where you are, or how
to get to where you want to go? In other words, do you
want help?"

"What kind of help?" The question was asked with
suspicion.

"First off," said Calhoun, "you broke out of overdrive. Have you checked your circuit-breaker?"

"We don't call it that," said the voice. *"What is it?"*

Calhoun could have sworn. Instead, he closed his
eyes. He felt a diminishing of his sense of balance. He
was annoyed at the prospective loss of dignity, but he
said, "A circuit-breaker . . ." Then with his eyes closed
he told what a circuit-breaker was, and where it would
be in a power line. There should be an indicator saying,
"Off." There had to be a circuit-breaker or the other
ship would be full of smoke from burned-out insu-
lation.

It occurred to him how the other ship came to be what
it was. It was a salvage job. It had been found somewhere and cobbled back to precarious operation by men
who had to guess at the functions of what they repaired.
They'd lifted off to space with it, probably by rocket. It
was hair-raising to think of it!

All he could do was give them advice and possibly a
course in drive-time so they wouldn't over-shoot, for
now. . . .

"When you find the circuit-breaker, turn off the
overdrive switch in the control-board," he said.
"Then—not before!—throw the circuit-breaker back
on. Then you can go into overdrive again. How about
your fuel? This is a repaired spaceboat, isn't it?"

A strained silence, and then a suspicious assent.

Calhoun had them report on the fuel, the air-pressure and the air-renewal apparatus. His sense of balance began to come back. He called for more and more instrument readings.

"You haven't too much fuel," he said briefly, "but you can get to a nearby spaceport. That's all! Where do you want to go?"

"That's our business!"

"You've only so many possible destinations," Calhoun told them. "Wait a minute."

He worked the computer and the data-retrieval device. He got courses from here to the nearest inhabited planets. There were four that they could reach handily. Calhoun named them and the time in overdrive required to get reasonably close to them—to a distance the Lawlor drive could traverse in a practicable interval. . . . One of the four was Lanke, and Calhoun frankly advised against taking the agglomeration of patches that was a ship to Lanke. His reason was the considerable likelihood that there was plague on Lanke now.

"I've written down the courses and drive-times," he observed. "Write them down as I dictate."

He dictated them. Murmurings. Discussion in the background of the other spacecraft. The harsh voice said, *"Those drive-times are pretty long. There's a yellow sun that looks close."*

"It's Delhi," said Calhoun, from memory. "It has an Earth-type planet and there may have been a colony on it once. But there's nothing there now! There's something wrong with it and no ship is known to have gotten back to its home spaceport after landing on it." He added conscientiously, "It's near enough. The drive-time's only—" He gave the drive-time and the course. "But I advise you to go to one of the other nearby worlds, go into orbit around it, and call down. They'll land you somehow. And when they get you down to ground, stay there!"

His eyes were better. He looked at the screens. The freakish, patched-up boat was very, very close, not more than a score or two of miles away. He opened his mouth to protest indignantly. He was practically a dead man. At the moment, to be sure, he felt only feverish. Otherwise, nothing serious seemed to be wrong. However, he knew that a mirror would show his own self with the plague marks he'd seen on a dead man back on Lanke.

"Meanwhile," he added, "you'd better not come closer to me."

There was no answer. There were, though, murmurings near the microphone in the other ship. Someone protested against something. The rasping voice growled. There was a click, and the murmuring stopped. The other microphone had been cut off.

Calhoun's eyes improved still more. He looked at the electron telescope image of the other ship. It was turning to face him directly, the pipe at its bow bore exactly.

Suddenly, there was a mad, violent swirling of vapor or gases from the tube at the other ship's bow. Emptiness snatched at it, grasped it, separated it to atoms and threw them away.

The Med Ship was alone. Something minute remained where the preposterous other spacecraft had been. It was very, very small. It was only a moving speck of reflected starlight. Then the electron telescope screen showed it clearly. It was bright metal, it was torpedo-shaped, and it moved with a certain high, fixed velocity toward the *Aesclipus Twenty*.

Calhoun stared at it. He knew at once what it was, of course, but his reaction was modified by the situation he found himself in. Normally, he'd have been angered by the sending of a missile, probably charged with chemical explosive, to destroy the Med Ship after the attacking vessel had vanished in overdrive. He was acutely aware that he happened to be in one of the remission-periods of the plague which undoubtedly would kill him. If he'd thought of the future as one usually does, he'd have been angry that somebody had tried to destroy him. Now he had no future to be robbed of. If this shell shattered the Med Ship, it wouldn't be doing very much. It would deprive him of one—two—maybe three days of vanishing satisfactions, in which he could accomplish nothing whatever.

It didn't seem to matter. He found himself smiling wryly at the thing that came swiftly to destroy him. Suddenly, he changed his mind. He threw the Lawlor-drive switch and the Med Ship moved. When the explosive missile passed through the spot the ship had occupied, and went sturdily on and on to nowhere, he grimaced a little.

"I dodged that on your account," he told Murgatroyd. "But for you, I'd have no reason to bother. I can't live to reach headquarters, though with warning they could receive me without danger and soothe my final hours. I can't land on a nearer, colonized planet without introducing a plague and being a murderer. So I'll compromise and put you down where you just barely may have a sporting chance of surviving—where if you die, it won't be by starving in this ship. I'll do whatever futile things my condition permits."

He began to set up a course and drive-time on the ship's automatic pilot. A little later he said, "Overdrive coming, Murgatroyd!"

Then came the intolerable accompaniments of going into overdrive. Vertigo and nausea and all the sensations of an unconscionable, spinning plunge toward oblivion. Calhoun endured them doggedly. He was convinced that presently his eyes wouldn't work again and he'd probably have to crawl to move about on the ship. Anticipation of such undignified behavior was much more annoying than a mere attempt to kill him. He didn't bother to be angry about the missile.

While he felt relatively himself, he readied a meal for Murgatroyd and ate what he could, himself. He viewed with a certain detached amusement the idea that since he couldn't live to reach headquarters, and couldn't land anywhere else without introducing the plague, he was using all the splendid technical equipment of a Med Ship, representing tens of millions of credits and the life achievements of many scientists and inventors, to put a small furry creature aground on an uninhabited world rather than leave him alone in an undirected spaceship.

"This," he told Murgatroyd while the little *tormal* zestfully ate the food he'd set out, "this is ridiculous!

You'll be left alone anyhow and I've no idea how you'll make out—but . . ."

He shrugged. It would be absurd to make a dramatic production out of the business of dying.

"I'm going to put you aground and you'll have to fend for yourself. You'll probably think I'm unkind. You can't imagine my being unable to take care of you. But that's the fact. It's typical. I haven't done anything in particular."

Murgatroyd said cheerfully, *"Chee-chee!"* and finished his plate.

The *Aesclipus Twenty* drove on. Presently, Calhoun's eyes went bad again. Later, he lost all ability to distinguish up from down, or sidewise from either. He sat grimly in the pilot's chair, with a cord knotted to keep him from falling out, which for some reason he considered necessary.

He probably slept. He waked, and he was horribly thirsty. He loosened the cord and let himself fall to the floor. With all his senses assuring him that the ship revolved, he made his way on all-fours—with several falls—to where there was drinking water. He drew a glass, and then solemnly poured it out on the way to his lips, which were responsive to the feeling that he had to turn the glass to prevent it from spilling as the Med Ship turned; but the ship didn't turn and the water was wasted.

Finally, he wedged himself against the wall and refused to believe anything but his eyes. He watched the surface of the water and denied all other evidence. He drank. He drank again and again and again.

Abruptly, he slept. Then he awoke, and acute nausea was just past, but dizziness had not woken him, and the feeling of spinning fall was only slightly different from the feelings he had all along. Now, Murgatroyd was plucking at him and chattering agitatedly, *"Chee! Chee-chee! Chee!"*

Then he knew that breakout had come, and the vision screens were lighted, and he looked and saw a blazing yellow sun and innumerable stars. The ceiling speaker crackled and whispered as in normal space. The Med

Ship had arrived at the solar system of Delhi, where there was an Earth-type planet from which no ship had ever returned to its home spaceport.

There was a planet to be found, a world mostly of marshy sea with a single continent and the ruins of an abandoned, depopulated human settlement. He would present Murgatroyd to this planet and that continent and those ruins, to make what he could of them. Because he, Calhoun, was shortly to be released from all obligations and could no longer take care of Murgatroyd.

When he was back in the pilot's chair he realized how weak he'd become, obviously, the effect of the plague nearing its terminal stage. He heard someone talking. It was himself, and he paid no attention. He searched for the planet, the planet that was of no use to anybody, from which no ship returned. He found it. It was astonishingly near. One part of his brain labored gravely with the computer and inexpertly made observations while another part talked nonsense, which he resented.

There followed a period of very great confusion. There seemed to be two of him, as there appeared to be two Murgatroyds and two electron telescope screens and two control-boards. One part of his mind considered this improper, but another part gleefully took note that he had two right hands and two lefts, and watched with charmed attention as those hands simultaneously operated twin controls, and something gigantic grew more immense as the *Aesclipus Twenty* approached it. He was absurdly surprised when it became a monstrous black hole in the universe of stars. The Med Ship had swung around to its night-side in an orbit Calhoun's then-disregarded sane brain-fraction had contrived. He seemed to sleep, and to wake again, and he was extremely thirsty. Suddenly, the sane part of his mind declared loudly, that there was a settlement! It showed on the electron telescope screen! Then the part of his brain that was angry with the fevered part forcibly took charge.

The confusion he experienced did not lessen, to be sure. The part of a man which is his total consciousness, the part that uses brain-cells to store memories and present data for judgment, the part that uses brain-cells to control his body, the part which recognizes the phenomena of consciousness, that part, still functioned. One's brain can become an unreliable instrument, from fever or alcohol, but there is an ego, an id, a something, which struggles to make sane use of it. There were moments when he knew that he was singing and that his body was behaving in a fashion totally irrelevant to his situation and his purpose. There were other moments when he seemed to control his body which was astonishingly feeble, and he was clearly aware that he had turned on the Med Ship's emergency rockets and that it was balancing on a pencil-thin, blue-white flame in mid-air.

Confusion came again. He was lecturing Murgatroyd on medical ethics. While he lectured, the Med Ship and all its contents turned somersaults, as did the planet outside. Calhoun knew that proper planets do not turn somersaults in their own skies, so he treated this behavior with the dignified contempt it deserved.

More chaotic sensations, so bewildering that they ceased to be impressions. Suddenly, there was a distinct thump, and he was shocked into rationality. He realized that the Med Ship had touched ground. He had cut off the rockets. He stared at the scene the vision screen showed.

The *Aesclipus Twenty* had landed in a swampy valley bottom among low mountains; there was vegetation outside which swayed gently in a strong breeze. On higher ground he saw white, man-made walls with empty window openings and tree tops showing where there should have been roofs. Close to the Med Ship there was swamp, marsh, stagnant puddles, and indigenous growing things.

Murgatroyd said, *"Chee-chee!"* in an anxious tone. Calhoun was weary beyond belief, but he roused.

"All right, Murgatroyd," he said dizzily, "I've done a very silly thing, and maybe I've done you no good at all, but if you'll follow me I'll finish it."

With an overwhelming lassitude, making his arms and legs seem to weigh tons, he left the chair by the control-board. He stayed on his feet almost half the way to the air-lock, by leaning heavily against the wall. Then his knees buckled under him and the rest of the way he crawled. At the inner air-lock door he reached up and by pure habit pushed the succession of buttons which opened both the inner and the outer doors. They rumbled wide, unsealing themselves. Air came in. There was the smell of mud and vegetation and unfamiliar life. There was also one particular odor which should have been unpleasing, but that it was so faint it seemed only strange.

"There!" said Calhoun. He waved his hand feebly. "There you are, Murgatroyd! There's a world for you. You'll be lonely, and maybe you'll die or be killed by some local predator, and maybe I'm doing you a dirty trick. But my intentions are of the best. Shoo! Get out so I can close the ports again."

Murgatroyd said, *"Chee!"* in a bewildered tone. It was not customary for Calhoun to crawl on his hands and knees and urge him out the air-lock. Calhoun was behaving strangely. Murgatroyd looked at him apprehensively.

"Chee!" he said. *"Chee-chee!"*

Calhoun did not answer. He felt himself slipping down to the Med Ship's floor. He was intolerably weary and weak. He was wholly confused. The sane part of his consciousness relaxed. He'd finished the task he'd set himself. If he rested, maybe he'd get back enough strength to close the air-lock door. It didn't really matter. It was annoying that he hadn't been able to get word of the Lanke situation to headquarters, but the plague had been on Lanke before. The doctors knew it. They were terrified by it, but maybe . . . maybe . . .

Wryly, at the moment he believed his moment of death, Calhoun conceded to himself that he'd done the best he could. It wasn't good enough.

III

WHEN CALHOUN AWOKE, or at any rate regained consciousness, Murgatroyd was saying, *"Chee-chee! Chee-chee!"* in his high-pitched voice. He sounded unhappy. There were smells in the air. Calhoun was not on the floor, but in his bunk. He heard footsteps and the sound of wind blowing. There were cracklings which were the sounds of the G.C. speaker reporting normal shortwave broadcasts from a nearby sun. There were other and unidentifiable sounds.

Calhoun opened his eyes. This instant, instinctive effort to sit up achieved nothing whatever. He was almost wholly without strength. He did manage to make a croaking sound, and someone came to the door of his sleeping cabin. He didn't even see clearly, just now, but he said in a fretful tone and with extreme exertion, "This is the devil! I've got a plague of some kind, and it's horribly infectious! You've got to set up some sort of quarantine around me. Get a doctor to the airlock—don't let him come in!—I'll tell him about it."

A voice—a girl's voice—said evenly, "That's all right. We know about the plague. This is Delhi. We should know, shouldn't we?"

Murgatroyd hopped up on the bunk on which Calhoun inexplicably lay. He said agitatedly, *"Chee! Chee-chee!"*

Calhoun found his voice improved. He said as fretfully as before, "No doubt. No doubt. But—this is the devil!"

A surpassing bitterness filled him. There were people here where he'd landed. Inhabitants. He was a Med Ship man and he'd brought plague here! Quite automatically, he assumed that in some moment of unrealized confusion he must have set up the wrong course and drive-time in the Med Ship's automatic-pilot. He'd had four courses and timings at hand to give to the other ship encountered in space. He must blindly have used the wrong one when setting course for Delhi. . . .

The girl's voice had said this was Delhi! But it couldn't be! No ship had ever gotten home from Delhi! It couldn't be colonized! It had been tried, and there were ruins to prove it, but there was something wrong with it, something yet unknown but utterly fatal. No ship had ever returned. . . .

He couldn't stop to think of such things now. He'd brought plague here!

"Get a doctor to the air-lock door," he commanded as fiercely as his weakness would allow. "Quick! I've got to tell him. . . ."

"We haven't any doctors," said the girl's voice, as evenly as before, "and you don't need one. This is Delhi. There's no use in having doctors on Delhi! Not for the plague! You're all right!"

He saw, with clearing eyes, that a figure bent over him. It was a girl with dark brown eyes. She lifted his head and gave him a drink from a cup.

"We heard your rockets, Rob and I," she said in a tone from which all warmth had been removed. "We could tell you were landing. We hurried, and we got here before anybody else. We found you halfway out of the air-lock with a tame little animal crying to you to wake up. So we brought you inside and Rob's watching now to see if anybody else heard you land. You can hope nobody did."

Calhoun decided that he was delirious again. He struggled to clear his brain. Murgatroyd said anxiously, *"Chee-chee?"*

"I suppose so," said Calhoun drearily. Then he said more loudly, "There has to be a quarantine! I'm carrying contagion. . . ."

The girl did not answer. Murgatroyd chattered at him. It sounded as if, relieved now, he were scolding Calhoun for not having paid attention to him before.

Calhoun fell, tumbled, dropped, back into slumber.

It was a very deep sleep. A dreamless sleep. He came out of it an indefinite time later, when he could not tell whether it was day or night. There was silence, now, except for the tiny background noises from the tape. The air-lock door was evidently closed. Murgatroyd was a warm spot touching Calhoun's leg through the bed covering. Calhoun noted that his brain was clear. His fever was gone. Which could mean either that it was burned out, or that he was. In the latter case, he was experiencing that clear-headedness sometimes granted to people just about to die.

He heard a peculiar small sound. Someone—a girl—was weeping while trying not to make a noise. Calhoun blinked. He must have moved in some other fashion too, because Murgatroyd waked instantly and asked, *"Chee-chee? Chee-chee-chee?"*

There was a stirring in the control-room. The girl who'd given him a drink came in. She looked as if she'd been crying; Calhoun said, "I feel very much better. Thanks. Can you tell me where I am and what's happened?"

The girl tried to smile, not very successfully. She said, "You're on Delhi, to stay. We've locked the air-lock doors and nobody can get in. They've only banged and called, so far. Rob's looking over the ship now, trying to find out how to smash it so it can't possibly be repaired. He says you can't lift anyhow. The ground here is swamp. Your landing-feet have sunk in the mud and you can't possibly get clear. So that's all right for the time being."

Calhoun stared at her. He ignored the statement that the Med Ship was permanently aground.

"Delhi—locked doors—" He said incredulously,

"Look! Delhi's not inhabited. Its air's wrong, or something! No ship that's ever landed on Delhi has ever gotten home again! Delhi doesn't have people. . . ."

"There are a good two thousand of them outside just now," said the girl as detachedly as before. "And every one of them will tear this ship apart with his bare hands rather than let you leave without taking them. But the swamp has taken care of that." Then she said abruptly, "I'll get you something to eat."

She went out and Calhoun groped for meaning in this addition to the improbabilities that had started on Lanke. They'd begun with a dead man who apparently came from nowhere, and the terror he evoked in the medical profession of Lanke. There'd been the plague Calhoun contracted from the most cursory of examinations of that dead man, and the patched-up lifeboat quite impossibly encountered in space. It also couldn't have come from anywhere. Above all there was the plague, which on Lanke was horribly dreaded, but which this girl disregarded. Now there were two thousand inhabitants on the uninhabited planet Delhi who wouldn't let the ship leave without them, and there was somebody—his name was Rob?—who intended to wreck the Med Ship so it couldn't leave at all.

The sum of all this was bewilderment. For example, the plague. He didn't have it anymore. It was a spontaneous recovery. If its victims recovered, why the terror on Lanke? Also, why were there two thousand people who wanted to leave Delhi, and somebody named Rob who didn't want anybody to leave—not even Calhoun?

He puzzled furiously while he waited for the girl to return. He heard movements. Somebody came up into the control-room from the storage decks below. He heard voices. If that was Rob, he'd reason to be uneasy. He called. A tall, broad young man of about his own age looked in the door.

"You're Rob," said Calhoun politely. His voice was stronger than he'd expected. "Would you mind telling me why you want to wreck my ship? I'm told that it's hopelessly bogged down in marshy ground now. Why add to the disaster by wrecking it?''

"Enough men," said the young man, with some grimness, "could dig it out. And then it could go away. That has to be made impossible!''

"But this is a Med Ship!" protested Calhoun. "It has a special status!''

"And this is Delhi," said Rob sternly. "There's a plague that's native to this planet. We who live here don't have it. If someone comes here with it, he recovers. But if we leave, we develop it, and if anyone from here landed on another world, he'd die of it with the people he took it to. So nobody must leave!''

Calhoun considered for a moment.

"But somebody has, not long ago. In fact, I caught the plague from him.''

He couldn't have proved the connection of the dead man on Lanke with the freakish spaceship and that with Delhi, but he believed the connection was there. The man named Rob proved it by grinding his teeth.

"A crime!" he said fiercely. "And maybe we'll be bombed for it! It's another reason this ship has to be wrecked. We're quarantined. We have to be! The quarantine mustn't be broken!''

Calhoun considered again. There were people on Delhi, not less than two thousand of them, who would seize this ship if they could, take aboard as many as could crowd into it, and go on to other worlds where—obviously—they did not believe the plague would appear. On the other hand, there were people who knew that they'd die of the plague if they ever landed on any other world, and the plague would spread from them. The two views were contradictory, and Calhoun was for the moment in between them. He was sure the plague could be spread, though. He'd caught it. Those who wanted to risk everything to leave Delhi and escape whatever they hated here, they wouldn't listen to argument or listen to evidence. Such states of mind are standard with a certain proportion of any population.

Calhoun rubbed his nose reflectively. "This plague

and this quarantine hasn't been reported to the Med Service," he observed. "When did it start, and why?"

"Delhi's been quarantined since the first ship landed," said Rob, grimly. "A ship came by and sent a lifeboat down to explore. It reported valuable minerals. The ship went back to Lanke—it hadn't landed—for equipment and supplies while the spaceboat explored further. They didn't know about the plague."

"It hadn't appeared?"

"No. The ship went back to Delhi and landed with machinery and supplies. They opened one mine. They built a settlement. They loaded the ship with ore. It went back to Lanke."

He paused dramatically. Calhoun said, "And . . ."

"It never got there! It simply never arrived. Months later an automatic distress-call was picked up from far out beyond the Lanke solar system. A ship went out to investigate. It was the ship from Delhi, floating where it had broken out of overdrive. There was no living creature aboard. Everybody was dead. It was the plague, but they didn't understand. They towed the ship to port and unloaded it; plague spread over the whole planet. They had to burn down cities to get rid of it! Delhi has been quarantined ever since, more than a hundred years!"

"The Med Service should have been told," said Calhoun, annoyed. "Something would have been done about it!"

There was a sudden metallic clanging. It was a blow of something heavy against the Med Ship's exterior air-lock door. There was another blow, and another, and another. Rob listened for a moment and shrugged.

"Sometimes," he said, "there's somebody dropped to us by parachute. They have the plague. They recover. They tell us what other worlds are like, now. They don't often get reconciled to staying here!"

The clanging continued. The girl came in from the control-room. She said in the same detached voice, "They're trying to break in with sledge-hammers. But some of them are cutting down trees and trimming them." She looked at Calhoun. "We can help you into the other room if you want to see."

Calhoun found himself struggling to rise. The tall man helped him. The girl said, "Rob has one thing wrong. Not all the people who're parachuted down to us have the plague!"

Rob made a deprecating sound. Calhoun began to move toward the cabin door. He was stronger than he'd thought. Once he was up, with the help of Rob on one side and the wall on the other, he made his way into the control-room. Rob helped him into the pilot's chair at the control-board.

He stared at the vision screens. The *Aesclipus Twenty* had landed in a marshy, meadowlike level space with mountains all around it. He could see the white walls of what had been a settlement on a mountain side, but it was plainly abandoned. There were only walls. Trees grew all the way down into the valley bottom, and men swung axes among them. As he looked, a tree toppled. Others had already been felled. He swung an outside pick-up to look down the Med Ship's side. A brawny, red-headed man was swinging a sledge-hammer against the sealing strip of the door. The impacts rang through the ship. Calhoun could see, too, where the flat parts of the landing-fins had pressed into the soggy soil. They'd sunk a good two yards below the surface and mud had flowed in over them. They were well buried.

"I'd guess," said Calhoun, "that they're cutting down the trees to make shears from which they can swing a battering ram. I doubt that a sledge-hammer can break the air-lock door. But a heavy enough log, swung hard enough, might do it. There are a lot of people here!"

The valley floor was black with human figures. There were at least two thousand of them, staring at the Med Ship, moving about restlessly, or standing in groups on the ground that might support a man, but not a spacecraft standing upright and heavy. Still others labored at the cutting and trimming of trees. There was somehow an air of tenseness, of impassioned feeling among the figures. Calhoun flipped on the outside microphones and the noise they made became audible. There was a growling, hurried murmur of voices. Sometimes, there were shouts. It was not a group of curiosity seekers, here to look at a spaceship come to ground where spaceships never came. It was a mob. It made the sound of a mob.

"Don't they know there's somebody alive in here?" asked Calhoun.

Rob said hesitantly, "I wanted to disable the ship. I thought it might take some time. So when we found they were coming we closed the air-lock and didn't answer the calls or their bangings on the hull. I think they've decided that somebody landed the ship and then died."

The girl said detachedly, "Not long ago they finished mending a lifeboat that was wrecked here generations ago. They went to Lanke, and they came back. One man didn't return. . . . They'd hidden their ship under water. Maybe he couldn't find it after he found what he was looking for. They may think that maybe he managed to steal this ship from the spaceport and has just gotten here. It could have been. He could have been wounded. He could have landed the ship and died."

"Only he didn't," said Calhoun with some dryness. "He didn't get at the spaceport. He developed the plague instead. He gave it to me. And I met the lifeboat, too. I think I was of some service to them."

He didn't mention that for payment the freak spaceboat had fired a missile at the Med Ship. Even that was reasonable as things became clearer. If Delhi was a quarantined world, with not enough of a population to maintain a modern civilization, it would have to go back toward the primitive and the savage. The desperation of its inhabitants would be absolute. If they could manage to cobble a long-wrecked spaceboat so it could take to space, and if because of the plague all nearby planets were its enemies, astronauts from Delhi would feel justified in destroying the Med Ship to keep their secret from becoming known. They'd do it in the hope of going on to a successful breaking of the quarantine that held them on this intolerable world. Yet the plague made that quarantine necessary.

"It must smell pretty bad out there, with all those people moving about," said the girl abruptly.

Calhoun turned his head.

"Why?"

"It's marsh," said the girl. "It smells when it's stirred up. It's strong! They say that on other worlds it isn't bad. Here it is. When new people are parachuted down to us, they hate it. We're used to the regular smell of things, I suppose. We don't notice. But we don't like to stir things up. Then we notice!"

Calhoun said, "Marsh . . . how about water?"

"At worst we boil it," she said evenly. "It isn't as bad, then, as un-boiled. Sometimes we filter it through fresh charcoal. That's better. There's a dam with electric generators that were installed for the mine. Some of us run that to electrolyze water into gases that we burn back together again. The flame destroys the cause of the smell, and then we condense the steam the flame combines to. That's the best, but it's a luxury and we can't afford luxuries." She looked at the vision screen. "There are charcoal breathing-masks for working when you have to stir things up. But making charcoal isn't fun, and it has to be fresh or it doesn't work. There aren't many masks out there. It must be pretty bad."

Calhoun looked at her for long seconds.

"Have you tried my drinking water?"

She shook her head. He made a gesture. She drew water from the spigot by the food-readier. Her expression changed.

"Water tastes like this? All the time?"

She pressed a glass on Rob. He tasted it and handed back the glass.

"That," she said fiercely, "is enough to want to leave Delhi forever! I'll never taste water again without thinking of this!"

Calhoun said suddenly, "You speak of new people parachuted down. Why are they sent here?"

Her lips compressed.

"Some have the plague, not many. A case turns up now and then, they say, leftover infection, maybe, from the plague they had on Lanke . . . from the other planets. . . ."

"Yes," said Calhoun. "The other planets! Which ones?"

She named three, besides Lanke. They were the three whose names and courses he'd offered to the cobbled spaceboat he'd encountered in space. They were the three colonized worlds closest to Lanke. If they sent unwilling colonists to Delhi, which they could not ever hope to leave, it was simple enough to understand that the men in the freakish ship wouldn't accept Calhoun's suggestion of them for destinations.

"How'd they get into the picture? It was Lanke that had the plague, wasn't it—and hid it?"

The girl shrugged.

"People were sent here later, from the other planets; they say that the government of Lanke got frightened, years and years ago, that another nearby planet might try to colonize Delhi as they'd tried to do. And it might get the plague, and it might re-infect Lanke. So as a state secret, it told the nearest planets why they mustn't explore Delhi. They checked on it. One of them sent a research team to try to make Delhi usable, because there are minerals here. But they couldn't do anything, and they couldn't go home. So for a while supplies were dropped to them. They lived all right, but they couldn't leave. Presently, it occurred to somebody that Delhi would be a good place to send life prisoners, criminals. So they did. Then they sent political offenders, it was very discreetly done—now . . ."

"Now what?"

"It's said that the crime rate on the four planets is very low," she told him bitterly, "because professional criminals—disappear. It saves the cost of some prisons and guards and the expense of a free criminal class to the others. So we're the sweepings of the four planets. Some of us were accused of having the plague when— we didn't. Naturally, it's all very secret!"

She looked at him defiantly. Calhoun nodded.

"That's quite possible," he admitted. "In any case it would be told, and the people who told it would believe it."

The girl looked at him with angry eyes and compressed lips.

"Some of us," said Rob severely, "accept the facts. We aren't all wrapped up in our own tragedies. Some of us think of our inevitable obligation to humanity at large. So we won't try to leave, and spread the plague!"

Rob frowned portentously. There was friction between these two. The girl clenched her hands. The sledge-hammer struck again, and again, and again. There was likely to be a quarrel between the man and the girl who between them had quite probably saved Calhoun's life. So he said dryly, "Swinging that sledge must be fatiguing. In fact the whole situation outside seems unfortunate. I'll change it."

He moved certain switches. He adjusted a dial. He pressed a button.

A pencil-thin flame shot down from between the Med Ship's landing-fins. It was pure, blue-white incandescence. It was the ship's emergency rocket, on which it had landed and by which it would have to take off again. For an instant the flame splashed out between the fins, and it was so bright that the daylight nearby seemed darkened by contrast. Then the flame bored down. In solid stone the *Aesclipus Twenty* could melt and boil away bed-rock to a depth of eighty feet. Here, in saturated meadow soil, enormous clouds of steam and smoke arose. Steam-loosened mud flew about. It looked as if the Med Ship squatted on a monstrous arc-flame which was blasting away the marsh on which it rested.

The flame cut off. It had burned for ten seconds or less, developing—under control from the pilot's chair—something less than one-eighth of its maximum power. The ship hadn't stirred.

"I suspect," said Calhoun, "that they think I tried to lift off then and couldn't. But maybe they'll think I could make a battering-ram crew very uncomfortable, close to the ship as they'd have to work.''

He watched the running figures below. There was no longer a crowd gathered about the Med Ship. Those nearest were in headlong flight. The red-headed man who'd been swinging the sledge crashed a way through those fleeing ahead of him. The roar of the rockets had stopped. Some fleeing men began to glance around them as they ran.

Then the mob ceased to flee. It formed a circle three hundred yards across, two thousand human beings facing inward. Some of them shook clenched fists. The outside microphones brought in a babbling, yapping noise that was not great in volume but appalling in the fury it expressed.

"They're not thinking straight,'' said Calhoun. "There are two thousand of them. Even if they could land somewhere and not die of the plague or carry it, even if they could, how many would this ship carry? How many could its air-renewer supply?'' Then he said in a different tone to the girl, "You said that not everybody who's parachuted down to Delhi has the plague. Why else should they be dropped here?''

She said fiercely, "It's a way to get rid of people! It's politics! It's crooked! Anybody can be accused of having the plague. Sometimes they do have it. But sometimes they haven't. My father didn't have it, and he was sent here. Rob's grandfather didn't, and he was too. There are others!''

Calhoun nodded. He said thoughtfully, "That may be true, because there was opportunity for it. But, true or not, people would believe it. And I guess, too, that you tell each other that the plague's worn itself out. Nobody has it here. Nobody who's landed here ever gets it. If they have it when they come, they're cured immediately. I was! So how could they give it to anybody else?''

"Yes!'' said the girl passionately. "That's it! How could we? Rob says we have to stay here! Here where the food has no taste, and the water. . . . Where we're made nauseated when we plow the ground to grow food! Where . . . Rob says we shouldn't marry and shouldn't have children because they'd be doomed in advance to become savages! He says . . ."

Rob said unhappily, "I think that's true, Elna."

"How could it be true? How could a disease that nobody can have be carried by anybody?"

Calhoun stirred in the pilot's chair.

"I think," he said apologetically, "that I have to get back to my cabin. The plague I had has made me ridiculously weak. But I have to admit, Elna, that I caught the plague from a man who left Delhi and went to Lanke and immediately developed the plague. Rob is right. Nobody must leave Delhi, but me. I have to get some help from Med Service Headquarters. Nobody else must leave. Nobody!"

Rob helped him into his cabin again. He sank gratefully down on his bunk. The girl Elna came in minutes later with another bowl of broth. Her expression was equal parts rebellion and despair. Calhoun was suddenly so sleepy that the spoon fell from his fingers. Rob supported him while Elna fed him, spoonful by spoonful. He was totally asleep the instant she'd finished.

Elna waked him by shaking his shoulder, he didn't know how long afterward. Murgatroyd made shrill protests. Calhoun waked easily and completely, and on the instant he knew that a surprising amount of strength had come back to him. With less than a desperate effort he actually sat up. He swung his feet over the side of the bunk. He became confident that he could walk, if in a wobbly fashion. However, he still wasn't up to rough-and-tumble exercise.

"Rob's gone down," said Elna desperately, "to start smashing up the ship's drive so it can't possibly be repaired!"

"Go tell him," said Calhoun, "that the drive-units from the lifeboat just back from Lanke can be used in this ship. They'll smash the quarantine. Wrecking my drive won't stop them. Anyhow the crowd outside will tear us all to small bits—including you and including

Rob—if they break in and find the ship's been smashed after landing. Tell him to come up and I'll give him better instructions."

She searched his face briefly and hurried away. He heard her footsteps clattering down the metal stair to the lower parts of the Med Ship. Murgatroyd said, *"Chee?"*

"Of course not!" said Calhoun severely. "We are members of the Interstellar Medical Service! We can't let a situation like this keep on! I should be able to stand up, now, and do something about it. Let's try!"

He found a handhold, and with arms and legs working together he got to a standing position. He was still uncertain in his steps, and his expression went wry. Finally, he got across the cabin. He opened a closet and found a robe. He put it on. He made his way unsteadily into the control-room. He opened another cupboard and brought out a blaster, almost a miniature, for the pocket. He adjusted the strength of its bolt and put it out of his robe. He went dizzily to the pilot's seat at the control-board. He threw the G.C. switch.

"General call!" he said into the transmitter. "General call! Med Ship *Aesclipus Twenty* calling repaired spaceboat or any other ship. General call!"

He waited, blinking at the vision screens. Ther⸱ were still very many people outside. A good proportion seemed to be laboring where the trees of the nearby mountainside ceased to grow because the ground was too marshy for their kind. He saw a disturbance. A chopped through tree trunk fell.

"General call," he repeated patiently. "General call. Med Ship *Aesclipus Twenty* calling repaired . . ."

A rasping voice interrupted. It was a familiar voice to Calhoun. He'd heard it during that improbable encounter of two ships in between-the-stars. Now it said unpleasantly, *"You followed us, eh? What for?"*

"Clinical information," said Calhoun. "One man of your crew didn't come back to Delhi with you. He had the plague. In fact, I got it from him. He's dead now, by the way. Why didn't the rest of you get it?"

The voice growled, *"What're you asking me for?"*

"I'm landed on Delhi, in a swamp," said Calhoun. "It looks like I can't lift off, because I'm mired here. There's a crowd—a mob—outside, trying to contrive a way to break into my ship so they can take it over, dig it out, and lift off for somewhere else. After they break in I'm not likely to get much information. Information like the information that tells me you hid your boat underwater while somebody went to figure out the chances of seizing a ship there by surprise and getting aloft on emergency rockets. That was the idea, wasn't it?"

The harsh voice was very harsh when it demanded, *"Who told you that?"*

"Never mind," said Calhoun. "But you didn't send only one man! How many?"

A pause. The other voice said cagily, *"There were two. But one began to see double and came back."*

"Which," Calhoun observed, "was proof that when people from Delhi land on another planet they develop the plague. You'd stopped believing in that. But it was so. It pretty well killed the idea of seizing a ship without warning, picking up a crew on Delhi and moving on to seize yet other ships and break the quarantine to small and quivering bits. Right?"

The voice grated, *"What are you driving at?"*

"I'd like some cooperation," said Calhoun. "You know you can't work that scheme now! You've promised to break the quarantine by force. Now you're afraid to admit it can't be done. Right?"

"What—are—you—driving—at?" rasped the voice.

"I'm Med Service," said Calhoun. "Tell me what you know about the plague, tell your followers to leave my ship alone and to gather information and biological specimens I ask for. Then we'll have the Med Service taking over as it should have done a hundred years ago. Shortly, there'll be no more plague and no more quarantine."

Silence. What Calhoun proposed was sound sense, but it was not the sort of sound sense that people would accept. The Med Service was not a reality to the people of Delhi, and the quarantine was, and was moreover the deliberate act of the nearby occupied worlds. They were imprisoned on a world which stank, and when its surface was disturbed it reeked, and even drinking water had to be boiled before it could endurably be drank. They could have no modern tools, lest they contrive some way to damage its enemies. They could have no science, because they had to be kept imprisoned. Men will not endure such conditions, necessary or not. They won't endure them!

Calhoun said evenly, "I know I'm asking a lot. There's a mob outside my ship now, contriving some way to break into it and seize it, so they can raid a spaceport somewhere and seize other ships to repeat and spread their revolt, and the plague! But you know it won't work! You can leave Delhi a thousand times over, but if you take the plague with you . . . it's no good!"

Silence. Calhoun, waiting, shook his head to himself. Delhi had had a century of isolation and hopelessness, and the arrival of other hopeless prisoners only reminded them of the intolerable nature of the lives they lived. Under such conditions men forget what they don't want to remember, and somehow come to believe everything they wish to be true. They'd developed a blind irrational belief that their imprisonment was unnecessary. They'd developed an unreasoned, impassioned faith in possible escape. They'd rebuilt a shattered spaceboat, learning the functions of the apparatus they rebuilt as they rebuilt it. They'd set out to accomplish the impossible.

Calhoun was asking them to abandon all efforts to help themselves, and depend on a Med Service of which most of them had not even ever heard. They couldn't do it. Especially not with the *Aesclipus Twenty* aground and needing only to be overwhelmed and then extracted from the marsh for their most desperate needs to be fulfilled. They'd only been told of the plague. They didn't have it. They didn't see it, and they were imprisoned because of it. Few of them really believed in it, as Rob did.

So Calhoun was not surprised when the rasping voice cursed him horribly and cut off communication without bothering to reply. It was a refusal.

His expression was wry as he said to Murgatroyd, "He's a disappointed man, Murgatroyd. That's why he's suspicious and angry. But I'm disappointed too. I think he could have found out things for me that I'll have trouble learning myself."

Extra movement in a vision screen drew his eyes to it. A felled and trimmed tree trunk moved from its place toward the Med Ship. It was carried by not less than fifty men, holding to short ropes passed under it. The people of Delhi had no wheeled vehicles to carry so great a load. If they'd owned them, the marsh would have made them useless. However, they did have arms and muscles. By pure brute strength, sweating in their toil, they brought the log slowly down into the valley. Calhoun had never seen the physical strength of fifty men applied to a single effort. Men used engines or machines for such work. This was like those legendary achievements of barbaric kings and pharaohs. Had they been moving stones, had there been whips cracking to urge them on, he'd have felt that he saw the process of the building of the pyramids on Earth, which were still mentioned in primary grade school texts all over the galaxy.

Then he heard the girl Elna and the man Rob coming up from below. Rob said in icy fury, "You're a woman and I'd have had to hurt you to keep you from interfering. It's because you've been listening to him! He persuaded you, but millions would die if this ship lifted off and went to another world! So I'm going to stop his persuading! Sick or well, if I have to hurt him . . ."

"But, Rob!" protested the girl. "Think, if it's true! Think! If there's a Med Service and if it can end the plague for always, think of us! You wouldn't feel that we mustn't marry. You wouldn't think there should be no children to become savages! And we could be so happy. . . ."

Calhoun raised his eyebrows. Murgatroyd said, *"Chee!"* in what happened to seem a very cynical tone. The heads of the man and girl appeared at the top of the stairwell. Rob's eyes were hot and accusing.

"You!" he cried furiously at sight of Calhoun. "This ship in the hands of the fools outside could mean all the human race wiped out! Don't you see it? Nobody must leave Delhi! Nobody! And as a beginning . . ."

They reached the floor of the control-room. Rob's hands clenched and unclenched. He moved slowly toward Calhoun, glaring in a very dramatic fashion.

"You display a very noble character, Rob," said Calhoun with some irony. "Self-sacrificing, too! It must be very satisfying to feel that way! But I almost agree with you. It's true that nobody must leave Delhi. Nobody but me. If you can't agree to that, we'll have to settle it right now!"

He drew the pocket-blaster from under his robe.

IV

THE SETTLEMENT WAS necessarily on Calhoun's terms. Calhoun had a weapon. Rob didn't. Calhoun wanted to do something. Rob wanted to keep something from being done. Calhoun was an essentially simple person, inclined to think of objective results in completely matter-of-fact terms. Rob reasoned emotionally, with much attention to noble ideals he was unable to compare with reality. Calhoun considered that he had a job to do. So the matter had to be settled as he decided. Rob had a very fine stock of invective and a splendid equipment of scorn. He made use of both in what he obviously considered an especially fine opportunity for stinging speech. But it was only speech. Calhoun listened unmoved.

"All right," he said presently, with some grimness. "That'll be enough. You've got it off your chest. What do you do now? Play along or sulk over it? I have to leave this place, for Med Headquarters. I need, right now, some mud from the swamp outside for what should be obvious reasons. You can get it. Will you?"

Rob ground his teeth. He refused, eloquently. Calhoun shrugged. Elna said, "I'll get it."

She did, while Rob glowered. It was only a matter of cracking the air-lock door and reaching down with a long ladle, while Calhoun watched the vision screens for signs of mob action. He literally wasn't up to the physical effort of getting a mud sample. There were in-furiated shoutings from the mob outside. Men hunted for stones to throw. There weren't any, on the surface of a semi-swamp. Elna brought up a ladleful of black stuff with evil-smelling water on top of it. She silently gave it to Calhoun. He put the mud into a centrifuge to separate the solid matter from the water that saturated it. He sat down, to rest while the centrifuge ran. Rob glared at him in the extremely unhappy state of a man with impassioned convictions he couldn't act on. He was doubtless quite capable of dying for the sake of an abstract humanity. The high drama of such an action would certainly help him do it.

The centrifuge delivered pellets of damp soil and a considerable amount of browning, malodorous water. It had been stirred and—as Elna had mentioned—it smelled very badly. The air in the ship was Delhi air, now, and doubtless it reeked also, but not so strongly that one couldn't get used to it. However, getting used to the smell of stirred swamp water was another matter.

Calhoun roused himself. He filled a culture slide almost full of the unpleasant stuff. He put it in the culture microscope which would let him watch living microbes living. A six-inch screen beside it showed the magnified image. He watched.

Without electronic amplification of the image, it was not possible to watch living microscopic creatures at high magnification. For genuinely high optical power, much light would be required on the slide. Beyond a certain point, that light would be lethal to microbes. But electronic amplification made a sharp, clear image of everything in the culture slide. He saw the equivalent of an amoeba. He noted that it seemed furry. He saw the equivalent of rotifers. They spun madly for a certain time, and then stopped and spun as madly in an opposite direction.

Then he saw the spherical, pigmented microscopic spheres he was looking for.

But these microbes did not dance. They did not fission feverishly. They moved, but very slowly. Doubtless, they did multiply, but Calhoun saw no example of it. Save for lack of activity, though, they were twins of the plague organism.

"Ever hear of ecology, Elna?" asked Calhoun. "I think I'm observing a micro-ecological system at work."

The girl shook her head. She looked at Rob. He sat with his arms grandly folded. Calhoun didn't notice. He said, pleased, "Microbes adjust to their environment, like larger things. And like larger things, their numbers in nature depend on very complicated processes. Small animals multiply fast, because they're eaten by larger things. Larger things multiply slowly, because if they multiply too fast they wipe out their food supply and starve. There are some very curious causes for the limitation of animal populations so they won't all starve to death. *If* this bug I'm looking at is what I think it may be, it's a most interesting example."

The girl did not seem to hear him. She looked at Rob. He ignored her, with conscious tragic dignity. She'd helped Calhoun.

"Here," said Calhoun, "are what look like plague microbes in their normal Delhian environment. They're sluggish and practically comatose. Phagocytes could take care of an invasion of them into a human body. But here—" He touched a culture bottle in which he had thriving plague microbes growing, cultured from a scrap of a dead man's clothing. "Here I have what may be the same bug in a Lanke environment. The bug is wildly active. It could cause the devil of a plague, on Lanke. I'm going to see what it would do on Delhi."

He looked up for an expression of interest. The girl looked unhappily at Rob. Calhoun stared, and frowned, and shrugged. He took up a pipette which might have been made for the smallest of dolls to use. He introduced dancing, swarming, preposterously proliferating microbes from the Lanke culture into the slide of Delhi swamp water.

Rob said harshly, "They're bringing a log to be a battering ram, since the sledge-hammer didn't work."

Calhoun looked at the outside vision screen. The log was moving slowly across the marshy ground on fifty pairs of feet. It looked like a monstrous creeping insect.

"They're stumbling," said Calhoun. "They can't batter while they're stumbling."

He turned back to the culture microscope. The half-drop of liquid from the pipette had contained thousands and thousands of the dark round microscopic spheres. They showed on the screen, now: dancing, swarming, dividing into half-globes and growing back to full spheres again. Their activity was more than feverish. It was frantic.

In minutes it diminished. The dancings and dartings slowed. The infinitesimal objects ceased their headlong multiplication. They became languid. Gradually, they seemed to sleep. Now and again they made trivial, stagnant motions. They were not dead. They were not spores, they were no longer active. Calhoun regarded them with satisfaction. He said, "Ah-h-h!"

It was a most gratifying development. It couldn't have been observed on Lanke, because there was no Delhian material to show it. It couldn't have been seen on Delhi. There were no super-active specimens on Delhi. Only a Med Ship man could have made the observation, with Med Ship equipment. Calhoun looked triumphantly about. Elna still looked unhappily at Rob, and Rob still wore an air compounded equally of fury and of martyrdom.

"Murgatroyd," said Calhoun, "at least you'll be interested! Things are looking up!"

"*Chee?*" said Murgatroyd.

He padded across the floor and swung up to the lab table unfolded from the wall. What Calhoun was doing meant nothing to Murgatroyd, of course, but Calhoun had invited him to conversation. Murgatroyd peered at the microscope screen as if it meant something to him. He said, "*Chee-chee! Chee-chee!*"

"Exactly!" said Calhoun. "This bug is comatose on Delhi, where there is no plague. It's wildly active on Lanke, where there has been, can be, and probably already is plague. We'll return these bugs to a Lanke environment.''

He made it, distilled water and a nutrient substance for them to feed on. It was practically the environment of Lanke. He returned the just-made-comatose microbes to the sort of environment in which plague germs throve. These microbes regained all the enthusiasm of multiplication and dancing and—doubtless—the production of deadly toxins they'd shown before.

''Something on Delhi,'' said Calhoun, ''slows down their activity and reduces their breeding rate as something on other worlds keeps the bigger predators from getting too numerous. Something here keeps their numbers down, and that something doesn't, on Lanke. What would you guess, Murgatroyd?''

Murgatroyd said, *''Chee!''* He moved about the lab table, with a very fine air of someone checking the various bits of equipment there. He picked up a culture slide. He sniffed at it and said, *''Chee-chee!''* in a very disapproving manner. He dropped it, and swamp water spilled. The odor was actively unpleasant. Murgatroyd sneezed, and retreated from it. He said, *''Chee!''* and rubbed his nose vigorously.

Calhoun shrugged. He mopped up the spilled half-spoonful. He had visions of living on a world where soil and swamp water stank when disturbed, and where even sea water might do the same. Where one boiled water before drinking it, not to make it germ-free but to drive out most of the taste. Elna had tasted normal water and had told Rob bitterly that she'd never taste water again without remembering how that pure water tasted.

He looked at the vision screens. There were fluffy white clouds in the bluest of blue skies. All oxygen atmosphere planets have blue skies, and those with habit-ability-one temperatures have winds and jet-streams and storm patterns of strictly standard types. On all the worlds with vegetation there were the equivalents of trees and brushwood and grass. The look of Delhi was not repellent, if one could only get used to the smell of the atmosphere, and not of the soil—if the reek of the swamp was simply an exaggeration of what everything smelled like and one could never fail to notice it . . . the passionate desire of its people to leave it could be understood.

The first log was almost at the Med Ship. A second was on the way. Smaller groups were bringing shorter logs. There were men coming with coils of rope.

Calhoun regarded them detachedly. He saw a man stumble and fall, and get up and be sick because of the stench of the mud he'd disturbed.

Calhoun went back to his work. He set out minute samples of swamp water, and added infinitesimal dosages of reagents to each, and then still more minute quantities of the Lanke environment, frantically active culture. Then a check to see what substance—or what substances made up a group—removed by a reagent would allow the spheres to thrive in swamp water.

It could almost have been predicted that the elaborate setup for research would be useless, and something insanely simple would give the answer. A strip of filter paper, wetted with the active culture and in a stoppered bottle with a trace of swamp fluid, that showed the active culture stopped dead. It did not touch swamp water. It was exposed only to the reek, the stench, the effluvium of the swamp. Calhoun said, "The devil!" Painstakingly, he repeated the test. He wanted to talk about it, to explain it for his own hearing so that he'd know if his reasoning made sense. He said, "Murgatroyd!"

Murgatroyd said with an air of charmed interest, *"Chee?"*

"I've got it," said Calhoun. "There is something in the swamp water that slows up the plague germs in multiplying and producing toxin to kill us humans. It's an inhibitive factor like the factors that on different worlds make large carnivores breed slowly, because if they bred fast they'd wipe out their own food supply and die of starvation. In the micro-ecology of germs in Delhi, there's something that holds down plague germs so nobody can get the plague. But on Lanke that inhibitive factor's missing.''

Murgatroyd said, *"Chee!"* and, beady-eyed, watched Calhoun's face.

''I'll bet you a hogshead of coffee to a cookie,'' said Calhoun exuberantly, ''that it's nothing but the smell, the reek, the stink of that—Ha!'' He referred to the Stellar Directory. He found Delhi. ''Here it is! There's a methane derivative to point oh four percent in the planet's air, about the same as carbon dioxide! Maybe there's a bug in the ocean that produces it. Maybe—oh, anything! There are microbes that can't live where there's oxygen and others that can't live where it isn't. This is a microbe that can just barely live where there's point oh four percent of this stinking stuff. But it goes wild where there's . . . now! You see, Murgatroyd? A ship from here, with Delhi air, could go to Lanke and nobody'd have the plague. But a man from it would develop the plague when he got out into Lanke air which hasn't the methane that holds the plague-germ back! A ship from Lanke that left Delhi without Delhi air in its reserve tanks . . . everybody aboard would die of the plague on the way home! You see?''

Murgatroyd said, *"Chee!"*

The girl Elna said uneasily, ''They're setting up some sort of—thing made out of the logs.''

Calhoun looked. There was no battering ram support being erected. There were two short logs upright, and heavy logs crosswise, and a very long log with numerous cross-pieces fastened to it lying in the disturbed ground. Men were working with ropes. It wouldn't make an effective battering ram. However, Calhoun was much too elated to give thought to the engineering feat in progress outside. He wanted to verify what was at once plausible and lacking proof. Proof would be finding a highly volatile liquid or a condensable gas in solution in the swamp water. He most definitely had the equipment for seeking it. He used his swamp-water sample recklessly. He did a reduced-pressure fractionating still-run, which could take a full tablespoon full of swamp water and by precise control of the temperature and pressure draw off dissolved air, dissolved carbon dioxide, dissolved . . .

He got enough of a condensable vapor to be visible under the microscope. With the beautifully exact temperature control he had, he found its boiling point by watching that infinitesimal droplet disappear as vapor, and recondense as a fluid as he sent the temperature up and down, watching through a microscope.

Elna said uneasily, "They're getting ready to do something. . . ."

Calhoun looked at the screen. Men swarmed about an area twenty or thirty feet from the Med Ship's outer plating. They had ropes fastened here and there. They were arranging themselves in long rows about the ropes. There were hundreds of them preparing to do something with the logs. Away over at the edge of the slanting ground, there was much smoke. Men worked at something involving fire. Men shook their fists at the Med Ship, ready to grasp and haul on the ropes they'd brought and placed.

Calhoun blinked. Then he said, "Clever! That's really a beautiful trick! They're sure we can't lift off, so they're going to take the ship with the minimum of damage. . . . That's really brilliant!"

Rob said fiercely, "When are you going to start smashing the ship?"

"I've much more important things to do," said Calhoun. "Much more important!"

Almost hilariously, he threw the G.C. switch and began to call: "General call! General call! To repaired lifeboat. Med Ship *Aesclipus Twenty* calling repaired lifeboat! Top emergency! Come in, repaired lifeboat!"

As he called, he regarded the work outside, which now approached a climax of activity. Men were making sure that ropes lying on the marshy ground were exactly laid to be pulled on. Other men were lining up to haul on those ropes. Leaders arranged them exactly to get the maximum of traction in exactly the proper directions-of-pull. A group of men were bringing something which gave off a thick white smoke. They kept out of the smoke.

"Calling repaired lifeboat! This is urgent! I've found out how the plague works! Calling repaired lifeboat. . . ."

A voice said in icy rage, *"Well?"*

"The plague," said Calhoun, "is a spherical microbe which can't be anything but sluggish in Delhian air, sea, ground, or swamp land, because there's some sort of methane derived compound which inhibits its growth. The compound that makes soil reek when it's disturbed, that you drive out partly when you boil water, that's the stuff that keeps the plague germ inactive. It was in the air you breathed when you went to Lanke. It was in the air you breathed when you kept your boat hidden underwater while two men tried to make it to the spaceboat. Do you understand?"

The rasping voice said suspiciously, *"What're you telling me for?"*

"Because when your two men tried to make it to the spaceport on Lanke, they were breathing air that didn't smell, and didn't hold back the plague germs from multiplying. One man went back when he saw double. Back in your ship the air stopped the germs from multiplying and he got over the plague. When I breathed Delhi air, I got over it. But one man panicked when he found he had the plague. He went to the Health Department and tried to give himself up as a plague victim. He hoped to be carried back to Delhi and to life. But they killed him."

There was a growling sound from the G.C. speaker. Calhoun said, "The Med Service can handle this, but I've got to get to headquarters! There's a mob outside my ship, getting ready to break in. I'll be wrecked! I need somebody to stop the mob from breaking in and wrecking this ship, which is needed to take these facts to Med Service Headquarters. As a matter of common sense, you'd better come here and stop them."

A pause. Then a growled, *"We'll be there!"*

Calhoun grinned. Murgatroyd said shrilly, *"Chee-chee-chee!"*

Ordinarily, when Calhoun held conversations over

the general communicator phone, it meant that the Med Ship would shortly go aground and people would pet Murgatroyd and feed him sweet cakes and coffee until he almost burst. His small brain made that association again. He began to lick his whiskers and otherwise make himself tidy and irresistible.

Rob said contemptuously, "Are you fool enough to expect him to protect this ship and let you go away in it? He'll never do that! Never!"

"I don't expect him to," said Calhoun mildly. "But he really shouldn't make trips like those to Lanke. It's dangerous! There may be plague on Lanke now, because of it. I expect him to try to get the ship for his own ideas."

"But he's coming . . ."

"Yes," said Calhoun.

He turned to the vision plates again. There were at least eight hundred men lined up beside ropes. There were shoutings and orders and cursings. Under exact instructions, the ropes tightened. Men heaved at the ends of the short logs. They rose. They stood up at an angle of forty-five degrees. More shoutings. Enormous, straining efforts . . .

The long log, the heaviest log, the one with the cross-pieces fastened to it, stirred. The shorter logs transferred the flat drag of the ropes to a slanting downward cable, so that the long log went wavering up from the ground. Men with ropes spreading out in every direction balanced it to a sharply vertical position. It stood on end, nearly forty feet long, with cross-pieces by which it could be climbed to its very top.

Now Calhoun observed the spike at its end. It was inches thick and six feet long. It pointed toward the Med Ship. The men with the smoking stuff were halfway across the marsh, now. They kept carefully out of the white vapor the thing they were carrying gave off.

Shoutings, making sure that everything was right.

"What . . ." That was Elna. Rob scowled, but he did not grasp the picture even yet.

The tall pole with the horizontal spike at its end

wavered a little, back and forth. A bellowing voice roared . . .

Half the men at the ropes—those that kept the spiked log from falling toward the ship—let go. The other half dragged frantically at the ropes to make it fall on the Med Ship.

It was very well handled. The log crashed into the small ship's plating. The spike went through, as no battering ram could possibly do. Then there were men swarming up the cross-pieces. Those who'd been bringing the smoking stuff ran desperately to arrive at the earliest possible instant. Containers of the strangling white smoke went up.

"Clever!" said Calhoun.

He sniffed. There was an uproar of triumph outside. The citizens of Delhi howled in triumph, and in their movements they stirred up the swampy pools and many were nauseated.

Calhoun sniffed again, and nodded.

"Sulfur," he commented. "They're blowing sulfur smoke in the hole they punched in our hull. In theory, we'll have to open the air-lock doors to get out or strangle. And when we go out they'll come in. Clever!"

The smell of burning sulfur became distinct. It grew strong. Calhoun adjusted a control governing the barometric pressure inside the ship. If by a rise in temperature or for other reasons the pressure in the ship went up, a pump would relieve the extra pressure by compressing it into one of the large air-tanks which carried fourteen times the volume of the Med Ship. Calhoun and Murgatroyd could live for a long time on stored air if the air-renewal system failed.

Now Calhoun had raised the pressure-control. The control called for a pressure of twenty pounds to the square inch instead of fourteen point seven. The tanks poured out vast volumes of air from the reserve-tanks. The pressure inside the ship went up. The sulfur smoke being pumped in the ship turned cold. An icy blast poured out on the sweating men atop the log. The burning sulfur itself was blown about . . .

The men on the log went down. The tumult of outcries outside the Med Ship was a frenzied rage.

Calhoun restored the pressure-control to normal. Elna shivered. The air in the ship was cold.

"What—what happens now?" she asked forlornly. "If you can't lift off . . ."

"I'm waiting for the spaceboat that went to Lanke," said Calhoun. "He's going to come here. Object, to take over the Med Ship."

The ceiling G.C. speaker rasped: *"Med Ship! You think you're smart, eh? Come out of that ship and leave the air-lock open or we'll kill you!"*

Calhoun said politely, "Hadn't we better talk it over? I really should get to Med Headquarters. . . ."

"We've a cannon," said the harsh voice. *"If we have to use it—we can rebuild what it breaks. Come out!"*

Calhoun did not reply. Instead, he carefully inspected the dials and the switches of the control-board. Rob said savagely, "Here comes the boat! If they fire an explosive shell into us, it'll destroy us!"

"And the Med Ship too," said Calhoun encouragingly. "Which is what you want. But they're not used to gunnery near a planet, which makes straight-line trajectories into parabolas."

He saw the lifeboat, patches on patches, dents and lumps in its hull, the very picture of makeshifts piled on each other to the point of lunacy. It landed, on what must have been a flat place on a mountain-flank. The voice came again, *"Come out, leaving the air-lock open, or we kill you!"*

Rob said as if reluctantly, "You should let Elna go out before they kill us."

Calhoun said, "I was just waiting for that ship. It really shouldn't go traveling about. Nobody should leave Delhi but me."

"But you're mired! You're stuck here! Your rockets can't lift you."

"I'm not counting on rocket thrust," said Calhoun cheerfully. "I'm going to use steam."

He pressed a button. As had happened once before in

this place, a slender blue-white flame appeared under the stern-most part of the Med Ship's hull. It was the emergency rocket, by which the ship had landed. Now the ship was held fast by mud. It would have required a pull or push of many times the Med Ship's weight to break the suction of the mud. The rockets, as rockets, could not conceivably have pushed the spacecraft clear.

But the rocket flame bored deep down into the ground. It vaporized the water beneath it. It volatilized the ground. For eighty feet down in the valley bottom's water-saturated soil, the flame bored its way. Steam pressure developed. Steam bubbles of enormous size came up. Steam broke surfaces, heaving up masses of semi-solid valley bottom and escaping at the jagged edges of the cracks between masses. The Med Ship ceased to rest upon an adhesive mass of muck, packed over the feet at the bottom of the landing-fins. The Med Ship actually floated on a mixture of solidities and semi-solidities and steam. It wasn't using the propulsive power of its rockets, at all. It used their steam-generating capacity.

She shot upward before the spaceboat could fire a shell at her. She went up three thousand feet before Calhoun cut down on the rocket power. Then he peered carefully, tilted the ship and let it drop. The valley bottom seemed to leap up. The spaceboat spouted rocket flame. Calhoun dashed at it, seeming to intend a crashing collision in mid-air. He missed it by feet. He swooped and circled and dashed in at it again. The spaceboat dodged frantically.

"I'm doing this in atmosphere," said Calhoun, with an air of apology, "because they made a leak in the hull. I have to take care of the spaceboat. It shouldn't leave Delhi."

The spaceboat fired a cannon-shell. It went completely wild. Calhoun swept in, flipped the Med Ship end for end, and his rocket flame would have cut the spaceboat in two had he swung one of his controls the quarter of an inch. He didn't. Instead he flung the Med Ship about until it was borne in upon the crew of the spaceboat. They had run up against a professional in spacecraft handling. He literally drove the spaceboat down and down and down—and he could have destroyed it a dozen times over—until at the last it made a panicky landing and figures leaped out of it and fled away.

Calhoun made the Med Ship hover above it, fifty feet high, with that deadly star-temperature flame of the rockets drilling through the hull, through the patches, and into the interior.

It was only when flames burst out of cracks and crevices all over the grounded freakish spacecraft that he lifted the Med ship and headed away over the horizon.

He landed once more on Delhi, some hundreds of miles away on the single continent this planet owned. He was very tired, then. He ordered Rob and Elna out of the ship.

"Nobody should leave Delhi but me," he repeated politely. "So you get out. There'll be a hospital ship here within a week, two at the outside. Are you two going to be married?"

Rob said with dignity, "Not unless the plague is defeated and we can go where we please, not if our children would have to stay on Delhi and gradually become savages."

"I'll send you a wedding present by the hospital ship," promised Calhoun. "You did me a great favor. Thanks."

He closed the air-lock. He looked at a dial. The reserve-tanks of the Med Ship had been emptied, in blowing sulfur smoke out of the single puncture in its hull. He had been pumping them up to normal reserve pressure again, and this was Delhi air. Anybody who got the plague had only to stay in Delhi air and he would be cured. However, there was work for the Med Service to do to arrange that he not relapse when he went out of Delhi air again, nor give the plague to anybody else. There'd be no difficulty about that. The Med Service had solved much more difficult problems.

Calhoun sealed the hull-puncture with a quick-setting plastic. He sealed off the compartment whose wall had been pierced. He went down to the control-room. He blinked as he set the rockets to roaring again and the Med Ship climbed for the sky.

An hour later he was intolerably tired. He aimed the Med Ship for that far-off small star-cluster which was its home. With extra care, because of his weariness, he verified what he'd done. Then he said, "Overdrive coming, Murgatroyd. Five—four—three—two—one."

There was a revolting dizziness and an appalling nausea and then the feeling of a spinning drop to nowhere. Then the Med Ship was in overdrive. It felt solid as a rock. There was no sound but the background tape producing almost inaudible noises of traffic, and rain, and surf, and music, and human voices. There was even faint laughter.

Calhoun yawned.

"Murgatroyd?"

"Chee-chee!" said Murgatroyd shrilly. *"Chee?"*

"Take over the ship," commanded Calhoun. "If any emergencies turn up, you take care of them. I'm going to bed!"

And he did.

THIS WORLD
IS TABOO

I

THE LITTLE MED SHIP came out of overdrive and the stars were strange and the Milky Way seemed unfamiliar. Which, of course, was because the Milky Way and the local Cepheid marker-stars were seen from an unaccustomed angle and a not-yet-commonplace pattern of varying magnitudes.

But Calhoun grunted in satisfaction. There was a banded sun off to port, which was good. A breakout at no more than sixty light-hours from one's destination wasn't bad, in a strange sector of the galaxy and after three light-years of journeying blind.

"Arise and shine, Murgatroyd," said Calhoun. "Comb your whiskers. Get set to astonish the natives!"

A sleepy, small, shrill voice said, *"Chee!"*

Murgatroyd the *tormal* came crawling out of the small cubbyhole which was his own. He blinked at Calhoun.

"We're due to land shortly," Calhoun observed. "You will impress the local inhabitants. I will get unpopular. According to the records, there's been no Med Ship inspection here for twelve standard years. And that was practically no inspection, to judge by the report."

Murgatroyd said, *"Chee-chee!"*

He began to make his toilet, first licking his right-hand whiskers and then his left. Then he stood up and shook himself and looked interestedly at Calhoun.

Tormals are companionable small animals. They are
charmed when somebody speaks to them. They find
great, deep satisfaction in imitating the actions of
humans, as parrots and mynahs and parakeets imitate
human speech. But *tormals* have certain valuable,
genetically transmitted talents which make them much
more valuable than mere companions or pets.

Calhoun got a light-reading for the banded sun. It
could hardly be an accurate measure of distance, but it
was a guide.

"Hold on to something, Murgatroyd!" he said.

Murgatroyd watched. He saw Calhoun make certain
gestures which presaged discomfort. He popped back
into his cubbyhole. Calhoun threw the overdrive switch
and the Med Ship flicked back into that questionable
state of being in which velocities of hundreds of times
that of light are possible. The sensation of going into
overdrive was unpleasant. A moment later, the sensation of coming out was no less so. Calhoun had experienced it often enough, and still didn't like it.

The sun Weald burned huge and terrible in space. It
was close, now. Its disk covered half a degree of arc.

"Very neat," observed Calhoun. "Weald Three is
our port, Murgatroyd. The plane of the ecliptic would
be . . . Hm . . ."

He swung the outside electron telescope, picked up a
nearby bright object, enlarged its image to show details,
and checked it against the local star-pilot. He calculated
a moment. The distance was too short for even the
briefest of overdrive hops, but it would take time to get
there on solar-system drive.

He thumbed down the communicator button and
spoke into a microphone.

"Med Ship *Aesclipus Twenty* reporting arrival and
asking coordinates for landing," he said matter-of-
factly. "Purpose of landing is planetary health inspection. Our mass is fifty tons, standard. We should arrive
at a landing position in something under four hours.
Repeat. Med Ship *Aesclipus Twenty* . . ."

He finished the regular second transmission and made

coffee for himself while he waited for an answer. Murgatroyd came out for a cup of coffee for himself. Murgatroyd adored coffee. In minutes he held a tiny cup in a furry small paw and sipped gingerly at the hot liquid.

A voice came out of the communicator, "*Aesclipus Twenty*, repeat your identification."

Calhoun went to the control board.

"*Aesclipus Twenty*," he said patiently, "is a Med Ship, sent by the Interstellar Medical Service to make a planetary health inspection on Weald. Check with your public health authorities. This is the first Med Ship visit in twelve standard years, I believe—which is inexcusable. But your health authorities will know all about it. Check with them."

The voice said truculently, "What was your last port?"

Calhoun named it. This was not his home sector, but Sector Twelve had gotten into a very bad situation. Some of its planets had gone unvisited for as long as twenty years, and twelve between inspections was almost commonplace. Other sectors had been called on to help it catch up.

Calhoun was one of the loaned Med Ship men, and because of the emergency he'd been given a list of half a dozen planets to be inspected one after another, instead of reporting back to sector headquarters after each visit. He'd had minor troubles before with landing-grid operators in Sector Twelve.

So he was very patient. He named the planet last inspected, the one from which he'd set out for Weald Three. The voice from the communicator said sharply, "What port before that?"

Calhoun named the one before the last.

"Don't drive any closer," said the voice harshly, "or you'll be destroyed!"

Calhoun said coldly, "Listen, my fine feathered friend! I'm from the Interstellar Medical Service. You get in touch with planetary health services immediately! Remind them of the Interstellar Medical Inspection

Agreement, signed on Tralee two hundred and forty
standard years ago. Remind them that if they do not
cooperate in medical inspection that I can put your
planet under quarantine and your space commerce will
be cut off like that!

"No ship will be cleared for Weald from any other
planet in the galaxy until there has been a health inspection! Things have pretty well gone to pot so far as
the Med Service in this sector is concerned, but it's being
straightened up. I'm helping straighten it! I give you
twenty minutes to clear this! Then I am coming in, and
if I'm not landed a quarantine goes on! Tell your health
authorities that!"

Silence. Calhoun clicked off and poured himself
another cup of coffee. Murgatroyd held out his cup for
a refill. Calhoun gave it to him.

"I hate to put on an official hat, Murgatroyd," he
said, annoyed, "but there are some people who demand
it. The rule is, never get official if you can help it, but
when you must, out-official the official who's of-
ficiating you."

Murgatroyd said, *"Chee!"* and sipped at his cup.

Calhoun checked the course of the Med Ship. It bore
on through space. There were tiny noises from the communicator. There were whisperings and rustlings and
the occasional strange and sometimes beautiful musical
notes whose origin is yet obscure, but which, since they
are carried by electromagnetic radiation of wildly
varying wave lengths, are not likely to be the fabled
music of the spheres.

In fifteen minutes a different voice came from the
speaker.

"Med Ship *Aesclipus*! Med Ship *Aesclipus*!"

Calhoun answered and the voice said anxiously,
"Sorry about the challenge, but we have the blueskin
problem always with us. We have to be extremely
careful! Will you come in, please?"

"I'm on my way," said Calhoun.

"The planetary health authorities," said the voice,
more anxiously still, "are very anxious to be cooperative. We need Med Service help! We lose a lot of sleep

over the blueskin! Could you tell us the name of the last
Med Ship to land here, and its inspector, and when that
inspection was made? We want to look up the record of
the event to be able to assist you in every possible way."

"He's lying," Calhoun told Murgatroyd, "but he's
more scared than hostile."

He picked up the order folio on Weald Three. He
gave the information about the last Med Ship visit.

"What," he asked, "is a blueskin?"

He'd read the folio on Weald, of course, but as the
ship swam onward through emptiness he went through
it again. The last medical inspection had been only per-
functory. Twelve years earlier—instead of three—a Med
Ship had landed on Weald. There had been official conferences with health officials. There was a report on the
birth rate, the death rate, the anomaly rate, and a break-
down of all reported communicable diseases. But that
was all. There were no special comments and no overall
picture.

Presently Calhoun found the word in a Sector dic-
tionary, where words of only local usage were to be
found:

> *Blueskin: Colloquial term for a person recovered
> from a plague which left large patches of blue pig-
> ment irregularly distributed over the body. Espe-
> cially, inhabitants of Dara. The condition is said
> to be caused by a chronic, nonfatal form of Dara
> plague and has been said to be noninfectious,
> though this is not certain. The etiology of Dara
> plague has not been worked out. The blueskin
> condition is hereditary but not a genetic modifica-
> tion, as markings appear in non-Mendelian dis-
> tributions.*

Calhoun puzzled over it. Nobody could have read the
entire Sector directory, even with unlimited leisure
during travel between solar systems. Calhoun hadn't
tried. But now he went laboriously through indices and
cross-references while the ship continued to travel onward.

He found no other reference to blueskins. He looked up Dara. It was listed as an inhabited planet, some four hundred years colonized, with a landing grid and, at the time the main notice was written out, a flourishing interstellar commerce. But there was a memo, evidently added to the entry in some change of editions: *"Since plague, special license from Med Service is required for landing."*

That was all. Absolutely all.

The communicator said suavely, "Med Ship *Aesclipus Twenty!* Come in on vision, please!"

Calhoun went to the control board and threw on vision.

"Well, what now?" he demanded.

His screen lighted. A bland face looked out at him.

"We have—ah—verified your statements," said the third voice from Weald. "Just one more item. Are you alone in your ship?"

"Of course," said Calhoun, frowning.

"Quite alone?" insisted the voice.

"Obviously!" said Calhoun.

"No other living creature?" insisted the voice again.

"Of—oh!" said Calhoun, annoyed. He called over his shoulder. "Murgatroyd! Come here!"

Murgatroyd hopped to his lap and gazed interestedly at the screen. The bland face changed remarkably. The voice changed even more.

"Very good!" it said. "Very, very good! Blueskins do not have *tormals!* You are Med Service! By all means come in! Your coordinates will be . . ."

Calhoun wrote them down. He clicked off the communicator again and growled to Murgatroyd, "So I might have been a blueskin, eh? And you're my passport, because only Med Ships have members of your tribe aboard! What the hell's the matter, Murgatroyd? They act like they think somebody's trying to get down on their planet with a load of plague germs!"

He grumbled to himself for minutes. The life of a Med Ship man is not exactly a sinecure, at best. It means long periods in empty space in overdrive, which is absolute and deadly tedium. Then two or three days aground, checking official documents and statistics, and asking questions to see how many of the newest medical techniques have reached this planet or that, and the supplying of information about such as have not arrived.

Then the lifting out to space for long periods of tedium, to repeat the process somewhere else. Med Ships carry only one man because two could not stand the close contact without quarreling with each other. But Med Ships do carry *tormals*, like Murgatroyd, and a *tormal* and a man can get along indefinitely, like a man and a dog. It is a highly unequal friendship, but it seems to be satisfactory to both.

Calhoun was very much annoyed with the way the Med Service had been operated in Sector Twelve. He was one of many men at work to corect the results of incompetence in directing Med Service in this sector. But it is always disheartening to have to labor at making up for somebody else's blundering, when there is so much new work that needs to be done.

The condition shown by the landing-grid suspicions was a case in point. Blueskins were people who inherited a splotchy skin pigmentation from other people who'd survived a plague. Weald plainly maintained a one-planet quarantine against them. But a quarantine is normally an emergency measure. The Med Service should have taken over, wiped out the need for a quarantine, and then lifted it. It hadn't been done.

Calhoun fumed to himself.

The world of Weald Three grew brighter and brighter and became a disk. The disk had icecaps and a reasonable proportion of land and water surface. The ship decelerated, voices notifying observation from the surface, and the little ship came to a stop some five planetary diameters out from solidity. The landing field's force-field locked on to it, and its descent began.

The business of landing was all very familiar, from the blue rim which appeared at the limb of the planet from one diameter out, to the singular flowing-apart of the surface features as the ship sank still lower. There

was the circular landing grid, rearing skyward for nearly
a mile. It could let down interstellar liners from emptiness and lift them out to emptiness again, with great
convenience and economy for everyone.

It landed the Med Ship in its center, and there were
officials to greet Calhoun, and he knew in advance the
routine part of his visit. There would be an interview
with the planet's chief executive, by whatever title he
was called. There would be a banquet. Murgatroyd
would be petted by everybody. There would be painful
efforts to impress Calhoun with the splendid conduct of
public health matters on Weald. He would be told much
scandal.

He might find one man, somewhere, who passionately labored to advance the welfare of his fellow
humans by finding out how to keep them well or, failing
that, how to make them well when they got sick. And in
two days, or three, Calhoun would be escorted back to
the landing grid, and lifted out to space, and he'd spend
long empty days in overdrive and land somewhere else
to do the whole thing all over again.

It all happened exactly as he expected, with one exception. Every human being he met on Weald wanted to
talk about blueskins. Blueskins and the idea of
blueskins obsessed everyone. Calhoun listened without
asking questions until he had the picture of what
blueskins meant to the people who talked of them. Then
he knew there would be no use asking questions at random.

Nobody mentioned ever having seen a blueskin.
Nobody mentioned a specific event in which a blueskin
had at any named time taken part. But everybody was
afraid of blueskins. It was a patterned, an inculcated, a
stage-directed fixed idea. And it found expression in
shocked references to the vileness, the depravity, the
monstrousness of the blueskin inhabitants of Dara,
from whom Weald must at all costs be protected.

It did not make sense. So Calhoun listened politely
until he found an undistinguished medical man who
wanted some special information about gene selection
as practiced halfway across the galaxy. He invited that

man to the Med Ship, where he supplied the information not hitherto available. He saw his guest's eyes shine a little with that joyous awe a man feels when he finds out something he has wanted long and badly to know.

"Now," said Calhoun, "tell me something? Why does everybody on this planet hate the inhabitants of Dara? It's light-years away. Nobody claims to have suffered in person from them. Why make a point of hating them?"

The Wealdian doctor grimaced.

"They've blue patches on their skins. They're different from us. So they can be pictured as a danger and our political parties can make an election issue out of competing for the privilege of defending us from them. They had a plague on Dara, once. They're accused of still having it ready for export."

"Hm," said Calhoun. "The story is that they want to spread contagion here, eh? Doesn't anybody"—his tone was sardonic—"doesn't anybody urge that they be massacred as an act of piety?"

"Yes-s-s-s," admitted the doctor reluctantly. "It's mentioned in political speeches."

"But how's it rationalized?" demanded Calhoun. "What's the argument to make pigment-patches involve moral and physical degradation, as I'm assured is the case?"

"In the public schools," said the doctor, "the children are taught that blueskins are now carriers of the disease they survived—three generations ago! That they hate everybody who isn't a blueskin. That they are constantly scheming to introduce their plague here so most of us will die and the rest will become blueskins. That's beyond rationalizing. It can't be true, but it's not safe to doubt it."

"Bad business," said Calhoun coldly. "That sort of thing usually costs lives in the end. It could lead to massacre!"

"Perhaps it has, in a way," said the doctor unhappily. "One doesn't like to think about it." He paused. "Twenty years ago there was a famine on Dara. There

were crop failures. The situation must have been very
bad: They built a spaceship.

"They've no use for such things normally, because no
nearby planet will deal with them or let them land. But
they built a spaceship and came here. There went in orbit around Weald. They asked to trade for shiploads of
food. They offered any price in heavy metals—gold,
platinum, irridium, and so on. They talked from orbit
by vision communicators. They could be seen to be
blueskins. You can guess what happened!"

"Tell me," said Calhoun.

"We armed ships in a hurry," admitted the doctor.
"We chased their spaceship back to Dara. We hung in
space off the planet. We told them we'd blast their
world from pole to pole if they ever dared take to space
again. We made them destroy their one ship, and we
watched on vision screens as it was done."

"But you gave them food?"

"No," said the doctor ashamedly. "They were
blueskins."

"How bad was the famine?"

"Who knows? Any number may have starved! And
we kept a squadron of armed ships in their skies for
years—to keep them from spreading the plague, we
said. And some of us believed it!"

The doctor's tone was purest irony.

"Lately," he said, "there's been a move for economy
in our government. Simultaneously, we began to have a
series of overabundant crops. The government had to
buy the excess grain to keep the price up. Retired patrol
ships, built to watch over Dara, were available for
storage space. We filled them up with grain and sent
them out into orbit. They're there now, hundreds of
thousands or millions of tons of grain!"

"And Dara?"

The doctor shrugged. He stood up.

"Our hatred of Dara," he said, again ironically, "has
produced one thing. Roughly halfway between here and
Dara there's a two-planet solar system, Orede. There's a
usable planet there. It was proposed to build an outpost

of Weald there, against blueskins. Cattle were landed to
run wild and multiply and make a reason for colonists
to settle there.

"They did, but nobody wants to move near to blueskins! So Orede stayed uninhabited until a hunting
party, shooting wild cattle, found an outcropping of
heavy-metal ore. So now there's a mine there. And
that's all. A few hundred men work the mine at fabu-
lous wages. You may be asked to check on their health.
But not Dara's!"

"I see," said Calhoun, frowning.

The doctor moved toward the Med Ship's exit port.

"I answered your questions," he said grimly. "But if
I talked to anyone else as I've done to you, I'd be lucky
only to be driven into exile!"

"I shan't give you away," said Calhoun. He did not
smile.

When the doctor had gone, Calhoun said deliberately, "Murgatroyd, you should be grateful that you're
a *tormal* and not a man. There's nothing about being a
tormal to make you ashamed!"

Then he grimly changed his garments for the full-
dress uniform of the Med Service. There was to be a
banquet at which he would sit next to the planet's chief
executive and hear innumerable speeches about the
splendor of Weald. Calhoun had his own, strictly Med
Service opinion of the planet's latest and most boasted-
of achievement. It was a domed city in the polar
regions, where nobody ever had to go outdoors.

He was less than professionally enthusiastic about the
moving streets, and much less than approving of the
dream broadcasts which supplied hypnotic, sleep-induc-
ing rhythms to anybody who chose to listen to them.
The price was that while asleep one would hear high
praise of commercial products, and might believe them
when awake.

But it was not Calhoun's function to criticize when it
could be avoided. Med Service had been badly managed
in Sector Twelve. So at the banquet Calhoun made a

brief and diplomatic address in which he temperately praised what could be praised, and did not mention anything else.

The chief executive followed him. As head of the government he paid some tribute to the Med Service. But then he reminded his hearers proudly of the high culture, splendid health, and remarkable prosperity of the planet since his political party took office. This, he said, despite the need to be perpetually on guard against the greatest and most immediate danger to which any world in all the galaxy was exposed.

He referred to the blueskins, of course. He did not need to tell the people of Weald what vigilance, what constant watchfulness was necessary against that race of deprived and malevolent deviants from the norm of humanity. But Weald, he said with emotion, held aloft the torch of all that humanity held most dear, and defended not alone the lives of its people against blueskin contagion, but their noble heritage of ideals against blueskin pollution.

When he sat down, Calhoun said very politely, "It looks as if some day it should be practical politics to urge the massacre of all blueskins. Have you thought of that?"

The chief executive said comfortably, "The idea's been proposed. It's good politics to urge it, but it would be foolish to carry it out. People vote against blueskins. Wipe them out, and where'd you be?"

Calhoun ground his teeth—quietly.

There were more speeches. Then a messenger, white-faced, arrived with a written note for the chief executive. He read it and passed it to Calhoun. It was from the Ministry of Health. The spaceport reported that a ship had just broken out from overdrive within the Wealdian solar system. Its tape-transmitter had automatically signaled its arrival from the mining planet Orede.

But, having sent off its automatic signal, the ship lay dead in space. It did not drive toward Weald. It did not respond to signals. It drifted like a derelict upon no course at all. It seemed ominous, and since it came from

Orede, the planet nearest to Dara of the blueskins, the
health ministry informed the planet's chief executive.

"It'll be blueskins," said that astute person firmly.
"They're next door to Orede. That's who's done this.
It wouldn't surprise me if they'd seeded Orede with
their plague, and this ship came from there to give us
warning!"

"There's no evidence for anything of the sort,"
protested Calhoun. "A ship simply came out of overdrive and didn't signal further. That's all!"

"We'll see," said the chief executive ominously.
"We'll go to the spaceport. There we'll get the news as it
comes in, and can frame orders on the latest information."

He took Calhoun by the arm. Calhoun said sharply,
"Murgatroyd!"

During the banquet, Murgatroyd had been visiting
with the wives of the higher-up officials. They had
enough of their husbands normally, without listening to
their official speeches. Murgatroyd was brought, his
small paunch distended with cakes and coffee and such
delicacies as he'd been plied with. He was half comatose
from overfeeding and overpetting, but he was glad to
see Calhoun.

Calhoun held the little creature in his arms as the
official ground-car raced through traffic with screaming
sirens claiming the right of way. It reached the spaceport, where enormous metal girders formed a monster
frame of metal lace against a star-filled sky. The chief
executive strode magnificently into the spaceport of-
fices. There was no news; the situation remained un-
changed.

A ship from Orede had come out of overdrive and lay
dead in emptiness. It did not answer calls. It did not
move in space. It floated eerily in no orbit, going
nowhere, doing nothing. And panic was the consequence.

It seemed to Calhoun that the official handling of the
matter accounted for the terror that he could feel
building up. The unexplained bit of news was on the air
all over the planet Weald. There was nobody awake of

all the world's population who did not believe that there
was a new danger in the sky. Nobody doubted that it
came from blueskins. The treatment of the news was
precisely calculated to keep alive the hatred of Weald
for the inhabitants of the world Dara.

Calhoun put Murgatroyd into the Med Ship and went
back to the spaceport office. A small spaceboat,
designed to inspect the circling grain ships from time to
time, was already aloft. The landing-grid had thrust it
swiftly out most of the way. Now it droned and drove
on sturdily toward the enigmatic ship.

Calhoun took no part in the agitated conferences
among the officials and news reporters at the spaceport.
But he listened to the talk about him. As the investigating small ship drew nearer to the deathly-still
cargo vessel, the guesses about the meaning of its
breakout and following silence grew more and more
wild.

But, singularly, there was no single suggestion that
the mystery might not be the work of blueskins.
Blueskins were scapegoats for all the fears and all the
uneasiness a perhaps over-civilized world developed.

Presently the investigating spaceboat reached the
mystery ship and circled it, beaming queries. No
answer. It reported the cargo ship dark. No lights anywhere on or in it. There were no induction-surges from
even pulsing, idling engines. Delicately, the messenger
craft maneuvered until it touched the silent vessel. It
reported that microphones detected no motion whatever
inside.

"Let a volunteer go aboard," commanded the chief
executive. "Let him report what he finds."

A pause. Then the solemn announcement of an
intrepid volunteer's name, from far, far away. Calhoun listened, frowning darkly. This pompous heroism
wouldn't be noticed in the Med Service. It would be
routine behavior.

Suspenseful, second-by-second reports. The volunteer had rocketed himself across the emptiness between
the two again separated ships. He had opened the air-

lock from outside. He'd gone in. He'd closed the outer air-lock door. He'd opened the inner. He reported—

The relayed report was almost incoherent, what with horror and incredulity and the feeling of doom that came upon the volunteer. The ship was a bulk-cargo ore-carrier, designed to run between Orede and Weald with cargos of heavy-metal ores and a crew of no more than five men. There was no cargo in her holds now, though.

Instead, there were men. They packed the ship. They filled the corridors. They had crawled into every space where a man could find room to push himself. There were hundreds of them. It was insanity. And it had been greater insanity still for the ship to have taken off with so preposterous a load of living creatures.

But they weren't living any longer. The air apparatus had been designed for a crew of five. It would purify the air for possibly twenty or more. But there were hundreds of men in hiding as well as in plain view in the cargo ship from Orede. There were many, many times more than her air apparatus and reserve tanks could possibly have taken care of. They couldn't even have been fed during the journey from Orede to Weald.

But they hadn't starved. Air-scarcity killed them before the ship came out of overdrive.

A remarkable thing was that there was no written message in the ship's log which referred to its takeoff. There was no memorandum of the taking on of such an impossible number of passengers.

"The blueskins did it," said the chief executive of Weald. He was pale. All about Calhoun men looked sick and shocked and terrified. "It was the blueskins! We'll have to teach them a lesson!" Then he turned to Calhoun. "The volunteer who went on that ship—he'll have to stay there, won't he? He can't be brought back to Weald without bringing contagion."

Calhoun raged at him.

II

THERE WAS A certain coldness in the manner of those at the Weald spaceport when the Med Ship left next morning. Calhoun was not popular because Weald was scared. It had been conditioned to scare easily, where blueskins might be involved. Its children were trained to react explosively when the word *blueskin* was uttered in their hearing, and its adults tended to say it when anything causing uneasiness entered their minds. So a planet-wide habit of irrational response had formed and was not seen to be irrational because almost everybody had it.

The volunteer who'd discovered the tragedy on the ship from Orede was safe, though. He'd made a completely conscientious survey of the ship he'd volunteered to enter and examine. For his courage, he'd have been doomed but for Calhoun.

The reaction of his fellow citizens was that by entering the ship he might have become contaminated by blueskin infectious material if the plague still existed, and *if* the men in the ship had caught it (but they certainly hadn't died of it), and *if* there had been blueskins on Orede to communicate it (for which there was no evidence), and *if* blueskins were responsible for the tragedy. Which was at the moment pure supposition. But Weald feared he might bring death back to Weald if he were allowed to return.

Calhoun saved his life. He ordered that the guardship

admit him to its air-lock, which then was to be filled
with steam and chlorine. The combination would
sterilize and even partly eat away his spacesuit, after
which the chlorine and steam should be bled out to
space, and air from the ship let into the lock.

If he stripped off the spacesuit without touching its
outer surface, and reentered the investigating ship while
the suit was flung outside by a man in another spacesuit,
handling it with a pole he'd fling after it, there could be
no possible contamination brought back.

Calhoun was quite right, but Weald in general considered that he'd persuaded the government to take an
unreasonable risk.

There were other reasons for disapproving of him.
Calhoun had been unpleasantly frank. The coming of
the death-ship stirred to frenzy those people who
believed that all blueskins should be exterminated as a
pious act. They'd appeared on every vision screen,
citing not only the ship from Orede but other incidents
which they interpreted as crimes against Weald.

They demanded that all Wealdian atomic reactors be
modified to turn out fusion-bomb materials while a
space fleet was made ready for an anti-blueskin crusade.
They confidently demanded such a rain of fusion bombs
on Dara that no blueskin, no animal, no shred of
vegetation, no fish in the deepest ocean, not even a
living virus particle of the blueskin plague could remain
alive on the blueskin world.

One of these vehement orators even asserted that
Calhoun agreed that no other course was possible,
speaking for the Interstellar Medical Service. And
Calhoun furiously demanded a chance to deny it by
broadcast, and he made a bitter and indiscreet speech
from which a planet-wide audience inferred that he
thought them fools.

He did.

So he was definitely unpopular when his ship lifted
from Weald. He'd curtly given his destination as Orede,
from which the death-ship had come. The landing grid
locked on, raised the small spacecraft until Weald was a
great shining ball below it, and then somehow scorn-

fully cast him off. The Med Ship was free, in clear space where there was not enough of a gravitational field to hinder overdrive.

He aimed for his destination, his face very grim. He said savagely, "Get set, Murgatroyd! Overdrive coming!"

He thumbed down the overdrive button. The universe of stars went out, while everything living in the ship felt the customary sensations of dizziness, of nausea, and of a spiraling fall to nothingness. Then there was silence.

The Med Ship actually moved at a rate which was a preposterous number of times the speed of light, but it felt absolutely solid, absolutely firm and fixed. A ship in overdrive feels exactly as if it were buried deep in the core of a planet. There is no vibration. There is no sign of anything but solidity and, if one looks out a port, there is only utter blackness plus an absence of sound fit to make one's eardrums crack.

But within seconds random tiny noises began. There was a reel and there were sound-speakers to keep the ship from sounding like a grave. The reel played and the speakers gave off minute creakings, and meaningless hums, and very tiny noises of every imaginable sort, all of which were just above the threshold of the inaudible.

Calhoun fretted. Sector Twelve was in very bad shape. A conscientious Med Service man would never have let the anti-blueskin obsession go unmentioned in a report on Weald. Health is not only a physical affair. There is mental health, also. When mental health goes a civilization can be destroyed more surely and more terribly than by any imaginable war or plague germs. A plague kills off those who are susceptible to it, leaving immunes to build up a world again. But immunes are the first to be killed when a mass neurosis sweeps a population.

Weald was definitely a Med Service problem world. Dara was another. And when hundreds of men jammed themselves into a cargo spaceship which could not furnish them with air to breathe, and took off and went into overdrive before the air could fail. . . . Orede called for no less of worry.

"I think," said Calhoun dourly, "that I'll have some coffee."

Coffee was one of the words that Murgatroyd recognized. Ordinarily he stirred immediately on hearing it, and watched the coffeemaker with bright, interested eyes. He'd even tried to imitate Calhoun's motions with it, once, and had scorched his paws in the attempt. But this time he did not move.

Calhoun turned his head. Murgatroyd sat on the floor, his long tail coiled reflectively about a chair leg. He watched the door of the Med Ship's sleeping cabin.

"Murgatroyd," said Calhoun. "I mentioned coffee!"

"Chee!" shrilled Murgatroyd.

But he continued to look at the door. The temperature was kept lower in the other cabin, and the look of things was different than the control compartment. The difference was part of the means by which a man was able to be alone for weeks on end—alone save for his *tormal*—without becoming ship-happy.

There were other carefully thought out items in the ship with the same purpose. But none of them should cause Murgatroyd to stare fixedly and fascinatedly at the sleeping cabin door. Not when coffee was in the making!

Calhoun considered. He became angry at the immediate suspicion that occurred to him. As a Med Service man, he was duty-bound to be impartial. To be impartial might mean not to side absolutely with Weald in its enmity to blueskins.

And the people of Weald had refused to help Dara in a time of famine, and had blockaded that pariah world for years afterward. And they had other reasons for hating the people they'd treated badly. It was entirely reasonable for some fanatic on Weald to consider that Calhoun must be killed lest he be of help to the blueskins Weald abhorred.

In fact, it was quite possible that somebody had stowed away on the Med Ship to murder Calhoun, so that there would be no danger of any report favorable to Dara ever being presented anywhere. If so, such a stowaway would be in the sleeping cabin now, waiting for Calhoun to walk in unsuspiciously, only to be shot dead.

So Calhoun made coffee. He slipped a blaster into a pocket where it would be handy. He filled a small cup for Murgatroyd and a large one for himself, and then a second large one.

He tapped on the sleeping cabin door, standing aside lest a blaster-bolt come through it.

"Coffee's ready," he said sardonically. "Come out and join us."

There was a long pause. Calhoun rapped again.

"You've a seat at the captain's table," he said more sardonically still. "It's not polite to keep me waiting!"

He listened, alert for a rush which would be a fanatic's desperate attempt to do murder despite premature discovery. He was prepared to shoot quite ruthlessly, because he was on duty and the Med Service did not approve of the extermination of populations, however justified another population might consider it.

But there was no rush. Instead, there came hesitant footfalls whose sound made Calhoun start. The door of the cabin slid slowly aside. A girl appeared in the opening, desperately white and desperately composed.

"H-how did you know I was there?" she asked shakily. She moistened her lips. "You didn't see me! I was in a closet, and you didn't even enter the room!"

Calhoun said grimly, "I've sources of information. Murgatroyd told me this time. May I present him? Murgatroyd, our passenger. Shake hands."

Murgatroyd moved forward, stood on his hind legs and offered a skinny, furry paw. She did not move. She stared at Calhoun.

"Better shake hands," said Calhoun, as grimly as before. "It might relax the tension a little. And do you want to tell me your story? You have one ready, I'm sure."

The girl swallowed. Murgatroyd shook hands gravely. He said, *"Chee-chee!"* in the shrillest of trebles and went back to his former position.

"The story?" said Calhoun insistently.

"There—there isn't any," said the girl unsteadily. "Just that I—I need to get to Orede, and you're going there. There's no other way to go, now."

"To the contrary," said Calhoun. "There'll undoubtedly be a fleet heading for Orede as soon as it can be assembled and armed. But I'm afraid that as a story yours isn't good enough. Try another."

She shivered a little.

"I'm running away . . ."

"Ah!" said Calhoun. "In that case I'll take you back."

"No!" she said fiercely. "I'll—I'll die first! I'll wreck this ship first!"

Her hand came from behind her. There was a tiny blaster in it. But it shook visibly as she tried to aim it.

"I'll shoot out the controls!"

Calhoun blinked. He'd had to make a drastic change in his estimate of the situation the instant he saw that the stowaway was a girl. Now he had to make another when her threat was not to kill him but to disable the ship. Women are rarely assassins, and when they are they don't use energy weapons. Daggers and poisons are more typical. But this girl threatened to destroy the ship rather than its owner, so she was not actually an assassin at all.

"I'd rather you didn't do that," said Calhoun dryly. "Besides, you'd get deadly bored if we were stuck in a derelict waiting for our air and food to give out."

Murgatroyd, for no reason whatever, felt it necessary to enter the conversation. *"Chee-chee-chee!"*

"A very sensible suggestion," observed Calhoun. "We'll sit down and have a cup of coffee." To the girl he said, "I'll take you to Orede, since that's where you say you want to go."

"I have a sweetheart there . . ."

Calhoun shook his head.

"No," he said reprovingly. "Nearly all the mining colony had packed itself into the ship that came into Weald with everybody dead. But not all. And there's been no check of what men were in the ship and what men weren't. You wouldn't go to Orede if it were likely your sweetheart had died on the way to you. Here's your coffee. Sugar or saccho, and do you take cream?"

She trembled a little, but she took the cup.

"I don't understand."

"Murgatroyd and I," explained Calhoun—and he did not know whether he spoke out of anger or something else—"we are do-gooders. We go around trying to keep people from getting sick or dying. Sometimes we even try to keep them from getting killed. It's our profession. We practice it even on our own behalf. We want to stay alive. So since you make such drastic threats, we will take you where you want to go. Especially since we're going there anyhow."

"You don't believe anything I've said!" It was a statement.

"Not a word," admitted Calhoun. "But you'll probably tell us something more believable presently. When did you eat last?"

"Yesterday."

"Would you rather do your own cooking?" asked Calhoun politely. "Or would you permit me to ready a snack?"

"I—I'll do it," she said.

She drank her coffee first, however, and then Calhoun showed her how to punch the readier for such-and-such dishes, to be extracted from storage and warmed or chilled, as the case might be, and served at dialed-for intervals. There was also equipment for preparing food for oneself, in one's own chosen manner—again an item to help make solitude not unendurable.

Calhoun deliberately immersed himself in the Galactic Directory, looking up the planet Orede. He was headed there, but he'd had no reason to inform himself about it before. Now he read with every appearance of absorption.

The girl ate daintily. Murgatroyd watched with highly amiable interest. But she looked acutely uncomfortable.

Calhoun finished with the Directory. He got out the microfilm reels which contained more information. He was specifically after the Med Service history of all the planets in this sector. He went through the filmed record of every inspection ever made on Weald and on Dara.

But Sector Twelve had not been run well. There was

no adequate account of a plague which had wiped out three-quarters of the population of an inhabited planet! It had happened shortly after one Med Ship visit, and was over before another Med Ship came by.

There should have been a painstaking investigation, even after the fact. There should have been a collection of infectious material and a reasonably complete identification and study of the agent. It hadn't been made. There was probably some other emergency at the time, and it slipped by. Calhoun, whose career was not to be spent in this sector, resolved on a blistering report about this negligence and its consequences.

He kept himself casually busy, ignoring the girl. A Med Ship man has resources of study and meditation with which to occupy himself during overdrive travel from one planet to another. Calhoun made use of those resources. He acted as if he were completely unconscious of the stowaway. But Murgatroyd watched her with charmed attention.

Hours after her discovery, she said uneasily, "Please?"

Calhoun looked up.

"Yes?"

"I don't know exactly how things stand."

"You are a stowaway," said Calhoun. "Legally, I have the right to put you out the air-lock. It doesn't seem necessary. There's a cabin. When you're sleepy, use it. Murgatroyd and I can make out quite well out here. When you're hungry, you now know how to get something to eat. When we land on Orede, you'll probably go about whatever business you have there. That's all."

She stared at him.

"But you don't believe what I've told you!"

"No," agreed Calhoun, but didn't add to the statement.

"But—I will tell you," she offered. "The police were after me. I had to get away from Weald! I had to! I'd stolen—"

He shook his head.

"No," he said. "If you were a thief, you'd say

anything in the world except that you were a thief.
You're not ready to tell the truth yet. You don't have to,
so why tell me anything? I suggest that you get some
sleep. Incidentally, there's no lock on the cabin door
because there's only supposed to be one person on this
ship at a time. But you can brace a chair to fasten it
somehow or other. Good night.''

She rose slowly. Twice her lips parted as if to speak
again, but then she went into the other cabin and closed
herself in. There was the sound of a chair being wedged
against the door.

Murgatroyd blinked at the place where she'd disappeared and then climbed up into Calhoun's lap, with
complete assurance of welcome. He settled himself and
was silent for moments. Then he said, *"Chee!"*

"I believe you're right," said Calhoun. "She doesn't
belong on Weald, or with the conditioning she'd have
had, there'd be only one place she'd dread worse than
Orede, which would be Dara. But I doubt she'd be
afraid to land even on Dara."

Murgatroyd liked to be talked to. He liked to pretend
that he carried on a conversation, like humans.

"Chee-chee!" he said with conviction.

"Definitely," agreed Calhoun. "She's not doing this
for her personal advantage. Whatever she thinks she's
doing, it's more important to her than her own life.
Murgatroyd . . .''

"Chee?" said Murgatroyd in an inquiring tone.

"There are wild cattle on Orede," said Calhoun.
"Herds and herds of them. I have a suspicion that
somebody's been shooting them. Lots of them. Do you
agree? Don't you think that a lot of cattle have been
slaughtered on Orede lately?''

Murgatroyd yawned. He settled himself still more
comfortably in Calhoun's lap.

"Chee, " he said drowsily.

He went to sleep, while Calhoun continued the examination of highly condensed information. Presently he
looked up the normal rate of increase, with other data,
among herds of *bovis domesticus* in a wild state, on
planets where there are no natural enemies.

It wasn't unheard-of for a world to be stocked with useful types of Terran fauna and flora before it was attempted to be colonized. Terran life-forms could play the devil with alien ecological systems—very much to humanity's benefit. Familiar micro-organisms and a standard vegetation added to the practicality of human settlements on otherwise alien worlds. But sometimes the results were strange.

They weren't often so strange, however, as to cause some hundreds of men to pack themselves frantically aboard a cargo ship which couldn't possibly sustain them, so that every man must die while the ship was in overdrive.

Still, by the time Calhoun turned in on a spare pneumatic mattress, he had calculated that as few as a dozen head of cattle, turned loose on a suitable planet, would have increased to herds of thousands or tens or even hundreds of thousands in much less time than had probably elapsed.

The Med Ship drove on in seemingly absolute solidity, with no sound from without, with no sight to be seen outside, with no evidence at all that it was not buried in the heart of a planet instead of flashing through emptiness at a speed so great as to have no meaning.

Next ship-day the girl looked oddly at Calhoun when she appeared in the control-room. Murgatroyd regarded her with great interest. Calhoun nodded politely and went back to what he'd been doing before she appeared.

"Shall I have breakfast?" she asked uncertainly.

"Murgatroyd and I have," he told her. "Why not?"

Silently, she operated the food-readier. She ate. Calhoun gave a very good portrayal of a man who will respond politely when spoken to, but who was busy with activities remote from stowaways.

About noon, ship-time, she asked, "When will we get to Orede?"

Calhoun told her absently, as if he were thinking of something else.

"What—what do you think happened there? I mean, to make that tragedy in the ship."

"I don't know," said Calhoun. "But I disagree with the authorities on Weald. I don't think it was a planned atrocity of the blueskins."

"Wh—what are blueskins?" asked the girl.

Calhoun turned around and looked at her directly.

"When lying," he said mildly, "you tell as much by what you pretend isn't, as by what you pretend is. You know what blueskins are!"

"But what do you think they are?" she asked.

"There used to be a human disease called smallpox," said Calhoun. "When people recovered from it, they were usually marked. Their skin had little scar pits here and there. At one time, back on Earth, it was expected that everybody would catch smallpox sooner or later, and a large percentage would die of it.

"And it was so much a matter of course that if they printed a picture of a criminal they never mentioned it if he were pock-marked. It was no distinction. But if he didn't have the markings, they'd mention that!" He paused. "Those pock-marks weren't hereditary, but otherwise a blueskin is like a man who had them. He can't be anything else!"

"Then you think they're human?"

"There's never yet been a case of reverse evolution," said Calhoun. "Maybe Pithecanthropus had a monkey uncle, but no Pithecanthropus ever went monkey."

She turned abruptly away. But she glanced at him often during that day. He continued to busy himself with those activities which make Med Ship life consistent with retained sanity.

Next day she asked without preliminary, "Don't you believe the blueskins planned for the ship with the dead men to arrive at Weald and spread plague there?"

"No," said Calhoun.

"Why?"

"It couldn't possibly work," Calhoun told her. "With only dead men on board, the ship wouldn't arrive at a place where the landing grid could bring it down. So that would be no good. And plague-stricken living men wouldn't try to conceal that they had the plague. They might ask for help, but they'd know they'd instantly be killed on Weald if they were found to be plague victims. So that would be no good, either! No, the ship wasn't intended to land plague on Weald.''

"Are you friendly to blueskins?" she asked uncertainly.

"Within reason," said Calhoun, "I am a well-wisher to all the human race. You're slipping, though. When using the word *blueskin* you should say it uncomfortably, as if it were a word no refined person liked to pronounce. You don't. We'll land on Orede tomorrow, by the way. If you ever intend to tell me the truth, there's not much time left."

She bit her lips. Twice, during the remainder of the day, she faced him and opened her mouth as if to speak, and then turned away again. Calhoun shrugged. He had fairly definite ideas about her, by now. He carefully kept them tentative, but no girl born and raised on Weald would willingly go to Orede, with all of Weald believing that a shipload of miners preferred death to remaining there. It tied in, like everything else that was unpleasant, to blueskins. Nobody from Weald would dream of landing on Orede! Not now!

A little before the Med Ship was due to break out from overdrive, the girl said very carefully, "You've been very kind. I'd like to thank you. I—I didn't really believe I would live to get to Orede."

Calhoun raised his eyebrows.

"I wish I could tell you everything you want to know," she added regretfully. "I think you're . . . really decent. But some thing . . ."

Calhoun said caustically, "You've told me a great deal. You weren't born on Weald. You weren't raised there. The people of Dara—notice that I don't say blueskins, though they are—the people of Dara have made at least one spaceship since Weald threatened them with extermination. There is probably a new food shortage on Dara now, leading to pure desperation. Most likely it's bad enough to make them risk landing on Orede to kill cattle and freeze beef to help. They've worked out—"

She gasped and sprang to her feet. She snatched out

the tiny blaster in her pocket. She pointed it waveringly at him.

"I have to kill you!" she cried desperately. "I—I have to!"

Calhoun reached out. She tugged despairingly at the blaster's trigger. Nothing happened. Before she could realize that she hadn't turned off the safety, Calhoun twisted the weapon from her fingers. He stepped back.

"Good girl!" he said approvingly. "I'll give this back to you when we land. And thanks. Thanks very much!"

She wrung her hands. Then she stared at him.

"Thanks? When I tried to kill you?"

"Of course!" said Calhoun. "I'd made guesses. I couldn't know that they were right. When you tried to kill me, you confirmed every one. Now, when we land on Orede I'm going to get you to try to put me in touch with your friends. It's going to be tricky, because they must be pretty well scared about that ship. But it's a highly desirable thing to get done!"

He went to the ships' control board and sat down before it.

"Twenty minutes to breakout," he observed.

Murgatroyd peered out of his little cubbyhole. His eyes were anxious. *Tormals* are amiable little creatures. During the days in overdrive, Calhoun had paid less than the usual amount of attention to Murgatroyd, while the girl was fascinating.

They'd made friends, awkwardly on the girl's part, very pleasantly on Murgatroyd's. But only moments ago there had been bitter emotion in the air. Murgatroyd had fled to his cubbyhole to escape it. He was distressed. Now that there was silence again, he peered out unhappily.

"Chee?" he queried plaintively. *"Chee-chee-chee?"*

Calhoun said matter-of-factly, "It's all right, Murgatroyd. If we aren't blasted as we try to land, we should be able to make friends with everybody and get something accomplished."

The statement was hopelessly inaccurate.

THERE WAS NO answer from the ground when breakout came and Calhoun drove the Med Ship to a favorable position for a call. He patiently repeated, over and over again, that the Med Ship *Aesclipus Twenty* notified its arrival and requested coordinates for landing. He added that its mass was fifty standard tons and that the purpose of its visit was a planetary health inspection.

But there was no reply. There should have been a crisp description of the direction from the planet's center at which, a certain time so many hours or minutes later, the force-fields of the grid would find it convenient to lock onto and lower the Med Ship. But the communicator remained silent.

"There is a landing grid," said Calhoun, frowning, "and if they're using it to load fresh meat for Dara, from the herds I'm told about, it should be manned. But they don't seem to intend to answer. Maybe they think that if they pretend I'm not here I'll go away."

He reflected, and his frown deepened.

"If I didn't know what I know, I might. So if I land on emergency rockets the blueskins down below may decide that I come from Weald. And in that case it would be reasonable to blast me before I could land and unload some fighting men. On the other hand, no ship from Weald would conceivably land without impassioned assurance that it was safe. It would drop bombs." He turned to the girl. "How many Darians down below?"

She shook her head.

"You don't know," said Calhoun, "or won't tell, yet. But they ought to be told about the arrival of that ship at Weald, and what Weald thinks about it! My guess is that you came to tell them. It isn't likely that Dara gets news directly from Weald. Where were you put ashore from Dara, when you set out to be a spy?"

Her lips parted to speak, but she compressed them tightly. She shook her head again.

"It must have been plenty far away," said Calhoun restlessly. "Your people would have built a ship, and made fine forged papers for it, and they'd travel so far from this part of space that when they landed nobody would think of Dara. They'd use make-up to cover the blue spots, but maybe it was so far away that blueskins had never been heard of!"

Her face looked pinched, but she did not reply.

"Then they'd land half a dozen of you, with a supply of make-up for the blue patches. And you'd separate, and take ships that went various roundabout ways, and arrive on Weald one by one, to see what could be done there to—" He stopped. "When did you find out positively that there wasn't any plague anymore?"

She began to grow pale.

"I'm not a mindreader," said Calhoun. "But it adds up. You're from Dara. You've been on Weald. It's practically certain that there are other . . . agents, if you like that word better, on Weald. And there hasn't been a plague on Weald so you people aren't carriers of it. But you knew it in advance, I think. How'd you learn? Did a ship in some sort of trouble land there, on Dara?"

"Y-yes," said the girl. "We wouldn't let it go again. But the people didn't catch—they didn't die. They lived—"

She stopped short.

"It's not fair to trap me!" she cried passionately. "It's not fair!"

"I'll stop," said Calhoun.

He turned to the control-board. The Med Ship was

only planetary diameters from Orede, now, and the electron telescope showed shining stars in leisurely motion across its screen. Then a huge, gibbous shining shape appeared, and there were irregular patches of that muddy color which is seabottom, and varicolored areas which were plains and forests. Also there were mountains. Calhoun steadied the image and squinted at it.

"The mine," he observed, "was found by members of a hunting party, killing wild cattle for sport."

Even a small planet has many millions of square miles of surface, and a single human installation on a whole world will not be easy to find by random search. But there were clues to this one. Men hunting for sport would not choose a tropic nor an arctic climate to hunt in. So if they found a mineral deposit, it would have been in a temperate zone.

Cattle would not be found deep in a mountainous terrain. The mine would not be on a prairie. The settlement on Orede, then, would be near the edge of mountains, not far from a prairie such as wild cattle would frequent, and it would be in a temperate climate.

Forested areas could be ruled out. And there would be a landing grid. Handling only one ship at a time, it might be a very small grid. It could be only hundreds of yards across and less than half a mile high. But its shadow would be distinctive.

Calhoun searched among low mountains near unforested prairie in a temperate zone. He found a speck. He enlarged it manyfold. It was the mine on Orede. There were heaps of tailings. There was something which cast a long, lacy shadow: the landing grid.

"But they don't answer our call," observed Calhoun, "so we go down unwelcomed."

He inverted the Med Ship and the emergency rockets boomed. The ship plunged planetward.

A long time later it was deep in the planet's atmosphere. The noise of its rockets had become thunderous, with air to carry and to reinforce the sound.

"Hold on to something, Murgatroyd," commanded Calhoun. "We may have to dodge some ack."

But nothing came up from below. The Med Ship

again inverted itself, and its rockets pointed toward the planet and poured out pencil-thin, blue-white, high-velocity flames. It checked slightly, but continued to descend. It was not directly above the grid.

It swept downward until almost level with the peaks of the mountains in which the mine lay. It tilted again, and swept onward over the mountaintops, and then tilted once more and went racing up the valley in which the landing grid was plainly visible. Calhoun swung it on an erratic course, lest there be opposition.

But there was no sign. Then the rockets bellowed, and the ship slowed its forward motion, hovered momentarily, and settled to solidity outside the framework of the grid. The grid was small, as Calhoun reasoned. But it reached interminably toward the sky.

The rockets cut off. Slender as the flames had been, they'd melted and bored thin drill-holes deep into the soil. Molten rock boiled and bubbled down below. But there seemed no other sound. There was no other motion. There was absolute stillness all around. But when Calhoun switched on the outside microphones a faint, sweet melange of high-pitched chirpings came from tiny creatures hidden under the vegetation of the mountainsides.

Calhoun put a blaster in his pocket and stood up.

"We'll see what it looks like outside," he said with a certain grimness. "I don't quite believe what the vision screens show."

Minutes later he stepped down to the ground from the Med Ship's exit port. The ship had landed perhaps a hundred feet from what once had been a wooden building. In it, ore from the mines was concentrated and the useless tailings carried away by a conveyer belt to make a monstrous pile of broken stone. But there was no longer a building.

Next to it there had been a structure containing an ore-crusher. The massive machinery could still be seen, but the structure was in fragments. Next to that, again, had been the shaft-head shelters of the mine. They also were shattered practically to matchsticks.

The look of the ground about the building sites was simply and purely impossible. It was a mass of hoof-prints. Cattle by thousands and tens of thousands had trampled everything. Cattle had burst in the wooden sides of the buildings. Cattle had piled themselves up against the beams upholding roofs until the buildings collapsed.

Then cattle had gone plunging over the wrecked buildings until there was nothing left but indescribable chaos. Many, many cattle had died in the crush. There were heaps of dead beasts about the metal girders which were the foundation of the landing grid. The air was tainted by the smell of carrion.

The settlement had been destroyed, positively by stampeded cattle in tens or hundreds of thousands charging blindly through and over and upon it. Senselessly, they'd trampled each other to horrible shapelessness. The mine shaft was not choked, because enormously strong timbers had fallen across and blocked it. But everything else was pure destruction.

Calhoun said evenly, "Clever! Very clever! You can't blame men when beasts stampede. We should accept the evidence that some monstrous herd, making its way through a mountain pass, somehow went crazy and bolted for the plains. This settlement got in the way and it was too bad for the settlement! Everything's explained, except the ship that went to Weald.

"A cattle stampede, yes. Anybody can believe that! But there was a man stampede. Men stampeded into the ship as blindly as the cattle trampled down this little town. The ship stampeded off into space as insanely as the cattle. But a stampede of men and cattle, in the same place? That's a little too much!"

"But what—"

"How," asked Calhoun directly, "do you intend to get in touch with your friends here?"

"I—I don't know," she said, distressed. "But if the ship stays here, they're bound to come and see why. Won't they? Or will they?"

"If they're sane, they won't," said Calhoun. "The

one undesirable thing, here, would be human footprints on top of cattle tracks. If your friends are a meat-getting party from Dara, as I believe, they should cover up their tracks, get off-planet as fast as possible, and pray that no signs of their former presence are ever discovered. That would be their best first move, certainly!"

"What should I do?" she asked helplessly.

"I'm far from sure. At a guess, and for the moment, probably nothing. I'll work something out. I've got the devil of a job before me, though. I can't spend but so much time here."

"You can leave me here. . . ."

He grunted and turned away. It was naturally unthinkable that he should leave another human being on a supposedly uninhabited planet, with the knowledge that it might actually be uninhabited, and the future knowledge that any visitors would have the strongest of possible reasons to hide themselves away.

He believed that there were Darians here, and the girl in the Med Ship, so he also believed, was also a Darian. But any who might be hiding had so much to lose if they were discovered that they might be hundreds or even thousands of miles from anywhere a spaceship would normally land—if they hadn't fled after the incident of the spaceship's departure with its load of doomed passengers.

Considered detachedly, the odds were that there was again a food shortage on Dara; that blueskins, in desperation, had raided or were raiding or would raid the cattle herds of Orede for food to carry back to their home planet; that somehow the miners on Orede had found that they had blueskin neighbors, and died of the consequences of their terror. It was a risky guess to make on such evidence as Calhoun considered he had, but no other guess was possible.

If his guess were right, he was under some obligation to do exactly what he believed the girl considered her mission—to warn all blueskins that Weald would presently try to find them on Orede, when all hell must break loose upon Dara for punishment. But if there were men here, he couldn't leave a written warning for them in default of friendly contact.

They might not find it, and a search party of Wealdians might. All he could possibly do was try to make contact and give warning by such means as would leave no evidence behind that he'd done so. Weald would consider a warning sure proof of blueskin guilt.

It was not satisfactory to be limited to broadcasts which might or might not be picked up, and were unlikely to be acknowledged. But he settled down with the communicator to make the attempt.

He called first on a GC wave length and form. It was unlikely that blueskins would use general communication bands to keep in touch with each other, but it had to be tried. He broadcast, tuned as broadly as possible, and went up and down the GC spectrum, repeating his warning painstakingly and listening without hope for a reply.

He did find one spot on the dial where there was re-radiation of his message, as if from a tuned receiver. But he could not get a fix on it: nobody might be listening. He exhausted the normal communication pattern. Then he broadcast on old-fashioned amplitude modulation which a modern communicator would not pick up at all, and which therefore might be used by men in hiding.

He worked for a long time. Then he shrugged and gave it up. He'd repeated to absolute tedium the facts that any Darians—blueskins—on Orede ought to know. There'd been no answer. And it was all too likely that if he'd been received, that those who heard him took his message for a trick to discover if there were any hearers.

He clicked off at last and stood up, shaking his head. Suddenly the Med Ship seemed empty. Then he saw Murgatroyd staring vexedly at the exit port. The inner door of that small air-lock was closed. The telltale light said the outer door was not locked. Someone had gone out quietly. The girl. Of course.

Calhoun said angrily, "How long ago, Murgatroyd?"

"Chee!" said Murgatroyd indignantly.

It wasn't an answer, but it showed that Murgatroyd was vexed that he'd been left behind. He and the girl were close friends, now. If she'd left Murgatroyd in the ship when he wanted to go with her, then she wasn't coming back.

Calhoun swore. He made certain she was not in the ship. He flipped the outside-speaker switch and said curtly into the microphone, "Coffee! Murgatroyd and I are having coffee. Will you come back, please?"

He repeated the call, and repeated it again. Multiplied as his voice was by the speakers, she should hear him within a mile. She did not appear. He went to a small and inconspicuous closet and armed himself. A Med Ship man was not ever expected to fight, but there were blast-rifles available for extreme emergency.

When he'd slung a power-pack over his shoulder and reached the air-lock, there was still no sign of his late stowaway. He stood in the air-lock door for long minutes, staring angrily about. Almost certainly she wouldn't be looking in the mountains for men of Dara come here for cattle. He used a pair of binoculars, first at low-magnification to search as wide an area down-valley as possible, and then at highest power to search the most likely routes.

He found a small, bobbing speck beyond a faraway hill crest. It was her head. It went down below the hilltop.

He snapped a command to Murgatroyd, and when the *tormal* was on the ground outside, he locked the port with that combination that nobody but a Med Ship man was at all likely to discover or use.

"She's an idiot!" he told Murgatroyd sourly. "Come along! We've got to be idiots too!"

He set out in pursuit.

There was blue sky overhead, as was inevitable on any oxygen-atmosphere planet of a Sol-type yellow sun. There were mountains, as is universal in planets whose surface rises and falls and folds and bends from the effects of weather or vulcanim. There were plants, as has come about wherever micro-organisms have broken down rock to a state where it can nourish vegetation. And naturally there were animals.

There were even trees of severely practical design, and underbrush and ground-cover equivalent to grass. There was, in short, a perfectly predictable ecological system on Orede. The organic molecules involved in life here would be made up of the same elements in the same combinations as elsewhere where the same conditions of temperature and moisture and sunshine obtained.

It was a distinctly Earthlike world, as it could not help but be, and it was reasonable for cattle to thrive and increase here. Only men's minds kept it from being a place where humans would thrive, too.

But only Calhoun would have considered the splintered settlement a proof of that last.

The girl had a long start. Twice Calhoun came to places where she could have chosen either of two ways onward. Each time he had to determine which she'd followed. That cost time. Then the mountains abruptly ended and a vast undulating plain stretched away to the horizon. There were at least two large masses and many smaller clumps of what could only be animals gathered together. Cattle.

But here the girl was plainly in view. Calhoun increased his stride. He began to gain on her. She did not look behind.

Murgatroyd said, *"Chee!"* in a complaining tone.

"I should have left you behind," agreed Calhoun dourly, "but there was and is a chance I won't get back. You'll have to keep on hiking."

He plodded on. His memory of the terrain around the mining settlement told him that there was no definite destination in the girl's mind. But she was in no such despair as to want deliberately to be lost. She'd guessed, Calhoun believed, that if there were Darians on the planet, they'd keep the landing grid under observation.

If they saw her leave that area and could see that she was alone, they should intercept her to find out the meaning of the Med Ship's landing. Then she could identify herself as one of them and give them the terribly necessary warning of Weald's suspicions.

"But," said Calhoun sourly, "if she's right, they'll have seen me marching after her now, which spoils her scheme. And I'd like to help it, but the way she's going is too dangerous!"

He went down into one of the hollows of the uneven plain. He saw a clump of a dozen or so cattle a little distance away. The bull looked up and snorted. The cows regarded him truculently. Their air was not one of bovine tranquility.

He was up the farther hillside and out of sight before the bull worked himself up to a charge. Then Calhoun suddenly remembered one of the items in the data about cattle he'd looked into just the other day. He felt himself grow pale.

"Murgatroyd!" he said sharply. "We've got to catch up! Fast! Stay with me if you can, but—" he was jog-trotting as he spoke—"even if you get lost I have to hurry!"

He ran fifty paces and walked fifty paces. He ran fifty and walked fifty. He saw her, atop a rolling of the ground. She came to a full stop. He ran. He saw her turn to retrace her steps. He flung off the safety of the blast-rifle and let off a roaring blast at the ground for her to hear.

Suddenly she was fleeing desperately, toward him. He plunged on. She vanished down into a hollow. Horns appeared over the hillcrest she'd just left. Cattle appeared. Four, a dozen, fifteen, twenty! They moved ominously in her wake.

He saw her again, running frantically over another upward swell of the prairie. He let off another blast to guide her. He ran on at top speed with Murgatroyd trailing anxiously behind. From time to time Murgatroyd called *"Chee-chee-chee!"* in frightened pleading not to be abandoned.

More cattle appeared against the horizon. Fifty or a hundred. They came after the first clump. The first group of a bull and his harem were moving faster, now.

The girl fled from them, but it is the instinct of beef cattle on the open range—Calhoun had learned it only two days before—to charge any human they find on foot. A mounted man to their dim minds is a creature to be tolerated or fled from, but a human on foot is to be crushed and stamped and gored.

Those in the lead were definitely charging now, with heads bent low. The bull charged furiously with shut eyes, as bulls do, but the cows, many times more deadly, charged with their eyes wide open and wickedly alert, and with a lumbering speed much greater than the girl could manage.

She came up over the last rise, chalky-white and gasping, her hair flying, in the last extremity of terror. The nearest of the pursuing cattle were within ten yards when Calhoun fired from twenty yards beyond. One creature bellowed as the blast-bolt struck.

It went down and others crashed into it and swept over it, and more came on. The girl saw Calhoun now, and ran toward him, panting. He knelt very deliberately and began to check the charge by shooting the leading animals.

He did not succeed. There were more cattle following the first, and more and more behind them. It appeared that all the cattle on the plain joined in the blind and senseless charge. The thudding of hoofs became a mutter and then a rumble and then a growl.

Plunging, clumsy figures rushed past on either side. But horns and heads heaved up over the mound of animals Calhoun had shot. He shot them too. More and more cattle came pounding past the rampart of his victims, but always, it seemed, some elected to climb the heap of their dead and dying fellows, and Calhoun shot and shot . . .

But he split the herd. The foremost animals had been charging a sighted human enemy. Others had followed because it is the instinct of cattle to join their running fellows in whatever crazed urgency they feel. There was a dense, pounding, wailing, grunting, puffing, raising thick and impenetrable clouds of dust which hid everything but galloping beasts going past on either side.

It lasted for minutes. Then the thunder of hoofs diminished. It ended abruptly, and Calhoun and the girl were left alone with the gruesome pile of animals which had divided the charging herd into two parts. They could see the rears of innumerable running animals, stupidly continuing the charge, hardly different, now, from a stampede, whose original objective none now remembered.

Calhoun thoughtfully touched the barrel of his blast-rifle and winced at its scorching heat.

"I just realized," he said coldly, "that I don't know your name. What is it?"

"Maril," said the girl. She swallowed. "Th—thank you."

"Maril," said Calhoun, "you are an idiot! It was half-witted at best to go off by yourself! You could have been lost! You could have cost me days of hunting for you, days badly needed for more important matters!"

He stopped and took breath. "You may have spoiled what little chance I've got to do something about the plans Weald's already making! You have just acted with the most concentrated folly, and the most magnificent imbecility that you or anybody else could manage!"

He said more bitterly still, "And I had to leave Murgatroyd behind to get to you in time! He was right in the path of that charge!"

He turned away from her and said dourly, "All right! Come on back to the ship. We'll go to Dara. We'd have to, anyhow. But Murgatroyd—"

Then he heard a very small sneeze. Out of a rolling wall of still-roiling dust, Murgatroyd appeared forlornly. He was dust-covered, and draggled, and his tail dropped, and he sneezed again. He moved as if he could barely put one paw before another, but at sight of Calhoun he sneezed yet again and said, *"Chee!"* in a disconsolate voice. Then he sat down and waited for Calhoun to come and pick him up.

When Calhoun did so, Murgatroyd clung to him

pathetically and said, *"Chee-chee!"* and again, *"Chee-chee!"* with the intonation of one telling of incredible horrors and disasters endured. And as a matter of fact the escape of a small animal like Murgatroyd was remarkable. He'd escaped the trampling hoofs of at least hundreds of charging animals. Luck must have played a great part in it, but an hysterical agility in dodging must have been required, too.

Calhoun headed back for the valley where the settlement had been, and the Med Ship was. Murgatroyd clung to his neck. The girl Maril followed discouragedly. She was at that age when girls—and men of corresponding type—can grow most passionately devoted to ideals or causes in default of a promising personal romance. When concerned with such causes they become splendidly confident that whatever they decide to do is sensible if only it is dramatic. But Maril was shaken, now.

Calhoun did not speak to her again. He led the way. A mile back toward the mountains, they began to see stragglers from the now-vanished herd. A little farther, those stragglers began to notice them. It would have been a matter of no moment if they'd been domesticated dairy cattle, but these were range cattle gone wild. Twice, Calhoun had to use his blast-rifle to discourage incipient charges by irritated bulls or even more irritated cows. Those with calves darkly suspected Calhoun of designs upon their offspring.

It was a relief to enter the valley again. But it was two miles more to the landing grid with the Med Ship beside it and the reek of carrion in the air.

They were perhaps two hundred feet from the ship when a blast-rifle crashed and its bolt whined past Calhoun so close that he felt the monstrous heat. There had been no challenge. There was no warning. There was simply a shot which came horribly close to ending Calhoun's career in a completely arbitrary fashion.

IV

FIVE MINUTES LATER Calhoun had located one would-be killer behind a mass of splintered planking that once had been a wall. He set the wood afire by a blaster-bolt and then viciously sent other bolts all around the man it had sheltered when he fled from the flames. He could have killed him ten times over, but it was more desirable to open communication. So he missed intentionally.

Maril had cried out that she came from Dara and had word for them, but they did not answer. There were three men with heavy-duty blast-rifles. One was the one Calhoun had burned out of his hiding place. That man's rifle exploded when the flames hit it. Two remained.

One—so Calhoun presently discovered—was working his way behind underbrush to a shelf from which he could shoot down at Calhoun. Calhoun had dropped into a hollow and pulled Maril to cover at the first shot. The second man happily planned to get to a point where he could shoot him like a fish in a barrel.

The third man had fired half a dozen times and then disappeared. Calhoun estimated that he intended to get around to the rear, hoping there was no protection from that direction for Calhoun. It would take some time for him to manage it.

So Calhoun industriously concentrated his fire on the man trying to get above him. He was behind a boulder, not too dissimilar to Calhoun's breastwork. Calhoun set

fire to the brush at the point at which the other man
aimed. That, then, made his effort useless.

Then Calhoun sent a dozen bolts at the other man's
rocky shield. It heated up. Steam rose in a whitish mass
and blew directly away from Calhoun. He saw that antagonist flee. He saw him so clearly that he was positive
that there was a patch of blue pigment on the right-hand
side of the back of his neck.

He grunted and swung to find the third. That man
moved through thick undergrowth, and Calhoun set it
on fire in a neat pattern of spreading flames. Evidently,
these men had had no training in battle tactics with
blast-rifles. The third man also had to get away. He did.
But something from him arched through the smoke. It
fell to the ground directly upwind from Calhoun. White
smoke puffed up violently.

It was instinct that made Calhoun react as he did. He
jerked the girl Maril to her feet and rushed her toward
the Med Ship. Smoke from the flung bomb upwind
barely swirled around him and missed Maril altogether.
Calhoun, though, got a whiff of something strange, not
scorched or burning vegetation at all. He ceased to
breathe and plunged onward. In clear air he emptied his
lungs and refilled them. They were then halfway to the
ship, with Murgatroyd prancing on ahead.

But then Calhoun's heart began to pound furiously.
His muscles twitched and tensed. He felt extraordinary
symptoms like an extreme of agitation. He swore, but a
Med Ship man would not react to such symptoms as a
non-medically trained man would have done. Calhoun
was familiar enough with tear gas, used by police on
some planets.

But this was different and worse. Even as he helped
and urged Maril onward, he automatically considered
his sensations, and had it—panic gas. Police did not use
it because panic is worse than rioting. Calhoun felt all
the physical symptoms of fear and of gibbering terror.

A man whose mind yields to terror experiences certain
physical sensations: wildly beating heart, tensed and
twitching muscles, and a frantic impulse to convulsive

action. A man in whom those physical sensations are induced by other means will, ordinarily, find his mind yielding to terror.

Calhoun couldn't combat his feelings, but his clinical attitude enabled him to act despite them. The three from Weald reached the base of the Med Ship. One of their enemies had lost his rifle and need not be counted. Another had fled from flames and might be ignored for some moments, anyhow. But a blast-bolt struck the ship's metal hull only feet from Calhoun, and he whipped around to the other side and let loose a staccato rat-tat-tat of fire which emptied the rifle of all its charges.

Then he opened the air-lock door, hating the fact that he shook and trembled. He urged the girl and Murgatroyd in. He slammed the outer air-lock door just as another blast-bolt hit.

"They—they don't realize," said Maril desperately. "If they only knew . . ."

"Talk to them, if you like," said Calhoun. His teeth chattered and he raged, because the symptom was of terror he denied.

He pushed a button on the control-board. He pointed to a microphone. He got at an oxygen bottle and inhaled deeply. Oxygen, obviously, should be an antidote for panic, since the symptoms of terror act to increase the oxygenation of the bloodstream and muscles, and to make superhuman exertion possible if necessary.

Breathing ninety-five percent oxygen produced the effect the terror-inspiring gas strove for, so his heart slowed nearly to normal and his body relaxed. He held out his hand and it did not tremble. He'd been affronted to see it shake uncontrollably when he pushed the microphone button for Maril.

He turned to her. She hadn't spoken into the mike.

"They may not be from Dara!" she said shakily. "I just thought! They could be somebody else, maybe criminals who planned to raid the mine for a shipload of its ore."

"Nonsense," said Calhoun. "I saw one of them

clearly enough to be sure. But they're skeptical characters. I'm afraid there may be more on the way here from wherever they keep themselves. Anyhow, now we know some of them are in hearing! I'll take advantage of that and we'll go on."

He took the microphone. An instant later his voice boomed in the stillness outside the ship, cutting through the thin shrill whirring of invisible small creatures.

"This is the Med Ship *Aesclipus Twenty*," said Calhoun's voice, amplified to a shout. "I left Weald four days ago, one day after the cargo ship from here arrived with everybody on board dead. On Weald they don't know how it happened, but they suspect blueskins. Sooner or later they'll search here.

"Get away! Cover up your tracks! Hide all signs that you've ever been here! Get the hell away, fast! One more warning! There's talk of fusion-bombing Dara. They're scared! If they find your traces, they'll be still more scared! So cover up your tracks and get away from here!"

The many-times-multiplied voice rolled and echoed among the hills. But it was very clear. Where it could be heard it could be understood, and it could be heard for miles.

But there was no response to it. Calhoun waited a reasonable time. Then he shrugged and seated himself at the control-board.

"It isn't easy," he observed, "to persuade desperate men that they've outsmarted themselves! Hold hard, Murgatroyd!"

The rockets bellowed. Then there was a tremendous noise to end all noises, and the ship began to climb. It sped up and up and up. By the time it was out of atmosphere it had velocity enough to coast to clear space and Calhoun cut the rockets altogether.

He busied himself with those astrogational chores which began with orienting oneself to galactic directions after leaving a planet which rotates at its own individual speed. Then one computes the overdrive course to another planet, from the respective coordinates of the world one is leaving and the one one aims for.

Then, in this case at any rate, there was the very finicky task of picking out a fourth-magnitude star of whose planets one was his destination. He aimed for it with ultra-fine precision.

"Overdrive coming," he said presently. "Hold on!"

Space reeled. There was nausea and giddiness and a horrible sensation of falling in a wildly unlikely spiral. Then stillness, and solidity, and the blackness outside the Med Ship. The little craft was in overdrive again.

After a long while, the girl Maril said uneasily, "I don't know what you plan now—"

"I'm going to Dara," said Calhoun. "On Orede I tried to get the blueskins there to get going, fast. Maybe I succeeded. I don't know. But this thing's been mishandled! Even if there's a famine people shouldn't do things out of desperation! Being desperate jogs the brain off-center. One doesn't think straight!"

"I know now that I was . . . very foolish."

"Forget it," commanded Calhoun. "I wasn't talking about you. Here I run into a situation that the Med Service should have caught and cleaned up generations ago! But it's not only a Med Service obligation; it's a current mess! Before I could begin to get at the basic problem, those idiots on Orede—it'd happened before I reached Weald! An emotional explosion triggered by a ship full of dead men that nobody intended to kill."

Maril shook her head.

"Those Darian characters," said Calhoun, annoyed, "shouldn't have gone to Orede in the first place. If they went there, they should at least have stayed on a continent where there were no people from Weald digging a mine and hunting cattle for sport on their off days! They could be spotted! I believe they were.

"And again, if it had been a long way from the mine installation, they could probably have wiped out the people who sighted them before they could get back with the news! But it looks like miners saw men hunting, and got close enough to see they were blueskins, and then got back to the mine with the news!"

She waited for him to explain.

"I know I'm guessing, but it fits!" he said distaste-fully. "So something had to be done. Either the mining settlement had to be wiped out or the story that blue-skins were on Orede had to be discredited. The blue-skins tried for both. They used panic gas on a herd of cattle and it made them crazy and they charged the settlement like the four-footed lunatics they are!

"And the blueskins used panic gas on the settlement itself as the cattle went through. It should have settled the whole business nicely. After it was over every man in the settlement would believe he'd been out of his head for a while, and he'd have the crazy state of the set-tlement to think about.

"He wouldn't be sure of what he'd seen or heard beforehand. They might try to verify the blueskin story later, but they wouldn't believe anything with certainty. It should have worked!"

Again she waited.

"Unfortunately, when the miners panicked, they stampeded into the ship. Also unfortunately, panic gas got into the ship with them. So they stayed panicked while the astrogator—in panic!—took off. They headed for Weald and threw on the overdrive—which would be set for Weald anyhow—because that would be the fastest way to run away from whatever he imagined he feared. But he and all the men on the ship were still crazy with panic from the gas they kept breathing until they died!"

Silence. After a long interval, Maril asked, "You don't think the Darians intended to kill?"

"I think they were stupid!" said Calhoun angrily. "Somebody's always urging the police to use panic gas in case of public tumult. But it's too dangerous. Nobody knows what one man will do in a panic. Take a hundred or two or three and panic them all, and there's no limit to their craziness! The whole thing was handled wrong!"

"But you don't blame them?"

"For being stupid, yes," said Calhoun fretfully. "But if I'd been in their place, perhaps—"

"Where were you born?" asked Maril suddenly.

Calhoun jerked his head around. "No! Not where you're guessing, or hoping. Not on Dara. Just because I act as if Darians were human doesn't mean I have to be one! I'm a Med Service man, and I'm acting as I think I should." His tone became exasperated.

"Dammit, I'm supposed to deal with health situations, actual and possible causes of human deaths! And if Weald thinks it finds proof that blueskins are in space again and caused the death of Wealdians, it won't be healthy! They're halfway set anyhow to drop fusion-bombs on Dara to wipe it out!"

Maril said fiercely, "They might as well drop bombs. It'll be quicker than starvation, at least!"

Calhoun looked at her, more exasperated than before.

"It is a crop failure again?" he demanded. When she nodded he said bitterly, "Famine conditions already?" When she nodded again he said drearily, "And of course famine is the great-grandfather of health problems! And that's right in my lap with all the rest!"

He stood up. Then he sat down again.

"I'm tired!" he said flatly. "I'd like to get some sleep. Would you mind taking a book or something and going into the other cabin? Murgatroyd and I would like a little relaxation from reality. With luck, if I go to sleep, I may only have a nightmare. It'll be a terrific improvement on what I'm in now!"

Alone in the control-compartment, he tried to relax, but it was not possible. He flung himself into a comfortable chair and brooded. There is brooding and brooding. It can be a form of wallowing in self-pity, engaged in for emotional satisfaction. But it can be, also, a way of bringing out unfavorable factors in a situation. A man in an optimistic mood can ignore them. But no awkward situation is likely to be remedied while any of its elements are neglected.

Calhoun dourly considered the situation of the people of the planet Dara, which it was his job as a Med Service man to remedy or at least improve. Those people were marked by patches of blue pigment as an inherited consequence of a plague of three generations past. Because of the marking, which it was easy to believe a sign of continuing infection, they were hated and dreaded by their neighbors. Dara was a planet of pariahs—excluded from the human race by those who feared them.

And now there was famine on Dara for the second time, and they were of no mind to starve quietly. There was food on the planet Orede, monstrous herds of cattle without owners. It was natural enough for Darians to build a ship or ships and try to bring food back to its starving people. But that desperately necessary enterprise had now roused Weald to a frenzy of apprehension.

Weald was, if possible, more hysterically afraid of blueskins than ever before, and even more implacably the enemy of the starving planet's population. Weald itself prospered. Ironically, it had such an excess of foodstuffs that it stored them in unneeded spaceships in orbits about itself.

Hundreds of thousands of tons of grain circled Weald in sealed-tight hulks, while the people of Dara starved and only dared try to steal—if it could be called stealing—some of the innumerable wild cattle of Orede.

The blueskins on Orede could not trust Calhoun, so they pretended not to hear. Or maybe they didn't hear. They'd been abandoned and betrayed by all of humanity off their world. They'd been threatened and oppressed by guardships in orbit about them, ready to shoot down any spacecraft they might send aloft. . . .

So Calhoun brooded, while Murgatroyd presently yawned and climbed to his cubbyhole and curled up to sleep with his furry tail carefully adjusted over his nose.

A long time later Calhoun heard small sounds which were not normal on a Med Ship in overdrive. They were not part of the random noises carefully generated to keep the silence of the ship endurable. Calhoun raised his head. He listened sharply. No sound could come from outside.

He knocked on the door of the sleeping cabin. The noises stopped instantly.

"Come out," he commanded through the door.

"I'm—I'm all right," said Maril's voice. But it was

not quite steady. She paused. "Did I make a noise? I was having a bad dream."

"I wish," said Calhoun, "that you'd tell me the truth just occasionally! Come out, please!"

There were stirrings. After a little it opened and Maril appeared. She looked as if she'd been crying. She said, quickly, "I probably look queer, but it's because I was asleep."

"To the contrary," said Calhoun, fuming. "You've been lying awake crying. I don't know why. I've been out here wishing I could, because I'm frustrated. But since you aren't asleep maybe you can help me with my job. I've figured some things out. For some others I need facts. Will you give them to me?"

She swallowed. "I'll try."

"Coffee?" he asked.

Murgatroyd popped his head out of his miniature sleeping cabin.

"Chee?" he asked interestedly.

"Go back to sleep!" snapped Calhoun.

He began to pace back and forth.

"I need to know something about the pigment patches," he said jerkily. "Maybe it sounds crazy to think of such things now—first things first, you know. But this is a first thing! So long as Darians don't look like the people of other worlds, they'll be believed to be different. If they look repulsive, they'll be believed to be evil.

"Tell me about those patches. They're different sizes and different shapes and they appear in different places. You've none on your face or hands, anyhow."

"I haven't any at all," said the girl reservedly.

"I thought—"

"Not everybody," she said defensively. "Nearly, yes. But not all. Some people don't have them. Some people are born with bluish splotches on their skin, but they fade out while they're children. When they grow up they're just like the people of Weald or any other world. And their children never have them."

Calhoun stared.

"You couldn't possibly be proved to be a Darian, then?"

She shook her head. Calhoun remembered, and started the coffee.

"When you left Dara," he said, "you were carried a long, long way, to some planet where they'd practically never heard of Dara, and where the name meant nothing. You could have settled there, or anywhere else and forgotten about Dara. But you didn't. Why not, since you're not a blueskin?"

"But I am!" she said fiercely. "My parents, my brothers and sister, and Korvan—"

Then she bit her lip. Calhoun took note but did not comment on the name she'd mentioned.

"Then your parents had the splotches fade, so you never had them," he said absorbedly. "Something like that happened on Tralee, once! There's a virus, a whole group of virus particles! Normally we humans are immune to them. One has to be in terrifically bad physical condition for them to take hold and produce whatever effects they do. But once they're established they're passed on from mother to child. And when they die out it's during childhood, too!"

He poured coffee for the two of them. Murgatroyd swung down to the floor and said, impatiently, *"Chee! Chee! Chee!"*

Calhoun absently filled Murgatroyd's tiny cup and handed it to him.

"But this is marvelous!" he said exuberantly. "The blue patches appeared after the plague, didn't they? After people recovered—when they recovered?"

Maril stared at him. His mind was filled with strictly professional considerations. He was not talking to her as a person. She was purely a source of information.

"So I'm told," said Maril reservedly. "Are there any more humiliating questions you want to ask?"

He gaped at her. Then he said ruefully, "I'm stupid, Maril, but you're touchy. There's nothing personal—"

"There is to me!" she said fiercely. "I was born among blüeskins, and they're of my blood, and they're

hated and I'd have been killed on Weald if I'd been
known as . . . what I am! And there's Korvan, who
arranged for me to be sent away as a spy and advised me
to do just what you said: abandon my home world and
everybody I care about! Including him! It's personal to
me!''

Calhoun wrinkled his forehead helplessly.

"I'm sorry," he repeated. "Drink your coffee!"

"I don't want it," she said bitterly. "I'd like to die!"

"If you stay around where I am," Calhoun told her,
"you may get your wish. All right, there'll be no more
questions."

She turned and moved toward the door to the cabin.
Calhoun looked after her.

"Maril."

"What?"

"Why were you crying?"

"You wouldn't understand," she said evenly.

Calhoun shrugged his shoulders almost up to his ears.
He was a professional man. In his profession he was not
incompetent. But there is no profession in which a really
competent man tries to understand women. Calhoun,
annoyed, had to let fate or chance or disaster take care
of Maril's personal problems. He had larger matters to
cope with.

But he had something to work on, now. He hunted
busily in the reference tapes. He came up with an explicit collection of information on exactly the subject he
needed. He left the control-room to go down into the
storage areas of the Med Ship's hull. He found an ultra
frigid storage box, whose contents were kept at the temperature of liquid air.

He donned thick gloves, used a special set of tongs,
and extracted a tiny block of plastic in which a sealed-
tight phial of glass was embedded. It frosted instantly it
took it out, and when the storage box was closed again
the block was covered with a thick and opaque coating
of frozen moisture.

He went back to the control-room and pulled down
the panel which made available a small-scale but sur-

prisingly adequate biological laboratory. He set the plastic block in a container which would raise it very, very gradually to a specific temperature and hold it there. It was, obviously, a living culture from which any imaginable quantity of the same culture could be bred. Calhoun set the apparatus with great exactitude.

"This," he told Murgatroyd, "may be a good day's work. Now I think I can rest."

Then, for a long while, there was no sound or movement in the Med Ship. The girl may have slept, or maybe not. Calhoun lay relaxed in a chair which at the touch of a button became the most comfortable of sleeping places. Murgatroyd remained in his cubbyhole, his tail curled over his nose.

There were comforting, unheard, easily dismissable murmurings now and again. They kept the feeling of life alive in the ship. But for such infinitesimal stirrings of sound, carefully recorded for this exact purpose, the feel of the ship would have been that of a tomb.

But it was quite otherwise when another ship-day began with the taped sounds of morning activities as faint as echoes but nevertheless establishing an atmosphere of their own.

Calhoun examined the plastic block and its contents. He read the instruments which had cared for it while he slept. He put the block—no longer frosted—in the culture microscope and saw its enclosed, infinitesimal particles of life in the process of multiplying on the food that had been frozen with them when they were reduced to the spore condition. He beamed. He replaced the block in the incubation oven and faced the day cheerfully.

Maril greeted him with great reserve. They breakfasted, with Murgatroyd eating from his own platter on the floor, a tiny cup of coffee alongside.

"I've been thinking," said Maril evenly. "I think I can get you a hearing for whatever ideas you may have to help Dara."

"Kind of you," murmured Calhoun.

In theory, a Med Service man had all the authority

needed for this or any other emergency. The power to declare a planet in quarantine, so cutting it off from all interstellar commerce, should be enough to force cooperation from any world's government. But in practice Calhoun had exactly as much power as he could exercise.

And Weald could not think straight where blueskins were concerned, and certainly the authorities on Dara could not be expected to be level-headed. They had a history of isolation and outlawry, and long experience of being regarded as less than human. In cold fact, Calhoun had no power at all.

"May I ask whose influence you'll exert?" asked Calhoun.

"There's a man," said Maril reservedly, "who thinks a great deal of me. I don't know his present official position, but he was certain to become prominent. I'll tell him how you've acted up to now, and your attitude, and of course that you're Med Service. He'll be glad to help you, I'm sure."

"Splendid!" said Calhoun, nodding. "That will be Korvan."

She started. "How did you know?"

"Intuition," said Calhoun dryly. "All right. I'll count on him."

But he did not. He worked in the tiny biological lab all that ship-day and all the next. The girl was very quiet. Murgatroyd tried to enter into pretended conversation with her, but she was not able to match his pretense.

On the ship-day after, the time for breakout approached. While the ship was practically a world all by itself, it was easy to look forward with confidence to the future. But when contact and, in a fashion, conflict with other and larger worlds loomed nearer, prospects seemed less bright. Calhoun had definite plans, now, but there were so many ways in which they could be frustrated.

Calhoun sat down at the control-board and watched the clock.

"I've got things lined up," he told Maril, "if only they work out. If I can make somebody on Dara listen, which is unlikely, and follow my advice, which they probably won't; and if Weald doesn't get the ideas it probably will get; and isn't doing what I suspect it is—why, maybe something can be done."

"I'm sure you'll do your best," said Maril politely.

Calhoun managed to grin. He watched the clock. There was no sensation attached to overdrive travel except at the beginning and the end. It was now time for the end. He might find most anything having happened. His plans might immediately be seen to be hopeless. Weald could have sent ships to Dara, or Dara might be in such a state of desperation. . . .

As it turned out, Dara was desperate. The Med Ship came out nearly a light-month from the sun about which the planet Dara revolved. Calhoun went into a short hop toward it. Then Dara was on the other side of the blazing yellow star. It took time to reach it.

He called down, identifying himself and the ship and asking for coordinates so his ship could be brought to ground. There was confusion, as if the request were so unusual that the answers were not ready. The grid, too, was on the planet's night side. Presently the ship was locked onto by the grid's force-fields. It went downward.

Calhoun saw that Maril sat tensely, twisting her fingers within each other, until the ship actually touched ground.

Then he opened the exit port—and faced armed men in the darkness, with blast-rifles trained on him. There was a portable cannon trained on the Med Ship itself.

"Come out!" rasped a voice. "If you try anything you get blasted! Your ship and its contents are seized by the planetary government!"

V

IT SEEMED THAT the smell of hunger was in the air. The armed men were emaciated. Lights came on, and stark, harsh shadows lay black upon the ground. Calhoun's captors were uniformed, but the uniforms hung loosely upon them. Where the lights struck upon their faces, their cheeks were hollow. They were cadaverous. And there were the splotches of pigment of which Calhoun had heard.

The man nearest the Med Ship's port had a monstrous, irregular dull-blue marking over half of one side of his face and up upon his forehead. The man next to him had a blue throat. The next man again was less marked, but his left ear was blue and there was what seemed a splashing of the same color on the skin under his hair.

The leader of the truculent group—it might have been a firing squad—made an imperious gesture with his hand. It was blue, except for two fingers which in the glaring illumination seemed whiter than white.

"Out!" said that man savagely. "We're taking over your stock of food. You'll get your share of it, like everybody else, but—"

Maril spoke over Calhoun's shoulder. She uttered a cryptic sentence or two. It should have amounted to identification but there was skepticism in the armed party.

"Oh, you're one of us, eh?" said the guard leader sardonically. "You'll have a chance to prove that. Come out of there!"

Calhoun spoke abruptly, "This is a Med Ship," he said. "There are medicines and bacterial culture inside it. They shouldn't be meddled with. Here on Dara you've had enough of plagues!"

The man with the blue hand said as sardonically as before, "I said the government was taking over your ship! It won't be looted. But you're not taking a full cargo of food away! In fact, it's not likely you're leaving!"

"And I want to speak to someone in authority," snapped Calhoun. "We've just come from Weald." He felt bristling hatred all about him as he named Weald. "There's tumult there. They're talking about dropping fusion-bombs here. It's important that I talk to somebody with the authority to take a few sensible precautions!"

He descended to the ground. There was a panicky *"Chee! Chee!"* from behind him, and Murgatroyd came dashing to swarm up his body and cling apprehensively to his neck.

"What's that?"

"A *tormal*," said Calhoun. 'He's not a pet. Your medical men will know something about him. This is a Med Ship and I'm a Med Ship man, and he's an important member of the crew. He's a Med Ship *tormal* and he stays with me!"

The man with the blue hand said harshly, "There's somebody waiting to ask you questions. Here!"

A ground-car came rolling out from the side of the landing-grid enclosure. The ground-car ran on wheels, and wheels were not much used on modern worlds. Dara was behind the times in more ways than one.

"This car will take you to Defense and you can tell them anything you want. But don't try to sneak back in this ship! It'll be guarded!"

The ground-car was enclosed, with room for a driver and the three from the Med Ship. But armed men festooned themselves about its exterior and it went bumping and rolling to the massive ground-layer girders of the grid. It rolled out under them and onto a paved highway. It picked up speed.

There were buildings on either side of the road, but few showed lights. This was night, and the men at the landing grid had set a pattern of hunger, so that the silence and the dark buildings did not seem a sign of tranquility and sleep, but of exhaustion and despair.

The highway lamps were few, by comparison with other inhabited worlds, and the ground-car needed lights of its own to guide its driver over a paved surface that needed repair. By those moving lights other depressing things could be seen: untidiness, buildings not kept up to perfection, evidences of apathy, the road, which hadn't been cleaned lately, litter here and there.

Even the fact that there were no stars added to the feeling of wretchedness and gloom and, ultimately, of hunger.

Maril spoke nervously to the driver.

"The famine isn't any better?"

He moved his head in negation, but did not speak. There was a splotch of blue pigment at the back of his neck. It extended upward into his hair.

"I left two years ago," said Maril. "It was just beginning then. Rationing hadn't started."

The driver said evenly, "There's rationing now!"

The car went on and on. A vast open space appeared ahead. Lights about its perimeter seemed few and pale.

"Everything seems worse. Even the lights."

"Using all the power," said the driver, "to warm up ground to grow crops where it ought to be winter. Not doing too well, either."

Calhoun knew, somehow, that Maril moistened her lips.

"I was sent," she explained to the driver, "to go ashore on Trent and then make my way to Weald. I mailed reports of what I found out back to Trent. Somebody got them back to here whenever it was possible."

The driver said, "Everybody knows the man on Trent

disappeared. Maybe he got caught, maybe somebody saw him without make-up. Or maybe he just quit being one of us. What's the difference? No use!"

Calhoun found himself wincing a little. The driver was not angry. He was hopeless. But men should not despair. They shouldn't accept hostility from those about them as a device of fate for their destruction.

Maril said quickly to Calhoun, "You understand? Dara's a heavy-metals planet. There aren't many light elements in our soil. Potassium is scarce. So our ground isn't very fertile. Before the plague we traded metals and manufactured products for imports of food and potash. But since the plague we've had no off-planet commerce. We've been quarantined."

"I gathered as much," said Calhoun. "It was up to Med Service to see that that didn't happen. It's up to Med Service now to see that it stops."

"Too late now for anything," said the driver. "Whatever Med Service may be! They're talking about cutting down our population so there'll be food enough for some to live. There are two questions about it. One is who's to be kept alive, and the other is why."

The ground-car aimed now for a cluster of faintly brighter lights on the far side of the great open space. They enlarged as they grew nearer. Maril said hesitantly, "There was someone, Korvan—" Calhoun didn't catch the rest of the name. Maril said hesitantly, "He was working on food plants. I thought he might accomplish something . . ."

The driver said caustically, "Sure! Everybody's heard about him! He came up with a wonderful thing! He and his outfit worked out a way to process weeds so they can be eaten. And they can. You can fill your belly and not feel hungry, but it's like eating hay. You starve just the same. He's still working. Head of a government division."

The ground-car passed through a gate. It stopped before a lighted door. The armed men hanging to its outside dropped off. They watched Calhoun closely as he stepped out with Murgatroyd riding on his shoulder.

Minutes later they faced a hastily summoned group of

officials of the Darian government. For a ship to land
on Dara was so remarkable an event that it called practically for a cabinet meeting. And Calhoun noted that
they were no better fed than the guards at the spaceport.

They regarded Calhoun and Maril with oddly burning
eyes. It was, of course, because the two of them showed
no signs of hunger. They obviously had not been on
short rations. Darians had this, now, to increase a
hatred which was inevitable anyhow, directed at all
peoples off their own planet.

"My name is Calhoun," said Calhoun briskly. "I've
the usual Med Service credentials. Now—"

He did not wait to be questioned. He told them of the
appalling state of things in the Twelfth Sector of the
Med Service, so that men had been borrowed from
other sectors to remedy the intolerable, and he was one
of them. He told of his arrival at Weald and what had
happened there, from the excessively cautious insistence
that he prove he was not a Darian, to the arrival of the
death-ship from Orede.

He was giving them the news affecting them, as they
had not heard it before. He went on to tell of his stop at
Orede and his purpose, and his encounter with the men
he found there. When he finished there was silence. He
broke it.

"Now," he said, "Maril's an agent of yours. She can
add to what I've told you. I'm Med Service. I have a job
to do here to carry out what wasn't done before. I
should make a planetary health inspection and make
recommendations for the improvement of the state of
things. I'll be glad if you'll arrange for me to talk to
your health officials. Things look bad, and something
should be done."

Someone laughed without mirth.

"What will you recommend for long-continued undernourishment?" he asked derisively. "That's our
health problem!"

"I recommend food," said Calhoun.

"Where'll you fill the prescription?"

"I've the answer to that, too," said Calhoun curtly.
"I'll want to talk to any space pilots you've got. Get

your astrogators together and I think they'll approve my idea."

The silence was totally skeptical.

"Orede—"

"Not Orede," said Calhoun. "Weald will be hunting that planet over for Darians. If they find any, they'll drop bombs here."

"Our only space pilots," said a tall man, presently, "are on Orede now. If you've told the truth, they'll probably head back because of your warning. They should bring meat."

His mouth worked peculiarly, and Calhoun knew that it was at the thought of food.

"Which," said another man sharply, "goes to the hospitals! I haven't tasted meat in two years!"

"Nobody has," growled another man still. "But here's this man Calhoun. I'm not convinced he can work magic, but we can find out if he lies. Put a guard on his ship. Otherwise let our health men give him his head. They'll find out if he's from this Medical Service he tells of! And this Maril . . ."

"I can be identified," said Maril. "I was sent to gather information and sent it in secret writing to one of us on Trent. I have a family here. They'll know me! And I—there was someone who was working on foods, and I believe he made it possible to use . . . all sorts of vegetation for food. He will identify me."

Someone laughed harshly.

Maril swallowed.

"I'd like to see him," she repeated. "And my family."

Some of the blue-splotched men turned away. A broad-shouldered man said bluntly, "Don't look for them to be glad to see you. And you'd better not show yourself in public. You've been well fed. You'll be hated for that."

Maril began to cry. Murgatroyd said bewilderedly, *"Chee! Chee!"*

Calhoun held him close. There was confusion. And Calhoun found the Minister of Health at hand. He looked most harried of all the officials gathered to question Calhoun. He proposed that he get a look at the hospital situation right away.

It wasn't practical. With all the population on half rations or less, when night came people needed to sleep. Most people, indeed, slept as many hours out of the traditional twenty-four as they could manage. It was much more pleasant to sleep than to be awake and constantly nagged at by continued hunger.

And there was the matter of simple decency. Continuous gnawing hunger had an embittering effect upon everyone. Quarrelsomeness was a common experience. And people who would normally be the leaders of opinion felt shame because they were obsessed by thoughts of food. It was best when people slept.

Still, Calhoun was in the hospitals by daybreak. What he found moved him to savage anger. There were too many sick children. In every case undernourishment contributed to their sickness. And there was not enough food to make them well. Doctors and nurses denied themselves food to spare it for their patients. And most of that self-denial was doubtless voluntary, but it would not be discreet for anybody on Dara to look conspicuously better fed than his fellows.

Calhoun brought out hormones and enzymes and medicaments from the Med Ship while the guard in the ship looked on. He demonstrated the processes of synthesis and autocatalysis that enabled such small samples to be multiplied indefinitely. He was annoyed by a clamorous appetite. There were some doctors who ignored the irony of medical techniques being taught to cure nonnutritional disease, when everybody was half-fed, or less. They approved of Calhoun. They even approved of Murgatroyd when Calhoun explained his function.

He was, of course, a Med Service *tormal*, and *tormals* were creatures of talent. They'd originally been found on a planet in the Deneb area, and they were engaging and friendly small animals. But the remarkable fact about them was that they couldn't contract any disease. Not any.

They had a built-in, explosive reaction to bacterial

and viral toxins, and there hadn't yet been any pathogenic organism discovered to which a *tormal* could not more or less immediately develop antibody resistance. So that in interstellar medicine *tormals* were priceless.

Let Murgatroyd be infected with however localized, however specialized, an inimical organism, and presently some highly valuable defensive substance could be isolated from his blood and he'd remain in his usual exuberant good health.

When the antibody was analyzed by those techniques of microanalysis the Service had developed, that was that. The antibody could be synthesized and one could attack any epidemic with confidence.

The tragedy for Dara was, of course, that no Med Ship had come to Dara three generations ago, when the Dara plague raged. Worse, after the plague Weald was able to exert pressure which only a criminally incompetent Med Service director would have permitted. But criminal incompetence and its consequences was what Calhoun had been loaned to Sector Twelve to help remedy. He was not at ease, though. No ship arrived from Orede to bear out his account of an attempt to get that lonely world evacuated before Weald discovered it had blueskins on it. Maril had vanished, to visit or return to her family, or perhaps to consult with the mysterious Korvan who'd arranged for her to leave Dara to be a spy, and had advised her simply to make a new life somewhere else, abandoning a famine-ridden, despised, and outcaste world.

Calhoun had learned of two achievements the same Korvan had made for his world. Neither was remarkably constructive. He'd offered to prove the value of the second by dying of it. Which might make him a very admirable character, or he could have a passion for martyrdom, which is much more common than most people think. In two days Calhoun was irritable enough from unaccustomed hunger to suspect the worst of him.

Meanwhile Calhoun worked doggedly; in the hospitals while the patients were awake and in the Med Ship, under guard, afterward. He had hunger cramps now, but he tested a plastic cube with a thriving biological culture in it.

He worked at increasing his store of it. He'd snipped samples of pigmented skin from dead patients in the hospitals, and examined the pigmented areas, and very, very painstakingly verified a theory. It took an electron microscope to do it, but he found a virus in the blue patches which matched the type discovered on Tralee.

The Tralee viruses had effects which were passed on from mother to child, and heredity had been charged with the observed results of quasi-living viral particles. And then Calhoun very, very carefully introduced into a virus culture the material he had been growing in a plastic cube. He watched what happened.

He was satisfied, so much so that immediately afterward he yawned and yawned and barely managed to stagger off to bed. The watching guard in the Med Ship watched him in amazement.

That night the ship from Orede came in, packed with frozen bloody carcasses of cattle. Calhoun knew nothing of it. But next morning Maril came back. There were shadows under her eyes and her expression was of someone who has lost everything that had meaning in her life.

"I'm all right," she insisted, when Calhoun commented. "I've been visiting my family. I've seen Korvan. I'm quite all right."

"You haven't eaten any better than I have," Calhoun observed.

"I couldn't!" admitted Maril. "My sisters, my little sisters so thin . . . There's rationing for everybody and it's all efficiently arranged. They even had rations for me. But I couldn't eat! I gave most of my food to my sisters and they—they squabbled over it!"

Calhoun said nothing. There was nothing to say. Then she said, in a no less desolate tone, "Korvan said I was foolish to come back."

"He could be right," said Calhoun.

"But I had to!" protested Maril. "And now I—I've been eating all I wanted to, in Weald and in the ship, and I'm ashamed because they're half-starved and I'm

not. And when you see what hunger does to them . . .
It's terrible to be half-starved and not able to think of
anything but food!"

"I hope," said Calhoun, "to do something about
that. If I can get hold of an astrogator or two—"

"The ship that was on Orede came in during the
night," Maril told him shakily. "It was loaded with
frozen meat, but one load's not enough to make a difference on a whole planet! And if Weald hunts for us on
Orede, we daren't go back for more meat."

She said abruptly, "There are some prisoners. They
were miners. They were crowded out of the ship. The
Darians who'd stampeded the cattle took them
prisoners. They had to!"

"True," said Calhoun. "It wouldn't have been wise
to leave Wealdians around on Orede with their throats
cut. Or living, either, to tell about a rumor of blueskins.
Even if their throats will be cut now. Is that the
program?"

Maril shivered.

"No. They'll be put on short rations like everybody
else. And people will watch them. The Wealdians expect
to die of plague any minute because they've been with
Darians. So people look at them and laugh. But it's not
very funny."

"It's natural," said Calhoun, "but perhaps lacking in
charity. Look there! How about those astrogators? I
need them for a job I have in mind."

Maril wrung her hands.

"C—come here," she said in a low tone.

There was an armed guard in the control-room of the
ship. He'd watched Calhoun a good part of the previous
day as Calhoun performed his mysterious work. He'd
been off-duty and now was on duty again. He was
bored. So long as Calhoun did not touch the control-
board, though, he was uninterested. He didn't even turn
his head when Maril led the way into the other cabin and
slid the door shut.

"The astrogators are coming," she said swiftly.
"They'll bring some boxes with them. They'll ask you
to instruct them so they can handle our ship better. They

lost themselves coming back from Orede. No, they didn't lose themselves, but they lost time, enough time almost to make an extra trip for meat. They need to be experts. I'm to come along, so they can be sure that what you teach them is what you've been doing right along."

Calhoun said, "Well?"

"They're crazy!" said Maril vehemently. "They knew Weald would do something monstrous sooner or later. But they're going to try to stop it by being more monstrous sooner! Not everybody agrees, but there are enough. So they want to use your ship—it's faster in overdrive and so on. And they'll go to Weald in this ship and—they say they'll give Weald something to keep it busy without bothering us!"

Calhoun said dryly, "This pays me off for being too sympathetic with blueskins! But if I'd been hungry for a couple of years, and was despised to boot by the people who kept me hungry, I suppose I might react the same way. No," he said curtly as she opened her lips to speak again, "don't tell me the trick. Considering everything, there's only one trick it could be. But I doubt profoundly that it would work. All right."

He slid the door back and returned to the control-room. Maril followed him. He said detachedly, "I've been working on a problem outside of the food one. It isn't the time to talk about it right now, but I think I've solved it."

Maril turned her head, listening. There were footsteps on the tarmack outside the ship. Both doors of the airlock were open. Four men came in. They were young men who did not look quite as hungry as most Darians, but there was a reason for that. Their leader introduced himself and the others. They were the astrogators of the ship Dara had built to try to bring food from Orede. They were not, said their self-appointed leader, good enough. They'd overshot their destination. They came out of overdrive too far off line. They needed instruction.

Calhoun nodded, and observed that he'd been asking

for them. They were, of course, blueskins. On one the only visible disfigurement was a patch of blue upon his wrist. On another the appearance of a blue birthmark appeared beside his eye and went back and up his temple. A third had a white patch on his temple, with all the rest of his face a dull blue. The fourth had blue fingers on one hand.

"We've got orders," said their leader, steadily, "to come on board and learn from you how to handle this ship. It's better than the one we've got."

"I asked for you," repeated Calhoun. "I've an idea I'll explain as we go along . . . Those boxes?"

Someone was passing in iron boxes through the airlock. One of the four very carefully brought them inside.

"They're rations," said a second young man. "We don't go anywhere without rations, except Orede."

"Orede, yes. I think we were shooting at each other there," said Calhoun pleasantly. "Weren't we?"

"Yes," said the young man.

He was neither cordial nor antagonistic. He was impassive. Calhoun shrugged.

"Then we can take off immediately. Here's the communicator and there's the button. You might call the grid and arrange for us to be lifted."

The young man seated himself at the control-board. Very professionally, he went through the routine of preparing to lift by landing grid, which routine has not changed in two hundred years. He went briskly ahead until the order to lift. Then Calhoun stopped him.

"Hold it!"

He pointed to the air-lock. Both doors were open. The young man at the control-board flushed vividly. One of the others closed and dogged the doors.

The ship lifted. Calhoun watched with seeming negligence. But he found occasion for a dozen corrections of procedure. This was presumably a training voyage of his own suggestion. Therefore, when the blueskin pilot would have flung the Med Ship into undirected overdrive, Calhoun grew stern. He insisted on a destination. He suggested Weald.

The young men glanced at each other and accepted the suggestion. He made the acting pilot look up the intrinsic brightness of its sun and measure its apparent brightness from just off Dara. He made him estimate the change in brightness to be expected after so many hours in overdrive, if one broke out to measure.

The first blueskin student pilot ended a Calhoun-determined tour of duty with more respect for Calhoun then he'd had at the beginning. The second was anxious to show up better than the first. Calhoun drilled him in the use of brightness-charts, by which the changes in apparent brightness of stars between overdrive hops could be correlated with angular changes to give a three-dimensional picture of the nearer heavens.

It was a highly necessary art which had not been worked out on Dara, and the prospective astrogators became absorbed in this and other fine points of space-piloting. They'd done enough, in a few trips to Orede, to realize that they needed to know more. Calhoun showed them.

Calhoun did not try to make things easy for them. He was hungry and easily annoyed. It was sound training tactics to be severe, and to phrase all suggestions as commands. He put the four young men in command of the ship in turn, under his direction. He continued to use Weald as a destination, but he set up problems in which the Med Ship came out of overdrive pointing in an unknown direction and with a precessory motion.

He made the third of his students identify Weald in the celestial globe containing hundreds of millions of stars, and get on course in overdrive toward it. The fourth was suddenly required to compute the distance to Weald from such data as he could get from observation, without reference to any records.

By this time the first man was chafing to take a second turn. Calhoun gave each of them a second grueling lesson. He gave them, in fact, a highly condensed but very sound course in the art of travel in space. His young students took command in four-hour watches, with at least one breakout from overdrive in each watch.

He built up enthusiasm in them. They ignored the discomfort of being hungry—though there had been no reason for them to stint on food on Orede—in growing pride in what they came to know.

When Weald was a first-magnitude star, the four were not highly qualified astrogators, to be sure, but they were vastly better spacemen than at the beginning. Inevitably, their attitude toward Calhoun was respect-ful. He'd been irritable and right. To the young, the combination is impressive.

Maril had served as passenger only. In theory she was to compare Calhoun's lessons with his practice when alone. But he did nothing on this journey which, teaching considered, was different from the two in-terstellar journeys Maril had made with him.

She occupied the sleeping cabin during two of the six watches of each ship-day. She operated the food-readier, which was almost completely emptied of its original store of food, it having been confiscated by the government of Dara. That amount of food would make no difference to the planet, but it was wise for everyone on Dara to be equally ill-fed.

On the sixth day out from Dara, the sun of Weald had a magnitude of minus five-tenths. The electron tele-scope could detect its larger planets, especially a gas-giant fifth-orbit world of high albedo. Calhoun had his four students estimate its distance again, pointing out the difference that could be made in breakout position if the Med Ship were mis-aimed by as much as one second of arc.

"And now," he said briskly, "we'll have coffee. I'm going to graduate you as pilots. Maril, four cups of coffee, please."

Murgatroyd said, *"Chee?"* The Med Ship was badly crowded with six humans and Murgatroyd in a space in-tended for Calhoun and Murgatroyd alone. The little *tormal* had spent most of his time in his cubbyhole, watching with beady eyes as so many people moved about on what had been a spacious ship before.

"No coffee for you, Murgatroyd," said Calhoun. "You didn't do your lessons. This is for the graduating class only."

Murgatroyd came out of his miniature den. He found his little cup and offered it insistently, saying, *"Chee! Chee! Chee!"*

"No!" said Calhoun firmly. He regarded his class of four young men with their blueskin markings. "Drink it down!" he commanded. "That's the last order I'll give you. You're graduate pilots, now!"

They drank the coffee with a flourish. There was not one who did not admire Calhoun for having made them admire themselves. They were, actually, almost as much better pilots as they believed.

"And now," said Calhoun, "I suppose you'll tell me the truth about those boxes you brought on board. You said they were rations, but they haven't been opened in six days. I have an idea what they mean, but you tell me."

The four looked uncomfortable. There was a long pause.

"They could be," said Calhoun detachedly, "cultures to be dumped on Weald. Weald is making plans to wipe out Dara. So some fool has decided to get Weald too busy fighting a plague of its own to bother with you. Is that right?"

The young men stirred unhappily. Young men can very easily be made into fanatics. But they have to be kept stirred up. They can't be provided with sound reason for self-respect. On the Med Ship there'd not been a single reference to Weald except as an object toward which the Med Ship was being astrogated. There'd been no reference to blueskins or enemies or threats or anything but space-piloting. The four young men were now fanatical about the proper handling of a ship in emptiness.

"Well, sir," said one of them, unhappily, "that's what we were ordered to do."

"I object," said Calhoun. "It wouldn't work. I just

left Weald a little while back, remember. They've been telling themselves that some day Dara would try that. They've made preparations to fight any imaginable contagion you could drop on them. Every so often somebody claims it's happening. It wouldn't work. I object!''

"But—"

"In fact," said Calhoun, "I forbid it. I shall prevent it. You shan't do anything of the kind."

One of the young men, staring at Calhoun, nodded suddenly. His eyes closed. He jerked his head erect and looked bewildered. A second sank heavily into a chair. He said remotely, "Thish sfunny!" and abruptly went to sleep. The third found his knees giving way. He paid elaborate attention to them, stiffening them. But they yielded like rubber and he went slowly down to the floor. The fourth said thickly and reproachfully, "Thought y'were our frien'!"

He collapsed.

Calhoun very soberly tied them hand and foot and laid them out comfortably on the floor. Maril watched, white-faced, her hand to her throat. Murgatroyd looked agitated. He said anxiously, *"Chee? Chee?"*

"No," said Calhoun. "They'll wake up presently."

Maril said in a tense and desperate whisper, "You're betraying us! You're going to take us to Weald!"

"No," said Calhoun. "We'll only orbit around it. First, though, I want to get rid of those damned packed-up cultures. They're dead, by the way. I killed them with supersonics a couple of days ago, while a fine argument was going on about distance-measurements by variable Cepheids of known period."

He put the four boxes carefully in the disposal unit. He operated it. The boxes and their contents streamed out to space in the form of metallic and other vapors. Calhoun sat at the control desk.

"I'm a Med Service man," he said detachedly. "I couldn't cooperate in the spread of plagues, anyhow, though a useful epidemic might be another matter. But the important thing right now is not keeping Weald busy with troubles to increase their hatred of Dara. It's getting some food for Dara. And driblets won't help. What's needed is thousands of tons, or tens of thousands." Then he said, "Overdrive coming, Murgatroyd! Hold fast!"

The universe vanished. The customary unpleasant sensations accompanied the change. Murgatroyd burped.

VI

A LARGE PART of the firmament was blotted out by the blindingly bright half-disk of Weald, as it shone in the sunshine. It had icecaps at its poles, and there were seas, and the mottled look of land which had that carefully maintained balance of woodland and cultivated areas which was so effective in climate control. The Med Ship floated free, and Calhoun fretfully monitored all the beacon frequencies known to man.

There was relative silence inside the ship. Maril watched Calhoun in a sort of despairing indecision. The four young blueskins still slept, still bound hand and foot upon the control-room floor. Murgatroyd regarded them, and Maril, and Calhoun in turn, and his small and furry forehead wrinkled helplessly.

"They can't have landed what I'm looking for!" protested Calhoun as his search had no result. "They can't! It would be too sensible for them to have done it!"

Murgatroyd said, *"Chee!"* in a subdued voice.

"But where the devil did they put them?" demanded Calhoun. "A polar orbit would be ridiculous! They—" Then he grunted in disgust. "Oh! Of course! Now, where's the landing grid?"

He worked busily for minutes, checking the position of the Wealdian landing grid, which was mapped in the Sector Directory, against the look of continents and seas on the half-disk so plainly visible outside. He found what he wanted. He put on the ship's solar system drive.

"I wish," he complained to Maril, "I wish I could think straight the first time! And it's so obvious! If you want to put something out in space, and not have it interfere with traffic, in what sort of orbit and at what distance will you put it?"

Maril did not answer.

"Obviously," said Calhoun, "you'll put it as far as possible from the landing pattern of ships coming in to the spaceport. You'll put it on the opposite side of the planet. And you'll want it to stay out of the way, where anybody can know it is at any time of the day or night without having to calculate anything.

"So you'll put it out in orbit so it will revolve around Weald in exactly one day, neither more nor less, and you'll put it above the equator. And then it will remain quite stationary above one spot on the planet, a hundred and eighty degrees longitude away from the landing grid and directly over the equator."

He scribbled for a moment.

"Which means forty-two thousand miles high, give or take a few hundred, and—here! And I was hunting for it in a close-in orbit!"

He grumbled to himself. He waited while the solar system drive pushed the Med Ship a quarter of the way around the bright planet below. The sunset line vanished and the planet's disk became a complete circle. Then Calhoun listened to the monitor earphones again, and grunted once more, and changed course, and presently made a noise indicating satisfaction.

He abandoned instrument control and peered directly out of a port, handling the solar system drive with great care. Murgatroyd said depressedly, *"Chee!"*

"Stop worrying," commanded Calhoun. "We haven't been challenged, and there is a beacon transmitter at work, just to make sure that nobody bumps into what we're looking for. It's a great help, because we do want to bump, but gently."

Stars swung across the port out of which he looked. Something dark appeared, and then straight lines and exact curvings. Even Maril, despairing and bewildered as she was, caught sight of something vastly larger than the Med Ship, floating in space. She stared. The Med Ship maneuvered very cautiously. She saw another large object. A third. A fourth. There seemed to be dozens of them.

They were spaceships, huge by comparison with *Aesclipus Twenty*. They floated as the Med Ship did. They did not drive. They were not in formation. They were not at even distances from each other. They did not point in the same direction. They swung in emptiness like derelicts.

Calhoun jockeyed his small ship with infinite care. Presently there came the gentlest of impacts and then a clanking sound. The appearance out the vision port became stationary, but still unbelievable. The Med Ship was grappled magnetically to a vast surface of welded metal.

Calhoun relaxed. He opened a wall panel and brought out a vacuum suit. He began briskly to get it on.

"Things moving smoothly," he commented. "We weren't challenged. So it's extremely unlikely that we were spotted. Our friends on the floor ought to begin to come to shortly. And I'm going to find out now whether I'm a hero or in sure-enough trouble!"

Maril said drearily, "I don't know what you've done, except—"

Calhoun blinked at her, in the act of hauling the vacuum suit up his chest and over his shoulders.

"Isn't it self-evident?" he demanded. "I've been giving astrogation lessons to these characters. I certainly didn't do it to help them dump germ cultures on Weald! I brought them here! Don't you see the point? These are spaceships. They're in orbit around Weald. They're not manned and they're not controlled. In fact, they're nothing but sky-riding storage bins!"

He seemed to consider the explanation complete. He wriggled his arms into the sleeves and gloves of the suit. He slung the air tanks over his shoulder and hooked them to the suit.

"I'll be back," he said. "I hope with good news. I've

reason to be hopeful, though, because these Wealdians are very practical men. They have things all prepared and tidy. I suspect I'll find these ships with stores of air and fuel, maybe even food, so that if Weald should manage to make a deal for the stuff stored out here in them, they'd only have to bring out crews.''

He lifted the space helmet down from its rack and put it on. He tested it, reading the tank air-pressure, power-storage, and other data from the lighted miniature instruments visible through pinholes above his eye-level. He fastened a space rope about himself, speaking through the helmet's opened faceplate.

''If our friends should wake up before I get back,'' he added, ''please restrain them. I'd hate to be marooned.''

He went waddling into the air-lock with the coil of space rope over one vacuum-suited arm. The inner lock door closed behind him. A little later Maril heard the outer lock open. Then silence.

Murgatroyd whimpered a little. Maril shivered. Calhoun had gone out of the ship to nothingness. He'd said that what he was looking for, and what he'd found, was forty-two thousand miles from Weald. One could imagine falling forty-two thousand miles, where one couldn't imagine falling a light-year.

Calhoun was walking on the steel plates of a gigantic spaceship which floated among dozens of its fellows, all seeming derelicts and seemingly abandoned. He was able to walk on the nearest because of magnetic-soled shoes. He trusted his life to them and to a flimsy space rope which trailed after him out the Med Ship's air-lock.

Time passed. A clock ticked in that hurried tempo of five ticks to the second which has been the habit of clocks since time immemorial. Very small and trivial noises came from the background tape, preventing utter silence from hanging intolerably in the ship.

Maril found herself listening tensely for something else. One of the four bound blueskins snored, and stirred, and slept again. Murgatroyd gazed about unhappily, and swung down to the control-room floor, and then paused for lack of any place to go or anything to do. He sat down and began half-heartedly to lick his whiskers. Maril stirred.

Murgatroyd looked at her hopefully.

"Chee?" he asked shrilly.

She shook her head. It became a habit to act as if Murgatroyd were a human being. "No," she said unsteadily. "Not yet."

More time passed. An unbearably long time. Then there was the faintest of clankings. It repeated. Then, abruptly, there were noises in the air-lock. They continued. They were fumbling noises.

The outer air-lock door closed. The inner door opened. Dense white fog came out of it. There was motion. Calhoun followed the fog out of the lock. He carried objects which had been weightless, but were suddenly heavy in the ship's gravity-field. There were two spacesuits and a curious assortment of parcels. He spread them out, flipped aside his faceplate, and said briskly, "This stuff is cold! Turn a heater on it, will you, Maril?"

He began to work his way out of his own vacuum-suit.

"Item," he said. "The ships are fueled *and* provisioned. A practical tribe, the Wealdians! The ships are ready to take off as soon as they're warmed up inside. A half-degree sun doesn't radiate heat enough to keep a ship warm, when the rest of the cosmos is effectively near zero Kelvin. Here, point the heaters like this."

He adjusted the radiant-heat dispensers. The fog disappeared where their beams played. But the metal spacesuits glistened and steamed, and the steam disappeared within inches. They were so completely and utterly cold that they condensed the air about them as a liquid, which re-evaporated to make fog, which warmed up and disappeared and was immediately replaced.

"Item," said Calhoun again, getting his arms out of the vacuum-suit sleeves. "The controls are pretty nearly standard. Our sleeping friends will be able to astrogate them back to Dara without trouble, provided only that nobody comes out here to bother us before they leave."

He shed the last of the spacesuit, stepping out of its legs.

"And," he finished wryly, "I brought back an emergency supply of ship provisions for everybody concerned, but find that I'm idiot enough to feel that they'll choke me if I eat them while Dara's still starving."

Maril said, "But there isn't any hope for Dara! No real hope!"

He gaped at her.

"What do you think we're here for?"

He set to work to restore his four recent students to consciousness. It was not a difficult task. The dosage mixed in the coffee given them as a graduation ceremony—the ceremony which had consisted solely of drinking coffee and passing out—allowed for waking-up processes. Calhoun took the precaution of disarming them first, but presently four hot-eyed young men glared at him.

"I'm calling," said Calhoun, holding a blaster negligently in his hand, "I'm calling for volunteers. There's a famine on Dara. There've been unmanageable crop surpluses on Weald. On Dara, the government grimly rations every ounce of food. On Weald, the government has been buying surplus grain to keep the price up.

"To save storage costs, it's loaded the grain into out-of-date spaceships it once used to stand sentry over Dara to keep it out of space when there was another famine there. Those ships have been put out in orbit, where we're hooked on to one of them.

"It's loaded with half a million bushels of grain. I've brought spacesuits from it, I've turned on the heaters in its interior, and I've set its overdrive unit for a hop to Dara. Now I'm calling for volunteers to take half a million bushels of grain to where it's needed. Do I get any volunteers?"

He got four. Not immediately, because they were

ashamed that he'd made it impossible to carry out their original fanatic plan, and now offered something much better to make up for it. They raged. But half a million bushels of grain meant that people who must otherwise die might live.

Ultimately, truculently, first one and then another angrily agreed.

"Good!" said Calhoun. "Now, how many of you dare risk the trip alone? I've got one grain ship warming up. There are plenty of others around us. Every one of you can take a ship and half a million bushels to Dara, if you have the nerve!"

The atmosphere changed. Suddenly they clamored for the task he offered them. They were still acutely uncomfortable. He'd bossed them and taught them until they felt capable and glamorous and proud. Then he'd pinned their ears back. But if they returned to Dara with four enemy ships and unimaginable quantities of food with which to break the famine . . .

There was work to be done first, of course. Only one ship was so far warming up. Three more had to be entered, in spacesuits, and each had to have its interior warmed so breathable air could exist inside it, and at least part of the stored provisions had to be brought up to reasonable temperature for use on the journey.

Then the overdrive unit had to be inspected and set for the length of journey that a direct overdrive hop to Dara would mean, and Calhoun had to make sure again that each of the four could identify Dara's sun under all circumstances and aim for it with the requisite high precision, both before going into overdrive and after breakout. When all that was accomplished, Calhoun might reasonably hope that they'd arrive. But it wasn't a certainty.

Still, presently his four students shook hands with him, with the fine tolerance of young men intending much greater achievements than their teacher. They wouldn't speak on communicator again, because their messages might be picked up on Weald.

Of course, for this high heroic action to be successful,

it had to be performed with the stealth of sneak-thieves.

What seemed a long time passed. The one ship turned slowly upon some unseen axis. It wavered back and forth, seeking a point of aim. A second twisted in its place. A third put on the barest trace of solar system drive to get clear of the rest. The fourth—

One ship vanished. It had gone into overdrive, heading for Dara at many times the speed of light. Another. Two more.

That was all. The remainder of the fleet hung clumsily in emptiness. And Calhoun worriedly went over in his mind the lessons he'd given in such a pathetically small number of days. If the four ships reached Dara, their pilots would be heroes. Calhoun had presented them with that estate over their bitter objection. But they would glory in it—if they reached Dara.

Maril looked at him with very strange eyes.

"Now what?" she asked.

"We hang around," said Calhoun, "to see if anybody comes up from Weald to find out what's happened. It's always possible to pick up a sort of signal when a ship goes into overdrive. Usually it doesn't mean a thing. Nobody pays any attention. But if somebody comes out here . . ."

"What?"

"It'll be regrettable," said Calhoun. He was suddenly very tired. "It'll spoil any chance of our coming back and stealing some more food, like interstellar mice. If they find out what we've done they'll expect us to try it again. They might get set to fight. Or they might simply land the rest of these ships."

"If I'd realized what you were about," said Maril, "I'd have joined in the lessons. I could have piloted a ship."

"You wouldn't have wanted to," said Calhoun. He yawned. "You wouldn't want to be a heroine. No normal girl does."

"Why?"

"Korvan," said Calhoun. He yawned again. "I've asked about him. He's been trying very desperately to deserve well of his fellow blueskins. All he's accomplished is develop a way to starve painlessly. He wouldn't feel comfortable with a girl who'd helped make starving unnecessary. He'd admire you politely, but he'd never marry you. And you know it.''

She shook her head, but it was not easy to tell whether she denied the reaction of Korvan, whom Calhoun had never met, or denied that he was more important to her than anything else. The last was what Calhoun plainly implied.

''You don't seem to be trying to be a hero!'' she protested.

''I'd enjoy it,'' admitted Calhoun, ''but I have a job to do. It's got to be done. It's more important than being admired.''

''You could take another ship back,'' she told him. ''It would be worth more to Dara than the Med Ship is! And then everybody would realize that you'd planned everything.''

''Ah,'' said Calhoun, ''but you've no idea how much this ship matters to Dara!''

He seated himself at the controls. He slipped headphones over his ears. He listened. Very, very carefully, he monitored all the wave lengths and wave forms he could discover in use on Weald. There was no mention of the oddity of behavior of shiploads of surplus grain aloft. There was no mention of the ships at all. There was plenty of mention of Dara, and blueskins, and of the vicious political fight now going on to see which political party could promise the most complete protection against blueskins.

After a full hour of it, Calhoun flipped off his receptor and swung the Med Ship to an exact, painstakingly precise aim at the sun around which Dara rolled. He said, ''Overdrive coming, Murgatroyd!''

Murgatroyd grabbed. The stars went out and the universe reeled and the Med Ship became a sort of cosmos all its own, into which no signal could come, no danger could enter, and in which there could be no sound except those minute ones made to prevent silence.

Calhoun yawned again.

"Now there's nothing to be done for a day or two," he said wearily, "and I'm beginning to understand why people sleep all they can, on Dara. It's one way not to feel hungry. And one dreams such delicious meals! But looking hungry is a social requirement, on Dara."

Maril said tensely, "You're going back? After they took the ship from you?"

"The job's not finished," he explained. "Not even the famine's ended, and the famine's a second-order effect. If there were no such thing as a blueskin, there'd be no famine. Food could be traded for. We've got to do something to make sure there are no more famines."

She looked at him oddly.

"It would be desirable," she said with irony. "But you can't do it."

"Not today, no," he admitted. Then he said longingly, "I didn't get much sleep on the way here, while running a seminar on astrogation. I think I'll take a nap."

She rose and almost ostentatiously went into the other cabin to leave him alone. He shrugged. He settled down into the chair which, to let a Med Ship man break the monotony of life in unchanging surroundings, turned into a comfortable sleeping arrangements. He fell instantly asleep.

For very many ship-hours, then, there was no action or activity or happening of any imaginable consequence in the Med Ship. Very, very far away, light-years distant and light-years apart, four shiploads of grain hurtled toward the famine-stricken planet of blueskins. Each great ship had a single semiskilled blueskin for pilot and crew.

Thousands of millions of suns blazed with violence appropriate to their stellar types in a galaxy of which a very small proportion had been explored and colonized by humanity. The human race was now to be counted in quadrillions on scores of hundreds of inhabited worlds, but the tiny Med Ship seemed the least significant of all possible created things.

It could travel between star-systems and even star-clusters, but it was not yet capable of crossing the continent of suns on which the human race arose. And between any two solar systems the journeying of the Med Ship consumed much time. Which would be maddening for someone with no work to do or no resources in himself, or herself.

On the second ship-day Calhoun labored painstakingly and somewhat distastefully at the little biological laboratory. Maril watched him in a sort of brooding silence. Murgatroyd slept much of the time, with his furry tail wrapped meticulously across his nose.

Toward the end of the day Calhoun finished his task. He had a matter of six or seven cubic centimeters of clear liquid as the conclusion of a long process of culturing, and examination by microscope, and again culturing plus final filtration. He looked at a clock and calculated time.

"Better wait until tomorrow," he observed, and put the bit of clear liquid in a temperature-controlled place of safekeeping.

"What is it?" asked Maril. "What's it for?"

"It's part of a job I have on hand," said Calhoun. He considered. "How about some music?"

She looked astonished. But he set up an instrument and fed microtape into it and settled back to listen. Then there was music such as she had never heard before. It was another device to counteract isolation and monotonous between-planet voyages. To keep it from losing its effectiveness, Calhoun rationed himself on music, as on other things.

Any indulgence frequently repeated would become a habit, in the sense that it would give no special pleasure when indulged in, but would make for stress if it were omitted. Calhoun deliberately went for weeks between uses of his recordings, so that music was an event to be looked forward to and cherished.

When he tapered off the stirring symphonies of Kun Gee with tranquilizing, soothing melodies from the Rim School of composers, Maril regarded him with a very peculiar gaze indeed.

"I think I understand now," she said slowly, "why

you don't act like other people. Toward me, for
example. The way you live gives you what other people
have to get in crazy ways—making their work feed their
vanity, and justify pride, and make them feel significant. But you can put your whole mind on your work.''

He thought it over.

''Med Ship routine is designed to keep one healthy in
his mind,'' he admitted. ''It works pretty well. It satis-
fies all my mental appetites. But there are instincts . . .''

She waited. He did not finish.

''What do you do about the instincts that work and
music and such things can't satisfy?''

Calhoun grinned wryly, ''I'm stern with them. I have
to be.''

He stood up and plainly expected her to go into the
other cabin for the night. She went.

It was after breakfast time of the next ship-day when
he got out the sample of clear liquid he'd worked so
long to produce.

''We'll see how it works,'' he observed. ''Murgatroyd's handy in case of a slip-up. It's perfectly safe so
long as he's aboard and there are only the two of us.''

She watched as he injected half a cc. under his own
skin. Then she shivered a little.

''What will it do?''

''That remains to be seen.'' He paused a moment.
''You and I,'' he said with some dryness, ''make a perfect test for anything. If you catch something from me,
it will be infectious indeed!''

She gazed at him utterly without comprehension.

He took his own temperature. He brought out the
folios which were his orders, covering each of the
planets he should give a standard Medical Service inspection. Weald was there. Dara wasn't. But a Med
Service man has much freedom of action, even when
only keeping up the routine of normal Med Service.
When catching up on badly neglected operations, he
necessarily has much more. Calhoun went over the
folios.

Two hours later he took his temperature again. He
looked pleased. He made an entry in the ship's log. Two

hours later yet he found himself drinking thirstily and looked more pleased still.

He made another entry in the log and matter-of-factly drew a small quantity of blood from his own vein and called to Murgatroyd. Murgatroyd submitted amiably to the very trivial operation Calhoun carried out. Calhoun put away the equipment and saw Maril staring at him with a certain look of shock.

"It doesn't hurt him," Calhoun explained. "Right after he's born there's a tiny spot on his flank that has the pain-nerves desensitized. Murgatroyd's all right. That's what he's for!"

"But he's your friend!" said Maril.

Murgatroyd, despite his small size and furriness, had all the human attributes an animal which lives with humans soon acquires. Calhoun looked at him with affection.

"He's my assistant. I don't ask anything of him that I can do myself. But we're both Med Service. And I do things for him that he can't do for himself. For example, I make coffee for him."

Murgatroyd heard the familiar word. He said, *"Chee!"*

"Very well," agreed Calhoun. "We'll all have some."

He made coffee. Murgatroyd sipped at the cup especially made for his little paws. Once he scratched at the place on his flank which had no pain nerves. It itched. But he was perfectly content. Murgatroyd would always be contented when he was somewhere near Calhoun.

Another hour went by. Murgatroyd climbed up into Calhoun's lap and with a determined air went to sleep there. Calhoun disturbed him long enough to get an instrument out of his pocket. He listened to Murgatroyd's heartbeat, while Murgatroyd dozed.

"Maril," he said. "Write down something for me. The time, and ninety-six, and one-twenty over ninety-four."

She obeyed, not comprehending. Half an hour later, still not stirring to disturb Murgatroyd, he had her write down another time and sequence of figures, only slightly different from the first. Half an hour later still, a third set. But then he put Murgatroyd down, well satisfied.

He took his own temperature. He nodded.

"Murgatroyd and I have one more chore to do," he told her. "Would you go in the other cabin for a moment?"

Disturbed, she went into the other cabin. Calhoun drew a small sample of blood from the insensitive area on Murgatroyd's flank. Murgatroyd submitted with complete confidence in the man. In ten minutes Calhoun had diluted the sample, added an anticoagulant, shaken it up thoroughly, and filtered it to clarity with all red and white corpuscles removed. Another Med Ship man would have considered that Calhoun had had Murgatroyd prepare a splendid small sample of antibody-containing serum, in case something got out of hand. It would assuredly take care of two patients.

But a Med Ship man would also have known that it was simply one of those scrupulous precautions a Med Ship man takes when using cultures from store.

Calhoun put the sample away and called Maril back.

"It was nothing," he explained, "but you might have felt uncomfortable. We simply had a bit of Med Service routine that had to be gone through. It's all right now."

He offered no further explanation. She said, "I'll fix lunch." She hesitated. "You brought some food from the first Weald ship. Do you want to—"

He shook his head.

"I'm squeamish," he admitted. "The trouble on Dara is Med Service fault. Before my time, but still . . . I'll stick to rations until everybody eats."

He watched her unobtrusively as the day went on. Presently he considered that she was slightly flushed. Shortly after the evening meal of singularly unappetizing Darian rations, she drank thirstily. He did not comment. He brought out cards and showed her a complicated game of solitaire in which mental arithmetic and expert use of probability increased one's chance of winning.

By midnight she'd learned the game and played it absorbedly. Calhoun was able to scrutinize her without appearing to do so, and he was satisfied again. When he mentioned that the Med Ship should arrive off Dara in eight hours more, she put the cards away and went into the other cabin.

Calhoun wrote up the log. He added the notes that Maril had made for him, of Murgatroyd's pulse and blood pressure after the injection of the same culture that produced fever and thirstiness in himself and later, without contact with him or the culture, in Maril. He put a professional comment at the end:

> The culture seems to have retained its normal characteristics during long storage in the spore state. It revived and reproduced rapidly. I injected .5 cc. under my skin and in less than one hour my temperature was 30.8° C. An hour later it was 30.9° C. This was its peak. It immediately returned to normal. The only other observable symptom was slightly increased thirst. Blood-pressure and pulse remained normal. The other person in the Med Ship displayed the same symptoms, in prompt and complete repetition, without physical contact.

He went to sleep, with Murgatroyd curled up in his cubbyhole, his tail draped carefully over his nose.

The Med Ship broke out of overdrive at 1300 hours, ship-time. Calhoun made contact with the grid and was promptly lowered to the ground.

It was almost two hours later, at 1500 hours ship-time, when the people of Dara were informed by broadcast that Calhoun was to be executed immediately.

VII

FROM THE VIEWPOINT of Darians, who were also blue-skins, the decision of Calhoun's guilt and the decision to execute him were reasonable enough. Maril protested fiercely, and her testimony agreed with Calhoun's in every respect, but from a blueskin viewpoint their own statements were damning.

Calhoun had taken four young astrogators to space. They were the only semiskilled space pilots Dara had. There were no fully qualified men. Calhoun had asked for them, and taken them out to emptiness, and there he had instructed them in modern guidance methods for ships of space.

So far there was no disagreement. He'd proposed to make them more competent pilots; more capable of driving a ship to Orede, for example, to raid the enormous cattle herds there. And he'd had them drive the Med Ship to Weald, against which there could be no objection.

But just before arrival he had tricked all four of them by giving them drugged coffee. He'd destroyed the lethal bacterial cultures they'd been ordered to dump on Weald. Then he'd sent the four student pilots off separately, so he and Maril claimed, in huge ships crammed with grain. But those ships were not to be believed in, anyhow.

Nobody believed in shiploads of grain to be had for

the taking. They did know that the only four partially experienced space pilots on Dara had been taken away and by Calhoun's own story sent out of the ship after they'd been drugged.

Had they been trained, and had they been helped or even permitted to sow the seeds of plague on Weald, and had they come back prepared to pass on training to other men to handle other spaceships now feverishly being built in hidden places on Dara, then Dara might have a chance of survival.

But a space battle with only partly trained pilots would be hazardous at best. With no trained pilots at all, it would be hopeless. So Calhoun, by his own story, appeared to have doomed every living being on Dara to massacre from the bombs of Weald.

It was this last angle which destroyed any chance of anybody believing in such fairy-tale objects as ships loaded down with grain. Calhoun had shattered Dara's feeble hope of resistance. Weald had some ships and could build or buy others faster than Dara could hope to construct them.

Equally important, Weald had a plenitude of experienced spacemen to man some ships fully and train the crews of others. If it had become desperately busy fighting plague, then a fleet to exterminate life on Dara would be delayed. Dara might have gained time at least to build ships which could ram their enemies and destroy them that way.

But Calhoun had made it impossible. If he told the truth and Weald already had a fleet of huge ships which only needed to be emptied of grain and filled with guns and men, then Dara was doomed. But if he did not tell the truth it was equally doomed by his actions. So Calhoun would be killed.

His execution was to take place in the open space of the landing grid, with vision cameras transmitting the sight over all the blueskin planet. Half-starved men with grisly blue blotches on their skins, marched him to the center of the largest level space on the planet which was not desperately being cultivated. Their hatred showed in their expressions. Bitterness and fury surrounded Calhoun like a wall. Most of Dara would have liked to have seen him killed in a manner as atrocious as his crime, but no conceivable death would be satisfying.

So the affair was coldly businesslike, with not even insults offered to him. He was left to stand alone in the very center of the landing-grid floor. There were a hundred blasters which would fire upon him at the same instant. He would not only be killed; he would be destroyed. He would be vaporized by the blue-white flames poured upon him.

His death was remarkably close, nothing remaining but the order to fire, when loudspeakers from the landing-grid office froze everything. One of the grain ships from Weald had broken out of overdrive and its pilot was triumphantly calling for landing coordinates. The grid office relayed his call to loudspeaker circuits as the quickest way to get it on the communication system of the whole planet.

"Calling ground," boomed the triumphant voice of the first of the student pilots Calhoun had trained. "Calling ground! Pilot Franz in captured ship requests coordinates for landing! Purpose of landing is to deliver half a million bushels of grain captured from the enemy!"

At first, nobody dared believe it. But the pilot could be seen on vision. He was known. No blueskin would be left alive long enough to be used as a decoy by the men of Weald! Presently the giant ship on its second voyage to Dara—the first had been a generation ago, when it threatened death and destruction—appeared as a dark pinpoint in the sky. It came down and down, and presently it hovered over the center of the tarmac, where Calhoun composedly stood on the spot where he was to have been executed.

The landing-grid crew shifted the ship to one side, and only then did Calhoun stoll in a leisurely fashion toward the Med Ship by the grid's metal-lace wall.

The big ship touched ground, and its exit port revolved and opened, and the student pilot stood there

grinning and heaving out handfuls of grain. There was a
swarming, yelling, deliriously triumphant crowd, then,
where only minutes before there'd been a mob waiting
to rejoice when Calhoun's living body exploded into
flame.

They no longer hated Calhoun, but he had to fight his
way to the Med Ship, nevertheless. He was surrounded
by ecstatically admiring citizens of Dara. They shouted
praise and rejoicing in his ears until he was half-
deafened, and they almost tore his clothing from him in
their desire to touch, to pat, to assure him of their
gratitude and affection, minutes since they'd thirsted
for his blood.

Two hours after the first ship, a second landed. Dara
went wild again. Four hours later still, the third arrived.
The fourth came down to ground on the following day.

When Calhoun faced the executive and cabinet of
Dara for the second time his tone and manner were very
dry.

"Now," he said curtly, "I would like a few more
astrogators to train. I think it likely that we can raid the
Wealdian grain fleet one more time, and in so doing get
the beginning of a fleet for defense. I insist, however,
that it must not be used in combat. We might as well be
sensible about this situation! After all, four shiploads of
grain won't break the famine! They'll help a lot, but
they're only the beginning of what's needed for a
planetary population!"

"How much grain can we hope for?" demanded a
man with a blue mark covering all his chin.

Calhoun told him.

"How long before Weald can have a fleet overhead,
dropping fusion-bombs?" demanded another, grimly.

Calhoun named a time. But then he said, "I think we
can keep them from dropping bombs if we can get the
grain fleet and some capable astrogators."

"How?"

He told them. It was not possible to tell the whole
story of what he considered sensible behavior. An
emotional program can be presented and accepted im-

mediately. A plan of action which is actually intelligent, considering all elements of a situation, has to be accepted piecemeal. Even so, the military men growled.

"We've plenty of heavy elements," said one. "If we'd used our brains, we'd have more bombs than Weald can hope for! We could turn that whole planet into a smoking cinder!"

"Which," said Calhoun acidly, "would give you some satisfaction but not an ounce of food! And food's more important than satisfaction. Now, I'm going to take off for Weald again. I'll want somebody to build an emergency device for my ship, and I'll want the four pilots I've trained and twenty more candidates. And I'd like to have some decent rations! The last trip brought back two million bushels of grain. You can certainly spare adequate food for twenty men for a few days!"

It took some time to get the special device constructed, but the Med Ship lifted in two days more. The device for which it had waited was simply a preventive of the disaster overtaking the ship from the mine on Orede. It was essentially a tank of liquid oxygen, packed in the space from which stores had been taken away. When the ship's air supply was pumped past it, first moisture and then CO_2 froze out.

Then the air flowed over the liquefied oxygen at a rate to replace the CO_2 with more useful breathing material. Then the moisture was restored to the air as it warmed again. For so long as the oxygen lasted, fresh air for any number of men could be kept purified and breathable. The Med Ship's normal equipment could take care of no more than ten. But with this it could journey to Weald with almost any complement on board.

Maril stayed on Dara when the Med Ship left. Murgatroyd protested shrilly when he discovered her about to be closed out by the closing air-lock.

"Chee!" he said indignantly. *"Chee! Chee!"*

"No," said Calhoun. "We'll be crowded enough anyhow. We'll see her later."

He nodded to one of the first four student pilots, who crisply made contact with the landing-grid office, and very efficiently supervised as the grid took the ship up. The other three of the four first-trained men explained every move to sub-classes assigned to each. Calhoun moved about, listening and making certain that the instruction was up to standard.

He felt queer, acting as the supervisor of an educational institution in space. He did not like it. There were twenty-four men beside himself crowded into the Med Ship's small interior. They got in each other's way. They trampled on each other. There was always somebody eating, and always somebody sleeping, and there was no need whatever for the background tape to keep the ship from being intolerably quiet. But the air system worked well enough, except once when the reheating unit quit and the air inside the ship went down below freezing before the trouble could be found and corrected.

The journey to Weald, this time, took seven days because of the training program in effect. Calhoun bit his nails over the delay. But it was necessary for each of the students to make his own line-ups on Weald's sun, and compute distances, and for each of them to practice maneuverings that would presently be called for. Calhoun hoped desperately that preparations for active warfare did not move fast on Weald.

He believed, however, that in the absence of direct news from Dara, Wealdian officials would take the normal course of politicos. They had proclaimed the ship from Orede an attack from Dara. Therefore, they would specialize on defensive measures before plumping for offense. They'd get patrol ships out to spot invasion ships long before they worked on a fleet to destroy the blueskins. It would meet the public demand for defense.

Calhoun was right. The Med Ship made its final approach to Weald under Calhoun's own control. He'd made brightness-measurements on his previous journey and he used them again. They would not be strictly accurate, because a sunspot could knock all meaning out of any reading beyond two decimal places. But the first breakout was just far enough from the Wealdian system for Calhoun to be able to pick out its planets with the electron telescope at maximum magnification. He could aim for Weald itself, allowing, of course, for the lag in the apparent motion of its image because of the limited speed of light. He tried the briefest of overdrive hops, and came out within the solar system and well inside any watching patrol.

That was pure fortune. It continued. He'd broken through the screen of guard ships in undetectable overdrive. He was within half an hour's solar system drive of the grain fleet. There was no alarm, at first. Of course radars spotted the Med Ship as an object, but nobody paid attention. It was not headed for Weald. It was probably assumed to be a guard boat itself. Such mistakes do happen.

Again from the storage space from which supplies had been removed, Calhoun produced vacuum suits. The four first students went out, each escorting a less-accustomed neophyte and all fastened firmly together with space ropes. They warmed the interiors of four ships and went on to others. Presently there were eight ships making ready for an interstellar journey, each with a scared but resolute new pilot familiarizing himself with its controls. There were sixteen ships. Twenty. Twenty-three.

A guard ship came humming out from Weald. It would be armed, of course. It came droning, droning up the forty-odd thousand miles from the planet. Calhoun swore. He could not call his students and tell them what was toward. The guard ship would overhear. He could not trust untried young men to act rationally if they were unaware and the guard ship arrived and matter-of-factly attempted to board one of them.

Then he was inspired. He called Murgatroyd, placed him before the communicator, and set it at voice-only transmission. This was familiar enough, to Murgatroyd. He'd often seen Calhoun use a communicator.

"Chee!" shrilled Murgatroyd. *"Chee-chee!"*

A startled voice came out of the speaker, "What's that?"

"Chee," said Murgatroyd zestfully.

The communicator was talking to him. Murgatroyd adored three things, in order. One was Calhoun. The second was coffee. The third was pretending to converse like a human being. The speaker said explosively, "You there, identify yourself!"

"*Chee-chee-chee-chee!*" observed Murgatroyd. He wriggled with pleasure and added, reasonably enough, "*Chee!*"

The communicator bawled, "Calling ground! Calling ground! Listen to this! Something that ain't human's talking at me on a communicator! Listen in an' tell me what to do!"

Murgatroyd interposed with another shrill, "*Chee!*"

Then Calhoun pulled the Med Ship slowly away from the clump of still-lifeless grain ships. It was highly improbable that the guard boat would carry an electron telescope. Most likely it would have only an echo-radar, and so could determine only that an object of some sort moved of its own accord in space. Calhoun let the Med Ship accelerate. That would be final evidence. The grain ships were between Weald and its sun. Even electron telescopes on the ground—and electron telescopes were ultimately optical telescopes with electronic amplification—could not get a good image of the ship through sunlit atmosphere.

"*Chee?*" asked Murgatroyd solicitously. "*Chee-chee-chee?*"

"Is it blueskins?" shakily demanded the voice from the guard boat. "Ground! Ground! Is it blueskins?"

A heavy, authoritative voice came in with much greater volume. "That's no human voice," it said harshly. "Approach its ship and send back an image. Don't fire first unless it heads for ground."

The guard ship swerved and headed for the Med Ship. It was still a very long way off.

"*Chee-chee,*" said Murgatroyd encouragingly.

Calhoun changed the Med Ship's course. The guard ship changed course too. Calhoun let it draw nearer, but only a little. He led it away from the fleet of grain ships.

He swung his electron telescope on them. He saw a space-suited figure outside one, safely roped, however.

It was easy to guess that someone had meant to return to the Med Ship for orders or to make a report, and found the Med Ship gone. He'd go back inside and turn on a communicator.

"Chee!" said Murgatroyd.

The heavy voice boomed. "You there! This is a human-occupied world! If you come in peace, cut your drive and let our guard ship approach!"

Murgatroyd replied in an interested but doubtful tone. The booming voice bellowed. Another voice of higher authority took over. Murgatroyd was entranced that so many people wanted to talk to him. He made what for him was practically an oration. The last voice spoke persuasively and suavely.

"Chee-chee-chee-chee," said Murgatroyd.

One of the grain ships flickered and ceased to be. It had gone into overdrive. Another. And another. Suddenly they began to flick out of sight by twos and threes.

"Chee," said Murgatroyd with a note of finality.

The last grain ship vanished.

"Calling guard ship," said Calhoun dryly. "This is Med Ship *Aesclipus Twenty*. I called here a couple of weeks ago. You've been talking to my *tormal*, Murgatroyd."

A pause. A blank pause. Then profanity of deep and savage intemperance.

"I've been on Dara," said Calhoun.

Dead silence fell.

"There's a famine there," said Calhoun deliberately. "So the grain ships you've had in orbit have been taken away by men from Dara—blueskins if you like—to feed themselves and their families. They've been dying of hunger and they don't like it."

There was a single burst of the unprintable. Then the formerly suave voice said waspishly, "Well? The Med Service will hear of your interference!"

"Yes," said Calhoun. "I'll report it myself. I have a message for you. Dara is ready to pay for every ounce of grain and for the ships it was stored in. They'll pay in heavy metals—irridium, uranium, that sort of thing."

The suave voice fairly curdled.

"As if we'd allow anything that was ever on Dara to touch ground here!"

"Ah! But there can be sterilization. To begin with metals, uranium melts at 1150° centigrade, and tungsten at 3370° and irridium at 2350°. You could load such things and melt them down in space and then tow them home. And you can actually sterilize a lot of other useful materials!"

The suave voice was infuriated. "I'll report this! You'll suffer for this!"

Calhoun said pleasantly, "I'm sure that what I say is being recorded, so that I'll add that it's perfectly practical for Wealdians to land on Dara, take whatever property they think wise—to pay for damage done by blueskins, of course—and get back to Wealdian ships with absolutely no danger of carrying contagion. If you'll make sure the recording's clear . . ."

He described, clearly and specifically, exactly how a man could be outfitted to walk into any area of any conceivable contagion, do whatever seemed necessary in the way of looting—but Calhoun did not use the word— and then return to his fellows with no risk whatever of bringing back infection. He gave exact details.

Then he said, "My radar says you've four ships converging on me to blast me out of space. I sign off."

The Med Ship disappeared from normal space, and entered that improbably stressed area of extension which it formed about itself and in which physical constants were wildly strange. For one thing, the speed of light in overdrive-stressed space had not been measured yet. It was too high. For another, a ship could travel very many times 186,000 miles per second in overdrive.

The Med Ship did just that. There was nobody but Calhoun and Murgatroyd on board. There was companionable silence, with only the small threshold-of-perception sounds which one did not often notice.

Calhoun luxuriated in regained privacy. For seven days he'd had twenty-four other human beings crowded into the two cabins of the ship, with never so much as one yard of space between himself and someone else. One need not be snobbish to wish to be alone sometimes!

Murgatroyd licked his whiskers thoughtfully.

"I hope," said Calhoun, "that things work out right. But they may remember on Dara that I'm responsible for some ten million bushels of grain reaching them. Maybe, just possibly, they'll listen to me and act sensibly. After all, there's only one way to break a famine. Not with ten million bushels for a whole planet! And certainly not with bombs!"

Driving direct, without pausing for practicing, the Med Ship could arrive at Dara in a little more than five days. Calhoun looked forward to relaxation. As a beginning he made ready to give himself an adequate meal for the first time since first landing on Dara. Then, presently, he sat down to a double meal of Darian famine-rations, which were far from appetizing. But there wasn't anything else on board.

He had some pleasure later, though, envisioning what went on in the normal, non-overdrive universe. Suns flared, and comets hurtled on their way, and clouds formed and dropped down rain, and all sorts of celestial and meteorological phenomena took place. On Weald, obviously, there would be purest panic.

The vanishing of the grain fleet wouldn't be charged against twenty-four men. A Darian fleet would be suspected, and with the suspicion would come terror, and with terror a governmental crisis. Then there'd be a frantic seizure of any craft that could take to space, and the agitated improvisation of a space fleet.

But besides that, biological-warfare technicians would examine Calhoun's instructions for equipment by which armed men could be landed on a plague-stricken planet and then safely taken off again. Military and governmental officials would come to the eminently sane conclusion that while Calhoun could not well take active measures against blueskins, as a sane and proper citizen of the galaxy he would be on the side of law and order and propriety and justice—in short, of Weald. So they ordered sample anticontagion suits made according to Calhoun's directions, and they had them tested. They worked admirably.

On Dara, while Calhoun journeyed placidly back to it, grain was distributed lavishly, and everybody on the planet had their cereal ration almost doubled. It was still not a comfortable ration, but the relief was great. There was considerable gratitude felt for Calhoun, which as usual included a lively anticipation of further favors to come. Maril was interviewed repeatedly, as the person best able to discuss him, and she did his reputation no harm. That was all that happened on Dara . . .

No. There was something else. A very curious thing, too. There was a spread of mild symptoms which nobody could exactly call a disease. They lasted only a few hours. A person felt slightly feverish, and ran a temperature which peaked at 30.9° centigrade, and drank more water than usual. Then his temperature went back to normal and he forgot all about it. There have always been such trivial epidemics. They are rarely recorded, because few people think to go to a doctor. That was the case here.

Calhoun looked ahead a little, too. Presently the fleet of grain ships would arrive and unload and lift again for Orede, and this time they would make an infinity of slaughter among wild cattle herds, and bring back incredible quantities of fresh-slaughtered frozen beef. Almost everybody would get to taste meat again, which would be most gratifying.

Then, the industries of Dara would labor at government-required tasks. An astonishing amount of fissionable material would be fashioned into bombs—a concession by Calhoun—and plastic factories would make an astonishing number of plastic sag-suits. And large shipments of heavy metals in ingots would be made to the planet's capital city and there would be some guns and minor items.

Perhaps somebody could have predicted any of these items in advance, but it was unlikely that anyone did. Nobody but Calhoun, however, would ever have put them together and hoped very urgently that things would work out. He could see a promising total result.

In fact, in the Med Ship hurtling through space, on the fourth day of his journey, he thought of an improvement that could be made in the sum of all those happenings when they got mixed together.

He got back to Dara. Maril came to the Med Ship. Murgatroyd greeted her with enthusiasm.

"Something strange has happened," said Maril, very much subdued. "I told you that sometimes blueskin markings fade out on children, and then neither they nor their children ever have markings again."

"Yes," said Calhoun. "I remember that you told me."

"And you were reminded of a group of viruses on Tralee. You said they only took hold of people in terribly bad physical condition, but then they could be passed on from mother to child, until sometimes they died out."

Calhoun blinked.

"Yes?"

"Korvan," said Maril very carefully, "has worked out an idea that that's what happens to the blueskin markings on Darians. He thinks that people almost dead of the plague could get the virus, and if they recovered from the plague pass the virus on and be blueskins."

"Interesting," said Calhoun, noncommittally.

"And when we went to Weald," said Maril very carefully indeed, "you were working with some culture material. You wrote quite a lot about it in the ship's log. You gave yourself an injection. Remember? And Murgatroyd? You wrote down your temperature, and Murgatroyd's?" She moistened her lips. "You said that if infection passed between us, something would be very infectious indeed?"

"This is a long discussion," said Calhoun. "Does it arrive at a point?"

"It does," said Maril. "Thousands of people are having their pigment-spots fade away. Not only children but grownups. And Korvan has found out that it always seems to happen after a day when they felt feverish and very thirsty, and then felt all right again. You tried out something that made you feverish and thirsty. I had it too, in the ship. Korvan thinks there's been an epidemic of something that is obliterating the blue spots on everybody that catches it. There are always trivial epidemics that nobody notices. Korvan's found evidence of one that's making *blueskin* no longer a word with any meaning."

"Remarkable!" said Calhoun.

"Did you do it?" asked Maril. "Did you start a harmless epidemic that wipes out the virus that makes blueskins?"

Calhoun said in feigned astonishment, "How can you think such a thing, Maril?"

"Because I was there," said Maril. She said, somehow desperately, "I know you did it! But the question is, are you going to tell? When people find they're not blueskins any longer, when there's no such thing as a blueskin any longer, will you tell them why?"

"Naturally not," said Calhoun. "Why?" Then he guessed. "Has Korvan—"

"He thinks," said Maril, "that he thought it up all by himself. He's found the proof. He's very proud. I'd have to tell him how the ideas got into his head if you were going to tell. And he'd be ashamed and angry."

Calhoun considered, staring at her.

"How it happened doesn't matter," he said at last. "The idea of anybody doing it deliberately would be disturbing, too. It shouldn't get about. So it seems much the best thing for Korvan to discover what's happened to the blueskin pigment, and how it happened. But not why."

She read his face carefully.

"You aren't doing it as a favor to me," she decided. "You'd rather it was that way."

She looked at him for a long time, until he squirmed. Then she nodded and went away.

An hour later the Wealdian space fleet was reported massed in space and driving for Dara.

VIII

THERE WERE SMALL scout ships which came on ahead of the main fleet. They'd originally been guard boats, intended for solar system duty only and quite incapable of overdrive. They'd come from Weald in the cargo holds of the liners now transformed into fighting ships. The scouts swept low, transmitting fine-screen images back to the fleet, of all they might see before they were shot down. They found the landing grid. It contained nothing larger than Calhoun's Med Ship, *Aesclipus Twenty*.

They searched here and there. They flittered to and fro, scanning wide bands of the surface of Dara. The planet's cities and highways and industrial centers were wholly open to inspection from the sky. It looked as if the scouts hunted most busily for the fleet of former grain ships which Calhoun had said the blueskins had seized and rushed away. If the scouts looked for them, they did not find them.

Dara offered no opposition to the ships. Nothing rose to space to oppose or to resist their search. They went darting over every portion of the hungry planet, land and seas alike, and there was no sign of military preparedness against their coming. The huge ships of the main fleet waited while the scouts reported monotonously that they saw no sign of the stolen fleet. But the stolen fleet was the only means by which the planet could be defended. There could be no point in a pitched battle in emptiness. But a fleet with a planet to back it might be dangerous.

Hours passed. The Wealdian main fleet waited. There was no offensive movement by the fleet. There was no defensive action from the ground. With fusion-bombs certain to be involved in any actual conflict, there was something like an embarrassed pause. The Wealdian ships were ready to bomb. They were less anxious to be vaporized by possible suicide dashes of defending ships which might blow themselves up near contact with their enemies.

But a fleet cannot travel some light-years through space to make a mere threat. And the Wealdian fleet was furnished with the material for total devastation. It could drop bombs from hundreds, or thousands, or even tens of thousands of miles away. It could cover the world of Dara with mushroom clouds springing up and spreading to make a continuous pall of atomic-fusion products. And they could settle down and kill every living thing not destroyed by the explosions themselves. Even the creatures of the deepest oceans would die of deadly, purposely contrived fallout particles.

The Wealdian fleet contemplated its own destructiveness. It found no capacity for defense on Dara. It moved forward.

But then a message went out from the capital city of Dara. It said that a ship in overdrive had carried word to a Darian fleet in space. The Darian fleet now hurtled toward Weald. It was a fleet of thirty-seven giant ships. They carried such-and-such bombs in such-and-such quantities. Unless its orders were countermanded, it would deliver those bombs on Weald, set to explode. If Weald bombed Dara, the orders could not be withdrawn. So Weald could bomb Dara. It could destroy all life on the pariah planet. But Weald would die with it.

The fleet ceased its advance. The situation was a stalemate with pure desperation on one side and pure frustration on the other. This was no way to end the war. Neither planet could trust the other, even for minutes. If they did not destroy each other simultaneously, as now was possible, each would expect the other to launch an

unwarned attack at some other moment. Ultimately one
or the other must perish, and the survivor would be the
one most skilled in treachery.

But then the pariah planet made a new proposal. It
would send a messenger ship to stop its own fleet's bom-
bardment if Weald would accept payment of the grain
ships and their cargos. It would pay in ingots of irridium
and uranium and tungsten, and gold if Weald wished it,
for all damages Weald might claim.

It would even pay indemnity for the miners of Orede,
who had died by accident but perhaps in some sense
through its fault. It would pay. But if it were bombed,
Weald must spout atomic fire and the fleet of Weald
would have no home planet to return to.

This proposal seemed both craven and foolish. It
would allow the fleet of Weald to loot and then betray
Dara. But it was Calhoun's idea. It seemed plausible to
the admirals of Weald. They felt only contempt for
blueskins. Contemptuously, they accepted the semi-
surrender.

The broadcast waves of Dara told of agreement, and
wild and fierce resentment filled the pariah planet's
people. There was almost revolution to insist upon
resistance, however hopeless and however fatal. But not
all of Dara realized that a vital change had come about
in the state of things on Dara. The enemy fleet had not a
hint of it.

In menacing array, the invading fleet spread itself
about the skies of Dara, well beyond the atmosphere.
Harsh voices talked with increasing arrogance to the
landing-grid staff. A monster ship of Weald came
heavily down, riding the landing grid's force-fields. It
touched gently. Its occupants were apprehensive, but
hungry for the loot they had been assured was theirs.
The ship's outer hull would be sterilized before it returned to Weald, of course. And there was adequate
protection for the landing party.

Men came out of the ship's ports. They wore the
double, transparent sag-suits Calhoun had suggested,
which had been painstakingly tested, and which were
perfect protection against contagion. They were double

garments of plastic, with air tanks inside the inner flexible envelope.

Men wearing such sag-suits could walk about on Dara. They could work on Dara. They could loot with impunity and all contamination must remain outside the suits, and on their return to their ships they would simply stand in the air-locks while corrosive gases swirled around them, killing any possible organism of disease. Then, for extra assurance, when air from Weald filled the air-lock again, the men would burn the outer plastic covering and step into the ship without ever having come within two layers of plastic of infection.

What loot they gathered, obviously, could be decontaminated before it was returned to Weald. Metals could be melted, if necessary. Gems could be sterilized. It was a most satisfactory discovery, to realize that blueskins could be not only scorned but robbed. There was only one bit of irrelevant information the space fleet of Weald did not have.

That information was that the people of Dara weren't blueskins any longer. There'd been a trivial epidemic. . . .

The sag-suited men of Weald went zestfully about their business. They took over the landing grid's operation, driving the Darian operators away. For the first time in history the operators of a landing grid wore make-up to look like they did have blue pigment in their skins. They didn't. The Wealdian landing party tested the grid's operation. They brought down another giant ship. Then another. And another.

Parties in the shiny sag-suits spread through the city. There were the huge stockpiles of precious metals, brought in readiness to be surrendered and carried away. Some men set to work to load these into the holds of the ships of Weald. Some went forthrightly after personal loot.

They came upon very few Darians. Those they saw kept sullenly away from them. They entered shops and took what they fancied. They zestfully removed the treasure of banks.

Triumphant and scornful reports went up to the

hovering great ships. The blueskins, said the reports, were spiritless and cowardly. They permitted themselves to be robbed. They kept out of the way. It had been observed that the population was streaming out of the city, fleeing because they feared the ships' landing parties. The blueskins had abjectly produced all they'd promised of precious metals, but there was more to be taken.

More ships came down, and more. Some of the first, heavily loaded, were lifted to emptiness again and the process of decontamination of their hulls began. There was jealousy among the ships in space for those upon the ground. The first landed ships had had their choice of loot. There were squabblings about priorities, now that the navy of Weald plainly had a license to steal. There was confusion among the members of the landing parties. Discipline disappeared. Men in plastic sag-suits roved about as individuals, seeking what they might loot.

There were armed and alerted landing parties around the grid itself, of course, but the capital city of Dara lay open. Men coming back with loot found their ships already lifted off to make room for others. They were pushed into re-embarking parties of other ships. There were more and more men to be found on ships where they did not belong, and more and more not to be found where they did.

By the time half the fleet had been aground, there was no longer any pretense of holding a ship down until all its crew returned. There were too many other ships' companies clamoring for their turn to loot. The rosters of many ships, indeed, bore no particular relationship to the men actually on board.

There were less than fifteen ships whose to-be-fumigated holds were still emptied, when the watchful government of Dara broadcast a new message to the invaders. It requested that the looting stop. No matter what payment Weald claimed, it had taken payment five times over. Now was time to stop.

It was amusing. The space admiral of Weald ordered his ships alerted for action. The message ship, ordering the Darian fleet away from Weald, had been sent off long since. No other ship could get away now! The Darians could take their choice: accept the consequences of surrender, or the fleet would rise to throw down bombs.

Calhoun was asking politely to be taken to the Wealdian admiral when the trouble began. It wasn't on the ground, at all. Everything was under splendid control where a landing force occupied the grid and all the ground immediately about it. The space admiral had headquarters in the landing-grid office. Reports came in, orders were issued, admirably crisp salutes were exchanged among sag-suited men. Everything was in perfect shape there.

But there was panic among the ships in space. Communicators gave off horrified, panic-stricken yells. There were screamings. Intelligible communications ceased. Ships plunged crazily this way and that. Some vanished in overdrive. At least one plunged at full power into a Darian ocean.

The space admiral found himself in command of fifteen ships only out of all his former force. The rest of the fleet went through a period of hysterical madness. In some ships it lasted for minutes only. In others it went on for half an hour or more. Then they hung overhead, but did not reply to calls.

Calhoun arrived at the spaceport with Murgatroyd riding on his shoulder. A bewildered officer in a sag-suit halted him.

"I've come," said Calhoun, "to speak to the admiral. My name is Calhoun and I'm Med Service, and I think I met the admiral at a banquet a few weeks ago. He'll remember me."

"You'll have to wait," protested the officer. "There's some trouble—"

"Yes," said Calhoun. "I know about it. I helped design it. I want to explain it to the admiral. He needs to know what's happened, if he's to take appropriate measures."

There were jitterings. Many men in sag-suits had still no idea that anything had gone wrong. Some appeared, brightly carrying loot. Some hung eagerly around the air-locks of ships on the grid tarmac, waiting their turns to stand in corrosive gases for the decontamination of their suits, when they would burn the outer layers and step, asceptic and happy, into a Wealdian ship again. There they could think how rich they were going to be back on Weald.

But the situation aloft was bewildering and very, very ominous. There was strident argument. Presently Calhoun stood before the Wealdian admiral.

"I came to explain something," said Calhoun pleasantly. "The situation has changed. You've noticed it, I'm sure."

The admiral glared at him through two layers of plastic, which covered him almost like a gift-wrapped parcel.

"Be quick!" he rasped.

"First," said Calhoun, "there are no more blueskins. An epidemic of something or other has made the blue patches on the skins of Darians fade out. There have always been some who didn't have blue patches. Now nobody has them."

"Nonsense!" rasped the admiral. "And what has that got to do with this situation?"

"Why, everything," said Calhoun mildly. "It seems that Darians can pass for Wealdians whenever they please. That they *are* passing for Wealdians. That they've been mixing with your men, wearing sag-suits exactly like the one you're wearing now. They've been going aboard your ships in the confusion of returning looters. There's not a ship now aloft, which has been aground today, which hasn't from one to fifteen Darians—no longer blueskins—on board."

The admiral roared. Then his face turned gray.

"You can't take your fleet back to Weald," said Calhoun gently, "if you believe its crews have been exposed to carriers of the Dara plague. You wouldn't be allowed to land, anyhow."

The admiral said through stiff lips, "I'll blast—"

"No," said Calhoun, again gently. "When you ordered all ships alerted for action, the Darians on each ship released panic gas. They only needed tiny, pocket-sized containers of the gas for the job. They had them. They only needed to use air tanks from their sag-suits to protect themselves against the gas. They kept them handy.

"On nearly all your ships aloft your crews are crazy from panic gas. They'll stay that way until the air is changed. Darians have barricaded themselves in the control-rooms of most if not all your ships. You haven't got a fleet. The few ships who will obey your orders—if they drop one bomb, our fleet off Weald will drop fifty.

"I don't think you'd better order offensive action. Instead, I think you'd better have your fleet medical officers come and learn some of the facts of life. There's no need for war between Dara and Weald, but if you insist . . ."

The admiral made a choking noise. He could have ordered Calhoun killed, but there was a certain appalling fact. The men aground from the fleet were breathing Wealdian air from tanks. It would last so long only. If they were taken on board the still obedient ships overhead, Darians would unquestionably be mixed with them. There was no way to take off the parties now aground without exposing them to contact with Darians, on the ground or in the ships. There was no way to sort out the Darians.

"I—I will give the orders," said the admiral thickly. "I do not know what you devils plan, but—I do not know how to stop you."

"All that's necessary," said Calhoun warmly, "is an open mind. There's a misunderstanding to be cleared up, and some principles of planetary health practices to be explained, and a certain amount of prejudice that has to be thrown away. But nobody need die of changing their minds. The Interstellar Medical Service has proved that over and over!"

Murgatroyd, perched on his shoulder, felt that it was time to take part in the conversation. He said, *"Chee-chee!"*

"Yes," agreed Calhoun. "We do want to get the job done. We're behind schedule now."

• • •

It was not, of course, possible for Calhoun to leave immediately. He had to preside at various meetings of the medical officers of the fleet and the health officials of Dara. He had to make explanations, and correct misapprehensions, and delicately suggest such biological experiments as would prove to the doctors of Weald that there was no longer a plague on Dara, whatever had been the case three generations before.

He had to sit by while an extremely self-confident young Darian doctor—one of his names was Korvan —rather condescendingly demonstrated that the former blue pigmentation was a viral product quite unconnected with the plague, and that it had been wiped out by a very trivial epidemic of such and such.

Calhoun regarded that young man with a detached interest. Maril thought him wonderful, even if she had to give him the material for his work. He agreed with her that he was wonderful. Calhoun shrugged and went on with his own work.

The return of loot, mutual, full, and complete agreement that Darians were no longer carriers of plague, if they had ever been—unless Weald convinced other worlds of this, Weald itself would join Dara in isolation from neighboring worlds. A messenger ship had to recall the twenty-seven ships once floating in orbit about Weald. Most of them would be used for some time, to bring beef from Orede. Some would haul more grain from Weald. It would be paid for. There would be a need for commercial missions to be exchanged between Weald and Dara. There would have to be. . . .

It was a full week before he could go to the little Med Ship and prepare for departure. Even then there were matters to be attended to. All the food-supplies that had been removed could not be replaced. There were biological samples to be replaced and some to be destroyed.

Maril came to the Med Ship again when he was almost ready to leave. She did not seem comfortable.

"I wanted you to meet Korvan," she said regretfully.

"I met him," said Calhoun. "I think he will be a most prominent citizen, in time. He has all the talents for it."

Maril smiled very faintly.

"But you don't admire him."

"I wouldn't say that," protested Calhoun. "After all, he is desirable to you, which is something I couldn't manage."

"You didn't try," said Maril. "Just as I didn't try to be fascinating to you. Why?"

Calhoun spread out his hands. But he looked at Maril with respect. Not every woman could have faced the fact that a man did not feel impelled to make passes at her. It is simply a fact that has nothing to do with desirability or charm or anything else.

"You're going to marry him," he said. "I hope you'll be very happy."

"He's the man I want," said Maril frankly. "And I doubt he'll ever look at another woman. He looks forward to splendid discoveries. I wish he didn't."

Calhoun did not ask the obvious question. Instead, he said thoughtfully, "There's something you could do. It needs to be done. The Med Service in this sector has been badly handled. There are a number of discoveries that need to be made. I don't think your Korvan would relish having things handed to him on a visible silver platter. But they should be known . . ."

Maril said, "I can guess what you mean. I dropped hints about the way the blueskin markings went away, yes. You've got books for me?"

Calhoun nodded. He found them.

"If we had only fallen in love with each other, Maril, we'd be a team! Too bad! These are a wedding present you'll do well to hide."

She put her hands in his.

"I like you almost as much as I like Murgatroyd! Yes! Korvan will never know, and he'll be a great man." Then she added defensively, "But I don't think he'll only discover things from hints I drop him. He'll make wonderful discoveries."

"Of which," said Calhoun, "the most remarkable is you. Good luck, Maril!"

She went away smiling. But she wiped her eyes when she was out of the ship.

Presently the Med Ship lifted. Calhoun aimed it for the next planet on the list of those he was to visit. After this one more he'd return to sector headquarters with a biting report to make on the way things had been handled before him.

"Overdrive coming, Murgatroyd!"

Then the stars went out and there was silence, and privacy, and a faint, faint, almost unhearable series of background sounds which kept the Med Ship from being totally unendurable.

Long, long days later the ship broke out of overdrive and Calhoun guided it to a round and sunlit world. In due time he thumbed the communicator button.

"Calling ground," he said crisply. "Calling ground! Med Ship *Aesclipus Twenty* reporting arrival and asking coordinates for landing. Purpose of landing is planetary health inspection. Our mass is fifty standard tons."

There was a pause while the beamed message went many, many thousands of miles. Then the speaker said, "*Aesclipus Twenty*, repeat your identification!"

Calhoun repeated it patiently. Murgatroyd watched with bright eyes. Perhaps he hoped to be allowed to have another long conversation with somebody by communicator.

"You are warned," said the communicator sternly, "that any deceit or deception about your identity or purpose in landing will be severely punished. We take few chances, here! If you wish to land notwithstanding this warning—"

"I'm coming in," said Calhoun. "Give me the coordinates."

He wrote them down. His expression was slightly pained. The Med Ship drove on, in solar system drive. Murgatroyd said, *"Chee-chee? Chee?"*

Calhoun sighed.

"That's right, Murgatroyd! Here we go again!"